THE COLOR OF OUR SKY

THE COLOR
OF OUR SKY

Amita Trasi

WILLIAM MORROW
An Imprint of HarperCollinsPublishers

THE COLOR OF OUR SKY. Copyright © 2017 by Amita Trasi. All rights reserved.
Printed in the United States of America. No part of this book may be used or repro-
duced in any manner whatsoever without written permission except in the case of
brief quotations embodied in critical articles and reviews. For information, address
HarperCollins Publishers, 195 Broadway, New York, NY 10007.

HarperCollins books may be purchased for educational, business, or sales pro-
motional use. For information, please email the Special Markets Department at
SPsales@harpercollins.com.

FIRST EDITION

Designed by Diahann Sturge

Library of Congress Cataloging-in-Publication Data has been applied for.

ISBN 978-0-06-247407-0

17 18 19 20 21   RS/LSC   10 9 8 7 6 5 4 3 2 1

In memory of my late father;
To Sameer, my husband extraordinaire;
And last but not the least,
To girls like Mukta—may you always find a
friend to help you through the darkness.

THE COLOR OF OUR SKY

CHAPTER 1

TARA
Mumbai, India—June 2004

THE MEMORY OF that moment hit me like a surging ocean wave—drawing me into it—the sour smell of darkness, those sobs erupting like an echo from a bottomless pit. I had tried to break away from it for so long I had forgotten that places can have memories too. I stood in the dimly lit corridor outside my childhood home and tried to unlock the door. The keys rattled in my hand and fell to the floor. This was proving to be more difficult than I had thought. *One deep breath and you will find the courage,* Papa used to tell me when I was a child. Now, in my mid-twenties, here I was, standing outside this locked door, feeling like a child once again.

I picked up the keys and tried again. The doors creaked as I managed to push them open. The apartment was dark. Outside, the sky thundered and rain rammed the rooftops. A stray slant of sunlight fell on furniture that had gathered dust over the years, and I stood in that unlit room looking at the old cobwebs crowding the corners of what had once been my home. I switched on the lights and wiped the dust off my writing desk with a smooth stroke of my hand. *It is just an apartment,* I told myself. But there were so many things from my childhood here—my writing desk where Papa had sat down next to me, teaching me how to write, and the sofa where we had watched television together as a family.

In my bedroom, my bed stood neatly covered, just the way I had left it. I could hear the sound of our laughter, smell my childhood—the food Aai used to cook and lovingly feed me—that wafting floral smell of saffron in the *pulao,* turmeric-perfumed *dal,* the sweet *rasgullas.* There wasn't any such smell of course, not anymore. All that was left was just a musty odor from closed doors, from buried secrets.

A cloud of dust erupted as I parted the curtains. Outside, the rain was falling softly, leaves cradling the raindrops. The scene was still the same as when Papa and I had moved away to Los Angeles eleven years ago: the zooming in and out of traffic, the honking of rickshaws and cars, the distant barking of stray dogs, the sprawled slums in the distance. Standing here, my suitcases lonely in the doorway, I understood why Papa had never tried to sell or rent this apartment. After making a home in America for eleven years, he had hoped to return one day to search for Mukta. After all, this was where she was kidnapped.

It is said that time heals everything. I don't think that's true. As the years have gone by, I've found it odd how simple things can still remind you of those terrible times or how the moment you try so hard to forget becomes your sharpest memory.

I STEPPED OUT of my apartment that day determined to find answers. The taxi drivers stood in a queue, waiting, hoping, begging you to take a ride from them. There was something about this city that I would never forget. I could see it everywhere, smell it, hear it—the dreams that lingered on people's faces, the smell of sweat and grime, the sound of distant chaos in the air. This was where it had happened—where walls had blown apart, vehicles had blown away, simple shards of glass had splintered lives, and our loved ones had become memories. Standing here, an image of Aai floated before my eyes, waiting for me somewhere, her kohl-lined eyes tearing up as she took me in her arms. It was different before the blasts had come and taken her away.

"Madam, I taking you anywhere you wanting to go," a taxi driver called out.

"No here, here . . ." another taxi driver waved.

I nodded to one of them and he hurriedly got behind the wheel. It began drizzling as I stepped inside. The rain fell softly around us.

"Take me to the police station in Dadar," I told him.

"Madam, you coming from foreign, no? I understanding from the way you speaking. I taking you to the bestest hotels in Mumbai. You will—"

"Take me to the police station," I repeated, sternly.

The driver was quiet the rest of the way, humming quietly to the tune of Bollywood music roaring through the speakers in his taxi. Outside, the slum dwellers and street children picking through garbage rolled past us. Heat hovered over the city despite the drizzle, and the wind smelled of smoke, curry, and drains. People still walked dangerously close to the speeding traffic, rickshaws sputtered alongside, and beggars knocked on my taxi window asking for money. The footpaths still housed many of the poor who lived in makeshift tents, women haggled with hawkers in the bazaars, and men loitered in corners giving vacant stares. Behind them, Bollywood movie posters on walls announced the latest movies.

When I was a child, Papa had taken me for a walk on these very streets. Once I had accompanied Aai to the bazaars and haggled with shopkeepers alongside her. And there was a time I had sat in the backseat of a taxi with Mukta next to me while Papa had taken us to the Asiatic library. How excitedly I had shown her the sea, the garden, and introduced her to my world. How many times had she walked with me to my school, carrying my schoolbag, or sat with me on the park bench slurping iced *golas*? Now, sitting in the backseat of this taxi, my stomach churned. These moments seemed to paralyze me; I was unable to breathe, as if the crime I had committed were slowly strangling me. I pressed my face closer to the open window and forced myself to breathe.

"Here, madam, that's the police station," the driver announced as he pulled over.

It was raining very hard when the taxi came to a stop, the wipers whipping wildly against the windshield. I stepped into ankle-deep water as I got down, the rain beating against my umbrella. I paid the taxi driver. In the distance, near the garbage cans, children in raincoats splashed water on each other, their giggles coming in waves.

AT THE STATION, I found a place on the bench in the corner and dropped my purse in my lap. Eleven years ago Papa and I had sat on one such bench in this police station, waiting for hours, to understand what had happened to us, trying to make sense of it all. Now, as I sat straight, sandwiched between strangers waiting their turn, I wished Papa were sitting beside me. In a way, I still carried him with me—his remains—his ashes, capped tightly in a bottle in my purse. I had brought them here to disperse in the Ganga river, something I needed to do, something that was in accordance with his last wishes.

A constable sat at a table nearby, his head behind a mountain of files; another sat behind him at another table, listening to complaints and noting them in a register, while yet another sat on a chair not far away, his head buried in a newspaper. A *chaiwalla* rushed past us carrying *masala* chai, placing the glasses of brown liquid on every table. Outside, police sirens pierced the air, and the policemen dragged two handcuffed men inside.

The woman before me sobbed and urged the constable to find her missing son. He yawned, scribbled something in the register, and then shooed her away. When it was my turn, I sat in front of him. He rubbed his eyes. "What is your complaint now?" he asked, sounding bored.

"I want to speak to your senior inspector."

He looked up from his register and narrowed his eyes, "About what, madam?"

The wooden board behind him had a chart of the number of murders and kidnappings this year and the cases they had solved.

"It is about a kidnapping that happened eleven years ago. A girl was kidnapped. My father filed a report then."

"Eleven years?" The constable raised his eyebrows. "And you want to search for her *now*?"

I nodded.

He looked at me curiously and sighed. "Okay, you wait," he said, then walked to a closed room and knocked on the door. An inspector opened the door; the constable pointed to me and whispered something. The inspector gave me a glance and then walked toward me.

"Inspector Pravin Godbole," he said, shaking my hand and introducing himself as the senior inspector of the station.

"I have . . . I am . . . looking for a girl who was kidnapped. Please, you *have* to help me. I-I just arrived after a long flight from America."

"Give me a few minutes, please; I have someone in my office. I can review your case after that."

IT TOOK A couple of hours for the constable to escort me to his office. Meanwhile, I ate a sandwich I'd stashed in my purse and watched the constable take down a few more complaints. People walked in, waited beside me, and left after the constable had filed their complaint. The *chaiwalla* offered me a glass of chai and I gratefully sipped it. I didn't mind waiting. I felt relief, even if it was only for a bit, to be able to finally speak to someone— someone important enough in this police station who could help me.

Inspector Godbole had sharp, intelligent eyes that I hoped would be able to see what others had been unable to see. He asked me to take a seat. His hat with the emblem *Satyamev Jayate*—truth alone triumphs—sat on the desk.

"What can I do for you?"

I introduced myself and sat down, opened my wallet, and

teased out the photograph. How young we looked then—Mukta and I—standing outside the Asiatic library. He took it from my hand and looked at the photograph.

"I am looking for her, for the girl in the photograph," I said.

"Which one?" he asked, squinting at the photograph.

"The one on the right, that's me. The other one—she was kidnapped eleven years ago."

His eyebrows angled upward. "Eleven years ago?"

"Uh . . . yes. She was kidnapped from our home just after the 1993 bomb blasts. I was in the room with her when it happened."

"So you saw the kidnapper?"

I paused.

"No . . . not really," I lied.

The inspector nodded.

"Her name was . . . *is* Mukta. She was a girl . . . an orphan my parents fostered." I explained, "My Papa was a kind man. He used to work with many NGOs and orphanages in his spare time to find a home for abandoned children. Sometimes he brought them back to our apartment. He rescued street children or poor kids from villages—one or two at a time—and let them stay in our home. They slept in the kitchen, ate food Aai made, and then in a few days Papa found them a place at one orphanage or another. Papa did good any opportunity he got. With Mukta . . . he tried so hard. Something happened to her back in her village. She just didn't speak for a long time. She—"

"I see, I see," he interrupted. "We'll try to find her."

I wanted to tell him that, unlike the other kids who had lived with us for barely a week or two, Mukta had been with us for five years. And that she was a good friend. I wanted to tell him how she liked reading poems and was afraid of the rain . . . and that we had wanted to grow up together.

"Ms. Tara?"

"My . . . my father had filed an FIR back then . . . of . . . of the kidnapping."

The inspector took a deep breath, scratched the stubble on his chin, and brought the photograph close to his face, staring at the picture. The photograph was worn out and wrinkled by age like a precious memory frozen in time, both of us smiling at the camera.

"Ms. Tara, this was such a long time ago. She will be . . . older now. And we don't have a recent picture. It will be very difficult to search for someone without a recent picture. But let me have a look at her file. I will have to contact the missing person's bureau. Why look for a poor village child after all these years? Has she stolen something precious from your home? Like an heirloom or something?"

"No. No . . . it's just . . . Papa worked so hard to give the other children a home. I suppose Papa thought Mukta was the only one who slipped through the cracks . . . someone he couldn't protect. He never forgave himself for that. At the time the police told us they had searched for her. Papa told me she was dead. Maybe a police inspector told him that. I don't know. Papa took me to America after that. I . . . I didn't know she was alive. I found some documents in his drawer after his death. He had been searching for her for a long time. And all this time he had been looking for her, I thought she was dead. He would have wanted me to search for her."

"Nobody looks for such children who have disappeared, madam. Look at all the children living in the slums—there is no one to take proper care of them, let alone worry how they are doing if they disappear."

I looked at him, not saying anything. There hadn't been a moment in the last eleven years that I hadn't wanted to wander back to that summer night, to that split second when I could have done something to stop it. I knew who the kidnapper was; I had always known. I had planned it, after all. But I didn't tell the inspector this, I couldn't. There would be way more things I would have to reveal than just that. In any case, I didn't want to concentrate on why I did it or who the kidnapper was; all I wanted to do now was look for Mukta.

The inspector flicked the photograph in his hand and sighed loudly. "Give me a few days. I will look through the files. We are backlogged with many cases now. You can give the constable all the details." He signaled to him and asked him to escort me outside.

"Thank you very much," I said, standing up.

At the door I turned to him again. "It would be great if you can help me find her." He lifted his head momentarily and gave me a slight nod before going back to his work. It took the constable a few minutes to take down the details.

I left the station and stood on the porch watching the police jeeps parked outside, constables carrying files, people waiting impatiently, and suddenly it seemed futile to have come to this place, to have asked for their help. They hadn't even asked the right questions: Did I remember the day when it happened? What were the sounds I heard before I knew what was happening? The exact time on the bedroom clock? Why did the kidnapper not kidnap me instead? Why did I not scream? Why did I not wake up Papa, who was sleeping in the next room? If they had asked me those questions, I was afraid the truth would come spilling out of me.

I LIT UP a cigarette, took a couple of puffs, and let the smoke drift through my nostrils. The two women constables standing on the porch gave me a dirty look. I smiled to myself. Not many women smoked here. My first cigarette had been in America with Brian when I was eighteen. Brian, my fiancé, had once been the love of my life, and I had conveniently left him behind in Los Angeles. If things hadn't changed, Brian and I would be lolling lazily on a beach right about now, watching the waves surge and recede. But now, it was over between us. I sighed as I noticed the lack of a ring on my finger, threw the cigarette butt on the floor, and squashed it under my foot.

A cold wet breeze hit me as I walked outside onto a noisy street. A six-year-old girl in tattered clothes scurried toward me, unmindful of her soiled and bleeding feet, spread out her palm, and looked at me pleadingly. I looked into her hopeful eyes for a second. She held my gaze. A team of child beggars watched me curiously from a distance. I searched my purse to find some rupee notes and handed them to her. Within seconds all the beggars enveloped me, begging for money. I distributed some notes between them. The children whooped and screamed in joy as they darted away.

"Is there a restaurant nearby?" I asked one of the beggar boys. He smiled; his pearly whites shone against his dark skin.

"There, madam, the best *masala* chai . . . very good, very *zhakas*," he said, and waved me a goodbye.

THE RESTAURANT WASN'T very busy this time of the day. I plopped my purse on a chair and ordered a sandwich and tea. Ten- to twelve-year-old boys were wiping the tables. Flies lingered on the damp surfaces. A waiter brought me a glass of chai. Outside the sky was clearing, the clouds making way for the clear blue. When Mukta had first arrived I had often found her sitting in our dark and dingy storage room, gazing out the window, staring at the stars in the sky as if seeking something in them. I remember a night when my parents had been asleep and I had tiptoed to her room to find her looking at the sky. She turned to me, surprised that I had appeared in the dark.

"What do you look for in the sky?" I had asked.

"Look," she said, pointing to the sky. "You can see for yourself."

I entered her room, sat beside her, and looked at the stars sparkling like diamonds in the night sky.

"Amma used to say that when we die, we become stars. She said when she died she would become a star and watch over me. But you see, there are so many of them. I don't know which one of them is Amma. Probably if I look hard enough, I will be able to see. She may send a signal to me. You don't believe it?"

I shrugged. "I don't know. If you believe it, it might be true."

"It *is* true," she whispered. "You just have to look hard enough."

We sat there for some time, watching the stars in the cloudless night sky.

I sat with her late that night and for many nights after that one. For many nights over the years, we sat under the moonlight in that dark, dingy room talking about our lives. It became our way of escaping the world. It was Mukta who taught me the sky was like a stage where clouds formed characters, morphed into different shapes, and drifted toward each other. It told us more stories than we could have ever read, more than our imaginations could afford.

CHAPTER 2

MUKTA
Village of Ganipur, India—1986

WE ARE LIKE the Datura flowers that unfurl at night—intoxicating, blossoming in the dark, wilting away at dawn. It's something my grandmother, Sakubai, used to tell me when I was a child. It sounded so poetic to me back then. I used to like listening to it, even giggling at it without understanding what it meant. It's the first thing that comes to my mind when people ask me about my life.

For a long time I did not know I was the daughter of a temple prostitute, that I was born into a cult that followed the sacred tradition of dedicating their daughters to the Goddess Yellamma. When the British ruled our country, Sakubai used to tell me, the kings and zamindars would act as our patrons and support us with money. People used to revere us as if we were priests. We danced in temples, sang songs of worship, and villagers sought our blessings for important occasions. The tradition is no different today. Except that patrons owned us and supported us then, but now there aren't any kings and very few upper-caste men who are willing to support us. Lower-caste girls as young as eight are married to the Goddess in a dedication ceremony. In this tiny village of South India we are also called *devdasis*—servants of God.

Coming from a long line of devdasis, I was bound to become one eventually. But as a child I did not know that. I did not know my body did not belong to me. I sometimes forget that I was a child once, that everything was foolish and naïve to my eyes. It all seems like a dream—those serene mornings, waking up in the village when all you could see were clear skies, sunshine pouring in—its slanting rays so thick you would be convinced that was all life had to offer. Our village had a lot of farms filled with rice, maize, and millet. Greenery swayed in every corner of the village. With every gentle whiff of wind that caressed my cheeks, Amma would say God's hands were patting my cheeks. She used to tell me that God overlooks my every move. I believed it then and feared God would punish me every time I plucked mangoes from the trees that did not belong to us. It was such a different life as a child, back when I didn't know what was coming for me.

My Amma was a beautiful woman. I once told her that her clear, honeyed complexion was like glittering gold, and the whites of her eyes shone like diamonds set in that gold, and she laughed. I didn't look anything like her. Sakubai used to say I was too fair for a lower caste, and it was clear I had inherited my looks and my green eyes from my father, who was an upper-caste Brahmin.

WHEN I THINK back to that time, I think of my Amma's soft brown eyes and the way she told me stories or sang to me. How her eyes portrayed every emotion in a story, how they would move with the music in her voice. She would sing to me in her smooth, melodious voice. I can still hear her at times.

The wind races through the woods,
Over the mountains and over the sea,
I hear it now, I hear it clear,
For all it does is whisper in my ear,
Of giant kingdoms, of gallant kings,
Of pretty princesses and their gentle grooms,
Oh! The wind, it speaks to me.

When I listened to her, my thoughts would race along with the wind, crossing our village, whistling through mountains, between boulders and rocks, ruffling the leaves on trees, flying with the birds, and reaching the city where my father lived. And I would wonder what my father was doing at that very minute. Was he looking out a window searching for my face, crossing the street thinking about me, or was he on his way here to meet me?

I've never met my father. Whatever little I knew of him I learned from Sakubai. Amma never spoke of him much. Whenever she did, there was a distant, dreamy look on her face—the glow of love. Sometimes, when Amma would take me to the village, I'd look at families shopping in the bazaar and I knew something was missing in ours. There were girls just like me, holding their father's hand or sitting on their father's shoulders. They looked happy and safe. Amma told me that fathers did anything to protect their daughters. It was something she said

I didn't have; something she knew would come my way. All we had to do was wait! I never asked Amma where my father was or who he was, although I yearned to ask. I was always afraid I might say something that would remind her of my father, and at times, when I did ask, her eyes would melt into that forlorn, heartbroken look. So I let her continue with her stories, never stopping her to ask if my father wanted to meet me. I'd wait, I told myself.

I LIVED WITH Amma and Sakubai in a house situated on the outskirts of our little village, Ganipur, at the foothills of the Sahyadri near the border of Maharashtra and Karnataka. It was a very old house built many years ago for Sakubai by the zamindar who owned the land and was her patron at the time. It wasn't a very big house—just two rooms. One of the two rooms belonged to Sakubai and the other was where Amma and I slept at night. In the corner of our room was a kitchen—a small space surrounded by blackened walls where we stoked the furnace. The house was fenced in, but the wooden fence in the backyard had rotted and fallen down long before I was born. Now the backyard was just an empty, open space.

Once Sakubai opened an old trunk and brought out a tattered black-and-white photograph of a house that looked different, a far cry from the house we lived in. When she showed me the snap, I gaped at the house in the photograph and refused to believe it was ours.

"That is not this house," I said stubbornly.

"Yes, it is," Sakubai insisted. She looked out the window as if looking at a different world, and I followed her gaze.

"There," she said, "that was where the garden was. Do you see the roses there by the gate and those patches of white flowers here on the side of this fence?"

I looked but still couldn't see. Nothing was remotely as beautiful as the house in the picture. Sakubai told me that this house—the house in the picture—had a lovely roof, a red-tiled roof with fresh cream paint. When she told me this I imagined the paint to be so fresh I could almost smell it. The house we lived in now . . . the roof was broken and leaked and the color of the walls was faded. Whenever I saw this house from a distance, I could see how the creepers had grown over the walls and climbed onto the roof; the cracks on the wall looked like a painting that came with the house.

For some reason I always thought the house we lived in was very sad. I don't know why I could never see this house the way Sakubai saw it; the way that photograph captured it. The window facing the gate was broken and drooped on the side like a wilting flower, much like a sad face. And when it rained we had to keep a bucket under the leaking roof. As a child I would watch the raindrops fall like tears into that bucket and imagine the roof was crying. It should have, I thought, because nobody looked after it well.

I could tell Sakubai was always sorrowful when she spoke of our house. "He left me for the younger devdasis," Sakubai said with a sigh. When I looked into her eyes she lowered them and rubbed off her tears with the end of her sari *pallu*. Amma explained to me that our broken-down house was a reminder of the love she once had, one that had withered away.

On days when I thought of it that way, I felt sad too.

I NEVER LET Amma know that the evenings were what I hated most about the day. Every evening, shadows would creep up to our doorstep—upper-caste men, often a different man every night—and offer Amma half a bag of grain or some clothes. There were some who brought sweets or small vessels or a bag of coconuts. I wondered if any of these men ever noticed Amma the way she wanted them to. They were too drunk to notice that she had let her hair fall loose on her shoulders, that she wore a bracelet of jasmine flowers on her wrist, or that the fragrance in our house was because of the lotus flowers she had spread on the floor.

At such times, Sakubai would disappear for the night. She'd tell me she was going to the village to visit a friend and I couldn't go with her. I wasn't allowed to enter the house. I was to sit in the backyard on the cold, concrete slab that would become my bed for the night. I'd eat my food there, and sleep there. It was a ritual I never questioned. I didn't know any better. But sitting there, watching the moon as lonely as me, I would often notice the ache that crept in my heart. In the morning I was to enter the house only after Amma allowed me, only after the man left. But one day, out of curiosity, I opened the back door and stood silently in the doorway. From there I could see into the room— the crumpled, unmade bed, the smell of perfume mixed with alcohol, the jasmine flowers strewn on the floor. I could also see the feet and hairy ankles of a man entwined with Amma's. I didn't know what to think or feel. I felt numb. I turned around and left. I sat in the backyard waiting for Amma to let me in. When Amma knocked on the back door as usual, opened it, and called out to me, I ran to her. She swept me in her arms and kissed me, apologizing for the night. Most days, that would have been enough. In a minute my pain would be gone; any anger, any questions would disappear. But that day the questions remained. And I didn't have the courage to ask Amma. So I decided that Sakubai could answer them for me.

That evening, Amma was churning butter in the backyard; the paddles inside the wooden container were spinning the milk inside it, the sound of agitation in that container similar to mine. Sakubai was in her room, playing the *tanpura*, singing a song to the Lord:

> *The night skies so utterly still,*
> *Even as the world sleeps*
> *My Lord, My Parameshwara*
> *Your voice rushes to us,*
> *Come to us, to our humble home.*

I tiptoed to her room and waited outside. There were days when music would echo through our house as if the house had a heartbeat, and my ears would fill up with the lilting tunes, my body full with the vibration of that music. But today I stood solemnly, waiting for her to finish.

"What do you want now?" Sakubai groaned, placing her *tanpura* beside her. It wasn't easy to ask, but I knew that I had to spit it out in one go.

"Why do these men come to visit Amma? Is one of them my father?" I asked softly, so softly it sounded like a whisper.

"Ah," Sakubai said," It is time you should know."

She waved to me to sit beside her on the cot. She seemed

oddly excited at my question. Her eyes lit up the way they would when she would gossip with Amma and she made a gesture of putting her finger to her lips, as if she was revealing some secret.

"I will tell you, what your Amma doesn't want to tell you. You see, we are one of many women whose great-grandmothers had taken a vow to dedicate all daughters born in this family to Goddess Yellamma. After your Amma's dedication ceremony, the men began visiting. That's what happens. Nowadays there is only one ceremony and the ceremonies are shorter but during my time, there were two ceremonies. For my dedication ceremony, I had to bathe in three holy ponds, and then guided by my mother and the village elders we went to meet the head priest. This was the main ceremony. I was eight then. The priest chanted prayers and told me about my duties toward the Goddess and the village."

"What duty?" I asked

"Don't interrupt. See there is a second ceremony, the *Uditumbuvadu*. I was twelve or thirteen when I was initiated in this ceremony. Oh! I glowed like a bride in a red sari and for hours the priest chanted mantras and flicked rice over my head. After that . . ." She let out a deep sigh. "Life was different after that. . . ."

I didn't understand what this had to with the men visiting Amma or why Sakubai wasn't answering my questions about my father. I thought, maybe Sakubai hadn't heard me well and I should repeat my question but Sakubai was so absorbed in telling me her story that I didn't interrupt.

". . . I had to take a bath every day early in the morning and go to the temple where the priest would perform a *puja* for the morning worship of Goddess Yellamma. I swept the compounds of the temple. There were days when the senior devdasis would teach me songs in praise of Yellamma. They are the ones that taught me the *tanpura*, taught me how to dance the *sadhir* dance performed in the temple as an offering to the Goddess. Some days we would go from house to house begging. Then one day the zamindar saw me at the temple, said he would keep me happy, even built this house for me. Life was beautiful back then, when the——"

"Why don't you tell her *how* your life was different and how *despite that* you pushed your daughter into this trade?"

It was Amma's voice. She had walked in from the backyard and now stood in front of us, her hand on her hip. Her long earrings dangled as she spoke. "And while you are at it, why don't you tell your granddaughter that it is nothing like a wedding? Wedding, you call it? Where is the groom?"

"You mustn't talk that way," Sakubai said, putting her hands to her ears. "You will anger the deity. We will have to live with her curse if you insult our tradition. It was decided for us the day we were born."

"What tradition? What was decided? That we were going to sleep with men in the name of God, that we are servants of God but the wife of the entire village?"

"Mukta's father has spoiled your mind, given you sinful thoughts. Don't you see? We are *nitya sumangali*—free from the evil of widowhood—because we never marry a man. We don't need one. We have the privilege of marrying the Goddess. You are crazy to be waiting all these years for him. Do you think he will return to the village and accept you after he abandoned you when you were pregnant with Mukta? Surely he has done some magic on you!" Sakubai sighed.

"There is no magic. And *this* is no privilege. You call this life a privilege? Look around you. Which world are you living in? Mukta's father, when he was around, only helped me see the truth. We aren't supposed to live like this."

"Oh? And how are we supposed to live then? I will not hear of it. Mukta's dedication ceremony is a couple of years away. You better prepare her."

"What do you want me to tell her? How all the men in the village use us and throw us away, or do you want me to teach her how not to wait for a man to love her, how it only brings disappointment, how not to have children, how not to . . ."

Amma voice was cracking now, trying to hold back her tears. When I saw the tears in her eyes, I burst into tears, cursed myself for asking stupid questions.

"You can have all the delusions you want. Women in our community do not know who their fathers are. They *don't* deserve a father. What makes you think Mukta deserves one?" Sakubai said, waving Amma away.

The words rang in my ear. Even when Amma yelled at me or beat me for my naughtiness, the pain wasn't as bad as it was now. I ran outside and sat in the backyard, watching the evening as it filled with darkness. It was peaceful outside, away from the noise of that house. There was no one to talk to, so I looked up at the sky, the full moon shining brightly as if smiling down at me. I talked to the moon and told him I thought I deserved a father, and if he thought so too, he should carry my prayer to God and send my father back to me. I thought that one day the moon would just get weary of listening to me, of watching over me, and offer me a solution to ease my confusion.

BACK IN MY village, when I didn't know what my life would be like, all I did was gallivant on the rocky terrain of the Sahyadris. I did not have any friends. The villagers did not allow their children to wander into the community of devdasis on the outskirts. Before I was born, there was a large community of women on the outskirts who were just like us—women who were destined to be slaves. But many years ago, they had moved away after a drought had affected our village. Amma had refused to go. So our house stood lonely on the outskirts just like me. The Sahyadri Mountains were my only friends. I climbed the rocks of that mountain as fast as a monkey climbs a tree. Amma was always scared I would get lost, hurt, or even injured by a wild animal. But those dense forests were my solace—the sounds, the air so fresh. Wandering in the scent of wildflowers, what did I have to fear? At night, the fireflies would light my way, and I ran after them while they led me out safely.

All my troubles started the moment Madam first came to see us. I was nine years old then. She arrived at our doorstep, her bangles clinking together, creating their own music as she knocked on our door. A strong, well-built man accompanied her. It was a gloomy day. Raindrops had begun falling early that morning and, as the day had progressed, the clouds thundered above us. The mud outside was pitted and slashed by heavy rain. I was looking out through the window, enjoying the sweet smell of earth, when they arrived with their muddy footsteps in our doorway.

Sakubai had been lingering by the door all morning. She was twirling the edges of her sari *pallu* as if anxiously waiting for someone. When she saw them through the window, she limped toward the door hurriedly. Her eyes lit up, and her face broke out in a smile. She waved to them to come in and gave both of them a long hug. I was standing behind Sakubai, hiding behind her, peering out briefly. Madam folded her umbrella and left it by the side of the door, then folded her hands in greeting.

"*Namaskar*, Sakubai, it has been many years. You are doing well?"

Sakubai nodded. She led Madam to a corner where they both sat cross-legged on the ground, facing each other. The man stood in the doorway, leaning against the door. His bloodshot eyes wandered around the house, stopping to look at me. His unshaven face gave him an unkempt appearance. He grinned at me as he loosened the handkerchief tied around his neck, then rubbed the triangle of hair on his chest that peeked through his half-unbuttoned shirt.

"This must be Mukta, your granddaughter?" Madam tilted her head to look at me. I peeped from behind Sakubai.

"Come here." Madam held my arm and tried to pull me away from Sakubai. I squirmed and held on to Sakubai's sari.

"It's all right. She is our friend," Sakubai said and loosened my grip from her sari. I found myself standing before Madam, her bright orange sari reflecting on her skin. Her lips shone red as if blood were oozing out of them. Despite the thick white powder on her face, her plump cheeks showed scars as if somebody had taken the time to carve very small holes into them.

"Look at how beautiful you are!" She gave my shoulders a squeeze. "Green eyes *and* a fair complexion. Sakubai, you have won a lottery!"

"Go inside, Mukta, and don't come out until I call you." Amma appeared from nowhere. I wriggled out of Madam's grip and ran inside.

I stood in the next room, my cheek against the wall, trying to listen. Every now and then I peeked from behind the curtain into the room.

"What is this? No *namaskar*, no nothing. Have you forgotten who I am, child?" Madam asked Amma.

"No, I haven't forgotten at all. How can I forget?" Amma crossed her arms over her chest; the hostility in her voice echoed through the room.

"Come, now, we don't treat guests like that." Sakubai tugged at Amma's arm.

"You should think about sending your daughter to Bombay with us; you know that is why I am here," Madam told Amma.

"I am *not* sending *my* daughter anywhere. I will offer you tea, and then I would like you to leave."

Sakubai sighed. She pressed her hands to her knees and massaged them, then sighed again.

"I will not be treated this way," Madam told Sakubai when Amma disappeared inside.

"You know my daughter. She is hot tempered. She doesn't know what she is saying."

Inside, Amma made tea. I watched as she poured the thick, brown liquid into short glasses that rattled in her hand as she placed them on a plate. I could see how her breath had quickened, how her eyes blinked rapidly. Outside, Sakubai and Madam chatted as if Amma's rudeness had been forgiven.

"So how is everything in Bombay?" Sakubai asked.

My heart skipped a beat. Bombay. They were from Bombay, the place where my father lived. Suddenly, as if I had forgotten what had happened, I wanted to jump, run outside, and ask them if they knew my father. I had questions, several of them. Did they know where my father was? Had they ever met him? What did this city, Bombay, look like? Several thoughts entered my mind, all of them together. Were they here to take me to Bombay? Had my father sent them here for me?

Everything seemed to be going well for a while. Amma had served tea and Madam was slurping hers with delight. Sakubai and Madam were so involved in their talk that I didn't think they could see me hiding behind that curtain.

Madam called out to me, "Come here."

I looked at Amma and she gave me a look that meant I was going to be in trouble for not listening to her.

"Come here!" Madam's voice was louder now, almost threatening. It prompted me to come out from my hiding place and walk toward her.

"What do you want?" Amma asked Madam, stopping me midway, her hands on my shoulders.

"What do *I* want?" She signaled to the man who left his place in the doorway, strode toward Amma, and held her hands behind her. Amma struggled and yelled at him.

"Let me go," she said, and I pounced on him, my shaky hands trying to assail him with blows. Of course he was stronger and looked at me as if I were a mere fly to be swatted away.

He picked up Amma like she was one of my cloth dolls and carried her inside, tied her hands with rope, and left her bound there. Before I knew what was happening, Madam had uprooted me and placed me before her. She held my jaw in her hand and tilted my head from side to side, looking for something on my face. Then she unbuttoned my blouse and loosened the *nada* on my skirt so it fell to the ground. Her hand slithered down my neck and crept down my body like a snake. I could hardly hold back my tears. I looked at the hazy form of Sakubai through my tears, waiting for a sign—any signal that would let me know what to do. But she wasn't looking at me at all. She kept looking out the window. Outside the rain still lashed against our roof, dripping into the bucket.

"Hmm, you are young," she said, looking at my naked body.

"What do you think?" she asked the man, who looked me up and down. His eyes wandered slowly over my body. Shame rose in me like a violent storm.

"She is ready, I think. If not, she will be in a year," he said, giving me a grin and patting my cheek.

Madam then picked up the blouse and skirt and dressed me delicately, as if she wasn't the woman who had been so harsh just a minute ago. "Do you know how much money you can make if you come with me to Bombay?" she asked me. "Oh, don't cry; look at your eyes, like emeralds. They don't look good when you cry."

She walked up to Amma, who was still bound and squirming on the floor.

"You are an intelligent woman to give birth to a girl, and she's a beautiful, fair one too. Only people in our community realize how important a girl child is, to carry our tradition forward, to receive the blessings of the Goddess. You cannot escape your fate by hiding your daughter."

"We will definitely spend our money on the girl for the dedication ceremony," Madam told Sakubai as they were leaving.

"Whatever is in the girl's destiny," Sakubai said resignedly, looking out the window, already bidding me goodbye. After they left, Sakubai limped inside, untied Amma, and caressed her back. Amma jerked her hand away. I could see the trail of tears that had left their mark on her cheeks. She gathered me in her arms and let me cry. Sakubai put her arms around us trying to comfort us.

"You called them, didn't you, Sakubai?" Amma asked.

"Yes. You don't listen. You are sitting in some stupid hope that Mukta's father will come. I cannot sit by and do nothing. We have a tradition to follow."

"I will never let it happen," Amma said.

"You have no choice," said Sakubai.

MANY DAYS LATER I was still wondering if it was a bad dream, if what had happened was merely my imagination. I would have liked to think it was and that I had woken up from a deep slumber in the forest, woken up under the shade of the trees with dappled sunlight on my face. The air was so warm and rich with the smells of the forest—the sounds of my life before that day. Truthfully, I had not understood why the strangers had treated us so badly or why Sakubai had invited them to our home, but I had begun to understand the pull of fear—how my heart beat faster for no apparent reason, how the heaviness in my chest never went away, and how I could hardly breathe in the open space of my beautiful forests.

Quietness descended on our lives at home. Amma and I mixed the spices while we cooked. There was a distant look in our eyes. We were afraid that if our eyes met even for a second, the bitter memory of that day would come spilling out. Sakubai left us alone. Most days she sat in her room looking out of the window or tottered around the house without glancing at us. Silence crept into our lives, allowing us to keep our nightmares and our thoughts to ourselves. We simply carried on, pretending it had never happened.

One morning I heard Amma's sweet voice calling out to me, "Mukta, Mukta, come here my child."

She sat by the furnace, a pot of rice boiling behind her. She gave me a slow, strained smile and patted the ground beside her. I sat down but remained very still, worried that any slight movement on my part could change what we seemed to have in that moment. Amma cupped my cheeks in her hands.

"I have been thinking about what happened that day," she said, and we both lowered our eyes, not looking at each other.

"I will call your father. I don't know which part of Bombay he lives in, but I know someone in this village—your father's mother—your grandmother—and she has promised to give me a telephone number where I can call him. You and I can visit the village and talk to him then. Your father is different than any other man I have known, Mukta. He always helps people in need. People come to him for advice. I am sure he will understand how desperately I want you to get away from this life. I want it to be different for you. I want it to be better." She looked away, a wistful look in her eyes. I nodded, still feeling very numb. I had never known that my father's mother lived in our village or that Amma was in touch with her. And once again, I did not ask.

"I couldn't protect you that day," Amma whispered, caressing my hair.

I looked at her then and felt as if my heart would burst. Tears poured relentlessly down my face. She put her arms around me, and I clung to her. I don't remember how long we sat there, near the furnace, holding each other, its warmth surrounding us, the rice boiling over behind us. Through my tears I could see the flames in the furnace rising high and low like the turns about to come into my life.

CHAPTER 3

TARA
2004

WHEN I WOKE up that morning, it was with a feeling of puzzlement. For a few seconds, I stared at the dusty arms of the ceiling fan that whirred overhead and listened to the wind chime as it tinkled in the breeze. The faded cream-colored walls around me added to my confusion. Where was I? Then it came to me. I was in my childhood home—Papa's apartment in Mumbai—far away from my tiny apartment in Los Angeles. It had been two weeks since I had returned, two weeks since I had contacted the police, and yet I didn't have the slightest clue where Mukta could be.

I took a deep breath and fumbled for my purse on the bedside table, delved into it, and opened the list of NGOs I had downloaded from the Internet. There were five names on it—centers that dealt with missing or kidnapped children. I started dialing the numbers. The numbers for the first three organizations rang, but there were no replies. The fourth organization politely took down the details and said they would contact me if they heard anything. When a man picked up the phone at the fifth agency, I hoped I could find an answer there.

"My father had hired a detective agency to search for Mukta," I told the man at the other end of the phone after I let him know all the basic details of the case.

"I see. And you said this detective agency that had been looking for her isn't responding to any of your calls?" He spoke in a low, rough voice.

"Yes. I have tried calling their office several times. Nobody picks up. I have been to their office almost daily since the day I've returned, but it's always closed. I just . . . I don't know how or where to start looking for her. Even the police aren't much help. I've been here for two weeks and there has been no progress." I was surprised at my frustration and how easily I'd spewed it at a stranger.

The man let out a sigh. "What did you say your name was?"

"Tara."

"Tara. I suggest you keep trying the detective agency; they may have some information. We don't like to turn people away, but you say she has been missing for eleven years, and we don't take cases more than five years old. We are a new setup and are trying to expand our services, but we won't be able to help. I don't like to tell this to people who are searching for a loved one, but the reality is there are about ten children missing every hour in India and more than seventy percent are never found. Also there is the possibility—"

I hung up the receiver as the words continued to pour out of it. I got up and walked toward the balcony of our second-floor apartment. I watched the city from up there. The street outside the apartment complex was flooded. Multicolored umbrellas fluttered in midair as pedestrians waded through knee-deep water. A *chaiwalla* served hot tea and *pakoras* in his street-side stall. Beside him, a hawker roasted corn for passersby. Red sparks flew in the air as he fanned the burning coals. As a child, I used to love the rain, mostly for its dramatic presence, the way it rammed down on this city, and brought life to a screeching halt. Only the rains, I used to think, had the power to humble this city.

There were memories of sailing paper boats in the gutters created by Bombay rains, of playing cricket on the wet playground with the neighborhood boys, of coming back home drenched and muddy, of Aai admonishing me for my tomboyish ways. If I closed my eyes, I could see my Aai, her soft eyes flashing with anger, that red *bindi* quivering on her forehead when she scolded me. I remember the time Aai used to invite the neighboring ladies to our home. They would gather in our living room eager to gossip, the cacophony of their cackling voices surging from our apartment. Meena-ji, our neighbor and Aai's best friend, a round-faced woman with a sharp tongue, was the one known to carry tales.

"I have always wanted to tell you this—about your daughter," Meena-ji would often tell Aai. "It is not good for a girl to have so much *josh* . . . so much spirit. How do you say this to a mother? How will she find a husband? Only we women know how difficult it is to get a suitable boy for our girls. How will she look after the house? Beating up boys, playing with them? Terrible! Teach her this or else you will never find a husband for her. You will spend the rest of your life collecting dowry but no one will marry her."

I smiled at the memory now, wondering what Meena-ji would think of me now—unmarried and not a person in the world to call family. If Papa were alive we could have laughed off her remarks together. Papa had always been my closest supporter, warding off such loose talk and rumors.

My Papa was such a tall, handsome man, and neighbors often knocked on our door for his advice. They would sit on our sofa in the living room and rattle off their woes while Papa listened carefully. Sometimes, I would hide in the kitchen, trying to listen in. I could always hear the grief-stricken tone in which those muffled voices spoke and how after my Papa had spoken to them—softly, reassuringly—they would emerge from our home with faces so cheerful I thought Papa had sprayed magic mist on them. I used to ask Papa if he knew magic, and he would laugh. "The magic is in the words, my dear girl. When you bend one's thoughts with words that touch the soul, they call it inspiration."

I thought of Papa and how he used to enjoy a chat with his best friend, Anupam chacha, here on this balcony, sharing a smoke, blowing curls of smoke into the air while Aai served them *samosas*, our apartment smelling of a mixture of smoke and fried food. Sometimes Papa would sit here by himself, his head buried in a book, and I would interrupt him and pester him to tell me about his life in his village.

"How many times are you going to listen to the same story?" he would laughingly ask.

I loved listening to it—over and over again. In those moments, he would take me with him as he wandered into his memories of when he grew up in the village of Ganipur. I would sit on Papa's lap; the eyes with which he watched this world became mine in that moment. His fair skin would acquire that flush of youth, his green eyes pondering over a distant memory of playing *kabaddi* and cricket with the other boys in the village. He told me about the mangoes hanging from trees and peacocks dancing in the rain, about the swaying rice and millet fields and the huge banyan tree in the middle of the village square where he and Aai had first met.

"Wherever you looked, Tara, the sky was clear and blue, bringing peace to the heart. You took one breath, and ah, the air was pure . . . so fresh."

It was a world different than the one I knew—this city of Bombay, where there were buildings after buildings, and when there were no buildings there were construction sites. I hadn't ever seen any green swaying farm fields with peacocks dancing in the middle of them. Those images would unravel in my mind's eye like one of the fictitious stories I read.

"I will take you to my village one day," he used to tell me. And I waited for that day to come. It never did.

I WASN'T EVEN born, Papa used to tell me, when my parents eloped from the village and arrived in this bustling city. They made their home in Dadar in this very apartment. Now, standing here, looking at the city from up here, I realized that nothing much had changed about this place. A row of *ashoka* trees and coconut palms still lined the walls of this complex, and a lonely *badam* tree still stood on the corner, its branches swaying in the breeze. I remember a board that hung crooked on the gates outside, with the words "Vijaya Co-operative Housing

Society," which greeted us when we entered the complex. That dull *chowkidar* who sat outside the gates always reminded me of Suppandi—the simpleton who appeared in my comic books. Every time we passed the gates, my best friend Navin, who was two years older than me, nudged me, reminding me of the resemblance, sending me into a bout of giggles.

It was on this balcony that Navin and I watched wedding processions that went by, staring in awe at the horse carrying the groom and the people who danced to the loud music around it. Before Mukta arrived in our lives, there wasn't a time when neighbors couldn't find Navin and me together—talking, laughing, or arguing—walking to school together, playing with the other boys, running after the ice cream carts during the summers, or trapping butterflies in plastic bottles.

I remember waking up waiting to hear the music resonating from Navin's sitar, the rhythm of the *raga*, and Navin's voice filling the air with melody. I would get out of bed, finish my breakfast in a hurry, and race to his apartment to hear him sing. Papa would laugh and tease me saying, "Except for one boy, nothing in the world is able to get you out of bed this early."

Papa used to say my friendship with Navin was destined to happen, written into our lives even before we were born. After all, Navin's father, Anupam chacha, and Papa had been childhood friends. Anupam chacha was a tall, broad-shouldered man, built like Papa with similar green eyes. While Papa got his engineering degree from IIT and joined a top firm, Anupam chacha started his own business in Bombay. Papa said they were brought up like brothers even though they were neighbors back in the village. They played together as children, went to the same school, and studied together. Anupam chacha was always telling us how as children they played pranks on the innocent villagers. I remember Anupam chacha telling Papa about his wife—Navin's mother—who died of cancer when he was six years old. Anupam chacha often reminisced about her, talking to Papa about her melodious voice, her singing talent. I learned from their conversation that she had been a gifted sitar player, and her last wish had been for her son to become a famous musician. Anupam chacha, wanting to honor his wife's last wishes, subjected Navin to hours of music lessons every day. I never heard Navin complain, not once, about these long music lessons even though I used to think they were torturous.

I looked across at the balcony next door—the apartment where Navin and Anupam chacha used to live. It had been silent since I had arrived. I had looked into its darkness through the windows; watched the locked doors hoping they'd appear there someday. Perhaps they had moved away too, trying to escape like we had. All our friendships had come to an end on that fateful day when Papa had taken me to America. I had not spoken to Navin or Anupam chacha after that day. And I had always wondered why Papa had stopped talking to Anupam chacha, why he never called him after we set foot in America. I thought of how the good memories from my childhood had disappeared so suddenly, like fleeting moments that I had to rummage through to remember. Next door, a neighbor hung clothes to dry on an indoor clothesline. A radio rang out with an old Hindi song in another home. "I have lost too much here," I said aloud. "I don't know what I can do to make it right." Birds chirped in the distance and the crows on the electrical line fluttered their wings at me.

THAT AFTERNOON, I decided to give the detective agency another go. I didn't know what Papa had been thinking, wasting his time and money on a detective agency that didn't respond to any calls. I fetched the document the detective agency had faxed over to Papa in the United States. There were two branches listed on their letterhead. I decided to visit the head office.

I caught a taxi and read the address to the taxi driver. He didn't know my destination but promised to take me anyway. As we neared the place, we stopped every few minutes to ask pedestrians for guidance. People were helpful, patiently giving directions. When we finally reached the building, I stood outside, watching the taxi roar away. The building was old, the walls cracked and uncared for. I entered the corridor and read the nameplate, "M/s Dharam Private Detective Agency."

There was no elevator, so I walked up three stories. To my surprise, the door was open. I peered inside. It didn't look like a detective's office at all. There were two tables littered with files, surrounded by empty walls. A girl in her early twenties sat at one of the tables. She lifted her head momentarily, her kohl-lined eyes peering above the files.

"Hello," I said.

"Yes?"

"Well, my father is . . . was a client."

She didn't reply.

"May I speak to someone who runs this place?" I asked.

"Wait, please."

I looked around. There were too many files fallen on the floor.

"Name?" the girl asked after she started her computer.

"Ashok Deshmukh—that's my father's name."

She typed the name on the keyboard, and then sifted through the files on the table.

"Yes, I remember. His file is not here. My boss has taken it with him."

"Your boss?"

"Yes—the one who owns this agency—Mr. Dharam Deo."

"Oh, yes. See, I have all the letters my father wrote to Mr. Dharam Deo from America. And here are the receipts for the payments my father made. But I can't find any response from Mr. Deo detailing the task he had undertaken. He was searching for a girl who was kidnapped years ago."

"I am sorry. I don't know anything about it, madam. You will have to wait. He may be back in two hours, or I can ask him to call you when he returns."

"I'll wait," I said and took a chair near the window.

The girl did not seem happy about me waiting in the office. She kept typing furiously on the keyboard. I waited for five hours, listening to the faint honking of cars, watching her work, wiping the sweat off my neck as the ceiling fan whirred above us.

When I was tired of waiting, I walked up to her and asked, "May I have this detective's cell number? A card maybe? The number I have been trying to call doesn't work."

She rummaged through her drawer, managed to find a card with oil stains on it, and flicked it on the table.

"Here's his card, but his number won't work."

"Really? I should complain to your boss, tell him how rude you are."

She looked up at me for a second. Then put up her hands.

"All right, all right," she said. "Let me look at those files in the cabinet and see if I can find something."

She shuffled through the files in the cabinet and looked at some papers in the drawers.

"Your father's name is Ashok Deshmukh? See, this looks like a list of the NGOs your father used to work with. I can't find the file. But you might learn something from them."

"Thanks."

The girl nodded but didn't smile. I walked down the three floors with the list in my hand. It had the names of seven NGOs Papa used to work with. How many children had Papa placed in good homes in his lifetime? How many children had lived with us during that time? Honestly, I didn't even remember all their names now. There was Abdul, the sweet five-year-old who peed in every corner of the house while my Aai cleaned up after him. There was Shobha, the eleven-year-old girl who chewed chocolates and spit them on the floor, and there was that beggar boy with matted hair Papa brought home—the one who stunk like garbage. Aai had been so scared I would catch lice from him that she had run after me for weeks to rub my hair with coconut oil. I smiled at the memory now.

A taxi screeched in front of me. The driver lowered the window and looked at me expectantly. I gave him the address of the first NGO on the list. Perhaps Mukta's name would be buried in some file . . . I hoped.

CHAPTER 4

MUKTA
1987

I WONDER IF every girl yearns for her father's love, almost like waiting to catch the moon hiding in the trees. After Amma told me we would telephone my father, the hum of thoughts in my head was like the buzz of honeybees—unsteady, unsettling. A ripple of excitement ran through me when I thought about hearing my father's voice for the first time. I hoped his voice would be gentle, the way I had imagined. I wondered if he would like my voice. But most of all, I worried about what I would say to him after the customary greetings. I thought of different things and rehearsed them like a mynah over the next few days. "My name is Mukta," I would begin. But it sounded foolish because he would already know my name. So I thought of saying, "How are you? How is Bombay?" but that was stupid too. I struck down sentence after sentence, thought after thought, until finally I decided to tell him what I really felt: "I miss you, Appa." Appa—that was what I would call him.

I didn't know what the telephone was; I had never seen it. Amma said she had seen it in the village but never used it. She described it as some sort of magical instrument that spoke to us in the voice of the person we wanted to speak to. It was a miracle, she said. I imagined a tiny person inside this box, no bigger than the box I hid stray cats in. This tiny person must be the one who had this magical power to be able to talk to both ends.

We left early in the morning on a sunny day before Sakubai woke up, before she had a chance to find out and question us. It was such a bright day. The sun peeked out from behind the clouds, and happiness danced on Amma's face, lingering in her smile. I couldn't have imagined our day to be any more different than it turned out. Before we left, I agonized over the dress I was going to wear, finally choosing a yellow skirt and blouse, then fussed over the way Amma fixed my hair, even took a bath longer than usual until Amma shouted, "Your father is not going to be able to see you through the telephone!"

I didn't know that. I told her I thought it was important to feel good so my father could hear that in my voice. Amma rolled her eyes at me.

On our way to the village I skipped behind Amma, raking up a mild flurry of dust that blew from the narrow road we walked on, a lonely stretch with only the occasional bullock cart passing us or a couple of tractors rumbling past us on their way to the farms. A few weary laborers passed by, too tired to notice us. I remember this walk with my mother, how a gentle breeze raced across the tall trees that lined the road, causing the grass amid the trees to flicker slightly—how the birds chirped along the way as we walked, and most of all, the happiness that bloomed in my heart even though my feet were soiled and hurting.

I remember there was a banyan tree standing in the middle of the village square, its aerial roots spread around it. Not far from there was the bazaar where women cheerfully bargained with shopkeepers who squatted on the floor with their weighing scales. At the grocer's shop there was a long queue to use the telephone. It was a hot day, and we joined the queue, waiting our turn, the sun gleaming down on us. The telephone was placed on a stool. When it was our turn, Amma picked it up but didn't know to use it and fumbled with it. The grocer sighed, took the chit from her hands, and dialed the number.

"Tell Sahib I helped." His tone was suddenly polite and gentle. I could tell from his reaction that my father was someone important in this village.

"It's me. It's me," Amma said, her eyes joyful, her lips spreading into a smile. I couldn't hear the voice on the other end. Amma held the earpiece in her trembling hands. The square black box with a round dial, sitting on the stool, looked interesting to me.

"Mukta is here if you want to speak to your child." There was a hint of moisture in her eyes as he spoke.

Many feelings floated in me: an ache for the father I never knew, the thrill of hearing his voice, but mostly, a sudden feeling of safety that overcame me. And I spread my hands waiting for Amma to place the earpiece in my hands, but she didn't. She continued listening, a frown spreading on her face.

"But, but . . . she is your child. You have to trust me. She *is* your child."

THE COLOR OF OUR SKY

She listened again, then stuttered, "She . . . she isn't . . . safe here."

Then, as if there was no more that she could listen to or say, she held the earpiece to her bosom, as if she were holding a baby in her arms, and looked wistfully in the distance. I could hear the distant flat dial tone echoing through the earpiece. We should have known it was the sound of rejection, the sound of being cast off. But Amma, she wouldn't let go.

"He will come to get you . . ." she kept muttering as we walked back home that evening.

Then, just a few days after we had tried to telephone him, I almost met my father—a moment that I replay again and again in my mind. It was Sakubai who brought the news, who stood outside our window, grinning, and bellowing, "There is a party in the next few days—the zamindar is throwing a party for the upper castes from the next village. The zamindar's son is coming from Bombay. Mukta's father is coming!"

Amma ran outside, holding the sides of her skirt. "I knew it. I knew it. He will come here to this house." She hugged Sakubai.

This time we should have known better, but hope always outweighs reason. On the evening my father was supposed to arrive from Bombay, our house looked like the house in one of Sakubai's pictures. It wasn't painted, of course, and the cracks still remained, and the roof still leaked, but there were many flowers Amma bought in the village—lilies, jasmines, sunflowers, roses. Their colors surrounded the house, filling it with their fragrance. There were *diyas* everywhere, the cotton wicks in them burning brightly, keeping the house aglow in their yellow light. She washed my hair and scented it with a special perfume. I wore the green dress Amma had bought especially for the occasion. Amma drew her own hair in a big bun and wound clumps of *gajra* on her hair. When we were ready we waited on the steps outside, looking at the desolate street that led up to our house. The sun loomed large on the horizon, threatening to descend behind the mountains, while we waited and watched. With every passing minute, the light grew dimmer and dimmer and the darkness spread around us. The flames in the *diyas* outside the house danced in the dark, their shadows on the walls, as if mocking us. Soon the moonlight was here to wash over our hopes.

Sakubai sauntered outside holding her aching hip and lowered herself gently on the steps.

"I told you, daughter, I told you," she whispered.

Amma wasn't listening. Her eyes were locked in the distance.

"Let's go," Amma said, standing up. There was a determination on her face, a sudden strength in her voice.

"Get up." She pulled me up by the wrists, dragging me behind her.

"Where are you going?" Sakubai asked.

"The zamindar's mansion."

The moon led our way. Our bare feet were grimy; dust clung to the hem of our new skirts. The village was silent this time of the night. We walked, not thinking about anything. We stopped only when we reached the zamindar's house. It was then I realized my wrist hurt from Amma's tight grip.

"This is where your father lives . . . lived until he decided to leave us and go away to Bombay," she said, looking accusingly at the house in front of us.

The house was huge, its roof peeping over brick walls so high I could not see what lay beyond them. It gleamed from beautiful yellow lights that spilled outside; the music playing inside the house and the sound of the dancers' anklets floated outside. I had never seen this house, the one where the zamindar lived, the one where my father was brought up and lived for many years.

Amma walked toward the house; I followed. Two hefty men stood outside the gates in uniform, holding *lathis* in their hand, looking vigilant. Behind them, the gates were decorated with marigolds and jasmines, ready to welcome guests.

"Go away before Sahib comes outside and shouts at us for allowing a lower-caste whore to come close to his property!" one of the guards shouted.

"I won't go until I meet Sahib," Amma insisted.

They stared at us, then looked at each other and burst into laughter.

"Yes, yes, Sahib will come running outside because you called." They laughed even louder.

"I will not go. You cannot make me go."

The guard shrugged. "Wait then."

"If you want to wait, you cannot come within ten feet of the door," the other guard said. He pointed to a place below the banyan tree. "Go there; sit down there if you want."

We sat under the banyan tree, hiding in its shadow, carefully protected from the eyes of the upper-caste visitors who arrived one by one in their cars. We watched the women who arrived outside the zamindar's house—how the gold around their neck glittered, and the borders on their silk saris sparkled, their *pallus* swaying in the breeze. I saw how every time a man stepped out of his car, looking dignified in a crisp *kurta,* Amma's eyes would scan his face for the man she loved. The music grew louder every time the guards opened the gates to let visitors in and softened as the gates closed behind them.

Amma allowed me to climb the tree to watch the feast inside. I had never seen a celebration of this kind, with so much extravagance. The courtyard was bigger than any I had ever seen; five houses like ours could easily fit in it. People were mingling, laughing and chatting, their faces, their jewelry shining under the bright yellow lights. I wondered if the light shining on their faces was the wisdom of knowing a world people like us would never know.

Even from this distance, I could see the long tables in the courtyard, the white tablecloths spread over them, silver vessels that held the pickles and the chutneys, the rotis and rice, different vegetables, curries. Men talked at one end with serious expressions on their faces, smiling now and then, while women gathered in the corner whispering and giggling. There were many servants pandering to their demands, some serving water and sherbet, some carrying plates of *kachoris.*

After some time, visitors no longer arrived at the gates. I got tired, climbed down, and sat beside Amma. We sat silently amid the night sounds and the music wafting from the house. We could hear the guards outside the gates, smoking their hookahs and drinking *daru,* telling tales of their family and laughing over their kids' pranks.

Amma said this was how it had been when she had first met

my father. She had been invited to dance at a party the zamindar had thrown for his son—my father.

"He took an interest in me. We would sit under this tree where no one could see us." She giggled. "When your grandparents were away attending a party in the neighboring village, we would meet on the terrace, talk about our lives, little things, even about the stars in the sky."

I couldn't fathom that Amma had actually entered this mansion. It seemed such a faraway thought, so beyond anything I could dream of.

"I was barely sixteen then; he was twenty, about to go to college in Bombay." She looked at the sky wistfully.

"Your Appa was fond of pointing out the stars to me. The stars, they make their own pictures in the sky, he used to say. Did you know? When we die, we become stars in the sky so we can watch over the ones we love."

I watched the stars that night. Someday, I hoped, my father would show me the stars in the sky the way he had shown them to Amma.

"I think our life is like the sky," Amma sighed, as she still looked at the sky. "Sometimes, Mukta . . . when you look at the sky it will be dark. You will not know who to rely on. You will wonder if anyone will be able to get you out of that darkness. But believe me, someday our sky will be bright again. And it will look and smell full of hope. I don't want you to forget that. I want you to hope, not give up."

I nodded. I told her I'd remember that.

We must have fallen asleep under that banyan tree because

when we woke up sunshine had already begun pouring behind the trees. There wasn't any music coming from the house anymore, and the gates were wide open, the guards fast asleep on the side. Beside me, Amma was sleeping soundly. I saw a man leave the mansion, saunter past the sleeping security guards, and walk up to the car waiting for him outside the gates.

I walked slowly toward the mansion and looked at this man as if I already knew him. I could hardly see his face, but I could see from the way he carried himself, the way his clothes were ironed crisp, that he must have been someone important. I remember how worried I became about my disheveled look—my skirt was torn in places from climbing up the tree; my plait had come undone. Then, something strange happened. I started running toward the man. I don't know what I was thinking when I called out, "Appa!"

The man turned to look, squinted through the sunlight.

"Appa!" I yelled again, even louder, as I stopped a few yards away.

I still couldn't see his face very clearly; the sun was too bright and on my face. But I could feel him watching me, hesitating, thinking about it. He took a step toward me, then turned, got in the backseat of his car, and sped away. I ran after the car, waving, screaming for it to stop, but it was too fast for me. I watched the car disappear around the corner, leaving behind a cloud of dust.

When I told Amma later, she said it couldn't have been my father, that my father was a very righteous man who could never leave us behind. But I knew better. When I ran behind the car, the man had looked behind briefly as if he was sorry he had to leave me behind. And I knew then, I knew as the dust that the car left behind blew on my face, that my father did not want me, that he would never come to get me. Sakubai had been right all along; I did not deserve a father.

CHAPTER 5

TARA
2004

"MY FATHER HAD always been looking for this girl. He worked with you and many other NGOs in his spare time and helped find a home for many children," I told the man at the NGO. "I just want to know more about this girl he rescued—Mukta. You must maintain some records of the children you rescue."

"I wouldn't know." He shrugged. "I am new here."

"Is there somebody else I can speak to?"

He looked at me confused. "Maybe," he said. "There is a senior person here—Mr. Chitale. He may be able to help. I'll call him." He disappeared behind a door.

So far I had discovered there had been two girls by the name of Mukta who had been rescued on the same day Papa had brought Mukta home. But, with one look at the attached photographs, I knew neither of them was the girl who had lived with us for five years. A couple of the agencies couldn't find a Mukta in their files, and others said they didn't maintain such records because the orphanages were supposed to maintain them.

"Yes, I am Mr. Chitale. What can I do for you?" He was an old man who limped toward me with a walking stick.

"I am looking for a girl. Her name is Mukta. My Papa—his name is Ashok Deshmukh—he had rescued this girl. I just want to know if there is any information in her file, anything that can help me find her."

"Ashok Deshmukh . . ." He frowned and adjusted his glasses. "*Haan haan* Ashok Sahib. Yes, he rescued so many children. How can we forget? How is he these days?"

"He . . . he's all right," I lied. I didn't want to tell him about Papa's suicide and invite questions. "He wanted me to look for Mukta, a girl he brought home in 1988. I am trying to find her."

"All right," he said nodding, "but we didn't have any computers back then, so we only maintained the names in a file. Five years ago the cupboard had termites, and we threw away the files."

"Oh."

"But before we destroyed the files, we put all the information into the computer. Let me see if I can find her in here." He took his glasses out and set them aside on the table. "What name did you say?"

"Mukta."

He typed the name many times, opening many records, leaning into the computer.

"There are five Muktas in our system. But they are girls who have been placed in orphanages recently. We didn't place a girl by that name in 1988."

"Could it be there was a loss of data when the transfer of files happened?'

"I don't think so. We are a very small organization. Many volunteers work for free but there wouldn't be any mistake. I wish I could have helped you. Ashok Sahib was such a good friend and a kind person. I've never really met anyone who has helped children as he had in those years. Wait . . . didn't you say this girl, Mukta, came from the same village as your father?"

I nodded.

"Then why don't you go there. You might find something."

"I can't," I explained. "It might sound weird when I say this, but I think . . . I think they'd kill me if I stepped foot in that village, if they knew I was Ashok Deshmukh's daughter."

"Hmm . . . no, no, nothing weird about it at all; your father had that effect on people. In his zeal to do good, he made many enemies. Don't I know that?" He sighed. "But wait. Maybe, I can help you with a list of the children he rescued. You might find some answers there."

He typed something on the computer, then handed me a printout.

"It's a complete list of all the children he helped. He wanted me to maintain the list so he knew where the children he rescued were at all times—if the families that adopted them were treating them well. He always looked out for them. You see, these adoption programs never really worked well . . . Couples want their own child, you know. Who wants to look after *such* children? So we sometimes allowed Ashok Sahib to bend the law a bit and let the children stay with him for a while so he could help them. It wasn't legal, but it was for a good cause. But this girl, Mukta . . . there doesn't seem to be any official record of her . . . anything that says your parents fostered her . . . so I don't know. Many children slip through the cracks. Some who get rescued land up as indentured servants. We try to make sure that doesn't happen, but we all know such things are always happening. I am sorry we couldn't be of more help."

"No problem. Thank you for your help," I said, and parked the list in my purse without looking at it. This search didn't seem to be going anywhere. As I was walking out of there, I wasn't sure if it was a gallant or a foolish choice to fly all the way back to Mumbai to look for a friend who had disappeared eleven years ago. Maybe there was no coming back from what I had done. Back in Los Angeles I had been a waitress at a small restaurant, besides having two other jobs. I worked all the time and barely managed to pay the bills, while Brian played in a band. Out here in this city, I did not know a single person who could help me. Maybe someone like me didn't know how to go about a search like this one. There was an easy way out of all this. I could simply leave—go back to Los Angeles to the life I had built. But I knew that could never be an option for me.

I thought of Papa and what he would have told me if I wanted to give up so early in my search. *We are strong people, Tara— you and I. We will survive no matter what.* I thought of his bright, smiling eyes that always gave me courage. Then I realized he himself had given up easily—committed suicide—given up on the search for Mukta, given up on *me*. I had told Papa's friends he had died of a heart attack, never letting them know he had hung himself. There was a certain shame in saying those words out loud. Perhaps it was the way Papa had raised me—to never *ever* quit.

I SPENT THE next few days cleaning Papa's apartment. I scrubbed the floors on my haunches; I stood on my tiptoes to get the cobwebs off the ceiling, wiped the dust off the tables, and rinsed the windowpanes. Some photo frames toppled to the floor as I opened the windows in the living room. Most of them were empty—I had taken the pictures with me to America. The ones that remained looked old—black-and-white pictures where the color was left to one's imagination. There was one of Aai beside me, celebrating my fifth birthday. Another where, as a three-year-old, I am sitting on Papa's left shoulder and Papa is clutching both my hands tightly. How proud he looked holding a daughter on his shoulder. Then there was that wedding picture of my parents—Aai dressed in a green sari, glowing as a bride, and Papa in a white kurta bordered with golden threads. There had been no big wedding for them, neither of their parents running around to make arrangements, no henna on my Aai's hands, no jewelry on her except for a simple gold chain and bangles, which her grandmother had given her. There was no ravishing hairstyle embellished with hair jewelry or jasmine flowers that all brides seek to have. Instead there was a flower that dangled from her hair bun, as lonely in her hair as she must have felt on that day. Aai and Papa are smiling in the photograph, but to me, their eyes always said something else. Tears had glistened in Aai's eyes whenever she spoke of her wedding day, and all I had ever seen was the disappointment in her eyes that her marriage would go unacknowledged by their parents.

Once, my desire to know my grandparents had known no bounds. The question of why both sets of grandparents never wanted to meet me crossed my mind now and then, but the desire to know them grew stronger during summer vacations when my friends would rush home excitedly to meet their grandparents who were visiting for the summer. I had wondered aloud to Aai once, asked her if I had done something wrong because my grandparents weren't keen to meet me. Aai said it wasn't my fault but *theirs*—Papa and hers. They were the ones who had eloped from their village and married without their parents' permission. Aai used to sigh and say the shadow of their elopement had fallen on their lives and followed them wherever they went, and that if she ever dared to step inside that village, her father would have killed her.

"That is what fathers do in my village when their daughter does something so dishonorable. It is not safe for you to go there. If you step foot in that village, your life is in danger too." She used to sigh and say, "Only your Papa is forgiven. Only he is allowed to visit the village."

I never again asked about my grandparents or tried to persuade my parents to take me to the village.

Once, I overheard Aai telling the neighboring women in her bashful way of talking to people, "The first time I saw this tall, inspiring man who stood in the middle of the village square telling us why we shouldn't serve the upper caste. Crowds followed him as if he were God." When she told her friends that many women in the village fell for his brave, defiant ways, no one doubted it.

"He sent me a letter. The milkman delivered it. Can you believe it? I was so shocked that he asked me to meet him by the banyan tree in the village square. As if I'd go . . ."

It was clear that Papa had chosen Aai. Of course, being her

usual shy self, she didn't dare venture out. Only after Papa's persistent efforts did she meet him after sunset in stealth, when no one was looking. My parents were upper-caste Brahmins from Ganipur but there was a flaw in Aai's horoscope that made Papa's parents vehemently against the match. It hadn't stopped Papa. He had married Aai anyway. "It is love that blinds you, doesn't make you think straight," Aai used to say. I always knew it was my Papa's charm that led Aai to take such a bold step. For it wasn't possible that my usually quiet mother, who believed it was her duty as a woman and a wife to always serve and obey the man she had married, could ever be so brave to defy her own parents. It must have been an enigma to anybody who knew this about her. Aai told me she did not have the good fortune of finishing her studies in the village. Her parents wanted to educate her brothers, so they had pulled her out of the village school in the fifth grade to help out at home.

"But that doesn't bother me, Tara. What would I have done studying anyway? I don't have your Papa's brains," my Aai used to tell me. "A good woman's life is in her husband's happiness, in being a good wife and a good mother, taking care of the family. And you better learn it too. Even six-year-old girls in the village know how to make *dal* and *sabji*. You better learn too."

It was Aai who told me about their life back in the village. "I was a moneylender's daughter. Your Papa," she told me in awe, "was always different. He married *me*, a dark-skinned girl, and could never see any wrong in it. Still can't. Even then, when he was hardly eighteen years old, instead of accepting the rules set by the upper-caste Brahmins for the lower-caste villagers, he rebelled against the zamindars, telling them the lower castes should be treated well. The zamindars were shocked. His parents thought this rebellious spirit of his would wear off if they sent him to Bombay for further studies." She laughed. "They must have thought being in Bombay would keep their son away from the village. But your Papa was a smart man; he finished his degree in engineering and returned to the village, causing so much unrest. Someone in the village once said your Papa's words were like lightning that lit souls on fire."

I used to gather these tales from Aai, and in all of them, Papa always emerged the hero in my eyes—like the one in the movies who saves young children and makes everything all right.

Once I had asked Papa why he did it, why he went against his parents and caused such a revolution in the village. He had laughed when he told me, "I was young then—I knew no other way of making the upper-caste society understand that the lower caste deserved respect." He looked away with a solemn expression. "But I was . . . I am honoring someone's wishes . . . When I was a child, about your age, my Rakesh mama would visit us in the village. He was my mother's brother and had joined the air force at a very young age. He was such a fearless man; always willing to help everyone. Whenever I knew he was going to visit us, I'd race down the stairs and wait for hours on the veranda outside. He'd drive down in his old ambassador car. We would sit on that veranda outside after we'd finished our meal and he would tell me stories. He'd often tell me of the time when he flew a plane and crashed into an unknown village. The villagers thought he was God because he had come down from the skies." Papa chuckled.

"They took him to the village hospital. He was unconscious

for several days and recovered only after several surgeries. He was inspired by how all those villagers, strangers really, helped him recover, prayed for him. They didn't care where he came from or which caste he belonged to . . . That's humanity, he used to say. I used to admire his courage. He used to take me around the village and tell me that all people are equal and that people from the lower caste should not be treated the way we were treating them. Initially, I couldn't understand what he was trying to tell me. But later on, slowly, I discovered that there is one thing that we all have in common, irrespective of anyone's caste or religion: we all get hurt in life, we all want to survive and be happy, and we all deserve to be treated well. After all, we don't choose where we are born but we can work hard and pave our way to success. And every person on earth deserves to have that chance."

"What happened to Rakesh mama?" I asked.

Papa gave out a long sigh. "He was killed in a car accident trying to save a pedestrian from getting hurt. He died trying to help somebody . . . You know, Tara, I grew up wanting to be just like him. In a way, he still lives in me. When I was young, I took too many liberties with my ideas of freedom and tried to create a revolution in the village. Now I think there are more peaceful ways of making people understand. I still very much wish though, that people would open their eyes and understand that humanity is more important than caste or even religion. And every human being has rights; treating others badly is a sin."

For Papa, these weren't just words. He put every good thought into practice. I remember the first time Papa brought a kid home to live with us. Eight-year-old Aram, with burn marks on his face, was abandoned at a train station. Papa said no couple was willing take him in, let alone adopt him.

"Let him stay here for a few days. I'll find him a home," Papa had assured Aai.

"Do you think such children should live in our home?" Aai had responded gently.

Papa glared at her but didn't say anything.

The first night Aram had managed to break almost all the glassware in the kitchen before my parents could get up and restrain him. The second night Aram had taken the scissors to the curtains and made a rip in every cloth he could lay his hand on. The next morning Aai had cried at the dining table. She reminded Papa gently about finding a home for Aram. After this she tried to keep me away from all such children who passed through our lives, determined that I not talk to any of them.

"They are not good for you," she would tell me.

I think it must have been a way to indulge Aai's misgivings when Papa told her that learning household chores would make such children self-reliant. Aai seemed thrilled to hear this, and she made sure all such kids who lived with us learned all household chores, from washing dishes and clothes to mopping floors and running errands. Until Mukta's arrival, she never complained to Papa, not once, about looking after children who were badly behaved and angry at being abandoned. And then Mukta arrived in our lives—lost and lonely—and Aai's tirade just wouldn't stop.

It is only now that I understand how my Aai suffered because of Papa's kindhearted nature. Every time my Papa dumped another poor, homeless child on us, my Aai had quietly cooked and cleaned and taken care of a child that was not hers. Not all of them listened to Aai, nor did all of them try to do their household chores. Angry at being abandoned, some even treated her badly. Perhaps everyone reaches their breaking point, because the arrival of Mukta had brought out Aai's worst side. After Mukta's arrival, however, she would often tell me softly, "If I had known this was what was in store for me, I never would have eloped."

Now, as I mopped the floors, I thought of my Aai's upper-caste upbringing, which had taught her to look down upon such children, and my Papa's free spirit, which had always prompted him to help. Despite their opposing value structures, they had always loved each other. At least, I'd like to remember it that way. After I finished dusting a part of the living room, I looked around at the rest of the apartment that still needed cleaning and told myself I would get to it the next day. I wolfed down the energy bars I had brought with me and crashed on the sofa. I glanced up to look at the sun setting in the sky and thought of the summer of 1988 when Mukta had first entered our lives.

CHAPTER 6

MUKTA
1988

I WAS ALMOST ten when I began to accept my life without a father. Amma, too, had resigned herself to the fact that my father would never return. In the days that followed after the incident outside the mansion, she never spoke of him, and her eyes never recovered from the loss of hope. There must be something about pain, about the way it touches you so deeply that sometimes you never get back to being the person you once were. You can even fall sick and never recover. That is what happened with *my* Amma. It was the beginning of bad times.

Amma was falling seriously ill; the disease that would ravage her body was just setting in. I did not know this then. Then all I could see was how her days had grown morose and her nights weary with thoughts, how there were dark half-moons under her eyes and how her glowing complexion had dwindled to paleness. The men had stopped visiting a long time ago, and most days I grappled with housework alone— boiling the *dal* and rice, hauling water from the well, cleaning the house, washing the dishes—the work was never-ending without Amma by my side.

It was Sakubai who was the first to point out that Amma had shrunk to almost half her size.

"Men don't want to hold a woman's corpse in their hands when they are paying for a visit. No wonder no man shows his face in the house anymore. Who will earn for the family now? I am tired of using my savings to run this home. I even had to sell my favorite earrings to the jeweler the other day. This won't do . . ." she lamented.

She went on, complaining that Amma lost her temper at the slightest thing nowadays, and that was not acceptable. Since Amma didn't say anything and lay there pale and tired, I thought I should speak for her. For the first time, I managed to open my mouth to tell Sakubai that Amma was a withered flower, one that hadn't been watered with the seed of hope for days, and that she, Sakubai, should have understood this without my having to say anything.

Sakubai snickered. "Withered flower? Seed of hope? What have you become? A poet?" She laughed as she limped to her room.

ONE EVENING, AMMA fell down in the kitchen. There was a resounding thud that made me scream in terror. I ran to Amma and tried to wake her up. I shook her so hard, but all I could see were the tears streaming from her closed eyes. I didn't know what to do, so I sat there sobbing, wiping her tears, until it occurred to me to run to the village to get the medicine man, the *vaidya*.

When I reached his house, I could see the smoke from the oven curling from the open windows, his wife cooking at the stove. I knocked on the door vigorously; the *vaidya* opened the door and yawned when he looked at me.

"Hurry, please. There is something wrong with Amma. She fell down, and she isn't opening her eyes."

He yawned again and tossed himself comfortably on a cushion in his living room.

"Please help me. You can give her medicines that will make her better, can't you?"

"Yes, but it's time to have my dinner now. Come back later."

I could see his wife near the furnace, slapping the dough on the pan, the smell of warm rotis wafting in the house, six children huddling in the corner biting into their share.

"I will wait," I said.

He shrugged. "Don't be so sure I will come to your house after my dinner. I might want to sleep after."

His wife looked out from her veil, her face flushed from the warmth of the oven, and I could see in her eyes that she felt sorry for me. She gently told her husband, her voice barely above a whisper, that I was a child.

"Shut up. They are lower-caste whores, what do you care?" he scolded her.

The woman hurriedly slapped another flattened piece of dough on the pan and didn't look at me anymore.

"I will tell my father," I said.

He looked up from his plate as he was about to have his first bite.

"I will tell my father you didn't help," I repeated.

"Your father does not even know you exist." He laughed.

"That's not true. I have met my father many times. He just asks us to not let the villagers know," I lied.

His laughter stopped. I didn't know what I was doing, but it was a ruse that worked. I had seen the villagers' eyes widen and their bodies stiffen at the mention of my father—after all, he was the zamindar's son. This time I used the power my father had over them to my advantage. I wasn't thinking; I just said what came to my mind. It didn't take him long to push his plate away, fling the medicine bag in my hands, and follow me. I wished he would walk faster, but I did not dare say anything in case he changed his mind. I remember how I could hear my heart pounding all the way and feel the moisture on my forehead.

When we neared our house, I ran inside not knowing what to expect. I was relieved to see Amma sitting on the kitchen floor, leaning back against the wall, and sipping a glass of water that Sakubai held in her hands. I dropped the *vaidya*'s bag, ran toward her, and put my arms around her. The *vaidya* pinched his nose in disgust at entering a lower-caste home but didn't say anything. He sat cross-legged beside Amma, checked her pulse, opened her eyelids to check her eyes, and then dipped into his bag to get some green and yellow herbs. He thrust them in Sakubai's hands. "Mix this with honey and milk and give it to her three times a day," he said to her before leaving.

AMMA FELT BETTER over the next few days, and her sudden cheerful mood put joy in my heart. But then there was Sakubai, who complained about every meal I prepared: the rice was too watery, the *dal* too salty, and the vegetables too spicy. Then Amma's health began to deteriorate rapidly. At night her body would burn, and she would mumble in her delirium, telling me not to worry, assuring me I would find love. Most nights I sat up with her, placing a wet cloth on her forehead, hoping her fever would die down. Days weren't any better; she was too frail to walk by herself, and I had to carry her with one of her arms on my shoulder whenever she wanted to go to the bathroom. When I tried to make her eat, she would retch violently.

One afternoon I was sitting by the window looking at the forests, trying to sew a tear in one of my old skirts. Amma was sleeping beside me when Sakubai staggered out from her room and began screaming loudly at me, saying it was all my fault. "Your mother is ill because you aren't willing to dedicate yourself, not willing to take the sacred oath that all women in our family have taken for generations. It is the Goddess's curse. What else could it be?"

"Mukta will never become one of us," Amma said faintly, her eyes red with the discomfort of her fever.

Sakubai mumbled something as she returned to her room: ". . . don't understand what she is doing . . . Where we will get food to eat if she doesn't earn . . . ? How long can we live on our savings?"

I thought about what Sakubai had said, thought about how right Sakubai had been all along about my father never returning to us. Probably she was right about this too—Amma was ill because of me. Maybe the solution *was* in my hands. After all, what could it mean to be dedicated? Clean the temple daily? Make food for the priests? Isn't that what Amma did when she went to the village? It did not occur to me that the men visiting Amma had anything to do with the dedication ceremony.

IT WAS A gray morning when I sat in the backyard thinking about what Sakubai had said. I decided I was going to do what Sakubai had planned for me, what the Goddess had in mind for me. After that, surely the Goddess could grant my wish and let Amma recover.

I thought I had mustered enough courage to tell Amma about my decision, and I stood outside the bedroom eager to let her know. Amma lay on the cot, coughing, looking outside the windows with pained eyes that had a layer of black beneath them. Her body looked so shriveled under the blanket. She didn't look like *my* Amma at all. I decided not to let Amma know about my decision. It was better that way.

I HAD NEVER seen Sakubai so pleased.

"You will find a special place in heaven for saving your mother," she said, taking me in her arms for the first time in my life.

It all happened so quickly after that, I couldn't believe it. It didn't feel real. Madam arrived from Bombay. Her jasmine flowers fell from her hair as she walked up to our house, and her red lips danced with delight as she spoke to me. "If you hadn't agreed you would still have to do it. Nobody was going to wait for you to make up your mind. You are born to do this," she said as she patted my head.

Over the next few days, Sakubai and Madam sat on our mud floor drawing up plans, making long lists of items, of errands to run, offerings to be made, things to be bought. But as they worked together, the silent tug of war between them was apparent. Madam wanted to finish the ceremony as quickly as possible, without much fuss, while Sakubai, who believed in the traditions of our ancestors, wanted everything to be done according to the right rituals.

"What is the need to spend so much money?" Madam asked.

Sakubai glared at her. "If we are dedicating Mukta we will do it properly, spending all the money we can. What do you care about how much money we borrow anyway? She will earn it back for you, won't she?"

Madam shrugged. "Have it your way then. Mukta will repay this debt for a long time."

The priest arrived in his white silk *dhoti* and sat cross-legged on our mud floor. Madam and Sakubai sat across from him as he consulted chart after chart and came up with an auspicious date that would bring great fortune to this village.

"This is the day," said Madam, spitting out her *paan*, the red stain spreading on our floor. "This is the day we will dedicate the girl."

The ceremony was to take place on the auspicious day—a full moon day—which was in three days. Sakubai explained that a bus would take us to the temple.

"What about Amma?" I asked.

"What about her?"

"How will we take her with us?"

"We are not taking her with us. A lower-caste woman from the village will come by to look after her while we are away," Sakubai said and limped back to her room.

I wasn't very happy leaving Amma behind and not telling her where we were disappearing to, and I told Sakubai I thought we should let Amma know in case she got worried. But Sakubai said Amma would get better because of what I was doing, and by the time we were back, she would be her smiling, usual self. I nodded and immediately pictured the Amma I once knew, before she had fallen ill, both of us working together in the kitchen, life going back to the way it was before all this happened.

IT WAS A Tuesday—an auspicious day to worship Goddess Yellamma. We started early. Sakubai and I took a dip in a holy pond nearby. Sakubai draped me in a sari, twirling it around me many times, arranging the end of it on my shoulders and pleating the rest of it around my waist.

"Pay attention. This is the way you will have to dress from now on. You can't wear childish clothes anymore," she said.

Then she lined my eyes with *kajal* and smeared red on my lips. She painted my face with a cream paste, then propped a mirror against the wall in front of me, looking approvingly at my reflection. When I looked, I was taken aback. The face staring back at me wasn't mine.

"How beautiful you look," Sakubai said, curling her fingers and cracking her knuckles on her head for good luck.

When I stepped out, a group of devdasis who had arrived from the neighboring village applauded and said, "What a lovely girl." The bullock cart stood outside the hut, loaded with the items required for the ceremony. Madam had already joined the group of senior devdasis and advised them that it was appropriate for all the girls who were to be dedicated to walk half a kilometer to the temple, and so we began walking barefoot. Until then, I hadn't realized there were other girls. I looked around and searched the faces that would participate in this ceremony with me. There were five other girls walking beside me, three of them younger than me, about eight years old. I wondered, since they were young, if they would be able to understand the great task ahead of them—to be devoted to the Goddess and be blessed by her. How foolish I was! When I think of those unaware faces now, I see myself in them, not knowing what life I was leading myself into. They walked unwittingly beside their mothers like I walked beside Sakubai. The older girls knew what was happening; their faces were soaked with tears and a shriek or a sob would emerge from them now and again. The senior devdasis played the *tanpura* and sang songs like the ones Sakubai often sang at home, but the music failed to fill me today, failed to quiet my fear.

The temple was at an elevation; the road to it went uphill, and Sakubai complained that at her age climbing was difficult. We thronged a narrow street lined with houses on both sides, and people watched us from their windows, gathering outside their homes to get a glimpse of us. There were many shops outside the temple; the shopkeepers were yelling away, encouraging passersby to buy the neatly stacked coconuts, the colorful bangles, and the plantain leaves. There were women wandering outside the temple, trying to sell us braided orange and yellow marigold garlands.

"Here we are," the devdasis announced; the noise and chaos of their instruments and their singing momentarily stopped.

The shopkeepers stared at us. Some of the younger girls cried for water, but Madam admonished all of them. All girls to be dedicated were supposed to be fasting, so we hadn't eaten or drunk anything since morning. As Madam explained this, the eight-year-olds cried even louder and had to be carried inside the temple. The moment we climbed the steps of the temple, we were in the presence of the Goddess. I truly felt that the Goddess would be there for me; she would certainly make Amma all right.

I could smell the premises—clean, purified with water and cow dung, different colors merging in a design on the floor—a beautiful *rangoli*. Sweets and fruits had been arranged for the feast after the ceremony, and my stomach growled for them.

The priest who entered the temple had a shaved head with three bands of white on his forehead; a *rudraksha mala* dangled on his bare chest. He sat before a large pit of fire and threw oil into it, making it leap up in flames, then chanted verses nobody there seemed to understand. Madam announced I would be the first girl to be dedicated and asked me to sit in front of the fire opposite the priest. Four senior devdasis sat in the four corners surrounding us, each holding a *kalash* in her hands. Each of these four pots contained plantain leaves, coconuts, and betel nut leaves. Many of the devdasis sang and played the *tanpura* so loudly I could hardly hear the priest. As they tied a single thread around the four pots in the four corners of the room, chanting mantras as they circled the room, enveloping us, I remember feeling like I was sitting in a boat floating in a river that was taking me from one corner of my life to another.

Everybody stood up and threw turmeric in the air, which fell on us thick and plentiful, yelling, "*Udheyo! Udheyo!* Rise up to the Mother!"

I scanned the crowd searching for my Amma even though I knew she wasn't there. How I missed her! Then the priest tied the *mutku* around my neck, the necklace that bound me to the temple, to the Goddess.

The priest asked Sakubai, "Are you willing to dedicate your granddaughter to the Goddess?"

Sakubai nodded. "Yes," she said just as easily as I had expected she would, without a second thought.

Then the priest addressed me, while leaning forward and planting a red *tilak* on my forehead. "You cannot marry any man. You are married to the deity and only after worshipping her will you be able to have a meal. You have to fast two days a week and oblige any man who comes to you. If he beats you, you must not retaliate."

He repeated this with the other five girls and the hours drifted in the chaos of the music and the mantras. When it was over, Sakubai came to me and said, "You made your mother proud. You are a devdasi like the rest of us."

That night, as Madam, Sakubai, and I left for home, I tried to climb the bus in my sari but stumbled over it until one of the devdasis lifted me and put me on the bus. When I fidgeted with my necklace, Sakubai slapped my hand and said, "You will get used to it."

As the bus ambled down the road, Sakubai brought out an apple and a sweet, and I gulped it down ravenously—the only meal I'd had that day. Along the way, we changed our mode of transport to a bullock cart for our journey back to our house.

I became impatient at the thought of Amma standing by the door, waiting for me, healthy, happy, and smiling. I imagined I would run into her arms and let her know how sorry I was for not letting her know why we had left without her. I truly believed that was the way the Goddess worked. I didn't think for a moment that any of these thoughts, these simple desires, were foolish. I was about to ask Sakubai if she was expecting it too, if she was waiting to see Amma the way I was, when the bullock cart took a wrong turn. Instead of taking us to the outskirts, it advanced straight toward another village. I was about to point that out to Sakubai, but she gave me a look that meant I had to be very quiet—which also meant it wasn't a wrong turn at all, and Sakubai knew where we were heading.

Squinting in the darkness, I could make out that this village was different than mine. We stopped outside a mansion with guards outside the gates who stopped our bullock cart, asked for our names, and immediately opened the gates as if they were expecting us. The courtyard around this mansion had yellow lights pouring over the garden, flowers swaying in the night breeze, and a light ripple in the pond that stood in the middle. We climbed the stone steps that led to an iron door where a servant was waiting for us. This mansion was bigger than the zamindar's mansion in our village. The servant asked all three of us to wait in the living room. A chandelier glimmered above us; photos of well-groomed rajahs and their queens adorned the long walls that surrounded us, and the ceiling seemed as if it were built halfway into the sky. Sakubai asked me to behave at this zamindar's house. She asked me to join my hands and say a *namaskar* as soon as he appeared, and all three of us squatted on the tiled floor, waiting.

A stocky man who caressed his belly like a pregnant woman appeared through one of the doors, waved to Madam, then walked outside with her. They spoke in whispers. The zamindar's voice was stern and Madam's a bit nervous, but even in her nervousness, she was adept at negotiating. They haggled about money, with her going higher and him preferring to stay closer to what he had initially offered. I hadn't understood most of the conversation I heard that day.

". . . but I am giving you a virgin," Madam said.

"I can have others . . ."

"But it is a reasonable price."

I tried to let my thoughts wander, but they bounced off the high ceiling back to Amma. I whispered to Sakubai, telling her Amma was waiting for us.

"Shh . . ." she said, glaring at me.

Madam called out to Sakubai, and they walked to the corner.

"I don't know . . . shouldn't we wait till she is older?" There was confusion in Sakubai's voice.

"Sakubai, if you are caught up in rituals, we will have to wait two or three years. Do you want the money or not?"

Sakubai took a deep breath and nodded. She led me to a room. "Sit here and I will be back," she told me.

I had no idea why I was supposed to wait in this room by myself, so I held on to Sakubai's hand, not letting go, until she knocked my hand away and left the room. The room was spacious, with an antique bed in the corner whose headboard had a gold carving embedded in it. I sat on the bed and looked at the chest of drawers; a table with a mirror balanced on it stared back at me. A certain anxiety crept upon me. I decided to leave the room, but just then the stocky man who was chatting with Madam entered and closed the doors behind him. He stood near the entrance for some time looking at me, then lit a cigarette and blew smoke as he walked toward me. Even in my fear I remembered what Sakubai told me to do. I folded my arms and greeted him, bowing my head slightly. "Namaskar," I mumbled. I didn't know whether he heard me because he did not smile at me. He tipped my chin towards him with his hands, scrutinized my face with his drowsy eyes, and said this had to be done so the Goddess could bless his family.

Without another word the man began unbuttoning his shirt and loosening his belt—shedding his clothes one by one and flinging them onto the chair. I slid under the bed and hid there, trying unsuccessfully not to cry. Everything was quiet for a while until his large, hairy hands reached for me, grabbed me, and dumped me on the bed. He said, "Look, don't cry. You are unnecessarily making things difficult for yourself."

I screamed for Sakubai, but he cupped his hand over my mouth. I whimpered under his firm grip, became quiet for a minute, and when he seemed convinced I wouldn't squirm anymore, he let go of me and tried to explain to me that this had to be done. Instinctively, I scrambled for safety in the corner and cowered under the table the mirror was balanced on. I told him I didn't want to be here and begged him to let me go back.

"Amma is waiting for me," I said, but he didn't seem to hear me.

He laughed as he grabbed my wrist in his hand. "You will get used to this."

I tried to loosen his grip with my other hand, but he pulled me out from under the table toward him—his breath smelling of garlic and cigarettes—with a force that shook the table, toppling the mirror. As it came crashing down, I could see myself in it—shattered into a million pieces.

CHAPTER 7

MUKTA
1988

I DID NOT know how long I had cried, how long the pain below had lasted, how much longer it would last. Most of what I remember was my face wet with tears, and thinking this was my punishment for not letting Amma know.

"Now, now," the man had said. "All girls cry their first time." He was putting his shirt back on and tightening the belt over his stomach.

For a while I lay there watching the ceiling, as bare as my skin. Even when the man opened the windows to let sunlight in, I could not move toward its warmth. When he left, Madam was waiting outside the door. I could see her spreading her palm as soon as he set foot outside the room. He thrust a few notes in her hand; she tucked them away in her blouse before waving to Sakubai, who entered the room and covered me with a white bedsheet that blotted the blood from the bed.

"Come, my dear girl," she said lovingly, softly, unlike her

usual self. "This has happened to all of us." Then she pulled my blouse over my head. "Can you walk?" I nodded and walked slowly toward the door. I don't think I knew what was happening to me; I had found a way out of my body and was watching myself move.

Sakubai loaded me in a bullock cart, and we headed home. I didn't notice the familiar farms calling out to me, didn't hear the swish of the trees. I realized later that this journey was the one where I had begun to lose the smells of my childhood. All I really remember is waking up to the sound of commotion, and I might have gone back to sleep had it not been the strangely familiar voice drifting to us.

The clouds loomed large and dark when we reached the village square, where villagers had gathered around a woman outside the temple, spewing insults at some villagers. "All you upper castes are responsible for allowing us to rot. All of you use her name—Goddess Yellamma—as if she were the one making us do this. You destroyed my daughter too."

It was Amma. She stood there, her hands trembling from sickness, her agony spread on her tired face. I wanted to jump from the bullock cart and run to her, but Sakubai held me back. I watched the villagers grow desperate in their anger.

"You cannot talk about us in that manner. You are insulting our traditions. The Goddess will curse the entire village," one said.

Above us, the sky thundered and flashes of lightning sparkled. Amma yelled profanities I had never heard her utter in my life. I could see the anger spreading like wildfire, each villager saying something that lit a flame in another.

"You whore . . . you cannot insult us . . . you cannot speak against the Goddess . . ."

One of them brought his *lathi* down on Amma's back, and in one blow she was crawling on the floor. Their backs were to me so I could only see their hands rise, their *lathis* coming down with a thud. I must have started walking because I remember nudging people to make my way through the crowd. I saw her lying there in a pool of blood. I lay down next to her. She looked at me, smiling through the pain, and held my hand. It began to drizzle; small drops of rain fell one by one on our faces, the sky weeping for us. I knew then that I had lost her, that the rains had come down to take her away from me—forever. The rain quickened its pace and fell so hard and strong it blurred everything around me. I remember watching how it mingled with the blood, trickling down into a steady reddish stream. My eyes closed, and I was enveloped in darkness.

MY EYES OPENED to the whirring of a ceiling fan above me, the yellow lights on the wall staring down at me. I found myself in somebody else's house in the village. There was a feeling of unbearable pain from the bruises on my body. There was a sense of numbness as an old man's face hovered over me, his bushy eyebrows raised in concern, his tiny eyes looking down at me. His hands, wrinkled with experience, quivered as he reached out to caress my hair.

"You must take this medicine," he said, repeating it twice before I understood what he was trying to tell me.

I was trying to piece every hazy bit of memory together—Amma lying on the floor, the pool of blood, the rain. I tried to speak, tried to tell this man that the person I loved the most in this world was now dead but the man put a finger on his lips and said, "Shh . . . shh . . . you shouldn't speak. I am the doctor, and you must do as the doctor says."

I fell asleep again, and when I woke up the morning birds had returned to their nest, and night had fallen. I could hear my name being mentioned outside. The voice was distant at first, bouncing off the corridor walls and approaching my room. I could hear footsteps and a woman's gentle voice, comforting and maternal, saying, "You work with that organization in Bombay. You help so many kids. Help this one. She is a child. If you leave her here, you know what will happen. She will live like all those women. Take her, I beg you." I imagined her to be elderly with gray hair.

A man's voice boomed in the corridor outside. "But Aai, I cannot take her. I work with street kids in Bombay and children who don't have a family. Her grandmother is alive. I cannot take a child away from her grandmother . . ."

"Look, her grandmother will only make her life worse. The police will arrest the villagers who killed her mother and find out who did this to the girl. But you know how that works. Nobody is going to go to jail. Money will solve that problem. Then what will happen to this girl? You are my son and I expect no less from you. She is all alone unless you take her with you." The woman's voice was soft yet stern.

The man sighed resignedly.

The sound of their footsteps entered the room now. The old woman sat by my bedside, tucked a strand of hair behind my ear, and gave me a warm smile.

I wanted to ask where Sakubai was, why she wasn't with me. I wanted to yell at Sakubai and ask her why she hadn't intervened and saved Amma. But there were no words that came out. Instead, that moment when Amma had died came back to me. I remembered watching her as her breathing grew softer and softer and her eyes closed slowly as if she didn't want to go, as if she didn't want to let me go. She held my hand tightly, and all I could see of her face was blood dripping out of every wound. But I remembered her eyes, I'd always remember what I saw in them one last time—fear—the fear that my life would be just like hers.

"There, there, you are safe now. They will leave you alone, your grandmother will also keep away." the old woman said, wiping away my tears. She looked at the man hopefully, perhaps expecting him to say something, but the man looked at me blankly, said nothing, shook his head, and sighed again.

"My dear, you will go with this Sahib to the city of Bombay and live with his family. You will do as he says from now on. Do you understand, my dear?" she asked.

I nodded.

Before we left, I watched the funeral pyre of my mother from afar, its flames leaping and rising into the sky. Amma's body was placed on the logs of wood, and I wondered how her once-living body could so easily go up in smoke, how ashes were all that remained of a lively, smiling face. The priest said a mantra that drifted in the emptiness and disappeared along with the flames. There was nobody there, not even Sakubai, nobody to sing mourning songs, nobody to say a goodbye to Amma except Sahib and me. Sahib paid the priest and stood at a distance, watching the fire after the priest left. We both waited until the fire had died down, then he turned his back toward the charred remains and walked away, leaving me to catch up to him. That's when Sahib told me he had offered Sakubai some money and asked her to stay away from me.

"It's better that way." He smiled at me.

IN THE DAYS after my life had taken a turn, I must have been in a daze because nothing made sense anymore. So it never occurred to me to question why any of this was happening to me. I didn't even grieve over the death of the one person I loved the most. I felt like an empty bucket tossed out in the sea, drifting at the whim of the waves.

I don't remember exactly how we arrived on a train to Bombay—if it was a bullock ride or a bus ride from the village to the railway station. There are faded memories of this journey to Bombay—of hawkers peddling *samosas*, chai, and cold drinks as they ran alongside the train, the wind blowing on my face from the window, and a dim image of Sahib sitting beside me, offering me a packet of biscuits as he adjusted his glasses on his nose and continued to read.

It was 1988 and many things changed in my life from that time on. When the train came to a stop in Bombay, I watched it from the window. This was the city Amma had talked about for so long. It was where my father lived. Sahib and I stood by the door, only to be thrust back into the train by a crowd eager to step out. It was alarming—the sudden crowd of people on the railway platform—some running toward a train, others waiting anxiously for another train to arrive. I worried that all these people would know what had happened that night with that man; they would stare at me, spit on me. How ashamed I felt imagining their eyes on me! I walked behind Sahib, keeping my eyes lowered, hugging my bundle of clothes closer to me, trying to hide my face in it. But when I looked around, I realized people were passing me by and not giving me even a glance.

A terrible void filled me as Sahib lifted me and put me in the backseat of a taxi. Immediately after, I felt a sense of panic when the crowded city rushed past me through the windows—the sounds and the noises of the rumbling buses, the cars that raced through crowded streets, the beggars who knocked on the taxi windows asking for food. Everything around me was spinning. I wanted to scream, let my terror out, but I admonished myself to be very quiet. We stopped outside the gates of a building, and a *chowkidar* opened the gates for us. But I had almost stopped breathing, and Sahib had to take my hand and pull me inside the apartment complex, into a world that forever changed my life.

CHAPTER 8

TARA
2004

THAT MORNING AT the police station, Inspector Pravin God-bole told me Mukta was sold as a maidservant to one of the middle-class families and had lived with them as a slave ever since. I imagined Mukta crouched in the corner of some house, shivering at the touch of another man, waiting and hoping someone would rescue her.

"It is her," he said confidently. "She's got green eyes just like this girl in the picture you showed me the other day. A local NGO needs our help in raiding the apartment and rescuing her. They told me her name was Mukta, and she had lived with a family in a building on the same street as your apartment . . . wait, what is the address you gave me the other day?"

He opened a file and read my address aloud: "Vijaya Co-operative Housing Society. Yes, that's it!"

"Are you sure?" I asked.

"Of course," he said.

I was suspicious. Could it be that easy finding someone after eleven years? *Maybe I was just lucky,* I told myself. I rode in the jeep with the police to a part of town I had never been to. The jeep sliced through narrow alleys, took many twists and turns, and rushed toward pedestrians who moved out of the way just in time. By the time we reached the place, I was feeling motion sick.

"Here, here," Inspector Godbole directed the driver of the jeep as he squeezed past a car and parked in a small space near an apartment building. A large truck barreled down the street, honking past us just as the inspector was about to get out of the jeep.

"You wait here," he instructed me as if I were a little child. I watched him run up the stairs and felt a need to run up the stairs after him. I wanted to knock on that apartment door and call out to Mukta. Then she would recognize me. I would envelop her in my arms and take her home, tell her how sorry I was for whatever happened. That was the hope.

Upstairs, I heard screaming and yelling. The constables handcuffed a man and dragged him down the stairs to the police jeep.

"I didn't do anything to her," the man kept repeating. He was in his underwear.

The inspector pulled a girl outside. She was trembling, sobbing, as Inspector Godbole brought her down the stairs. She had a deep cut on her forehead, a black eye, and a purple bruise spread across her right cheek.

"Mukta?" I called out as she climbed down the stairs.

Her green eyes fixed on me for a while, and then she looked away. I got out of the jeep.

"Mukta?" I said again, trying to hold her hand as she neared me. She knocked it off.

"My name is not Mukta. Mind your own business," she hissed and walked away from me to the police jeep. She was young, in her late teens. It wasn't Mukta.

"She said her name is not Mukta." The inspector shrugged as he knew that already.

"This girl must not be more than eighteen. Mukta was fifteen when she was kidnapped. She is about twenty-six now. I thought you knew that. I thought I had made myself clear."

"Madam Tara, look . . . it is so much hard work just to rescue one girl. You saw what happened today. There are so many such cases. You are coming from Amreeka, and you wouldn't understand there has to be some incentive to look for that girl . . . what's her name . . . Mukta."

He looked at me expectantly and cleared his throat. Behind him the constables waited patiently in the jeep.

"What do you think, Madam?" There was a glint of greed in his eyes.

I took a deep breath. This entire morning had been a ruse to extract a bribe from me. I wondered if that girl in the jeep would even have been rescued if I hadn't been desperately looking for Mukta. Or was it all just a setup? Had she been paid to act a part so I would hand over some money? I could refuse to pay him and never find Mukta. But that wasn't something I was willing to do. I sighed, put a few thousand rupee notes in an envelope, and slipped it to him.

"You better help me find her."

"Yes, yes," he said and returned to the jeep.

I hailed a taxi to take me home. When I looked behind, the girl sitting in the jeep continued to stare at me. I felt as if I were eight years old again, watching a girl with similar green eyes walk into our lives.

As THE YEARS have gone by, I have often thought about the day when I first met Mukta—a sunny evening in the summer of 1988—the year I turned eight. The sun had barely begun its downward journey. It was a Sunday, the day Papa was supposed to return from his weekend trip to his village. I was playing cricket with the neighborhood boys on the playground. But my attention was hardly on the game. My eyes turned every now and then to the gates of our apartment complex, searching for Papa, hoping he would appear there anytime.

Papa went on official trips to different countries and brought back souvenirs for me. I treasured those souvenirs, not because they were from some exotic, foreign land but because they were a gift from *my* Papa. It meant the world to me that Papa thought of me despite his work and worries. Perhaps Papa thought the anticipation of those impending gifts would distract me from his absence. But they always failed to console me. Every day he was away, I got up hoping I would be able to see his face, sit on his lap, and listen to the poetry he read out loud to me. This time, he had been away to visit his parents in his village and, as usual, had promised to bring me a gift.

When I saw the *chowkidar* opening the gates to let them in, I left the game I was playing and ran toward him, flying into his arms. I did not notice the girl walking beside him. Papa picked me up and gave me a peck on my forehead.

"What did you get for me from the village, Papa?" I asked.

"Nothing this time, Tara."

He sounded tired; he did not promise me something for the next time, neither did he apologize for not getting me a gift. His mind was somewhere else, a light crease appearing between his eyebrows. I didn't pester him with my thoughts, didn't ask him anything about his trip as I usually did, didn't ask why he had returned from his village empty-handed. I put my arms around him and allowed him to carry me home. It was then I saw this scrawny girl following us, carrying a bundle of clothes and a solemn expression. That evening when she entered our lives . . . I remember how her fair complexion shone in the orange hues of the setting sun, how her brown hair, tied into pigtails and braided with red ribbons, dangled on the side as she walked, and how her eyes—her brilliant green eyes—stood out like emeralds on her skin. She looked at me with those forlorn eyes for a moment, and then lowered them.

The women in the courtyard, watching over their children as they played, looked at us and whispered. The girl walked slowly as she climbed the steps, following us into our apartment. She stood in our living room.

"Who is she?" Aai had asked, emerging from the kitchen, looking her up and down. The girl took two steps back; her eyes filled up.

"Let her stay with us for a while," Papa said. "I'll find her a place in the orphanage soon."

"What is your name?" Aai asked the girl.

But the girl looked at her feet. Her eyes brimmed with tears. Aai asked her many questions, but she did not reply. At best, she nodded or shook her head. I thought I saw her lips move, but I didn't hear anything.

"Can't she speak? Is she mute?" Aai asked Papa. "What's her name?"

"Her name is Mukta. She has to get used to the city. She will take her time." Papa settled on the couch, opened the newspaper, and hid behind it.

"Hope she doesn't take too much time." Aai sighed and mumbled something else as she led the girl into the kitchen.

"Let's give her the extra room—the storage room. Didn't you clean it up last weekend? Let her have it."

"You want her to stay in there?" Aai was shocked.

"Yes. It might be nice for her to have her own room."

"In that room?" Aai repeated.

Papa nodded. Aai sighed again, loudly.

"You can sleep here," Aai said, and there, in our small apartment, in that even smaller room, the girl came to stay.

Our apartment wasn't as spacious as many other apartments in the building. Apart from the living room and the kitchen, it had two bedrooms; one of them belonged to my parents and the other was mine, next to the storage room. When she first arrived, all I did was share a wall with her. I heard her crying herself to sleep at nights, her sobs rising and falling in the silence of our home. Some nights, I would jump out of bed and stand outside that room, wondering if I should ask her if she needed something. But I never dared enter that room. Instead, I tried telling Papa that the girl cried throughout the night. He patted my cheek. "Oh, you shouldn't worry about it. It is a new place. She is getting used to it."

Yet I couldn't help but wonder if it was the room she lived in that made her cry. It was so tiny, dingy and dark, with faded paint that looked like the designs of a monster to me. As far as I remember, sunlight was never kind to this room, though the moonlight did spare it a few moments of light.

As the days passed, we grew accustomed to her stifled sobs and choked whimpers and let them mingle with the ambient sounds—the noise of traffic, the chirping of crickets, the distant barking of dogs. For a long time she never spoke. Neighbors made strange sounds as they called out to her. Perhaps we were so absorbed in our own sweet lives that we were unable to see the sadness in her eyes.

AAI TRIED TO train the girl, teach her household chores—to cook for us and clean the dishes, sweep and mop the floors, wash and hang our clothes to dry—but she was always clumsy, dropping things at the slightest pretext. Her hands shivered at the smallest sound, her eyes welled up with the gentlest scolding, and the rings around her eyes darkened as time passed. Soon her silent sobs turned into screams. I remember one night the lights came on in my parents' bedroom. I watched their shadows saunter to the storage room, and I curiously hurried behind them. Papa sprinkled water on Mukta's face as she quivered on the floor, hysterical from her nightmares. When she woke up, she cowered in the corner, her eyes frantically darting from one side of the room to the other, searching for something that was not there.

Neighbors came knocking on our door on one such night. It was windy and the breeze blew on our faces as Papa opened the door. I peeked from behind him at all the angry faces gathered outside. One man with a bald pate and tufts of hair sticking from his ears looked at us with his sleepy eyes and warned us, quite politely, that every night the girl screamed and wailed she invited evil into our home.

"After all," he said, "how can a mute girl scream?"

A lady standing beside him made a sign of the cross and said the devil must be in her. Papa laughed, said there was no such thing as the devil, and there was nothing evil about crying. All the people spoke respectfully to Papa, some talking in hushed tones, then a man grumbled loudly, "You should keep her under control. Waking us up in the middle of the night?"

It emboldened the rest of them.

"We all have to go to work tomorrow."

"Yes, yes. Take her to someone who can cure her of her mental illness, you know. We don't want such children spoiling our peace of mind."

"You should take her to the *jandeshwar Bhaba* outside the temple. He cures all ailments with a touch of his hand, I hear," a woman said.

"I am not taking her to any quack," Papa said firmly. "She is new to the city, new to this place, and she will get used to it."

That silenced the crowd for a minute, then someone mumbled something, and they began to rail again. By now Anupam chacha had woken up, appeared outside his apartment, rubbed his eyes, and asked, "What's happening?" I saw one of the neighbors say something to him after which Anupam chacha patted him on the back and said, "We will sort it out. Come on, *Challo,* let us go to sleep." And with a wave of his hand he herded all the neighbors away to their homes.

When they left, Papa and Anupam chacha sat on the balcony discussing the situation in the middle of the night. "Maybe I should take her to a doctor." Papa sighed.

Whether he made that doctor's appointment or not, I don't know. I never saw him take her to a doctor.

"SHE IS A lowly girl," Aai reminded me every night before she put me to bed. "Your Papa has all these fancy ideas about equality. Society doesn't function that way. We have to know our place in society."

Back then I always did as Papa asked. Every time Papa brought home a street child, he took me aside and said, "You have to be kind. Everyone is equal in the eyes of God." He repeated the same thing to me when he brought Mukta home.

My Aai was troubled by the arrival of Mukta, but she incited a deep curiosity within me. I yearned to know more about my grandparents from her; after all, she came from the same village as Papa. One afternoon I stood by the kitchen door and watched the girl cutting vegetables while the sunlight poured through the window. I walked toward her, contemplating the question I wanted to ask, and stood beside her near the kitchen sink, expecting her to look up at me. When she didn't, I asked anyway, "Do you like the village you come from? Do you think of it?"

She lifted her head, looked at me as if I was causing her pain by asking that question, and continued chopping the vegetables, the sound of the slicing on the wooden board slicing through the silence between us.

"I wanted to know more about the village, that's all, but if you don't want to tell me . . ." I shrugged and left the sentence open-ended, like the ache in my heart. I walked toward the door and thought of what Papa would have wanted me to say. So I turned around and said to her, "Navin and I play in the court-yard with the other boys. You can play with us if you want to."

She looked at me with surprise. I expected her to smile, but she didn't respond, leaving me to wonder if God had forgotten to put a smile on her face when He sent her into this world.

CHAPTER 9

MUKTA
1988

OUTSIDE OUR HOUSE in the village there was a sacred pipal tree not far from where we lived. Amma would pray to it and walk around it, circling a thread around its thick trunk in the hope that her wishes would be fulfilled. I would watch her as the thread enveloped itself around the tree; the dried leaves would fall and gather at its roots, then flutter away in the wind. I often wondered what it would have felt like to be that leaf, blowing away in the rage of the wind without a will of its own, traveling far away from the tree it called home, not knowing at whose doorstep it would land. But here I was—far away from the only home I knew, in a city, among strangers. You would probably ask me why I didn't run away, why I was willingly carried whichever direction the wind was taking me. But where could I go? There *was* nowhere to go. Truthfully, the idea hadn't occurred to me then. Those first few days in Bombay, whatever I did, I did in a daze.

That day I followed Sahib into the apartment, she came

running out of nowhere, like a gust of sudden wind. That was the first time I saw Tara—Sahib's daughter—rushing into her father's arms, the joy of seeing him spreading on her face. Watching her father take her in his arms and plant a kiss on her forehead, I couldn't help but feel a pang of envy jab my heart. She had kind eyes, just like Sahib. She smiled at me as if I was her friend. She was a couple years younger than me, and she adored her father—anybody could see that. Whenever I saw them together, I would have to stop myself from wondering what that felt like—to have a father who loved you so much.

When I entered their apartment I told myself Sakubai wasn't here to spoil the air with her complaints, which should have been a relief, I suppose, but it failed to quell that terrible feeling of emptiness inside me.

"What is your name?" Tara's mother asked, and out of nowhere Amma's face appeared before my eyes and tears slowly dripped down my cheeks. Tara's mother must have asked me many questions, but as I tried to speak, I couldn't hear myself, and it astonished me. This was the first time after my Amma died that I had tried to open my mouth and say something. I knew then that sometimes even the tongue dries up, just like the heart, and withers away in pain.

Looking back, I don't know if I had truly lost my voice. Maybe I chose not to speak. Sometimes, words defy the pain, the sadness in our hearts. Even if I could have spoken, had begun talking, what would I have said? My memories are very hazy about that time. In the first few days in this apartment with this family, learning to work in the kitchen by myself while everybody around me was asking why I didn't speak, I remember feeling lost—things happening to me didn't seem to really be happening at all. Sometimes when I stared at myself in the mirror, I let my fingers trace my image to understand if it really was me.

TARA'S MOTHER WAS a slim, good-looking woman with skin the color of honey, who always wore her sari *pallu* as a veil, hiding her face in it every time a man appeared at our doorstep. She was a dutiful wife who never raised her voice against her husband. I was instructed to call her Memsahib even though I did not speak back then. She was very strict about the housework and would not spare me if I missed a single detail. If I missed a stain on any of the clothes I washed, I earned two hours of extra cleaning time, and when one of the washed dishes still showed grime caked on its inside, I would spend hours cleaning the grout on the bathroom tiles as my punishment. I didn't mind the work; it kept my mind off the images from my past that came back to haunt me, especially the image of that night, which refused to leave me. Each morning she asked me to hold Tara's school bag and walk her to school.

The way things functioned in the city was very different from where I had lived. For one, every evening the lightbulbs would glimmer down at us, and the electric fans whirred on the ceilings like ghosts at work. There was an electrical grinder so noisy that the first time Memsahib tried to teach me how to use it, I ran and hid behind the door. I was so afraid of it. Memsahib laughed until tears came to her eyes. I only came out when Memsahib assured me repeatedly that it wasn't going to hurt me. During such times, I could almost hear Sakubai in my head saying the demon was running his vile powers through this apartment.

AT THE VERY beginning I knew there was something about Sahib—the warmth that shone through him—that I saw in no other. He was a man of few words, but when he spoke, everyone listened. And then of course, there was Tara—a zeal glowing through her. There was a strange energy in the girl that made her stand up to the world, stand up to anybody who got in her way. One day I watched from my window in my quarters as she played with the boys on the playground. It was a game of marbles and a boy who lost the game to her said, "She is a cheat."

Tara advanced on him, but Navin held her hand. He turned to the boy and said, "You are new here. You don't know anything about her."

"Look at her buck teeth, her short hair. My mother says girls who are good don't look like that."

"Don't look at me then," Tara said and punched him hard in the face before he knew what was coming.

Oh, it was a sight to watch! Such spirit! I wondered about it that night and asked myself if I would have the courage to do what she had done. Of course I didn't have a shred of that courage. Back in the village, I couldn't open my mouth when the villagers accused Amma or me.

Some days I liked, and even looked forward to, when Tara would make an attempt to talk to me. Every now and then she would appear from behind, tap me softly on the shoulder, and when I turned to look, run away and hide behind a door, peering out and smiling at me. I know she did this on purpose to make me smile, make me speak. Unlike everybody else who was either asking me to get something for them or was talking about me as if I were invisible, she said she wanted to be my friend.

Memsahib used to shout at her, tell her that she couldn't be friends with a girl like me, but that didn't stop Tara. She continued to pester me with questions, her mind like a beaver burrowing in, never seeming to stop. And on some days, I wished I could speak so I could tell her that she should never try to talk to a girl like me.

YOU SEE, I don't think I have quite explained the kind of strength Tara had. If she put her mind to it, I am confident she could do just about anything she wanted to.

One day, a couple of years after I had lived with them in Bombay, she asked, really pestered me about my father, and I told her he lived in Bombay. After all, it was true. When I told her about this on our way back from school one day, she marched me straight to the police station. I kept pulling at her hand, saying that was not a good idea. An inspector sat before us, smiled, and humored her. "What can I do for you?" he asked.

"She is searching for her father," she told him, pointing at me. I sat next to her, her school bag in my lap, utterly dumbfounded; all I could do was stare at her with my mouth open. The inspector called Sahib while we each drank a bottle of Limca. He took us back home, all the while telling her that was a foolish idea. I have never forgotten that episode. She was ten years old. Even *now*, I don't have that kind of boldness.

I WAS BECOMING quite a nuisance to everybody around me. The neighboring people complained about me constantly, saying I was keeping them up at nights with my crying. But I wasn't doing it deliberately, so it was not something I could have stopped, although I tried to. Looking back, I didn't know who I was crying for—my dead mother or the child in me I had left behind. I didn't think of all these reasons then, but I tried to figure out a reason and came to the conclusion that I must cry *just* for him—*for* my father—in some vain hope that my wails would reach him somewhere in this vast city. Why else would my wails spread so far in the night that people would complain?

Memsahib wasn't happy when Sahib said he would take me to a doctor. That morning I should have realized Memsahib was in a bad mood because of it. I was drying the glasses and one slipped from my hand and fell to the floor, shattering. Memsahib, who was wiping a glass plate, put the plate down, lay her hands over the counter, and took a deep breath. Her eyes flashed with anger as she leaned toward me and brought her face closer. I thought she was going to admonish me for what I had done, but instead she said, "I know who you are. I come from the same village. I know everything about you and your filthy mother. You have trickery in your blood. Don't try to trick me."

I knew then that she knew everything about me, and shame pierced my heart. After this I always kept to myself and put all my energy into trying to do my work properly. That way I hoped Memsahib wouldn't tell anybody what had happened to me. But no matter how hard I worked, it didn't seem enough, because for the next two nights, she dumped all the leftovers in the dustbin, leaving me nothing to eat for dinner. I must admit, at times I felt it was better this way—she gave me what I deserved, unlike the gentleness and warmth Tara and her father offered, which was such a shock.

THE NEXT AFTERNOON, after lunch, I was standing in the kitchen washing the dishes, daydreaming about Amma, imagining we were walking along a narrow street to the village as I watched the sparrows hopping on the branches of the nearby trees. I was suddenly brought to reality, ripped from my daydream, when Sahib's loud voice boomed across the living room, telling Tara he was going to the library to search for a book he had wanted to read for a long time. I think this was actually meant for Memsahib to hear; she was in the kitchen at the time with me. Those days, that was how they communicated with each other—by letting Tara know what they were doing. I presumed this still had something to do with Sahib trying to take me to the doctor, although I knew Memsahib had already convinced Sahib I did not need one.

I could hear Tara pester her father to take her along, like the way I used to pester my Amma. I didn't expect Sahib to come in, wave his hand at me, and ask me if I wanted to come along. I was so shocked; I kept staring at him, then looked at Memsahib for approval. She was standing near the stove, chopping ginger, and she lifted her head but barely looked at me.

"Come now, don't worry about Memsahib," Sahib said, so I left the dirty dishes in the vessels, wiped my hands on the towel on my shoulder, and hurried along as the chopping sounds from the kitchen behind me grew faster and louder.

Navin wanted to come along too, but his father looked up

from the newspaper he was reading, frowned at him, and said, "Your music lessons?" Navin returned home with a dismal expression.

Like I said before, the street outside this apartment complex was lined with shops and we walked for a distance—Tara holding her father's hand, walking ahead. Many shopkeepers poked their heads outside, joined their hands in greeting as Sahib nodded at them. My fear could have easily overtaken me, I suppose, but today for some reason thoughts of my father invaded my mind. I imagined to see him in every face that passed by, imagined that one day he would recognize me on the street and call out to me the way Amma would lovingly call out, "Mukta, come here my child." It was a remote possibility, but I hung on to it like a spider hangs on to the weave of its damaged web.

It took us a while to find a taxi on this sleepy afternoon. Tara pointed out to the sea, to the temple, or the garden that we passed, jabbering away, imbuing it with her own colors, and I watched everything around me through her eyes. The waves of the sea didn't seem as threatening anymore; instead I heard music in them. I didn't seem to be overwhelmed by the crowd anymore—I saw them as people having their own worries—and when she talked about her mother, I could see Amma and me together in that garden we passed by. I realized then that her presence was giving me more comfort than anything had in the past few days.

When the taxi stopped, Tara opened the door to a world I had never seen before. It was the Asiatic library, she said. I didn't know what a library was, but as I saw this structure and several steps leading to it, I understood it was a temple—a temple for books. Its presence was so commanding with its white paint gleaming in the sun. I stood at the bottom of the stairs, watching this structure before me, astonished at the tricks my eyes were playing on me. Tara held my hand and led me up the stairs. Her sudden touch, its warmth without warning, astonished me.

The smell inside was musty, but I didn't mind it. There were elderly people poring over local newspapers and a spiral staircase that led to more books. I wondered as I looked at those books, trying to distribute a treasure of experiences. How I wanted to gather those thoughts for myself! I opened a book and caressed the letters on the pages, wondering about the strength of those words that had caused people to build a temple for them. I wasn't listening very well when Sahib pointed to the marble statues, explaining each of them to Tara, telling her about the rare gold coin that belonged to Emperor Akbar. A deep longing to be able to read rose in my heart, just like that day when Amma and I had walked through the village and she had shown me the village school for the first time. I couldn't believe I was allowed to see a place as great as this.

When we exited the library a bus full of tourists arrived, clicking pictures. As people posed on the steps, Tara insisted on getting a photograph. Overhearing her tantrum, one of the photographers with the tourist group offered to click a snap of us and spoke to Sahib, assuring him, "Don't worry. I will post the negative and the snaps to you."

Tara stood on the steps outside the library and insisted I stand beside her. There is a photograph of us when we were little, those eight commanding columns behind us, Tara's arm around me. Later, the envelope arrived with two identical photos and a negative—one of which Tara gave me to keep. I saved it in a special hiding place under a loose tile in the kitchen.

In the taxi, when we were returning home, Sahib asked Tara, "So, are you excited that school begins soon?"

She made a face and shrugged. Then out of the blue, she pointed to me and asked, "Papa, will she be going to school too?"

I looked at her shocked. Sahib turned behind to look at me.

"What do you think? You will want to study, won't you?" he asked, and before I could digest the thought, I could see myself in his eyes, flying like a bird in the sky.

CHAPTER 10

TARA

1988–1992

I REMEMBER THE argument my parents had that night—it was one of their first fierce fights. The voices came from their bedroom. I could hear them through the wall while I lay wide awake in my bed. A frog croaked somewhere in the distance, and I could hear the sputter of a vehicle on the street below, but I tried to concentrate on these sounds instead.

"Why are you doing this to me? Asking such a child if she wants to study?" Aai sobbed.

"Shh, be quiet," Papa said, "unless you want the neighbors to hear."

"This is all because I could not give you a son, *haan*?"

"It has nothing to do with *us* having a son. I think everyone deserves to have an education. And if she is going to live here, shouldn't she at least be allowed to study?"

"That isn't the way our society sees it. She is not our child. Why pay for this child to go to school? What is so important about her that you won't find her a place in the orphanage? Why does she have to live with us?"

"I . . . I . . . think she needs us. She needs us," Papa repeated.

"All my friends will laugh at me for taking care of a lower-caste child."

"It is their problem if they don't understand. You married me because you like my ideas, remember? Or have you forgotten? And I already think you make her do too much work around the house. You—"

"It is my father's curse. The day I decided to run away, elope with you, I chose my fate. How can you . . . ?"

I didn't listen anymore; their voices put a fear in my heart; a warm feeling of uncertainty rose up in my throat. Before this, I had never witnessed an argument between my parents, and I wondered when Papa's calmness or Aai's faithful reticence had disappeared.

I blamed myself.

I wasn't thinking when I had asked if she would be going to school too. It was an absurd question to begin with, because if I had given it thought, I would have realized all such children who came to stay with us for a while never went to school. They stayed at home and earned their keep. But words once released cannot be taken back.

I lumbered out of my bedroom and walked up to the window, hoping that watching the serene night might drown their argument. I don't know what made me amble across to the storage room. I sat outside the storage room near the sill where a door should have been and watched the girl as she sat there—looking out the window, wiping her tears.

"Why are you crying?" I whispered, the sill a line that divided us.

She looked at me, then looked back at the sky. I thought she hadn't heard me, so I hollered the question a little louder. When she didn't respond, I put one foot across the sill and crossed over into that dark room. Without realizing it, that was my first step into her world, a place I had never before set foot, and I remember how the air smelled musty and stale, how hopefully she was looking out the window, sitting with her back against the wall, her knees drawn to her chest. I sat down next to her, knowing that if Aai saw me, she would scold me and say, "You should never sit next to such children."

BUT THERE MUST have been something comforting about it, about having another person next to me in my moment of chaos. We didn't say anything to each other. The only sounds were the chirping of crickets, distant traffic, and her intermittent choked whimpers.

I REMEMBER TRYING so very hard to follow Papa's ways, to try to be kind to Mukta. But I am not sure if I was always kind to her. There are many things I don't remember now; I don't recollect when she began speaking or when we became friends or when the bond between us strengthened. I don't think Aai was ever kind to her, although that is a memory I would like to have. What I do remember are moments Mukta and I shared—like on that first rainy day of school in 1989 when it began to drizzle.

Mukta was carrying my school bag for me as she walked me to school. I was telling her how Papa loved the rain.

"Aai says Papa should have been a poet. Because Papa said," I jabbered on, "when the first raindrops smudge the soil, the smell that wafts into the air is like . . ."

I had the sudden feeling I was walking all alone. When I looked behind me, Mukta was nowhere in sight. I retraced my steps. She was standing in the middle of the street, looking up at the sky with frightened eyes. The sky roared above us as dark clouds gathered. I walked to her.

"What happened? We will be late for school."

She was still staring at the sky. It began raining hard then, the raindrops falling with such force and ferocity that people took cover in nearby shops and under tarpaulin roofs put up by hawkers.

"We should go too. There . . ." I pointed to a shop. Mukta stood rooted to the spot, quivering, tears rolling down her cheeks, clutching my school bag to her chest. I pulled at her hand, trying to wake her up from her reverie.

"Come on," I urged. But she didn't give me a glance.

The rain poured even harder. Sudden lightning bolts in the sky made everybody on the street wary. I was completely drenched and mad at her. I told her that I'd complain to Aai. Before I said anything else, she dropped my school bag on the street and started running.

"Mukta!" I called after her.

She had disappeared in the rain. I picked up my soaking school bag and ran in the same direction. I couldn't see through the heavy rain, so, squinting, I searched for her, and then spotted her sitting somewhere. As I neared, I realized it was a shop that was closed for business. Its shutters were down and Mukta sat on the steps outside. I stood there watching her. The roof, a thin asbestos sheet, protected us from the rain ramming away on it.

She sat holding her knees to her chest, swinging back and forth. I sat down beside her, watching people fleeing the rain, searching for a shelter, escaping from the flurry around us.

"Are you all right?" I asked.

"Amma died . . ." Mukta whispered, looking toward the sky. "Amma died in the rain. They beat her and left her to die."

Suddenly, I wished Papa were there. He would have known what to say.

"She was ill for a very long time, and I thought . . . I thought she'd get better . . . but . . ." she sobbed, her words melting into tears.

I put my hand around her shoulder, and we huddled close together. In that moment I had forgotten she was just another homeless kid Papa had brought home. We were simply two girls sitting on the side of that street, watching the rain wash down the debris. When the rain diminished to a drizzle and the skies were clear, people stepped out of their shelters and went their way. I sat there for some time holding her close, hoping my warmth could dissolve her pain. I'd like to think *that* was the beginning of our friendship.

EVERY MOMENT WE spent together brought us closer. I remember I was eleven when she first asked me if I could teach her how to read. Amused, I had laughed out loud. But she had insisted, day after day, and so I thought I'd teach her a few alphabets and leave it at that. After all, how much could a girl like her be interested in learning? But unlike anybody I had ever met—among my friends

or in my class—her hunger for reading was unique, never seeming to stop. When I brought her the alphabet book, I thought
she would be bored with it and give up on her outrageous desire
to read, realizing it wasn't meant for her. Instead, she surprised
me. She kept going with it and learned how to read proficiently
within a year, probably less. When Aai wasn't around, she borrowed books from the library in our apartment, and I brought
her books from the library in my school. I always wondered what
she saw in them. Once I even asked her, "What do you get from
those books, anyway?"

She closed the book she was reading, thought for a while,
and said, "It is better than the world we live in."

"You are crazy," I said, shaking my head.

NOW, WHEN I think of my childhood, these are the images
that drift to me: I am sitting by her side talking to her as she is
busy with the household chores; we are sitting on the terrace,
huddled together, discussing books because she likes to do that
and discussing sports because I like to do that; we are walking
to school or are walking back from the crowded bazaars; we are
sitting on the park bench licking ice cream cones. These and
many more pictures remain, and it is what I think about the
most—our time together.

CHAPTER 11

MUKTA
1988–1992

YOU SEE, WHEN you find a true friend, a strange joy suddenly springs from within—one you could not find for yourself until then, and one you hope will carry with you as you go along. I would do just about anything for Tara if she asked. She was the only one who greeted me with a smile in the morning, making me feel as if I meant something to someone in this world. Memsahib woke her up and combed her hair lovingly, but I fussed over her while I served breakfast, giving her an extra helping. Memsahib watched with a frown on her face while she knitted but didn't seem to mind.

There were other things I liked doing for Tara—packing her lunch box, cleaning her room, collecting her scattered books and putting them in her school bag—but most of all I had begun to enjoy our long walks to her school. Following her, carrying her backpack, was all I looked forward to those days. The school wasn't far away, a half hour's walk, but listening to Tara's stories of school, of her day, of the friends she made, the teachers who bothered her—her nonstop chatter—was such a pleasure. I tell you, the way she could talk! You could travel the world but never be able to see it the way she could describe it to you.

When I asked her if she liked to study, she said studying wasn't that great. To prove her point she showed me a village on the map of India—a tiny area marked with red ink that looked so small I wondered how I must have lived in one such village, how all of us could have fit in such a tiny place. It confused me.

"See, they confuse you. Sometimes you are better off not knowing."

"But don't you like that you can get to know everything there is to know?" I asked. "If it meant that I had to search for a thousand villages on a map, I would be ready to do it."

She sighed and said nothing else. I knew I had overstepped my boundary. It wasn't like me to say what I liked to do, but she was the only person I could say anything to who would understand.

You see, there was only one thing I couldn't tell Tara—about the village I came from, although she insisted many times that I tell her about it. There were too many bad memories there, things I couldn't share with her or anyone, for that matter. And I knew she was annoyed with me for not telling her about my life back in the village. Some days she would be silent, not speak to me, and that was punishment enough for me.

Sometimes, I couldn't help but wonder what it would be like to study. To be educated would mean gaining respect in everybody's eyes. But did someone like me deserve that? Memsahib had made it very clear that I shouldn't have fancy ideas about school. She had spoken to Sahib about that. "As long as you live with us, you will not be going to school, you hear me?" she had said.

There were days when I walked Tara to school, watched her disappear inside the compound, then stood for a long time watching the premises fill with students in their brown uniforms. When all the parents and servants left and all the cars, rickshaws, and taxis disappeared, I stood outside the school, as if it were a dream. Of course Memsahib used to be livid with me for not being back in time, threatening me by saying she would put me back on the streets where I belonged or slapping me.

I think Memsahib was the only one who didn't like me. I remember how terrified I was of her. On some days, she increased my daily chores, and I struggled hard to complete them. It was in 1991, when Memsahib got an offer to use her embroidering skills in a garment shop opened by one of her friends near Century Bazaar, that I found relief from her hatred. That also gave Tara and me a lot of time with each other. Sahib was traveling and Memsahib was too busy with her work to worry if her daughter was mingling with a girl like me.

Once when Tara and I were walking back home, I commented on the bookshop next door and said jokingly, "I would never be able to go to a store like that. If I went in there it would be like a pig wanting a bath." I giggled. I thought it was a great joke, but Tara kept looking at me seriously.

"Maybe I will help you learn to read," she said. "You talk so much about it. Once you study we will be equals—you and I—just like sisters. Then Aai wouldn't treat you badly. But you have to learn English for that. Nobody can call you lowly if you know English. Aai says people who know English are very smart."

My eyes widened, and I felt like a brick sat in my throat. I couldn't believe she was willing to teach me.

Over the next few days she didn't bring it up again, so I thought it must have been a joke. But Tara kept her promise. One afternoon after Memsahib stepped out to Century Bazaar, she led me to the terrace. Under the warmth of the afternoon sun we laid down a blanket on the terrace floor and sat cross-legged on it. She handed me a book from her school bag; when I opened it, everything that looked back at me was foreign.

"It is an alphabet book. Let's start from there," she said.

Tara was the one who taught me how to hold a pencil, the one to hold my hand and make me draw the lines and the curves of the English alphabet.

"Okay, you have to repeat after me," Tara said, and I repeated every alphabet after her.

I practiced it many times over and over in my head as I washed dishes or cooked. I learned to form words and picture them as I repeated them to myself. I read under the candlelight at night and learned as fast as I could. Over the few years that I lived there, I learned from her and from listening to people around me, forming haphazard sentences as I spoke. Back then my grammar wasn't good, and Tara corrected me whenever we walked from school. For example, I might say, "I coming to pick you up," and she'd correct me, saying, "I've come to pick you up." And when no one was listening, we tried to speak in English so I could practice.

Every time I read a poem, I felt as if I had floated back into my world of forests. I yearned to know more, read more. Tara brought me books from the school library, and I hid them under my blanket in the kitchen. I never knew there was a language that had such utter beauty—something that could so easily take me to the time in the forests, when Amma was alive. In my short life, I had only ever spoken one language. Now there was this world I had been introduced to, and it took me to places I would never be able to travel. The more poems I read, the easier it became to glide into different lives, to know them better, to learn from them. I have often thought about the space we created for ourselves, away from the eyes of this world, on the terrace of that apartment building. Those couple of hours—there was just Tara and me.

I remember even at night, Tara didn't leave my side. When everybody was asleep, she leisurely walked into the storage room with two pillows tucked under her arms and a bedsheet trailing behind her, with no worry about what her parents might say. I insisted she sleep in her bed and suggested that I sleep in her room on the floor. That way I would be the one getting into trouble if we were ever caught.

"No," she said, laying the bedsheet on the floor, arranging one pillow on it and offering me the other.

We talked until late that night in whispers. I giggled as she told me tales, distracting me from anything untoward that happened that day. When she went off to sleep, I lay down beside her. In her sleep she put her hand around me and a warm feeling of joy crept through me. I told her how grateful I was—whispered it to her while she slept, hoping she had heard me.

She mumbled something in her sleep, held me tighter, and I knew she had heard me. Even in her sleep, her breath warm on my face, I knew she was there for me.

Those were the happiest few years of my life, until fate intervened.

CHAPTER 12

TARA
2004

THAT EVENING I was walking back to the bus stop from the police station, my head swirling with thoughts, when a voice called out.

"Tara," he called from behind. I stopped and looked back.

"Tara?" he asked, "I thought it was you. I saw you at the police station. You looked familiar, but I didn't recognize you. Then I heard some constables talking about your case, about Mukta, and I realized it was *you*—back from America!" He approached me and smiled as if he had known me for a long time.

I scanned his face, trying to recollect him from my memories. The pockmarks on his face revealed youth long gone by; his dark hair was neatly combed; his eyes looked like they held the experience of a lifetime; his broad shoulders and stubble made him look ruggedly handsome.

"I am sorry. I can't seem to place you." I smiled.

"Tara, it is Raza."

It didn't take long for the impressions of my past to come

flooding back. It had been such a long time ago when he had stood beside Salim, pinning me down in that lonely alleyway, unhindered by my violent screams, unperturbed by my rising sobs. His voice had changed from when I had last seen him. I turned to leave and began walking down the street, but he walked beside me without an invitation.

"After you left India, I heard about what happened to your mother in the '93 blasts. I am sorry."

I quickened my pace.

"Look, I just want to help. I saw you at the police station and thought I could help."

"So you *followed* me?"

I kept walking. He stood and hollered at me. "No, I had work with a detective agency here. I run a nonprofit now. I can help."

I stopped and looked back at him, surprised. I could feel the eyes of the people on the balconies in the surrounding buildings watching us with curiosity. Street children ran around us, chasing each other, running around us as if we were statues.

"I can help," he repeated, giving me a smile. The concern on his face seemed genuine. *He just might be able to help,* I thought.

"How?" I asked.

"Take my business card. My office is not very far from here. You can walk in anytime, and we can talk," he said, walking toward me and planting the card in my hand.

I dropped the card in my purse, turned around, and fled.

IT HAD BEEN years since Raza's face had loomed in my nightmares. At night, when I had tossed and turned in my sleep, I had seen him standing there, behind Salim, trying to restrain me in that lonely alleyway. In my dreams, their faces appeared as dark and deadly as they had on that day. They were tall, lanky teenagers then, no more than fifteen, but known to loiter around corners to leer at women and harass passersby. That evening Mukta and I had bought a few *jalebis* from the sweetmeat shop around the corner and were sitting next to each other in a lonely alleyway. We were busy devouring the sweets, the sugar syrup coating our hands and dripping down to our elbows. We were completely unaware of the day dimming around us. That is when they had appeared, out of nowhere, like apparitions, their faces shielded by darkness.

It was Salim who brought his face close to mine. His eyes were bloodshot, his grin vicious. His breath smelled of tobacco and the bitterness of beer. A high-pitched yelp escaped me; the *jalebis* in my hand scattered on the dusty ground. In the slant of the dim streetlight, Raza peeked from behind him and gave out a throaty laugh. I fell backward and pressed my palms onto the ground in an attempt to get away. He leaned forward and gripped my hands tightly behind me. I struggled and kicked at him in a futile attempt to escape.

"Tsk-tsk . . . it's useless to try," Salim chortled gleefully as he tied my hands, twisting and turning the rope around my wrists. A sharp stab of pain went through my hands as he tightened the knot.

"This here is my friend, my *bhai*, Raza. We are like brothers," Salim told me and patted Raza's back. Raza smiled and tried to get hold of Mukta.

"Leave her alone, she is only a poor village kid . . . lower caste, just like us!" Salim shouted at him. "We don't hurt our people. And no one would care if we did anything to her. But this girl here"—he pointed at me and continued talking to me—"we could take you away from this fancy life of yours. Do you know how much money we can get for a virgin these days? Or better still, we can make you a beggar on some corner in Bombay and make you bring your earnings to us. It will teach all middle-class bastards a lesson. They think they are all superior to us." He spit on my face.

Everything around me seemed blurry from my tears, all sounds amplified—the noise of a rickshaw engine passing by, the chirp of night crickets, the sound of shutters closing in the distance. After the shops closed for the day, there wasn't a soul on the street. I blinked at Mukta and tears rolled down my face. She was looking at a trailer that had roared to a stop near the new buildings under construction, a cloud of dust rising from it. I watched as she ran toward it.

"Look at me," Salim demanded as he pulled me to him. I flinched and let out a wail. My sobs rose in that dark, desolate street.

"Can't we leave her alone?" Raza asked timidly, his voice panic-stricken.

Salim turned around to stare at him, "Shut up," he barked. "You have much to learn. Don't worry, you will get used to it."

Out of the blue, I heard a sudden whoosh in the air behind me, and before any of us knew what was happening, Salim was kneeling down on the street, rubbing his eyes, and screaming in pain. Raza too had fallen back; his hands were covering his eyes. I could smell the sand scattered in the air around me. Mukta had gathered sand from the construction site, snuck behind me, and thrown it in their faces. I sat rooted to the spot, listening to my heart pound in my chest, still unable to grasp the sudden turn of events.

"Run," Mukta said, her eyes wide with urgency. She untied the knot on my wrists. But I stood there staring at her.

"Run," she repeated, tugging at my arms.

Then I ran, next to her. We ran as if our feet knew the way to carry us back home. Everything we passed and everyone we bumped into on the way was a blur. I remember now—that's when she began speaking. *Run* was her first word to me.

I never thanked her for what she had done—saved me from harm that day, from those two boys. Perhaps I had slipped *that* into her duties. Probably I didn't want to admit I hadn't been as brave as she'd been. I remember convincing myself that a lower-caste girl like her should be grateful to *us* and not the other way around; after all, we were the ones looking after her.

Several months later, the incident had still flashed before my eyes from time to time. It had still frightened me. I didn't tell my parents about it. There was the danger of being punished for wandering onto that lonely street at that hour of the day, but mostly I was ashamed of what had happened. I tried to behave as if it hadn't happened. When I couldn't sleep, I walked into the storage room to talk to Mukta. She was the only one who knew. Several nights in a row, we watched the sky together, the clouds floating around the moon, the sparkle of the stars. On starlit nights we would sneak up to the terrace, stand up on the parapet, and watch the city from up here. Below, the city was alive and throbbing, and above, the stars would be watching over us.

Mukta used to be afraid but I'd pull her up to me and hold her close. If someone had told me how dangerous this was, I'm afraid it wouldn't have stopped me. I was a child who wanted to escape the fear the two boys had introduced into my life. I wanted to unburden myself of the shame and feel free, and Mukta was the only one standing with me—the only one who understood how I felt.

In all those years we spent together, I don't think I ever considered her to be the same as my other friends. She was always someone who did as I asked. What I did not realize then is that I needed her. She had rescued me, prevented an assault on me, and what had I done?

THAT WAS MANY years ago, and yet, on this night, I was unable to sleep; the sheets rustled as I tossed and turned. Then I sat by the window in my apartment and thought of something Papa used to tell me: *The only way we can rectify our mistakes is to try to undo the wrong we have done.* His voice had faltered as he had said it, his hands clenched tightly into a fist as if he was speaking about himself. Was that even possible, undoing the wrong?

CHAPTER 13

TARA
2004

I AWOKE WITH a start. The birds were chirping, and I could hear the honking and chaos of traffic outside. It felt like the morning after Mukta had been kidnapped. I waited to hear Papa call out to me, for his voice to echo through this apartment. The sudden sense of foreboding was overwhelming. Maybe calling someone would help me forget. I tried to shake myself out of my reverie. I picked up the phone and made a call to Elisa, the only good friend I had made in America besides Brian. We had been friends since high school, and she was the only one I had come to rely on since I left India.

Three rings and Elisa picked up. "Hey, how're you doing?" she asked.

"Okay, I guess. This morning the sun seems sad . . . I don't know why . . ." I was babbling.

"Are you okay?" I heard the concern in her voice and sat up in my bed. My head ached.

"Yes, yeah . . . it's . . . I'm kinda trying to figure out my way here. I've been here more than three months, and I don't seem to be making much progress."

"You better be taking care of yourself."

"Elisa . . ." I said softly, "this place has too many memories."

I heard a long breath at the other end. I imagined her sitting by her bedroom window, the ocean roaring in the distance, her blond hair curled into perfect loose waves for a night out with her fiancé, Peter. "I want to tell you to come back," she exhaled, "but I know you are so stubborn you won't listen. But I'm sure you will figure out a way to deal with it."

I chuckled. That's something Papa would have told me.

"What happened to the search? Did you go to the cops? To the detective?"

"Yeah, but they don't seem to be a lot of help. I . . . actually . . . I met this guy—"

"Oh, that sounds interesting," she said mischievously.

"No, Elisa, not in the romantic way that you imagine. This guy . . . this man . . . he was involved in some bad stuff, criminal activities when I was a child. He had once tried to . . ." I let out a long sigh. "Anyway, he seems decent enough now. He says he runs a nonprofit organization now and can help me locate Mukta."

"So what are you waiting for?"

"I . . . don't know if I can trust him."

"Hmm, people change, you know. And he runs a nonprofit now, didn't you say?"

"Yes. But I'm still not sure—"

"Well, sometimes we have to take that chance."

"I'll think about it," I said. "How is Peter doing?"

"Good. You know, we're both busy with the wedding planning. Yesterday we went furniture shopping for the new house and found this most incredible deal, and Peter says . . ." There was a pause at Elisa's end. "Look at me, talking about my wedding when you are going through such a time. I should stop talking and let you go. We'll miss you at the wedding. I wanted you to be my maid of honor, you know."

"I know," I sighed. She didn't ask me about Brian, about how we broke up. I *yearned* to tell her I felt guilty that I didn't think of him anymore.

"The Realtor's been able to sell your dad's apartment here. It didn't go for much but I've transferred the money to your account in India. You'll see it soon. I am sure it'll help you survive in India."

"Sure. Thanks, Elisa." I had given Elisa the power of attorney to sell Papa's apartment in Los Angeles. Papa had already left me some money but it would definitely not hurt to have the money from the sale of his apartment. It would help while searching for Mukta.

"Okay. Call me later, honey," she said.

I ARRIVED AT Raza's office on that overcast Monday morning. It was still drizzling. For a while I stood outside the door wondering what I was doing there. Was I so desperate now that I wanted to seek the help of a man who once, as a boy, had threatened two girls? Did I really want to trust a man who hadn't stopped to think that he was hurting someone? Turns out, when it came to looking for Mukta, I was willing to do anything.

The door opened, and Raza walked out.

"Oh, I was just about to step out. I-I didn't think you'd come," he said, surprised.

"Yeah, well, I wanted to ask if there was anything you could do for me." I gulped, looking away, trying to let go of the fear I felt.

"Of course," he said, leading me inside and pulling out a chair for me. "Why don't you have a seat? I have an errand to run. I will be back very quickly. I have to meet someone to hand over something—*just* around that corner," Raza explained, pointing his finger at the window.

"No problem. I'll wait."

I watched him leave and took a deep breath. I could hear raindrops tapping on the windowpane. The office looked old. It clearly needed a touch of paint to freshen it. It had five cubicle spaces, but nobody was around. Raza's desk was in an open space; a pile of files and papers was on the desk not far from a small cooking space in the corner. There were pictures on his desk of a woman in a hijab, with his hand protectively around her shoulder while she beamed at the camera. There were other pictures of both of them, one in which they were distributing food at a shelter, another where they were smiling and a field of crops swayed behind them. A piece of paper with lovely handwriting was pinned to the wall:

Let's take a different road,

Find another way

Pick a road less travelled.

I walked up to the window and watched the rainfall as the

sky thundered and lightning bolted its way across the city. I wondered if Mukta was in the city somewhere, watching the rainfall and thinking of me the way I was thinking of her.

In the distance, I could see Raza returning, walking swiftly through the rain, his umbrella zigzagging in the heavy wind. He left his umbrella outside, entered the office, picked a towel out from a drawer, and wiped his wet hair with it.

"I didn't expect it to get that bad outside." He smiled, gesturing to me to sit down. "Can I make you a cup of tea?"

"That would be nice, thank you," I said as I came away from the window and took a seat in front of him. It was awkward, but I was trying to be friendly. After all, the memories I had of him were difficult to erase.

He walked to a corner in his office and lit the stove. "Most people who work with me are out today for a food drive," he said as he added the water and milk to the teapot.

"I like the three lines there . . . on that piece of paper beside your desk." I smiled, trying to make conversation.

"Yes," he said, turning back, "my wife wrote that. She believed that we have to take the difficult path—a different one from what most people choose. That is the only way, she said, we could make a difference in somebody's life." He looked away; smiled at the memory.

I pointed to the picture frame. "Your wife is beautiful."

He swallowed hard. "She was killed last year in the bomb blasts. Someone, in the name of religion, always takes our loved ones away from us. After eleven years, it is still the same."

"I'm sorry. I didn't know."

He nodded, turned to the stove, poured tea into glasses, and placed them on the table.

"Anyway, enough about me. Tell me, how can I help you?" He pulled a chair opposite me. This man sitting before me with a rugged smile was different from that lanky teenage ruffian I had met years ago.

"I am looking for the girl who used to live with us—Mukta."

"I know. I heard—the constables at the police station talk about your case. They seemed baffled that you would look for a girl who disappeared eleven years ago."

I smiled and shrugged.

"I need to ask you something."

"Sure." He narrowed his eyes.

I forced myself to take a deep breath and measured my words carefully. He was the only one close to the kidnapper—the only one who could locate him, and ask him what he had done with Mukta. I knew this was a chance I had to take. I looked him in the eye. I had definitely lost my mind.

"It was Salim that night; Salim kidnapped Mukta. But he must have already told you that, hasn't he?"

Those words had never been uttered before. Not once, not to anyone—not Brian, not Elisa, not even Papa. He raised his eyebrows.

"Why do you think I would know that? Because I was in Salim's gang once upon a time?" He gave out a laugh. "I left that life a long time ago. I have helped people since then. And why are you so sure Salim was the kidnapper? The Salim I knew back then . . . he always liked to scare people. It was his way of showing off, telling people he's the boss. But to kidnap some-body? He would never—"

"What do you mean?" I interrupted. "Are you saying I am lying? I am sure it was Salim. I *saw* him. I was in the room when Mukta was kidnapped."

He looked taken aback for a moment, then frowned. "*You* were in the room? You watched him kidnap Mukta?"

"Yes . . . I . . ."

"I am sorry. I had no idea." He shook his head.

"Do you . . . do you know where he is these days?"

"Who? Salim? We lost touch a long time ago." Raza sighed. A wave of despondency swelled in my heart.

"But I can find out," he said.

"You will? You can? That . . . that will be great. I mean thanks for the help." I was relieved.

He smiled.

"Tara, it may take some time to locate Salim—a few months maybe. I will have to put word out on the street. Mumbai is such a big city. I don't even know if he is somewhere in this city or if he has moved away. The Salim I knew was a scared little boy on the inside. Threatening younger children, robbing, sell-ing drugs maybe, but breaking into a home and kidnapping? I never thought he'd do anything so serious. If, just for a moment, we say Salim committed the crime, what makes you think he will admit to it?"

"I don't want him to admit anything. I just want him to tell me where he took Mukta. I just want to know where she is."

"Wouldn't you be better off working with other nonprofit

organizations that search for missing children? Maybe I could put you in touch with—"

I wasn't listening. "Salim will tell *you*, won't he? You were close to him once. I think you are the only person he would tell. Then we will know where she is," I said and felt the tremble in my voice. I left only after Raza assured me he would do whatever he could to find Salim.

ON MY WAY back, as my rickshaw bumped over potholes, I kept thinking back to the picture of Raza's wife, her smiling face disappearing within the chaos that had taken over our lives. I knew how much he missed her. I could see it in his eyes. I wondered how many of us there were, still living and breathing, confused as to why we weren't chosen to be there on that fateful day instead of our loved ones. If that day hadn't come into our lives, would things have been different?

March 12, 1993, is a day fixed in my memories. I was thirteen then.

"You want to talk on the terrace this afternoon, after school?" Mukta had asked me that morning. I had nodded, absentmindedly. As the day went by, I completely forgot about it. I was worried about a math test at school. I was never very good at math and my thoughts were milling around the test. The very thoughts I agonized over that morning, seemingly so important, would become nothing as the day came to an end.

It was a Friday and, after my test, I was planning on going to a friend's place to watch TV. Before I left that morning, Aai asked me if I could drop off a bundle of clothes at her friend's shop near Century Bazaar, where Aai worked.

"Once you come back from school, you can take these things. It isn't very far. I still have some work to do. I have asked everybody I know but they all seem busy. I would send Mukta, but she is not feeling well," Aai said to me.

I told her I couldn't go. I was sure Aai would find someone else or borrow a servant from a neighbor to get her work done. Now when I think of this moment, I can't remember the excuse I gave her. What was it I had said? Had I said I had to go to a friend's place because she had promised to help with my homework, or had I said that my friend needed help with her schoolwork?

It is hard to decide what my last words to my mother were.

It did not occur to me then that, before asking me, she had told Mukta to drop the clothes at the shop, and she, too, had made up an excuse. I had taught Mukta to feign illness if Aai asked her to run an errand when I needed to talk to her or share something. In the beginning she had been afraid to lie, but I had convinced her it was a white lie and could cause nobody harm. It always happened on my cue; we would discuss the reason in detail so Aai wouldn't find out that it was a lie. It had worked for many years, and I had warned Mukta to follow my orders, never stray from them. On this day, however, things would be different.

IT WAS LATE afternoon. After school, my friend and I were sitting on the sofa, watching television while we munched on chips, cribbing about cantankerous teachers and idiotic, bright-eyed students those teachers favored. The news flashed in the middle of the show. The woman on the news channel was strangely calm when she announced the bomb blasts. Behind her, scenes flashed—of walls blown apart, of vehicles whose roofs had landed elsewhere, shards of glass everywhere, wounded faces, bloodied bodies, and the air thick with black smoke.

Words poured out of the newscaster about the areas targeted: Bombay stock exchange, passport office, Century Bazaar, Zaveri Bazaar, Plaza Cinema . . .

The words rang in my head: *Century Bazaar*—that was where Aai was supposed to go that afternoon because she hadn't found anybody else to go to the shop. What if something had happened to her? Everything else the newscaster went on about sounded like gibberish to my ears. My thoughts came in waves, followed by moments of numbness. I dismissed the possibility that anything had happened. I remember running through alleys, racing past shops, tearing past people and honking vehicles, opening the gates of my apartment complex, and racing up the steps. I knocked hard on the door of my apartment, but no one opened it. Mukta should have been at home. Had she run out on an errand to the grocery store? Aai should have been back by now. But nobody answered the door. I tried opening the door with the key I had, but it kept trembling in my clammy hands. When I finally opened the door, there was silence in the apartment as I called out Aai's name. A deep pain throbbed in my heart.

"Aai? Aai?"

There was a muffled voice from outside. I followed it, stepped out of the apartment, and saw Mukta leisurely coming down the stairs, smiling at me. "I thought I heard someone open the door," she said. "What happened? I was waiting for you upstairs on the terrace. I thought you wanted to talk."

Watching her smile, the spring in her steps as she walked down, something inside me snapped.

"Talk? Which world do you live in? You are a useless village girl. What would you know?"

I saw the surprise, then the pain, on her face at my sudden outburst, but I didn't wait to explain before I turned around and ran down the stairs.

I knocked hard on a neighbor's apartment on the lower floor. The phone in our apartment hadn't been working for days, and I hoped to call Papa from somebody's phone. One of Aai's friends opened the door in her housecoat. She stood by her door and yelled at me, "What is it? Do you want to break down the door?"

"I want to call Papa. Aai is out there . . ." My voice trailed off.

"Oh," she said, examining my face, her voice softening. "The phone lines are jammed; we can't reach anyone."

I pretended not to hear and brushed past her. I entered her home and sat next to the phone, dialing the numbers. The phone at the other end didn't ring but gave me a busy signal instead. My fingers were heavy, my breathing belabored, but I kept dialing. The woman hovered over me with a worried expression. She paced the floor as I dialed again and again. I resignedly put the phone down.

"See, I told you," she said. "My husband is out there too. I have been trying to reach him. I—"

I wasn't listening.

I ran downstairs, thinking I would walk to Papa's workplace.

That way I could tell him what had happened. Some of the neighbors had gathered downstairs, back home early from work.

"Let's go then," I heard one of them say.

Anupam chacha pushed his way out of the crowd and approached me. "Yes, I heard—your Aai might be there," he said. However calm he wanted to sound, I could hear the fear in his voice and sense the sea of despondency surrounding us already. But he continued in the same vein. "Many residents of our building are out there. Your Papa is already out there. I saw him on my way here. We will find your Aai, don't worry." His hand reassuringly patted my shoulder.

"I will come with you," I insisted.

"*No*, I want you to be here in case your Aai gets back. You listen to me and stay right here. You understand?"

His voice was loud, commanding enough to make me stay. I must have nodded because he smiled at me and then disappeared into the crowd. I walked back and sat on the steps outside, hoping to see Aai anytime now, opening the gates, approaching me, telling me I was worried for nothing. Some people returned from work early but rushed past me, worried and wanting to check on their own. The scenes on the TV flashed in my head all over again: a woman beating her chest and crying, rocking her dead son back and forth. Around her, bloodied bodies lay on the ground. Shocked faces loitered on streets amid smoke and roofless damaged vehicles. The confusion and chaos made me wonder if my Aai was lost somewhere, shaken from the turn of events, trying to get back to her family, her home. And I wanted to appear calm as she opened the gates, so she could see she had nothing to worry about. As much as I wanted to stay strong, there was an odd tear that crept up at the edge of my eye and I had to keep wiping it off. Mukta sat beside me silently, holding my hand, afraid that if she uttered a word, I would erupt into tears. I sat there and made silent promises to God—I would never again offend Aai or speak back to her, and I would do as she said from now on. I promised to go with her to the temple every time she insisted, and most of all, I would never, *ever* say no to whatever errand she wanted me to run.

PAPA CAME HOME late. He had a frazzled look on his face; his hair was astray and his shirt was soaked in sweat and blood. He mumbled something about bodies, about how irresponsible people were. I had never seen Papa in such a state. To see a grown man dissolve in tears, to watch *my* Papa, who once told me tales of courage, was something that pulled at my heart. I brushed away my tears, tugged at his sleeves, and asked him, "Where is Aai?"

My voice sounded choked. He didn't say anything, just looked at me blankly. Navin whispered to me that Papa and Anupam chacha had sifted through bodies, turning them over, trying to identify Aai. Navin and I walked to the apartment silently following Papa and Anupam chacha. When we reached our apartment Papa knelt outside, leaning against the door as if he couldn't enter our home. Anupam chacha tried to get Papa up, held him as if he were a baby learning to walk.

"Tara, you have to be strong for your father," Anupam chacha said to me.

"What happened to Aai?" I asked.

"We don't know yet," he replied as he led Papa inside and

made him sit on the sofa. Then Anupam chacha left, taking Navin and Mukta with him. "They need to be alone for now," he told them as he led them outside.

Papa and I sat on that sofa in silence next to each other for a while, listening to the clock in our living room tick, hoping Aai would walk through our front door at any minute. Then Papa said he had to get out of the apartment.

"I have to search for your Aai. Sitting here is not going to accomplish a thing. You have to wait at home, Tara . . . in case . . . Aai returns," Papa told me as he left home.

I lay in bed that night, watching the moon stare down at me. I wondered how things could change so abruptly, so drastically. Just last night, Aai was telling me a story while she put me to bed. Just yesterday, she had made *jalebis* for me. I wanted to believe, if I closed my eyes tightly, it would all go away, and today never would have happened.

PAPA RETURNED HOME the next morning dejected. Even though we didn't say it out aloud, it was as if we both expected the worst—Aai was somewhere out there, her body mangled among the many corpses. We walked from hospital to hospital that day, searching for Aai's remains.

"You should have stayed home, Tara," Papa said from time to time, but I wanted to be there, holding his hand. I didn't want to wince when I saw the bodies; I was determined to have one last glimpse of my mother. I wanted to have one chance to bid her a goodbye.

Anupam chacha came with us and inquired for us when Papa

could no longer form words, when all he could do was give an exasperated grunt. There were crowds outside hospitals and police stations, with police officers trying to keep them under control. Occasionally a nurse would look at a sheet where names had become numbers, shake her head, and say, "Maybe she is at another hospital." And I would think of Aai's face on the morning when she coaxed me to go drop the clothes at the bazaar and how, by evening, nothing had remained of her, not even a body.

At each hospital, the nurse there would say something similar, and the color would drain from Papa's face. Or a glimmer of hope would rise in his eyes each time a nurse asked us to wait so she could check if Aai had been admitted to that hospital. Waiting there, I hoped to see Aai emerging from behind a curtain with few bruises, a scratch or two, smiling at us, telling us it was nothing, telling us how God was great and she had narrowly escaped. But nothing like that happened. There was only dismay and disappointment surrounding everybody, so much turmoil that nobody knew a way out of it. At each hospital we rushed in with hope and walked out in slow steady steps, the burden of defeat making our legs heavy. It was a strange scene—there were no actual bodies around us, but death was everywhere, the glistening of loss in everyone's eyes.

When I insisted on knowing, days later, Navin told me how they had searched for Aai at the bomb site and helped others in the process. "We lifted bodies, shoved them in taxis so they could get to hospitals. The thing is . . ." His voice trailed off and his eyes filled with tears. "The thing is, Tara, I didn't know if any of them were still alive."

Navin became quiet in the coming days—so quiet I wondered if he would ever talk again. All that remained at the end of all this were memories of those brokenhearted faces, the sound of chaos, and the smell of death that would shroud all of us from here on.

CHAPTER 14

MUKTA
March 1993

FOR DAYS SAHIB and Tara went out, searched for Memsahib, and then returned home, their faces drowned in anguish. I could do nothing but watch how the longing to see Memsahib each morning turned into despair by evening. Of course, in Memsahib's absence, I had no other recourse but to take charge of and care for the apartment by myself. I made sure I kept the apartment clean and the smell of food wafting in the home, and I ran the errands like clockwork. I didn't want them to feel that along with their life, their apartment too was falling apart.

Tara sat on the sofa watching the news as they endlessly repeated scenes from the bomb blast, her eyes searching for her mother in the middle of that tumult. I begged her several times to stop watching, to stop reliving that agony, but she refused to listen. I knew what she was trying to do—understand what her mother went through, just like I kept summoning in my mind that scene of my Amma dying. The scene on the TV was gory—bodies with missing limbs, body parts strewn on streets, the shards of glass scattered everywhere. I wondered at how strange life was—all those people who had died or had been injured that day probably had never met the people who had caused them so much pain.

Despite the smell of sadness in their home, Tara didn't cry much and kept to herself. Sahib asked her to go meet her friends, but she sat in her room looking out the window at the bustling street, waiting for her mother to appear. At night when I served dinner, she insisted I keep a plate for her mother in case she arrived. Every night that plate of food sat waiting for Memsahib while Sahib and Tara picked at their food. After they finished, I would gather the leftovers for my dinner and give the rest to a beggar outside the complex, hoping his prayers were with Tara and her Papa.

IT WAS ON the fourth day after the blasts that they discovered her body at a morgue. Sahib identified it by a gold necklace Memsahib always wore. They brought the bundled body on a stretcher and placed her in the middle of the playground. We couldn't see her face. Neighbors and many of Memsahib's friends gathered there dressed in white, wiped away tears silently beside the body, put bouquets and garlands of flowers at her feet, and then took her body straight to the crematorium. Since women were not allowed to go to the crematorium, many of Memsahib's friends stayed behind, waiting downstairs, crying softly. Tara and I watched from the balcony. Their gentle cries reminded me of Amma's funeral. I felt transported to a part of my life that I never could leave behind: I was watching Amma's lonely body burn on the funeral pyre. Then, as if life was taking

me backward, I was beside Amma holding her hand as the villagers beat her to death. She looked at me one last time, her face
filled with fear and then . . . a loud exhale.

A sudden wave of pain pinched my heart now and I heard
myself whimper. My face was wet with tears. I thought of Memsahib dying in the same way, not knowing what she had done
wrong; worried that she'd never be able to see her child again—
just like my Amma. I wanted to scream and yell at all those
people who had taken away our mothers from us. I looked at
Tara and yearned to tell her that I understood the pain of losing
a mother. But beside me, Tara stood quite stoically. I marveled at
the way Tara did not allow tears to fall from her eyes. I put my
arm around her and gave her shoulder a squeeze, but she pushed
it away. I didn't mind. I understood. You see, like a tortoise
withdraws itself into its shell for protection, we, too, sometimes
have to build a wall around ourselves. Maybe it is the only way
we can cope.

A HOUSE WHERE someone has died needs to be purified,
cleansed. If Amma had been there she would have told me
what to do. I did what I knew. I lit *diyas*, oil lamps, near Memsahib's photograph and kept flowers near it. I knew the oil
lamp could not be allowed to extinguish in the first few days
after someone dies, so I guarded it with my life, continually
pouring oil into it, keeping vigilance over it. But I didn't know
if it was enough.

Meena-ji, one of Memsahib's best friends, came the next
day, stood in the living room, and asked for Sahib. When I
offered her a glass of water, she knocked it from my hand.

"Don't you know," she screamed, "that you are not supposed to serve food or drinks to guests in a house where somebody has died?"

I didn't reply and kneeled down to wipe the water that had spilled to the ground. Sahib walked in then, his face puffy with sleeplessness, his beard unshaven. He folded his hands in greeting to Meena-ji and nodded his head, acknowledging her presence, but didn't utter a word.

"All the neighbors want to help with the thirteenth-day rituals. We can arrange everything—the priest, the food, the venue . . ." Meena-ji said.

"That is very nice of you, but I don't think that will be necessary. I don't believe in all that," Sahib said, politely.

"This is the least we can do for her. She *was* your wife," Meena-ji said as if reminding him.

Sahib looked away, took a deep breath, and said, "Whatever you think is right, go ahead."

Meena-ji left the apartment, beaming. What I didn't know was that for the next several days leading to the ritual, she would drive several servants, and me, to work like dogs.

I didn't mind, really. The thirteen days of mourning followed by the ritual was a must; Meena-ji thought so, even if Sahib didn't agree. Every day Meena-ji would make Tara place balls of rice and *dal* on a banana leaf with water on the terrace; I would hide and watch the crows come and peck at them. *Pind-daan*—Meena-ji called it. She said it was food for the soul of the departed on their journey to heaven. Meena-ji rattled off a set of instructions that we were meant to follow. Every servant had a particular chore to complete. Meena-ji also had chores for me. One of my main chores included cleaning the house thoroughly, and Rajni, another servant, was told to help me. Every day Rajni would arrive after completing her daily work for the family she worked for; we cleaned and wiped down every item in the apartment. Tara didn't talk much in those days, and Rajni had funny stories to regale me with. She would imitate people in the neighborhood. When Tara and Sahib weren't around, Rajni would mimic Meena-ji exactly the way she shouted or how her face contorted with anger when she scolded us. And our smothered giggles broke the silence in this home. It was Rajni who told me that the purpose of this ritual on the thirteenth day was important for the journey of the departed—to leave this life, settle in heaven, and come back in the afterlife in peace.

ONE DAY TARA stood by the table in the living room looking at framed photographs of her mother. Rajni looked at her and asked me, "She hasn't cried yet, has she? What daughter does not cry at her mother's funeral?" She rolled her eyes.

I was enraged. *We have our own ways of dealing with grief. I hadn't cried for my mother too. I remember how numb I had been,* I wanted to tell her but Rajni continued unabated. "She should consider herself lucky. They are lucky to find her mother's body. Many haven't yet recovered their loved ones' bodies."

"Shh . . ." I said loudly, trying to admonish Rajni, but she continued. "Why? Don't you think it's odd that she doesn't cry?"

I looked at Tara, afraid she might hear, but she was still standing there, lost in her thoughts, staring at her mother's photograph in the living room. I hadn't wanted anyone to go through the same pain that I had experienced a few years ago. It was as if my pain was now playing out in someone else— someone who was so dear to me. I went and stood beside Tara, telling her that it was going to be all right. I told her that I got through my grief because of her and that she'd be able to make it through this because I was with her. We'd face it together, I said. But Tara wasn't listening to me. She was lost in her thoughts and looking at Memsahib's photograph intently. Later, I admonished Rajni and told her we should pay more attention to cleaning the apartment and less to gossip. She twisted her face and never spoke to me again.

THAT SAME AFTERNOON, Meena-ji came home and sat on the sofa. "Go inside," she told me. "I have something important to discuss with your Sahib. And I don't want you listening in."

I ran into the kitchen and hid behind the door, waiting to hear what she had to say. Sahib offered her a seat on the sofa and pulled out a chair for himself.

"Have you ever thought she could be the reason—the bad omen?" Meena-ji didn't hesitate to ask.

"Who?"

"That girl! Who else? What's her name? Mukta. Ever since she has come to stay here, look at the confusion she has caused in your happy home."

Sahib got up from the chair. "Meena-ji," he said firmly, "I don't believe in such superstitions. My wife did, but I don't. So I would appreciate it if you don't bring such ridiculous tales to me." His voice was stern but not rude. He folded his hands as if saying a goodbye and walked back into his room, leaving Meena-ji flustered, looking small on that sofa.

I thought about what she had said. There was a high possibility it was my shadow, my bad luck that had befallen Tara. After all, how could she lose her mother like I had? It couldn't be a coincidence. I thought about it for many days after and wondered if there was something I could do to release the demons following me. But every time, this thought wound up as a knot in my stomach, and I didn't know what to do.

ON THE THIRTEENTH day, there was a huge ceremony, and all the residents of the building gathered in Tara's apartment. All the servants were shooed away and told they should stand outside lest their dark shadows fall on something so auspicious. I stood outside alongside them. We watched from outside. Meena-ji arranged the coconuts, the banana leaves, rice, *jaggery*, salt, and all the items required for the fire sacrifice. A priest arrived, sat down cross-legged on a low stool, closed his eyes, and recited mantras in front of the consecrated fire. A servant explained it was for the purification of the apartment and to give peace to the people Memsahib had left behind.

I saw Tara slip out and walk up the stairs to the terrace; I knew she wanted to be alone. But I followed her, watched her from a distance at first, and then sat down beside her. It was so quiet I was afraid to breathe. She kept staring into the distance. I finally whispered to her, "You know, I think that whenever the wind moves a branch, it is my mother trying to say something to me. I am sure your mother will try to say things to you too. You'll see."

She looked sideways, smiled at me, and asked, "Did they do all this, this ceremony, these rituals, for your Amma, too?"

"No, Amma didn't have any of this."

"Why?"

"Because . . ." I sighed, "maybe, our kind doesn't deserve it? Because, we aren't worthy. . . ."

She took my hand in hers, squeezed it, and then looked away. We sat there quietly, the wind whipping in our ears.

"Do you miss her very much?" She turned around.

"Every day."

Her eyes reddened but there we no tears. "How do you survive this then . . . this . . . this . . ."

She left the words unsaid but I understood.

"I don't know. I have her memories—good memories—and—I have you." I tightened my grip on her hand.

She nodded to herself without looking at me, and became silent once again.

"I wish I had gone that day when Memsahib told me to drop off the clothes, but I told her I was sick. I thought you wanted to talk. I regret it," I told her. It was something I wanted to get off my chest, something I thought she should know.

She looked at me for a while as if she was memorizing my face. Her mouth opened, then closed. Then, angry words. "You mean to say Aai wouldn't have died if you had gone, if you hadn't lied?" She jerked my hand away.

"I didn't lie; I just gave an excuse like you had taught me to. I thought you wanted to talk."

"But I didn't. And I didn't ask you to make any excuse. It's your fault isn't it? It's your fault Aai is dead."

The sudden realization in her eyes, her surging anger, made me afraid. She *was* right. As she walked away, wiping her tears, I couldn't say a thing. Her words looped over and over in my head that night, and by morning my heart felt like a stone sinking under the ocean.

CHAPTER 15

TARA
2004

RAZA THOUGHT IT would take a few weeks to locate Salim. So I spent another month of my life staring at my phone, hoping it would ring. I had always known looking for someone kidnapped eleven years ago was going to be a slow ordeal, that no matter how hard I looked, the clues to where she could be must have been buried a long time ago. But since I didn't know where to look, I spent most of my time at the police station sitting on that bench, watching people with harried expressions rushing in to make their complaints, seeing the hustle bustle of the station ebb and flow during the day. The constables took pity on me once in a while and asked me if I'd like to have a cold drink or chai. When Inspector Pravin Godbole walked by me he would tell me he was still looking and I should go home. Yet I sat on that bench, naïvely hoping it would be a reminder to them to work on the case.

Some evenings, I went to the ice cream shop that Mukta and I used to visit and sat on the same park bench, slurping my ice cream cone among mothers who watched their children play. Every morning before going to the police station, I'd walk down those long streets that Mukta and I had walked once, stand outside my old school, and watch the children in their brown uniforms gather in the courtyard for their morning prayers. Some nights, I'd sleep in the storage room on the floor and watch the sky while the chirping crickets and the hum of the traffic put me to sleep. Returning to my city should have been uncomplicated. If things hadn't turned out the way they did, I'd probably be happy just being back in this city. The familiarity of everything—the language, the people, the streets, even the honking of traffic—made me feel comfortable and yet, wherever I went, there were places and things that wanted to remind me. And maybe I didn't want to forget some of those moments. I had so many wonderful memories with my family and Mukta here. Those seemed to be the only ones that offered me respite in my times of desperation. And so I continued to visit all those places that Mukta and I had ever been to. I'd sit on the terrace and watch the birds fly in the sky on those late afternoons when the police had nothing more to tell me; I'd visit the Asiatic library every other weekend just so that Papa was back with me, pointing to the marble statues, telling me about them, explaining to me how important books were in expanding our knowledge. And I'd hear Mukta whisper to me, *a temple of books.* And so it went on, my days turning into weeks, then into months.

ON OCCASION, I followed up with the private detective as well, but whenever I entered the shabby office, the secretary would shuffle piles of paper on her desk, refusing to answer any of the phones that rang off the hook. Some days she wouldn't even lift her head to look at me. Then one day, when I could take it no longer, I shouted at her, "What is the point in telling me you will let me know if you aren't doing anything about it?"

"What can I do?" she asked, looking at me meekly, startled at my outburst. I left her there with her papers and her pile of files and told her I would never come back. And I didn't. I realized months later that perhaps the detective had finagled my father out of a good sum of money without having done anything on the case. My father had trusted him enough to ensure that he received a monthly payment for many years. And evidently, this detective hadn't done a shred of work. Perhaps avoiding me was his best chance of keeping the money. In any case, it wasn't something I was willing to probe at this point. My focus was on finding Mukta, but days went by with no help forthcoming from any quarters.

ON HOPELESS DAYS filled with dismay and darkness, I was reminded of the days after Aai's thirteenth-day ritual. It had taken days for the mourning, like a long death wail, to settle around us. Suddenly all we were left with was silence, and I had been surprised to see it creep into our lives so easily. After the ceremony, Meena-ji no longer knocked on our door to collect money from Papa for the ritual; there were no servants gathering in our apartment, cleaning the house, painting it with their banter, nobody dropping off items for the ceremony. Aai's death had pierced our hearts days ago, but it was only now that we were becoming aware of the void it had left in us.

Every morning I woke up startled by the unaccustomed shrill

ring of the alarm clock, expecting Aai's hands to shake me from my reverie, hoping to hear Aai's voice telling me to hurry up and get ready for school. When I got up I raced to the kitchen, expecting to see Aai there, standing next to Mukta, telling her how to knead the chapati dough or how much milk should go in the coffee. It was strange how I did this day after day, despite her absence. Every time I looked at Mukta, I knew all this pain was because of what she had done. For days after Mukta told me she had feigned illness and refused to run the errand, the thought raced through my head that if Mukta hadn't refused to go to the bazaar, my Aai would be alive. The more I thought about this, the more I began to understand what Meena-ji was referring to—that Mukta *was* the bad omen in our lives. Even if Papa didn't believe it, I could not refute the possibility that *Mukta* was the one responsible for Aai's death. After that, whenever I looked at her, it reminded me of her betrayal, her audacity to make a decision without consulting me. After all, she was a village kid and did not belong in our family. What a huge price I was paying for it!

When Mukta prepared food and set it on the table, she tried to arrange it the way Aai would—the *parathas* in the left hand corner, the bowl of *curd* in the middle, the coffee served in our mugs just the way we liked it. It was the way Aai had taught her, the way Aai had always been particular about. I wanted to snap at her, throw away all the food she had prepared and tell her that she could never cook as good as my Aai cooked. That she shouldn't even try. And she didn't deserve to be anywhere near me. As much as I wanted to yell at her, I couldn't do so because I knew it would upset Papa. And I couldn't afford to do that.

These days Papa, too, had become very subdued. He would have a small bite of breakfast in the morning or ignore it completely, gulping down only a cup of coffee. Having taken time off from work, he slept most of the day, waking up only to nibble on an apple or gulp down a glass of milk. On odd occasions, he would wearily ask me if I had eaten something or how I was doing, then without waiting for my response, he would turn around and walk toward his room. On the first few occasions, I had sincerely replied, only to see him shut the door behind him. Very soon I learned not to respond, and he learned not to ask. He would shut the door loudly—that slamming noise the only thing that pierced the silence in our home. This became my only means of communication with my Papa.

ONE LATE AFTERNOON, Anupam chacha came home. I was sitting on the balcony aimlessly, with my head on the railing, watching pedestrians walk on the street.

"Where is your Papa?" he asked.

I lifted my head, pointed to Papa's room, and followed him as he woke Papa and threw open the curtains. The sunlight poured through the windows and slanted across his face as he sat up straight, squinted at me, and began to look around him. "Close the curtain. The sun—"

"Let's go outside, get some fresh air. Moping will not help. You have a daughter to take care of."

Anupam chacha helped Papa out of bed, and they walked outside. They sat on the balcony in their usual chairs, but there was nothing usual about this scene. I watched from the living room, wishing, hoping that life could be more like a videotape.

Then I could have rewound it and relived some moments of my life.

"Maybe I should return to work. It will keep me occupied," Papa said, staring blankly at the ceiling.

Anupam chacha patted him on the back and poured him a beer. The drink sat there with them; it bubbled and foamed up but didn't spill out.

I HADN'T BEEN to school in two weeks, and Papa admonished me during dinner that night. "You should go to school. I will talk to the principal tomorrow. The teachers will help you with the schoolwork you missed," he said, picking at his food.

For the rest of the meal, we didn't say anything but listened to the scraping of utensils as Mukta served food to us. It was times like these I wished he would say it would be all right, that he would take care of everything and, whatever had happened, we would somehow survive. But this was the moment—right here, sitting at the dinner table—when I should have realized we had left behind those days when he would talk to me, teach me the workings of the world, when I would sit by him while he narrated stories or read poems to me.

Some days Mukta would come up to me and say, "Would you like to come to the terrace? You might feel better."

"No. I'm fine," I would answer, withdrawing to my room to avoid her.

When she would ask me if I needed something from the bazaar, I would pretend to read one of Papa's books, refuse to look up, shake my head, and then watch her leave. When I resumed school, I grabbed my school bag and set out earlier than the scheduled time so she wouldn't have a chance to accompany me. On the third day of this, she peered from behind the door to my room, twirling the edges of her dress. "I didn't do anything wrong, did I?" she asked, looking concerned.

"No," I said, setting aside the book and walking past her out of the door.

It didn't help that my teachers at school who knew I had lost my mother looked at me with pity in their eyes, patting me occasionally on my back, trying to give me comfort. The more I listened to them, the more aware I became of a sinking feeling in my chest. I didn't exactly know what it was, but if there was one thing I did know, it was that regret was slowly burning a hole in my heart—regret at not being able to change one minute on that unfortunate day, regret that I had even tried to befriend a girl like Mukta.

BY THE END of the month, I could take it no more. I couldn't bear to be anywhere near Mukta. I decided I had to do something about it. I mentioned it to Navin. We were sitting on a bench in the courtyard of our apartment complex. The place was barely lit, and we often sat there in the dark.

"I wish someone would take her away. I cannot bear looking at her knowing she is the reason Aai is dead. If only I could find a way."

"Don't say that, Tara."

"Well, what do you want me to say? It is the truth. I think . . . I think I should go find someone to take her back to the village. She will be happy there, and she will leave me in peace." I could feel the warmth of my anger on my cheeks. There was a look of surprise on Navin's face. He didn't have to say it. I could see it in his eyes. He didn't think I was capable of such a thought. That should have been enough to stop me, but now everything had changed. What we didn't recognize then is that death doesn't just bring with it stifling grief; it changes us in more ways than one. It had certainly changed me.

The next evening I overheard some women gossiping in our courtyard. "I am looking for a good electrician to rewire my apartment and what do I get? Nobody is willing to do it unless I give them good money. Gone are those days when people would charge reasonable prices for their services," said Meena-ji, slapping her forehead.

"*Arre*, everybody is a thug nowadays. All they want is money. Even if we pay them, nobody gets the work completed properly and on time. How different are they from the street-side *goondas*?"

I left them and their agitation behind as I walked home, but it sparked an idea in me. In that insane moment I knew exactly who to contact—the street-side thugs who would do anything for money. I thought about this for a while, thought if I could hand over some of the pocket money I had accumulated over the years, they would probably take her back where she belonged. What I wanted more than anything else was for somebody to take Mukta away from me, from Papa. The only street-side thugs I knew were Raza and Salim, and they always loitered at the corner of an alleyway a distance from Station Road. I had seen them there many times as Papa and I had driven past in a taxi. But, of course, I wasn't going to approach two people who had tried to hurt me. The thought scared me. I broke out in a cold sweat just thinking of it. It was impossible, I told myself. But the thought didn't leave me for the next few hours. It kept blooming in my heart, growing into a full-fledged plan, like a fantasy I was building in my head. If I really wanted Mukta out of my life, I'd swallow my fears and approach Salim. He seemed the stronger of the two, someone who'd definitely follow through. There was no other way out of my pain, I was convinced. Salim might not be willing to help me, but he would do the job if I gave him money, especially if I told him it was about helping a lower-caste girl, someone who belonged to the same class as he. I'd lie and tell him Mukta wanted to return home to her village. Hadn't he said he could never hurt a poor village child? But I quickly dismissed the idea again, and told myself these were the same boys Mukta had once saved me from, and I *must* feel grateful to her instead. By next morning, I was chiding myself for thinking about something so evil. And in a way, I was relieved that I wouldn't be seeing Salim again. But sometimes it seems a sense of gratitude is quickly overpowered by anger, and one can't see clearly.

It was a Wednesday, I remember. That afternoon Mukta walked with me to school.

"It is going to be all right," she said, her words soft and kind as she handed me my school bag. Those words gave new life to my thoughts. I remember her bright eyes and hopeful expression wanting to put an end to my misery, instead fueling my disgust for her.

I decided quickly. I left her standing near the flaming red

flowers on the *gulmohar* tree outside my school and walked toward the backyard of the school campus. I don't know what I was thinking when I climbed over the wall and jumped into an alleyway that lined the school. People walking in that alleyway gave me shocked stares and murmured to each other, one of them yelling behind me, asking me if I was in some kind of trouble. I ignored them and kept walking. I thought of the teachers who would look for me in class and wondered if Mukta would run home and squeal to Papa, telling him I had run away. But the fear Papa would have didn't stop me. There was only one thing on my mind.

I walked from one alley to another, passing food carts and harried mothers talking to their children, cars parked on the side, and children playing marbles in the middle of the street, until I saw them standing there—Salim and his buddies—laughing loudly, chatting on the corner of a street. They were just where I had hoped they would be. Behind them a garbage can overflowed onto the streets, but they seemed unhindered by the smell. I stood at the intersection between two streets, watching them for a while. I could feel the drops of sweat on my forehead. The wall behind me had graffiti—a girl with tears in her eyes and matted hair who looked at me longingly. Above her was a caption, *Help the girl child*.

I looked at Salim and saw the same boy who had viciously tied my hands behind me. I suddenly smelled the bitterness of beer on his breath as he chuckled in my memory. I wanted to run away, back home, back to Papa. I didn't have the guts to face Salim. *This is a bad idea*, a voice inside my head kept telling me. But I'd promised myself I'd swallow my fears and approach

Salim. It was the only way to get Mukta far away from us. I hurriedly brought out a notebook from my school bag, kneeled on
the street—not bothered by the gravel that scraped my knees—
and tore off an empty page. I wrote hurriedly whatever came to
my mind, cursing myself for not thinking of this sooner, then
folded the page and put it into an envelope with two hundred
rupees. I stood there, my uniform soaking in sweat, my eyes
darting toward Salim's gang from time to time, wondering how
I could get the note across to Salim.

I waited a long time, listening to their raucous laughter,
watching people carrying heavy bags of groceries and trucks
unloading their wares to shops on that street. Afternoon turned
into evening, and I could see people returning home from work
and the traffic waning. The pocket money I had saved for years
lay there in my school bag glaring at me, mocking me. For a
moment I thought of the things we would be doing at this time
had I been home. I thought of the chai Mukta would prepare
for Papa and imagined Papa sipping it. It would have been an
ordinary evening if I had not slipped away from school.

If the beggar boy hadn't approached me, I would have made
my way back home. But he stood before me, his bare feet soiled,
his clothes tattered, his face showing streaks of tears. I took one
look at his face and knew this was my chance. I dipped into my
school bag and offered him fifty rupees. He stared at the note in
his hand, stroked it with his other hand, and then looked back
at me with astonishment.

"You can take the money if you take this envelope to that
man standing there." I pointed to Salim down the street. The
boy took the envelope from my hands and hurried down the

street. I watched from a comfortable distance so that if Salim came after me I could run away quickly and join a crowd on a street, where it would be difficult for him to cause me any harm.

The beggar boy tugged at Salim's sleeve, handed him the envelope, pointed to me, ran down the street, and disappeared. Salim looked at the envelope, then at me, and opened it. He unfolded the note and the money fell to the ground, but even then, the brutality of what I was doing didn't occur to me. My note had three lines; I couldn't think of anything else in that moment: *Take the girl who lives with us away to her village. Her life will be better there, away from us. I am willing to pay you more than this if necessary.*

Salim burst out into laughter and read the note aloud to his friends, who laughed too. He bent down, picked up the money and put it into his back pocket, then started walking toward me, hollering, "I don't follow the command of little girls!"

He crumpled the note into a ball and threw it away. It rolled toward the side of the street and plopped into the gutter. I turned and ran as fast as I could, wiping away my tears with the sleeve of my uniform. Everything around me blurred as I ran.

PAPA WAS PACING nervously outside our apartment when I reached home.

"Where were you?" he shouted. "I called the school and was about to call the police. Isn't it enough that I lose your mother; now you give me trouble too?"

My heart was pounding; my breath was warm against my skin. He didn't wait for me to respond but went back to his bedroom and shut the door loudly behind him. He didn't come out for dinner that night.

"Are you all right?" Mukta asked.

I must have looked disheveled. I had fallen twice while running home and bruised my knees badly, but I didn't reply. She brought me a glass of water and wiped my wounds with an antiseptic. She also brought me dinner that night and sat beside me on my bed.

"I know you think it is my fault, but I didn't mean to let Memsahib go by herself. I misunderstood when you said you wanted to talk. I thought you had asked me to make an excuse. I didn't mean to do anything without your permission."

Anger rose in my throat, but I let it go down with my dinner. I didn't want to extend her the courtesy of acknowledging her presence.

AFTER SHE HAD switched off the lights, I lay awake in bed, the scene of Salim crumpling the paper and throwing it away playing in my mind. It was my last hope, and it hadn't worked. Then Mukta came to my room.

"I will sleep here, just in case." She spread a sheet on the floor. Before this, I had often relished the thought of Mukta sleeping beside my bed on the floor. She loved the thought of abandoning her dingy room, while I loved having her with me at night. Of course, Aai hadn't been very fond of the idea and had admonished me, which had never dissuaded me.

Now I thought of Aai—how badly she must have wanted me to listen to her. Today she would have been proud of me because I didn't want Mukta anywhere near me. I grumbled. I told Mukta she wasn't welcome in my room anymore. I shifted in my bed and turned my back toward her. She ignored me, crawling into a sleeping position on the floor. She might have thought I needed her, but it irritated me that she had ignored what I said—once again. I jumped out of bed, stood by the door, switched on the lights, and stared at her.

"I said I don't want you here anymore."

She patted the ground next to her, hoping I'd sit and share my heartache. The annoyance bubbling inside me came spilling out: "I hope the devil comes for you tonight, walks in right through that door." I pointed to the main door, walked up to it, and unlocked it. "I wish I never had to see you again. I wish you would burn in hell." I switched off the lights, jumped into my bed, and drew the blanket over me.

The words floated around us, trying to shrink the bond we shared. In the slant of the dim streetlight, she sat there watching me, despair engulfing her face, but I didn't regret what I had said, not on that night.

MUKTA DIDN'T LEAVE, in spite of my outburst. I remember feeling safe having her close by. In retrospect, I should have realized how much I needed her in my grief. But back then I was busy thinking of ways to get rid of her.

Something woke me up that night—I don't remember what. Was it the sudden whoosh of the wind through the window or the swishing of curtains? I hadn't opened my eyes, but I had already smelled the whiff of danger in the air. It was a sour smell, the smell of alcohol. I thought I was having a dream about Papa and Anupam chacha sitting on the balcony, laughing, drinking whiskey in the happier days. But when my eyes opened, I could see him, the man who dawdled around my bed, reeking of alcohol.

The streetlight was barely letting light in, but I could see Mukta sitting upright on the floor, her back against a cupboard, staring at him in horror. His shadow sauntering through the room looked deadly and sent a shiver through me. I could see a masked face with eyes scanning my room. *It is a bad dream.* He kneeled down on the floor beside Mukta, blotted a tape across her mouth, and tied her hands behind her. *Wake up.*

But there was no waking up because it was no dream. I was wide awake. Mukta squirmed and tried to push the man away. I remember trying to get up—I wanted to help her—but my body wouldn't move. My mouth opened to scream but snapped shut on its own. Tears crept down her cheeks, reached the borders of the tape on her mouth, and slid down her neck. All her attempts at screaming came out soft and garbled. It came to me then—Salim—it was Salim—it had to be. He picked Mukta up in his arms and flung her over his shoulder. When she looked at me one last time, her face on his shoulder as he turned his back to me, I could see the fear, the pain, the confusion on her face. But most of all, I remember—I am unable to forget—the hope I saw in her eyes as if she believed I was brave enough to save her—*I*, who had gone to all the trouble of seeking out Salim to get rid of her.

I don't know how long I lay there, my eyes shut, lingering in that silence, frozen in time, perspiration beading my forehead. When I opened my eyes, the room seemed bereft of all that had happened. I looked around and examined it. I tried to convince myself Mukta was still sleeping on the floor and whatever had happened was a figment of my imagination. The sequence of events buzzed in my head as I walked to the storage room, hoping to find Mukta there. It was empty—as empty as the space in my heart.

I didn't wake up Papa that night. I sat on the floor of that storage room, waiting for somebody to jolt me from my nightmare. The main door must have been left open by the intruder because I could hear it creak all night and could feel the cold breeze that blew inside as I waited for light to appear. In hindsight, I could have woken up Papa or at least screamed, both of which would have been good choices to catch a kidnapper. Was I actually afraid or had I not been able to move because I wanted Mukta out? For years I've tried to analyze that night in my head but have never gotten an answer.

The next morning Papa called my name several times, and it echoed in our apartment until he found me sitting in the storage room. I remember the way he looked at me, standing outside the room, peering inside, his eyes widening in alarm. I got up and rushed into his arms. I remember trying to tell him everything between sobs as he held me close and caressed my hair.

"Shh . . . it's all right, you can tell me later."

AT THE POLICE station, Papa pressed my trembling hands while we waited on a bench. The barred window let the dappled sunlight fall on my face. I saw his concern for me and knew that was what I had been missing. Ever since Aai died, there hadn't been a moment like this between us. It reminded me of why I had wanted Mukta gone from our home. With the bad omen no longer there to create any trouble, I felt reassured everything would be all right now, that though I would miss Aai, things between Papa and me would revert to normal. Guilt surged

through my heart, but I decided it was best not to tell anyone
what had really happened that night. Telling the truth would
mean leading the police to Salim and eventually to me. Not only
would I be in trouble, but Papa would know. He would know
the evil way in which his daughter had conspired to let a poor
village girl vanish from their lives. So I carefully planned what
I was going to say. I would tell the policeman I didn't remember anything. If he pestered me for information, I would make
something up.

"You shouldn't be here," Papa kept telling me, holding my
hands, clenching and unclenching them as we sat there. His
hands were cold although summer was at its peak.

We sat on that bench for a long time. The couple before
us complained about a stalker troubling them. The constable
scribbled something in the register. When it was our turn, we sat
in front of a constable who asked, "What is your complaint?"

"Someone broke into our apartment last night," Papa said.

The constable bent his head forward.

"The man kidnapped a girl . . . this girl who was staying at
our place. He—"

"Who was she?" the constable asked.

"She was an orphan from a village. She used to live with us."

"So she's a servant! I've seen people like you who bring young
girls from villages to be your servants. Now you want to complain about a man kidnapping a servant? What did you do to
her?" The constable raised his eyebrows.

"She wasn't a servant. She just did some chores in the house.
She helped out, that's all."

"I see. So you sent her to the same school as your daughter?

And your daughter did as many chores as her? Who are you fooling, sir?"

Papa's face tightened and flushed with anger. The chair scraped the tiled floor as he stood up. "I want to speak with your senior," Papa said. His voice boomed across the station. For a second, the din in the police station settled around us like dust.

A police officer emerged from an inner room and looked at the constable. "What's the issue?"

His attire was different than the others and gave him a presence of authority. The constable sitting before us got up and hurried toward him. "This man wants to complain about a kidnapped village girl," he said loudly.

The police officer looked at Papa.

"I am Inspector Chavan," he said. He led us to his office and asked us to have a seat.

"So how can I help you?" he asked with genuine interest. The grim expression on his face frightened me. I was afraid I might break down and narrate the sequence of events as they happened, but Papa began to speak. "A girl was kidnapped last night from our apartment. A man broke into—"

"Hmm, did he take anything? Rob you?"

Papa paused. "I didn't check. But the girl was sleeping in my daughter's room."

"Did you see the man?"

"My daughter was awake—"

"The question was meant for her." The inspector looked at me.

I was startled by his eyes on me. "I-I . . . couldn't see that well," I managed to say.

"I see. If you remember details like how tall he was, what he looked like . . . anything can help."

I lowered my eyes and shook my head.

"My daughter . . . she is in shock. In a day or two she may recollect something." Papa looked at me as if somewhere in my mind was a clue that could unravel his troubles.

"All right," the inspector sighed. "I will have to come to your home in a day or two to investigate."

I walked out of the inspector's office, holding Papa's hand, not knowing where my lie was leading me.

THE INSPECTOR KNOCKED on our door two days later. I hadn't expected it. I had overheard Meena-ji saying the other day that no one takes any interest in the disappearance of such a child. But here he was, with a bright smile as I opened the door.

"Hello, Tara," he said, tapping his *lathi* lightly on the door.

A constable stood behind him. I invited the inspector in and absentmindedly called out to Mukta to bring him some tea. It was just a force of habit. Behind me, the kitchen echoed its emptiness; the spoons hanging off a stand made a clanking sound in the breeze.

"Is your father here?" the inspector asked.

"Yes, yes, so nice of you to come," Papa said behind me. He shook hands with the inspector, asked him to sit on the sofa, and asked me to get him a glass of water. By the time I returned with the glass of water and handed it to him, the inspector was examining our apartment. Papa led him to my room. He stood in the doorway, studying the interior of my room.

"Where was she sleeping?"

"In there with Tara." Papa pointed to the floor beside my bed.

The inspector turned to me. "You, little girl, *must* tell me what happened."

"I would really appreciate it if you could keep her out of it. She recently lost her mother, and I am unsure if she is ready to—"

"I understand, but I can't keep her out of this. She is the one who saw everything."

"Can we . . ." Papa indicated with his fingers, asking the inspector to step aside, out of my earshot. They walked outside, out of the main door, and talked in whispers. When they were back, the inspector walked toward me.

"Now, I have spoken to your Papa. He says you are a smart girl. So you will understand that if you don't tell me what you remember it will be difficult to find her."

I looked at Papa. He nodded. "Tell him whatever you remember," he said.

The inspector looked at me suspiciously, his penetrating eyes trying to decipher the secret I held.

"Were you sleeping right there?" He pointed to the bed in my room.

I nodded.

"And you didn't wake up all night, not at the slightest sound?"

I let my eyes tear up at the question and looked to Papa to rescue me.

Papa walked up to me and squeezed my shoulder. "She isn't usually like this. If she knew, she would tell you. She is a brave kid."

The inspector sighed and stood up. "We will do what we can." He shook hands with Papa and was on his way out when he stopped.

"Do you lock the door every night?" he turned to ask Papa.

"Right before I go to sleep."

The inspector nodded and pursed his lips as if deep in thought, then walked to the door and examined the lock. "The lock is intact. Nobody has broken it. Somebody had to have unlocked the door from the inside and opened the door for the intruder."

"What rubbish," Papa said. "Why would anyone in this house do such a thing?"

I would, I wanted to say. In a way I had opened the door to an intruder, to Salim, by asking him to take Mukta away. But I had no clue as to how he had opened the door. I had unlocked the door but our door lock was such that without the keys to our apartment, one couldn't open it even if it was unlocked from the inside. How could he have possibly broken into our home without breaking the door?

The inspector ignored Papa's raised voice and continued: "Who else has the keys?"

"A few of our neighbors," Papa said, giving him some names. The inspector noted them down.

"We will talk to them and check if, by any chance, they have lost the keys to your apartment. They must have fallen into the hands of the intruder," he said. Then he smiled, shook Papa's hand, and left, leaving our empty home to us.

DAYS LATER, WHEN we went to the police station to inquire, the inspector said he had been busy and hadn't found time to inquire with our neighbors, let alone investigate the case. Papa said it was the inspector's way of telling us the kidnapping of a village child wasn't that important, at least when the police were still busy trying to weed out the culprits behind the bomb blasts. After this we went exactly four times to the station, although I am sure Papa must have taken this trip several times after work. Each time the inspector said they were investigating but had nothing so far. We returned home every time, Papa's feet heavy with disappointment, my mind burdened with guilt for making Papa search for a girl whom I had wanted out of our lives. But he probably knew that eventually we would have to stop looking for her, and we did.

I remember how those last few days in India went by—Navin and I walked around fruitlessly, silently, as if he understood what I had done. Most days when I tried to talk to him, he said he had an errand to run or had to meet another friend. Papa came home tired from work and grunted when I asked him anything. That's how he talked to me in those days. On some days, I wondered if this was what the rest of my life would be—watching happy families saunter down the road, reminding me of my childhood before all this happened. I tried to find that affection in the winds on the terrace—the winds Mukta used to talk about; I wondered if I could hear what she had wanted me to hear in them. I wished I could go back and cry in Aai's arms and tell her I had meant no harm to Mukta. But even this small delight wasn't meant for me anymore.

There were times when, looking up from my homework, I would see a pigeon fluttering its wings outside the window. Mukta would have discovered a hidden message in it. At times like those, I wanted to shout out and tell Papa everything, tell him what I had done, tell him Mukta must be back where she came from and we should go get her. That is what I hoped Salim had done—taken her back to her village. In my sanest moments it seemed implausible, but I didn't question it. Many times, sitting silently surrounded by the four walls of what was once home to me, I wondered if I should talk to Salim, ask him if Mukta was safe, but even this, I couldn't manage.

Papa came home one evening, let his briefcase drop on the floor, and said he had a surprise for me.

"What?" I asked excitedly.

It had been months since silence had overwhelmed our home—something I was still not quite used to. I waited as he loosened his tie and sat down on the sofa near the living room window, his arms spread on its back.

"Come here," Papa said.

I left my homework on the table and settled on the sofa near him.

"I have accepted a job with an international organization, Tara. Ever since I got my engineering degree at IIT, I've got a lot of job offers with companies abroad but I never once wanted to leave India. I thought your Aai wouldn't like it in a

foreign place. But now, I think it'll be better for us if we leave."
He took a deep breath and looked out the window; his arms
settled on my shoulder. Outside it was a bright evening, the
sky blue and cloudless; I could see birds flying together in a V
pattern. I looked at Papa anxiously, knowing there was more
to come.

"Tara, you understand what it means, don't you? We will
have to leave this apartment, leave this country for America. It
guarantees a good education for you. The dreams I have for you
can still come true. Besides, I think it is time we moved on from
this home, from the bitter memories it gives us."

I sat there watching the sky for a moment and thought of
Mukta, then of Aai—two people I had lost so quickly and without notice. In the last few months, the emptiness Mukta left was
beginning to haunt me, and in some strange way, since I could
never confess, I had hoped the police would search for her, unravel her whereabouts sooner or later, lead us back to where she
came from, and just maybe, we would be able to bring her home
once again.

"Tara, are you listening to me?"

"But Papa, we have to find Mukta."

Papa grew morose. "There . . . there is another thing I have
to tell you."

His expression, his sudden despair, was unsettling. He
blinked his eyes and looked away. "The police phoned me at the
office. They said she died a couple of days ago."

The silence resounding through our home echoed in my ears.
That night, her silent struggle, the look of anguish in her eyes,
and that hope on her face—everything came back. This was the

result of what I had attempted to do. How could I have done something so careless, with no thought or caution that something might happen to her? Worse, I had been naïve enough to think that Salim would never hurt her. What had I been thinking? I couldn't even bear to ask Papa how Mukta had died. Was she in pain? Had she suffered? Had she gotten a proper funeral? These were questions I was too afraid and ashamed to ask. They would linger in my heart for a long time to come.

The tears I hadn't shed all this while came free. Papa sat next to me, smoothing my hair until the sunlight faded around us.

THE DAY WE boarded the plane, I remember looking back at all the families who had come to drop off their loved ones, waving at them. I searched for faces I knew, but there was nobody there for us. As the plane took off, I remember watching the dimly lit city below us, wondering if I would ever return. I had heard about America from my teachers. They said it was a land of plenty. Some of my friends whose relatives lived there said it was a land where dreams are fulfilled. Looking back, I suppose, I had a lot of time on the flight to wonder about this country, to be excited about our life ahead or even feel apprehension about it. But at the time, these thoughts didn't occur to me. I didn't think of a new school or a new apartment or about making new friends. My head swirled with memories of Mukta, of that one day when I had stupidly tried to get rid of her.

"Tara, sometimes we have to find a new life, a new dream, especially when the old one doesn't work out," Papa told me as the plane was about to land. Around us people tightened their seat belts and awaited their destination. Papa didn't smile at me as he said this. He kept looking ahead, with a deep furrow between his brows, and I waited for him to look at me, to say something else. I wondered if he believed it himself—that we would be successful at building this new life that he talked about.

As the plane landed in America, I knew the weight of what I had done could never wash off in these foreign waters.

CHAPTER 16

MUKTA
Kamathipura, Mumbai—1993

HAVE YOU EVER had the feeling you are plummeting down a deep, dark hole? The worst part of it isn't the fear of what might happen to you but the desperate hope that someone will be there at the end of it, someone who loves you enough to save you. I woke up with that feeling that day. I thought I might drown in the darkness—it was everywhere around me. When I came to, my wrists and ankles ached from being bound. The ground was damp under me. I could hear a steady trickle of water, then a sob—a girl's sob, or perhaps it was the crying of a baby left on this wet floor beside me. I tried to feel the ground with my hands, to reach the baby, but the cries kept getting louder and louder. I couldn't speak so I started humming an old Hindi song, hoping the baby would quiet down, hoping I soon would hear its sweet gurgle. But it was the voice of a girl instead, and she was saying something. I tried to listen.

"Are you . . . ?"

I strained my ears and listened harder.

"Are you awake?" the voice whispered to me between sobs.

I whimpered—my attempt at a response.

"Don't worry. You will feel that way. It is because of the drugs they have given you." It was another voice from behind me.

How many people were here, wallowing in this darkness with me? Tara's face flashed before my eyes, startled as she lay in her bed, watching me being taken away from her. Then the images of our childhood together—of us sitting on the terrace watching birds, reading books, giggling frivolously, the walks to her school, the moments we stole to eat ice cream. It didn't seem real anymore; it was as if I had dreamed up my time with her. I felt I knew what was coming. Memories of that man back in the village trying to get a hold of eight-year-old me. I could smell his garlic breath, the cigarette fumes on my face. I could hear the mirror toppling and shattering to pieces. Then his hand on me . . . I couldn't bear it if it happened again. But maybe, a voice inside me said, this was where I was supposed to be—the place I had been trying to escape from for the last five years. And there was no escape from it. I tried to rouse myself from my fearful memories, and forced my body to move. But I was handcuffed and my legs were tied, and there wasn't much I could do. It was dark and I couldn't see a thing. I tried to look at the faces, the shapes floating around me, crying softly.

The voices drifted around me, whispering, lulling me to sleep. I slipped in and out of sleep, struggling to return to reality. When I came out of it, I could hear the girls around me sobbing, talking in hushed tones.

"Where are we?" I asked.

"Don't know." A girl's voice said, "They must have kept us

here for at least two days. I am Jasmine. I have been with this brothel for ten years. Every year I try to escape, and they trap me in here. This is what they do when anybody tries to escape from here. I am used to the drugs now. None of the new girls can take it like I can."

I thought I could hear the tiredness in her voice. And I was sure she would cry, but she laughed instead. The sound of her laughter echoed through the room for a while. Then the room became silent; maybe everybody there was as frightened as I was.

"Don't worry. This is the last time I will laugh. They will not keep me alive for too long," Jasmine said with a chuckle. "That is why they put me in with all of you—the new girls—so all of you know what happens to anybody who tries to escape. They will kill me in front of all of you as a lesson. You watch."

Someone sobbed softly, and then another joined in. Soon the sobs rose to wails.

"Shh, shh," Jasmine said. "That doesn't mean you can't escape. That is what I want to tell you. Don't give up hope. Sometimes one act of bravery is better than a life lived as a coward, as a slave."

The sobbing continued. But her words echoed in my ears. In the midst of my fear, her strength poured into me as if a dying plant had been watered, and I told myself I would remember what she had said, remember the strength in her voice, the way she had said it.

IN THE MORNING, rays of light were filtering through openings in windows covered with black paper, pouring through cracks in the walls. We could see each other now. Around me, there were many girls looking weary, hungry—some handcuffed to a pipe, some to the bar of a window. Only one girl had her hands untied. She sat with her hands around her knees, wrapped in a red silk sari, her face thickly painted with makeup, her *kajal* dripping from her eyes, and I knew as soon as she gave me a smile she was the girl whose words had rebounded in this darkness for me. She was Jasmine—whose face, like the flower, smelled of hope.

"I don't have the key to your handcuffs or I would help," she said to me. She smiled again, and I knew it was an attempt to hide the pain digging deep into her eyes. One of the girls squinted in the light. Her wrists were handcuffed like mine, and she whimpered either in pain or hopelessness. Hunger pangs had set in, and even in that brightened room, everything seemed bleak.

"Are you hurt?" Jasmine asked her.

She shook her head. There were two girls sitting next to Jasmine. One of them had a gash on her forehead with dried blood that had oozed out of it in a straight line down one side of her face. Neither of them could have been more than twelve, about three years younger than me. To me, they looked quite identical.

"They are sisters. Their father sold them. We are like vegetables—all of us—ready to be sold the day we are born. Have you seen potatoes being sold in the market—five rupees for two kilos? We are those potatoes, we are—" Jasmine's words erupted into laughter again. She didn't finish what she was saying, just kept laughing nervously.

"*Bas*, keep quiet!" another girl yelled at Jasmine. "You are frightening everyone. Stay calm. There will be a way out of this.

Let's think. My mother used to say to me, 'Neerja, we can always find a way out of difficult situations.' Maybe we can escape."

"Yes, yes, try and try . . . keep trying and trying." Jasmine burst into giggles again.

The twin girls huddled in the corner, staying close to each other, tears pouring from their eyes. Despite my alarm, I wanted to reassure them and distract them from their agony. I was about to open my mouth when the panel of light from under the door got broader and broader as the door opened. I could make out the silhouette of a woman with two men following her. She stood for a while in the dimly lit room, blinking her eyes several times to become accustomed to the darkness, then looked around at all of us, beaming with pride at our conquered spirits.

"Jasmine is of no use to me. You can take her away," the woman said to the two men behind her. Jasmine giggled deliriously.

The woman bent down to look at the two twelve-year-old girls, held their faces in both her hands, and said, "Virgins cure many diseases. You will be very useful to me."

The two girls whimpered and erupted into sobs.

She walked toward me and brought her face closer to mine. I lurched back, the handcuffs leaving their mark on my flesh.

"Remember me?"

Her eyes had the same bitterness, the same venom, I had seen years earlier. Many years ago she had sat in our living room, slurping the tea Amma had served. *Do you know how much money you can make if you come with me to Bombay?* she had asked me. I shuddered at everything that came after it. Sweat stung my eyes. I blinked it away. For the past five years, I had nightmares of meeting this woman again. For months after arriving in Bombay, I had sobbed in my sleep because of her. But then, as years had passed by, I had convinced myself that she was a thing of my past.

"You didn't think that ceremony at the Yellamma temple would come free, did you? Or did you think your debt could get repaid that quickly—with just one night with a zamindar? Did you think you could escape?" She glared at me.

Madam was older now, yet her smile was still sly. I could smell jasmine flowers mixed with sweat and a sweet smell of *supari*, just like I had years ago. It reminded me of times when Amma was still alive, when I would prance behind her as she took me into the village, of a time when Amma and I would cook together, of a time when my life was simple. Until she had taken away all those simple pleasures of my life. I wish I was strong enough to look this woman in her eye and tell her that she couldn't just continue to destroy many more lives. I turned away and focused my eyes on Jasmine. The men had pulled Jasmine to her feet and were still standing there with her.

"What are you waiting for? Take her away," Madam admonished them.

They hurriedly dragged her away. Jasmine turned sideways to glance at me and gave me a smile as if she didn't fear what was coming. I will always remember that smile, how her eyes knew no fear, and for years I would wonder if I could ever have the courage she had.

Madam stood up straight, addressing all of us: "See, this is a lesson I want all of you to learn. There never will be an escape from this place. Look at Jasmine—you live here or you die here."

IT DIDN'T TAKE them long to dump Jasmine's body next to us. You'd think it would be easier to see a dead body after I had seen my own mother die. But it wasn't. I was the first to crawl next to Jasmine's body. I wanted to think Jasmine was in a deep sleep, would wake up any time, and start giggling all over again. My hands were still tied together but I shook her body. Her eyes were open, staring at the ceiling, but there was no life inside them. I lurched back with a scream and slipped in the water on the floor. I scraped my elbow, and my head hit the damp floor; my tears came thick and strong. Any day now, this would become our fate. Neerja, who had previously been unhindered by our plight and spoke so bravely of finding a way to escape, cried the loudest. Locked up in that room that night, in the darkness with Jasmine's body beside us, I don't remember how long we cried . . . or vomited.

By next morning, a man obediently followed Madam and dropped a plate before us—a few rotis and pieces of potatoes— and put a jug of water beside it. We must have lost touch with reality because all of us put our hands into that plate and grabbed whatever food we could. It was the only meal I'd had in days. In that moment, we didn't think of what was coming our way; we didn't fear or worry about our fate or our lives; we just ate. It was only afterward I realized I hadn't stopped to look as they had carried away Jasmine's body. As I stuffed my mouth with food, I didn't even bother bidding her a goodbye. I kept chewing even as they dragged the two wailing, twelve-year-old girls away. What had happened to me? I didn't cringe at their tears; I didn't fear for them. Suddenly, for me, someone else's life had become cheaper than mine.

"YOU HAVE UNTIL tomorrow to clean up," Madam announced to everyone. "I have given a lot of money to whoever sold you. It is time to pay your debt now. As for you, Mukta, I didn't even realize Ashok Sahib had taken you from your village until it was too late. But I don't accept defeat. Nobody gets away from me. After five years of search, one of my men saw you entering that building in Dadar the other day. To think you were in Bombay all this time, right under my nose. Finally!"

She left, closing the door behind her.

I realized I was struggling to keep my eyes open. All the other girls must have been drowsy, because nobody said a word. They had drugged us again. I drifted off to sleep. That night I dreamt of Tara.

We are holding hands and walking on soft sand. It's a beach. She is sitting beside me on the warm sand, both of us looking at the calm sea in front of us, the wind blowing on our faces. I think to myself, it must be her presence beside me that is making everything look so radiant. She smiles at me, tells me she will take me with her wherever she goes. And when I turn to look, there is no one beside me. Tara is walking away from me. "It's because of you my Aai died, isn't it?" she asks me. Her words echo around me.

Another dream—*my father, my Appa, pulls me onto his lap and tells me stories. We are sitting outside my house in the village; in the distance the forest is looking at us. Amma is feeding the chickens in our yard, watching us with a smile on her face. It is so safe here, nothing could ever harm me. Sakubai hands me a glass of milk—— it looks so pristine sitting in my hands, nothing like me. Remember, she points out to me: you will always be dirt; you couldn't even save your own mother.*

"Wake up," said the gruff voice of a man. I felt like I'd been kicked. My back hurt. Perhaps I was in another dream.

"Get up," the voice again. I opened my eyes to see the peering faces of two men. "You can't sleep all day. Earn us some money," said one, and the other laughed behind him.

The room stank of our vomit, our waste—what else were we to do tied up? They took us out of the room onto the terrace. There were six of us there, trying to open our eyes and look at each other. After we had been in that dark room for so long, the sun was scorching hot and unwelcome. They made us walk for a bit in the sun to get rid of our drowsiness.

I was still dazed when they took me to a room. I heard some-one say, "This one doesn't have any windows, no escape." My eyes were still closing on me when a girl walked in, scrubbed my body with a warm towel scented with neem, changed my clothes, painted my face, and left me in that room. There was a slow-whirring ceiling fan above me, and a lightbulb flickering above the doorway, making me nauseous. Soon there was a man standing in the doorway, smoking a bidi and blowing rings of smoke into the room. Even in that dazed state, I could feel his eyes on my body as he looked me up and down.

"You are more beautiful than they said you would be," he said, flicking ashes in midair and strolling toward me.

I remember breaking into a cold sweat, standing up, and taking a few steps backward as he advanced, but there was a wall behind me and nowhere to go. He came close—so close I could smell the smoke on his breath. Without hesitating, he grabbed my hair and yanked it so hard my head hit the wall. He pinned me against it with one hand. I screamed and shivered as his other hand slid down my back and went lower and lower until it was pulling at my skirt.

"No, no," I gasped, but his hand was on my thigh now.

He loosened the drawstring of his pajamas and let them fall around his ankles. His body pressed against mine as he thrust himself into me. The pain was intense. My voice became a rasp as I gripped his shoulders, my nails digging into his flesh, but he didn't flinch. Even in my drug-induced state I could feel his un-shaven face pressed against mine, his breathing fast and vicious. I closed my eyes and wandered to the memories of better times: sitting on the terrace with Tara, listening to the tales she told me, cooking with Amma, skipping behind her to the village.

When he was done, he slumped next to me. For a while, I could hear our breathing slow down, my heart still beating wildly. Then he yanked my hair again and banged my head on the wall repeatedly. All I could hear was the repeated thumping; the whimpers that rose from my throat seemed like some other girl's distant cries.

When he let go of my hair, I sank against the wall. He gave a throaty laugh as I stroked the back of my head and brought out bloodied fingers.

"All you whores deserve it," he said.

He disappeared, leaving me behind in that smoky room. I don't remember what he looked like. I have wondered what his eyes looked like—were they calm and composed as he hurt me? But now there are too many men to remember, faces that come and go, merge into one another.

CHAPTER 17

TARA
2004

THAT EVENING, WALKING back home, I was surprised to see the door to the neighboring apartment open.

"Tara?" a man inside the apartment called out. He scanned my face.

It was Navin. His eyes still held that mischievous sparkle. His shoulder-length hair covered his wide cheekbones, and a ridiculous-looking goatee stood on his chin.

"Navin! You look *so* different." I gave him a grin.

"And you?" He smiled. "You look so much like your mother. I could almost swear it was her."

I smiled. The memories of Aai came flooding back.

"Come in, come in," he said, waving me inside. "The neighbors told me you were back from America. Daddy and I just got back today from our village, after more than six months away.

"My wife and child are still back there," he continued. "Daddy wanted to stay in Ganipur, where he grew up. Just for a while—fresh air, good food, you know." Navin chuckled. "How long have you been here?"

"About four months," I said.

It *had* been four months—*four months* of lingering unsuccessfully at the police station and the detective's office, *four months* of forgetting that the rest of the world existed.

"So what brings you here?" He pulled up a chair and urged me to sit.

"Papa died . . . a few months ago."

"Oh, I—"

"He . . . committed suicide . . . hung himself," I said. I didn't know why I wanted to tell him this.

"Oh." He looked alarmed. "Why? What happened?"

I shrugged, lowering my eyes.

"I wish I knew," I said. "When he was lying there . . . you know, at the funeral . . . I was wondering what must have been going through his head to do something like that." I blinked back my tears. It felt good to tell someone.

Navin let out a sigh. "I-I don't know what to say, but I'm sorry to hear that, sorry to know you had to go through all that. Bhagwan rest his soul."

"Thank you." I nodded. "So . . . I came here to disperse his ashes and . . . and I came to look for Mukta. She is alive, you know, or at least I think she is."

"That child your Papa brought home? Your friend? She . . . she is alive?" He looked nervous and wiped his hands on his shirt. "How . . . how do you know?"

"It's a long story. I'll tell you someday . . . Do you remember Raza?"

"That street *goonda*?"

"Yes, he runs an NGO now. He seems to have changed. He says he can help me find Mukta."

Navin seemed perturbed. "Do you trust him? I don't know how a boy like that becomes a good man, you know these days—"

"I have no choice, Navin," I interrupted, "I have no choice but to trust him. I have to find Mukta!" My voice was stern. Navin was taken aback.

"So how's Anupam chacha?" I changed the topic.

"He's . . . you know . . ." He gulped. "He's sleeping right now, but he would really like to see you. Let me get you something to eat." Navin disappeared inside.

I looked around me. This apartment took me back to when we were children—Navin and I arguing and chasing each other in this apartment. I used to love watching him play the sitar. "Do you still sing, play the sitar?" I asked Navin as he brought me a plate of snacks.

"No, I left that a long time ago." He smiled wryly, his eyes seeming to remember the friendship we once shared.

"HELLO *BETA*, THERE you are." Anupam chacha waved to me from a wheelchair in the doorway. I couldn't have imagined the man I knew once—Papa's best friend, the man who once ran five miles every day—to be in this condition.

"Look at you, Tara," he said, his breathing noisy and strained, "all grown up. You were so young when you left." He paused and coughed hard.

I watched his tired, pale face, which had been robbed of its youth. His scalp showed through splotches of hair; his eyes looked as if they were sinking under their own weight.

"Cancer . . . it's a slow killer," he said, giving me a feeble smile. "Everybody looks at me that way."

"I am sorry. I didn't mean to."

"Daddy, you need water?" Navin asked as he poured everybody a cup of tea.

Anupam chacha waved him away. "*Arre*, because I am sick you people treat me like I am some child."

Navin retired inside. I sat beside Anupam chacha, the teacup warming my hands.

"Don't worry about him. You can always catch up with him later, you know, after I am gone." He chuckled, as if it was a joke. "I am lucky—my son and daughter-in-law take care of me. Tara, tell me all about America. Is it true what they say about the land, that . . . everybody is . . . rich; that . . . everybody has . . . cars?" His breathing was more erratic now, his speech halting at intervals.

I felt guilty for not having kept in touch, for not having known he had been suffering so gravely. "I am sorry Papa and I couldn't call when we were in America. Sorry that—" The teacup rattled in my hand.

"Everybody has their reasons," he interrupted and gave me a gentle wave of his hand and a wobble of his head. "Forget that and tell me, are you married?" He spoke between coughs now. "I hear it is okay . . . to keep a boyfriend . . . there without . . . being married." He attempted to laugh. A picture of Brian flashed through my mind, strumming his guitar, a new girlfriend filling the space I had left.

"No, I didn't marry," I said and tried to take a sip of my tea.

"So you didn't marry *haan*? If your . . . Aai was here . . . she would have been throwing a fit." He laughed. "Of course . . . your Papa would have . . . supported you in anything you ever did. You were . . . the apple of his eye."

I made an effort to smile, to hide the dismay I felt at the mention of my dead parents.

"Navin just told me about your Papa. I never imagined that he'd commit suicide. May his soul rest in peace! I was very sorry to hear about it."

"I really don't know why he did it. I knew he was lonely and maybe . . . lost when we went to America but . . ." I paused.

"Sometimes, we just carry too big a burden in life. Who can tell when a person decides that he can't carry it anymore? Hmm . . ."

I nodded and lowered my eyes, not wanting to talk about it.

"So . . . we won't talk more about it if you don't wish to. Have you been to . . . your village yet?" Anupam chacha continued.

"What would I do there?" I asked, happy to talk about something else. "Aai used to say that if I stepped foot in the village they'd kill me. I don't know if that's true, but I certainly don't want to find out. And then both sets of grandparents are dead. Papa told me when they died. There is no one there for me now."

Anupam chacha sighed. "What your Aai used to say . . . about the villagers trying to kill her was true . . . once. I don't think . . . anyone cares anymore. Her parents are dead anyway. Besides . . . they revere your . . . father too much . . . in the village to bring . . . any harm to you. You shouldn't worry about that.

And . . . your father's mother . . . she is alive. I am sure . . . she would like to . . . meet you."

"No, no," I said with a chuckle, "that can't be true. Papa wouldn't lie to me about that. I mean, it was different when he told me Mukta was dead. He wanted me to get away from the grief of what had happened, have a better life in America. He—"

"There is a reason . . . he lied. That girl, Mukta . . . she was a prostitute's daughter . . . from our village."

"A prostitute's daughter?"

He nodded.

"You should go to the village . . . and talk to your grand-mother. How I wish . . . he was alive today—your Papa. He . . . would have wanted you . . . to know how badly . . . he had always wanted to help . . . that girl. I never got a chance . . . to speak to him after . . . that one phone call he made . . . from America. Never had . . . a chance to tell him . . ."

A bout of coughing overtook him. He held a towel to his mouth, and his face turned red. Before I knew it, Navin had rushed beside him, brought him a glass of water, and put the glass to his mouth, letting him sip the water and wiping the dribble from his chin.

"Are you all right, Daddy?" Navin asked. Anupam chacha nodded.

"Maybe you should go now," Navin said to me.

"Of course," I said, then stood up and placed the teacup on the table.

"No, no, don't leave," Anupam chacha said, having recov-ered. "There is so much . . . we have to talk about . . . so much I have to tell you—"

"Not now, Daddy. Maybe another time," Navin admonished him.

I knew Anupam chacha might have wanted to talk about Papa and their time together, and I would have loved to listen and talk about those old memories, but he was in no condition to do so.

"I have to be somewhere," I said, "so I should probably go. But I will be back again." I picked up my purse, letting the strap fall over my shoulders.

"Will you?" Anupam chacha asked, looking at me earnestly. "I would love it . . . if you come. I'd love . . . to hear you read . . . to me sometime, the . . . same stories that I . . . used to tell you." He chuckled to himself.

"Sure," I said.

"I'll walk you out," Navin told me. We walked down the corridor to the steps. I held on to the railing and looked at Navin. "How much time does he have?" I asked.

"Not much. A few months, a year maybe. Two if we are lucky. We had Rohan because Daddy wanted, you know, to see his grandchild before he died. So not much time—not much . . ." He shook his head, tears glistening in his eyes.

"Maybe I will come by to read to him some days, if that's okay?" I said.

"Of course, he would like that."

I squeezed his shoulder. "Take care," I whispered to him and walked back home.

THAT NIGHT AS I slept, my conversation with Anupam chacha replayed in my head. Was Mukta a prostitute's child? And how could my grandmother be alive? Why would Papa lie to me about that? It just wasn't possible. Papa knew how badly I had wanted to meet my grandparents my whole life. He would not have lied to me about that. Maybe Anupam chacha was confused. With the cancer and the pain medicines he was on, he must have gotten his facts mixed up. My conversation with Anupam chacha replayed in my head, and I reminisced about his friendship with Papa, about my childhood, about how little time he had left, about how Navin's son would never know his grandfather, just as I had never known mine. But what was Anupam chacha sorry about? Something Papa and he had disagreed on? Was that why Papa had stopped calling them when we were in America?

MY THOUGHTS DRIFTED to America. How quickly Papa and I had left this country back then. How quickly we had tried to escape from the pain, as if running away from it, moving to another country allowed us the luxury of leaving behind the memories.

For the first three months, we had stayed in a studio apartment that belonged to one of Papa's colleagues who had been kind enough to offer it to us for free until we rented an apartment in the city that would become my home for eleven years. I remember when Papa first took me to that apartment. Mustiness filled the air as he opened the doors and led me into the living room. The carpet was dirty and full of cat hair. Papa didn't seem to notice all this; he strolled along to the window and pointed to a faraway building, hidden in the shadow of other buildings.

"There, at the corner of that street is your school. See, now you can walk to it."

Just a few months ago, he would have asked me, "Do you like it?" Before Aai had become just a memory in our lives, he would have taken me in his arms and told me we could move if I didn't like the apartment. But now, all he did was stand by the window and point to the school as if that were the place where I could hope to find respite from my memories.

I barricaded myself in my room that afternoon. I knew Papa would knock on the door and ask me what was wrong. I sat on my bed and waited, straining my ears to listen for the smallest sound outside the door. He needn't have knocked on the door at all—I would have jumped out of bed and swung the door open *if only* I had heard him outside. But there was no such sound. When I opened the door hours later, I saw Papa's tall figure sitting on the couch, a book in his hands, his shadow on the wall turning the page. He looked up at me, smiled, and asked, "Are we having dinner here? Or do you want to go out?"

I searched his face, seeing how it portrayed the sadness that had crept deep into my heart. A memory came to me of how comfortable we had been when Mukta had sobbed through the nights, many years ago, but we had not understood how lonely she had been. Back then, I hadn't known what it felt like to have your mother taken away from you. Perhaps if I'd known even a fourth of this pain, I wouldn't have let Mukta sob alone those first few nights. I'd have stood by her, supported her when Aai shouted at her or forced her to work hard in the kitchen. It was ironic that I was exactly where Mukta stood a few years ago—we had both left home behind and arrived in a foreign place

where there was no one—not a soul to understand us. If only I
had realized this earlier, how could I have ever thought of getting rid of my only friend?

OVER THOSE FIRST days, I had arranged the apartment as best
as I could, the way Aai would have, had she been here. I covered the cream-colored walls with cheap paintings bought at
the supermarket; garish curtains from the Indian store adorned
the windows, and the tablecloth spread on the dining table had
been a gift to Aai from my grandmother, handed to her before
she had eloped with Papa. Aai had treasured it, spread it on the
dining table in our apartment in Bombay, and I had carried it
with me in my suitcase to this foreign land. I was afraid Papa
wouldn't like it, but he didn't seem to notice, or if he did, he
didn't comment on it.

In my closet was a special place for Aai's things—things I
had carried with me that made me feel closer to her—a half-
empty bottle of coconut oil and a spray bottle of rose water I
sprayed on my pillow so I could imagine her lulling me to sleep
the way she used to when we were in Bombay. Some nights I
would get out of bed, sit down on my bedroom floor, and look
at the stars through the window, pretending Mukta was by my
side, giggling with me as if nothing had ever happened.

There were times when the loss of a mother seemed unfath-
omable to me. Like on the day when I stood up to read a chapter
aloud during English period. A girl pointed out the blood on
my skirt, and I sobbed, thinking I had gotten a dreadful disease after coming to this foreign country. The teacher took me
aside while girls sneered, teasing me that I knew nothing, and

explained to me it was just the beginning of my womanhood. I stared at the teacher's face, wondering if that was what Aai had meant when she wanted me to remember I was a girl and had no business playing with boys.

I remember those first few days in this foreign country, I had wanted to learn their ways, wanted my accent to be different. I had wanted everything about me to be different. I had spent hours watching television, carefully listening to the dialogues, the way characters enunciated their words in movies, repeating after them hoping to decipher the country in which I had landed. When I looked out my window, there were no women wearing *shalwar kameez* or saris and I yearned for that familiarity. Cars obediently followed rules and stayed in their lane. Jaywalking was against the rules. Men and women both smoked and nobody would bat an eye! People here smiled even if they didn't know you. Hello, they said nodding their head, greeting me. It took me time to return their smiles, to understand that this was the norm.

I longed to be back in Bombay where everything was so much more comfortable, where I could run on streets and wave to shopkeepers, where there was always a neighbor somewhere around you watching over you. And of course, in America, the thing that I found most astonishing was those huge pet places that groomed animals. I could not believe it. It was strange to me that people held so much affection for their pets. It was more than we had ever placed in Mukta.

PAPA WOULD TAKE me to meet some of his friends who had left India behind to settle in America. *Like us,* Papa would say.

"Do I have to?" I would always ask, and every time Papa would look at me sharply, take a deep breath and say, "Come on, you don't have to make dinner for us today. Besides you will feel better. Meeting people from our own country!"

On one occasion I remember dragging myself to a dinner party. I wore a T-shirt and jeans, sat on the couch, surrounded by a bevy of boisterous women dressed in saris or *shalwar kameezes*, just like those moments when Aai would allow me to sit in with her friends. It should have been comforting but I felt out of place. Behind them, four-year-olds ran from one end of the room to another. If there were any teenagers there, I had nothing in common with them. When their parents weren't listening, they would secretly talk about their dating lives or the after-school parties or how they had already had a sip of beer. Teenagers didn't date in India and certainly didn't sip beer!

I wanted to sit in silence but my thoughts were interrupted by a woman with *sindoor* in her hair and a red sari to match.

"What are you wearing? Just because you're in Amreeka doesn't mean you have to wear jeans every time. You can wear some Indian dresses too," she teased me, nudging me laughing at her own sense of humor, her entire body shaking from her laughter.

"*Arre*, you leave her alone. Don't you know, she just lost her mother?" She looked at me with large, *kajal*-laden eyes and her arms as slender as a pencil, patted my head.

"I am Smita," she said to me as she let herself fall into the couch beside me. "So you must miss home, *haan*? Don't worry," she said patting my shoulders, "you will get used to Amreeka and its culture. Very soon, I promise. You come, come to eat," she said, and pulled me to the table laden with food—the *parathas,* the *samosas,* the *dahi wadas.* It conjured up memories, of Aai in the kitchen, Mukta trying to help her; a similar smell had wafted in our apartment in Bombay not very long ago. As I stood there with a plate in my hand, tears spontaneously burned in my eyes. Everything around me looked hazy as I searched for Papa in that crowd of people. People around me didn't seem to notice, gobbled their dinner, discussed the events happening in India, ranted about returning there. I saw Papa then, standing among them, looking as lost as I was. I knew then that in this sea of people, we were all alone. We looked at each other and as though in that one gaze, both of us knew that we would never share the dream that all these immigrants had—the dream of prosperity as they settled here. The promise of America would always be different for the both of us—to be able to forget all that had happened.

MOST DAYS, PAPA took me to school in his used Camry. He left me at the school gates, saying, "I'll see you at home. Be safe when you walk back."

I always wanted to ask if he would pick me up, but all I did was nod, shut the car door behind me, and stand there watching his car disappear around the corner.

As I watched other children carrying their school bags, heading toward school, I remembered what Mukta had asked me one day: *do you like school?* I wondered what I would have told her if she had asked that now.

One day when I stood outside my school, a girl's voice came from behind me. "You're new!" The accent was strange, something I was still getting used to. "Hey, you're that new girl!" she repeated as I turned around to face her.

Her hair was like spun gold; her eyes were shining as bright as hope. I nodded.

"I'm Elisa." She smiled.

She walked with me to class, and the day after that she was standing near the gates, looking for me. Soon she began sitting next to me in class, asking me if her dress looked pretty or wondering aloud if her mother had styled her hair properly that day. As days passed we walked to our lockers together, sat at the same table to eat lunch in the cafeteria, and walked home together. Usually she jabbered on and on about something at home, complaining about how her elder sister took advantage of her, while I wasn't even listening to her. Everybody at school assumed she was my best friend. I wasn't sure if she was; she knew nothing about me. But I didn't have the energy to clarify anything to anybody—most of all to tell Elisa she wasn't my friend. Admittedly, her dull babble gave me respite from the chatter in my mind, from the mélange of memories inflicted on me by the smallest whiff of Indian food from a restaurant we passed or the bickering and giggling of schoolgirls ahead of us, reminding me of my walks with Mukta.

One afternoon as we were buying food from the school cafeteria, I opened my wallet and she peered inside. "Who's that?" she asked. "Lovely girl, who is she?"

It was a photograph of Mukta and me standing outside the Asiatic library, something I had sneaked into my wallet before leaving India. I looked at Mukta's tired face beside my own excited one, at her beautiful green eyes that had taught me to see so many things differently, and I felt a sudden surge of guilt, of grief—tasted it like the bitterness of a pill sliding down my throat.

"None of your business!" I snapped, and everybody around me stared at us.

But Elisa didn't mind my tone or my loud voice. She followed me to the table as I carried the tray of food and let it crash on the table. The table rattled.

"Well, she must have been your best friend." Elisa shrugged as she sat down and bit into a cookie.

I tried to gulp down my food. I couldn't tell Elisa about Mukta because then I'd have to tell her what happened to her. And that was something no one could know because they'd know how vicious and vile my nature was. It frightened me to think of what I was capable of, of what Elisa would think of me, of what Papa would think of me—that I was responsible for my good friend losing her life, that I had planned it! There was no friendship or forgiveness in the world that could rectify that, I knew.

"She was a friend . . . a very good friend," I whispered to Elisa later when I had calmed down.

"Hmm . . ." Elisa said. "You know, you are just weird. What is the matter with you?"

SOMETIMES, I USED to think of the early morning *raga* Navin would sing—the music that used to float in the air and wake me up in Bombay. There was nothing of the sort here; sometimes the garbage trucks woke me up or a distant whoosh of traffic on the highway. I asked Papa a couple of times why we couldn't call

Navin or Anupam chacha and speak to them; after all, Anupam chacha was his best friend. Papa frowned when I asked him this, his expression hardened, and he looked away as if hiding something from me before he said, "Well, I did speak to him a couple of times. I also spoke to Navin the last time. But you know, Tara . . . it's . . ." He looked around as if fumbling for an excuse. "It's expensive. It's expensive to call India."

I left it at that.

Papa had tried to introduce me to several Indian girls my age—girls who had traveled to the United States like me, trying to establish an anchor in this country. But whenever one of the girls called, I would say I had something else to do, something more important, and soon they stopped calling.

"What's happened to you?" Papa asked when he heard me making an excuse over the phone. "You used to have so many friends in Bombay—running around, making *masti*. Neighbors used to come and complain about you, remember?"

"Papa, I really have something important to do," I said as I dropped the receiver.

What could I have told Papa? That the girls reminded me too much of the life I used to have in Bombay and everything that came with it? How could I tell him I desperately wanted to leave behind the girl I once was?

ONE DAY WHEN walking down a quiet corridor after class, I came across what I thought was the quietest place on earth. I took a peek inside at rows and rows of books, and the lady at the desk looked up at me from a book she was reading, adjusted her glasses, and smiled. I knew I was in a place that could give me some answers. I walked up to the shelf and picked a book. *The Arabian Nights.*

"Oh, that's a good one, honey; haven't you read it yet?" the librarian behind the desk called out softly.

I didn't let her know that Papa used to tell me the stories. I wanted to be Scheherazade—wise and brave—when I was eight years old. When I told this to Mukta once, she had listened in awe.

"You are just like her," she had told me. "Very brave. The things you do, I could never hope to do."

I took the book home that night, sat in my room, and watched the sky, book in hand. The rain fell silently outside, the drizzle too afraid to awaken anyone. I imagined Mukta beside me, heard her giggles, then pictured her looking at the sky solemnly, telling me the rain had a life of its own, making its journey from sky to earth—a long, tiring journey. I opened the book. I should have read this book many years ago, I told myself. I would have understood Scheherazade better and known then that I was nothing like her.

CHAPTER 18

TARA
America
1998–2004

By THE TIME I was eighteen and almost done with high school, I had learned to escape from my memories by delving into books. I read Eudora Welty, Patti Smith, Mark Twain, Jane Austen, the works of Rumi, and I agreed with what Mukta had once told me—*they are better than the world we live in*. Elisa didn't like that the library had become my sanctuary. She would hover around me in the library, telling me we needed to do something more interesting with our lives. She would come up with ideas and rattle them off to me, one after another, until people around us in the library shushed her.

"You are eighteen years old. You should be out with a boy, staring into his eyes. What do you find in those damn books anyway," she whispered to me one afternoon, peering over my shoulder into the book I was holding.

I chuckled. "You know, I asked somebody the same question years ago," I told her. "Maybe I am just trying to find the answer."

"Huh," she whispered. "I know who you are talking about.

It is the look you get in your eyes when you talk about her. It's that girl from the photograph, isn't it?"

I looked away and shut the book sharply between my hands. "What do you want, Elisa?" My voice was loud, my tone abrupt, and people shushed around us, but I didn't care.

We were quiet for some time, until people stopped staring and settled back into their reading.

"Oh nothing, it's just that you never tell me about what happened to her—to your best friend."

I gave her a glare. "What do you want?" I repeated.

Elisa never seemed to mind the tone I spoke in when I grew annoyed with her. Over the years, my exasperation with her grew on her as much as her talkativeness grew on me.

"Well, there's a party tonight at Frank's place. You might meet someone interesting."

Frank was her boyfriend. Elisa changed boyfriends with the season, which I had no problem with. What annoyed me was that she was always determined to set me up with someone whom I just didn't like. Two times before, she had set me up with guys I had nothing in common with, dim-witted guys who wanted to show off, quite unnecessarily.

"Not interested," I said, opening my book, drawing my eyes to it.

"You never come. This time I am not listening to any excuse. I will pick you up at seven P.M.," she said. When I lifted my head she was already walking out the door.

It was at Elisa's party that I met Brian. Everybody said that party was "happening." I remember, the table was set with finger foods—cheese, crackers, pepperoni, salami, chicken tenders, dips, chips. I wandered toward the punch bowl avoiding people. Some danced to music, spilling drinks on themselves, others kept talking to each other as if they hadn't met in a long time.

"You don't seem to enjoy the party very much," he said—his first words to me. His blue eyes caught me by surprise as I turned around—brown flecks floating in water—as hypnotic as the sea. He smiled and raised his eyebrows as he looked at me, his forehead wrinkling under stray strands of bronze hair.

"Oh, I didn't mean to stare . . . I . . ."

"It's all right," he said good-naturedly. "My name is Brian, by the way."

He looked a year older to me, if at all.

"Tara,"

"Tara—nice name. I always find such parties boring. Did you come here with a friend?"

"Elisa . . . With Elisa; she is my friend,"

"Yeah, I know Elisa. She said she was bringing a friend; she was the one who insisted I come—"

"Oh, there you guys are," Elisa interrupted. "I see you two have already met. Tara, Brian is a neighbor. His father is one of Los Angeles's best lawyers. Brian here is an awesome guitar player. You should ask him to play for you sometime. I wanted you guys to meet for such a long time. Cool," she said, clapping her hands. "Enjoy."

We watched her drift away from us, dancing to the tune of Backstreet Boys.

"Well, this party is getting boring anyway. Do you want to come for a drive?" Brian asked.

I nodded. I hadn't done anything like that before—go out with a boy by myself, with a stranger. But right there, it felt like I knew Brian, like I shared something with him. And I wanted to trust that feeling.

As he drove, the cold wind blowing on our faces, he asked me about myself. I told him where I was from, how long I had been in this country—the bare minimum that I had rehearsed when people asked me.

"Why did you leave India?"

"My father got a job here. . . . and my mother . . . she died." I looked out the window. After so many years, it was still difficult to say.

"I am sorry."

We didn't speak for a while. He hit the gas pedal, went around bends on roads, up winding steep roads. I could see the San Fernando Valley below—it looked breathtaking, lit up at night. We pulled over in a parking lot. As I got out of the car, he popped the trunk, got a couple of cans of beer. I sat on a bench near the clearing. It was like sitting on a mountaintop watching the lit-up city below us. After living here for so many years, I hadn't been here—not once—to see the city in action at night.

"I don't drink," I told him, as he offered me one.

"I like coming here," he said, popping open his can of beer and taking a sip. "So many millions out there—going about their own lives, their own heartbreaks, their own troubles. I think about them, wonder if grief piles on as heavy on everybody else."

The leaves rustled in the wind as I looked at his face and I knew *that* was what I shared with him.

"Ha! Don't mind me." He lit a cigarette.

"You don't talk much, do you?" he said, looking at me sideways.

"No, no, I . . . I think it is beautiful here!" I said, looking at the city below.

He chuckled.

"I know . . . I know," he said, "What it is like. Like animals smell fear from a distance, I smell grief on others. I don't know what happened with you but it is more to do than just your mother dying," he said, flicking the cigarette ash, having another gulp of beer.

Was that what it was—grief? Over what I had done? Or was it regret? Guilt? Maybe all of it.

Brian sighed.

"You should know this about me. Six months ago I was driving, not drunk or anything but driving like a normal teenager— *just* driving. My mom was in the front seat; my little sister, Tessa was sitting behind. She . . . she was six you know. "

He stopped looked in the distance. The streetlight at the end of our street flickered; his eyes shimmered with tears.

"I didn't stop at a red light. I was in a hurry, thought my mom was punishing me by making me drive to the store. She had hurt her arm, you know, that day." He gulped. "She . . . She couldn't drive. It happened in seconds. There were glass shards everywhere, everybody screaming, the pain unbearable and then the darkness—that *damn* darkness. I woke up in the hospital two days later. They told me, my mother and sister were dead— just like that—as if it was that simple."

He sighed, then puffed at his cigarette so hard it made his

eyes water. "You know, sometimes I think I didn't stop at the stop sign and crashed the car deliberately because I was *so angry.* I just didn't expect to lose anyone, you know." He rubbed his eyes, chuckled at himself, and offered me the cigarette. I did not refuse. I put it to my mouth and choked on it, coughed.

He laughed, patted me hard on the back, and said, "Your first cigarette!"

Through the smoke that surrounded us, I could clearly see the night when I could have stopped a kidnapping. *I am just like you, worse maybe,* I wanted to tell him but the smoke around us dispersed in the air and the words died in my mouth.

He smiled at me as if he understood.

"Nowadays," he sighed, "I keep turning back in the car to see if they are still around and it's all just a stupid dream. I have to live with it now, you know. Ever have that feeling that you have left someone behind?"

I sighed, looked into the dark sky. I knew exactly what he meant.

BRIAN WAS A rich kid. He took me out for lavish dinners on his pocket money and bought me expensive dresses and perfumes that I stowed away from Papa's eyes. He took me for long drives in expensive cars borrowed from his father. I loved the drives. We raced around bends on roads, up winding steep roads. We would sit and stare at the city for so long from up there—it was as if we didn't need words to say how each of us felt. On those warm summer afternoons when he played the guitar for me and sang songs, the honeyed tone of his voice melting my heart, I would consider telling him what happened to Mukta or how it happened, get it out in the open, but until the very end, it remained a secret locked away in my heart.

I REMEMBER WHEN, days before my high school graduation, Brian and I were sitting outside a coffee shop sipping coffee when he asked, quite casually, "How about we move in together?"

That took me by surprise; I put my coffee on the table. "We've known each other for what . . . ten months?"

He laughed, shrugged his shoulders. "Who cares? I am dead serious about us."

I considered it, thought of Papa, then Aai, wondered what she would have said about all this.

"So?"

"What's going on with you, Brian?"

He looked away, "My father . . . he wants me to go to the same college as him, then go to law school and be a lawyer. I don't want to do that . . . I want to be a musician. I want to get away from my father, not be like him. Do you know, he didn't shed a tear when my sister and mom died? He just went to the office even earlier and stayed later. He's the same selfish pig that he used to be. I want to show him that I can get away from him and have a family. After my mom and sister, you are the only one I love, Tara. I really . . . love you and want you to move in with me."

"I love you too, Brian, but I don't know about moving in. Papa likes you okay but if my Aai were alive, she would be horrified. Moving in is not exactly what a girl would do in India. We don't live in with a man unless we are married to him."

"But you are not in India any longer; you are here—in the United States."

"Yes, but in a way, I . . . I still belong there."

Brian was silent. His eyes wandered from me to the street. As much as I wanted to hold his hand, and tell him how much I loved him, I just couldn't. I told myself I wanted to get through graduation day without making any hurried, important decisions. That was the day I had been waiting for, hoping that I had finally done one thing that Papa would be proud of, which would draw a curtain over everything we had endured.

BRIAN DIDN'T SPEAK about moving in again until graduation day. As our valedictorian finished her speech and I stood in line to get my diploma, I scanned the crowd, tried to spot Papa. He was nowhere to be seen. Finally, seconds before my name was announced he came rushing inside, fumbling with his tie, wiping the sweat off his brow, and looked for a place to sit. I watched Papa's face intently as I climbed onto the stage. But as I moved my tassel from the right to the left he didn't look in my direction He sat there looking lost and lonely among those unknown faces that cheered and clapped for their loved ones. It took Papa a while to notice me, smile at me, and I saw the years of sadness still lingering on his face as he clapped.

I knew that there would be no photos of my high school graduation ceremony. I wished Aai were alive. If she was here, she would insist that he get a camera, and at the very least take one picture. I didn't have time to dwell on this thought because Brian came from nowhere, planted a kiss on my cheek, handed me a camera, and showed me the pictures he had clicked—of my graduation, of me standing in that queue, waving at Papa trying to catch his eye, of me accepting my diploma. I looked up at him, his eyes twinkling with joy, with that pride that I had wanted to see in Papa's eyes instead.

Before I knew it he was kneeling before me, holding out a ring. I glanced in Papa's direction, saw him departing, walking toward the car, where he waited impatiently beside it. And I knew then that if I wanted to be happy, I had to shed any belongingness to the land I was born in. I had to leave behind anybody or anything that reminded me of the past. In that moment, my answer seemed crystal clear to me,

"Yes," I said and Brian kissed me. In his arms I felt the warmth and affection that I had missed that evening, perhaps something I had missed ever since Aai had died.

"I AM MOVING out." I told Papa the next day.

I remember him sitting there on the couch, looking up from the book he was reading, the confusion on his face.

"What do you mean?"

"Brian asked me to marry him. He gave me a ring, see."

That hot afternoon, I was nineteen; standing in our living room and twirling the ring on my finger wanting Papa to blow up, tell me that all this was against our culture, *we are Indians and we don't do things this way.* But of course, it wasn't like Papa to say anything like that. It would have been Aai who would have told me something like that. Papa sat there and sighed, took his glasses off, and looked at me as if he were for the first time.

"What about college?"

"Well, I can work for some time and then go back to college.

It's not as if we are in a hurry to get married. We are just moving in together."

He sighed again, trying to take it all in. All of a sudden, I wished I could take it all back so that I could stay by his side.

Papa took a deep breath. "Aai wouldn't have liked it." He shook his head. "But you know, I am not one to worry about what society says. I married young, and against my parents' wishes and against all caste rules. So I think I have lost the right to tell you what is right or wrong in this matter but . . ."

I waited.

"You are young, Tara. And whatever you do, I hope you pursue college. Education is more important than you know."

I stood there hoping he had more to say, but he put on his glasses and went back to reading the book. I looked at this haggard man sitting before me. Papa had changed dramatically ever since we had landed in America. He withdrew more into himself with every passing year; some days I thought he looked so listless that I even asked him to see a therapist. But he had brushed off the suggestion. I wish he would have told me that he wanted me to stay. I had hoped he would forbid me to take such a drastic step and reassure me that he was proud of me, and would always be there for me. But that was not to be.

WHEN BRIAN AND I first moved in together we were both jubilant about getting into the University of California, Los Angeles—I had enrolled in journalism like Papa wanted. Brian had chosen music as his major. What Brian hadn't told me was that his father had thrown him out because he hadn't agreed to pursue law. And along with that went his trust fund. But when

I learned about it, I didn't mind. I wanted us to make a home in the tiny apartment we had discovered in East L.A. That was all we would need, I had thought. Both of us worked part-time to pay the rent—Brian at a coffee shop and I at Mc Donald's, serving burgers.

"Why are you in a hurry to work? Finish your college. You can take money from me," Papa had said.

I should have listened to him. But I had been—I was—determined, for once in my life to not give up, to keep at it, to do this on my own. I could finally prove to Papa that he had a daughter to be proud of. I regretted that decision as soon as Brian quit college to join a band.

"This is just the beginning . . . You watch . . . my band will become famous someday," he kept telling me.

I didn't ask him how we would pay the rent. I quietly quit college soon after that to take three jobs to support us. One of them, working part-time at a local newspaper office where I mostly sorted mail, was a job that allowed me to lie to Papa and tell him I was writing some articles. Some days when I heard Brian sing, I imagined Papa asking me, "What is the point of all this—staring into the distance and struggling to write songs?" But he never really asked.

Papa's face turned grim every time I mentioned Brian's name. He was annoyed that I gave up college for Brian, and I knew Papa thought he wasn't right for me. I wasn't willing to agree. Brian had qualities I adored. He belonged to a life different than the one I had, one in which he dared to live on his terms, follow his dreams. I could see why Papa could never see him as accomplished. If he did land a record deal he would never be the intellectual Papa wanted me to marry. There were times when I was compelled to wonder why I fell in love with Brian. Was it for the dreamy moments we had sitting on the sand at the beach, looking at the night sky, counting the stars like I had in my childhood, or was it for the poems he read to me or how his nose crinkled when he talked about lyrical moments like the ones I had shared with Mukta once? His music reminded me of Navin singing *ragas*, but more than anything it reminded me of the childhood I had left behind.

THEN THERE WERE other things about Brian people wouldn't understand. There was a certain naïveté he carried with him, his easy demeanor; his casual behavior made him more charismatic to me. He was cool about a lot of things—he had found an escape in his music and didn't seem to carry the burden I carried with me. It wasn't easy brushing off guilt, burying it under some other passion. But Brian seemed to do that with music while I carried my guilt and shame with me wherever I went. Those memories of kneeling on the street, scribbling a note trying to destroy Mukta's life, stayed with me every day, but with Brian I could forget, just for a few minutes, even for a few hours. I could breathe easy in his company, be myself. I smoked heavily in those days and allowed myself to wander into those inebriated moments of sexual pleasure. I didn't feel dragged down, bound by any expectations I had of myself. I felt . . . free.

Over the five years we lived together, Elisa asked many times, "When are you getting married?" as if finding a new boyfriend, Peter had given her the liberty to inquire about our relationship. Now and then she would point out, "Oh, the both of you are made for each other," or, "You look lovely together!" as if it justified us staying together. She was proud to take credit for introducing Brian and me.

Then came the day we met her and Peter for dinner. I was surprised when she said they were getting married. Brian and I congratulated them, but I couldn't wait to get out of there.

I don't know why I couldn't bear it that my best friend was getting married. I had been to many weddings before—the ones that Papa's friends invited me to. I suppose among Papa's friends' circle, Papa was the only man whose daughter wasn't married, the only girl who didn't go to college. So many weddings, so many ebullient faces, and yet I never felt as lonely when I attended a wedding. I always watched the bride and groom on the stage as the priest chanted a mantra, the sacred fire burning fiercely as they poured a spoonful of ghee into it, and wondered if that would be me someday sitting there beside Brian, the henna weaving its design on my hand, the *payal* on my feet tinkling as I took the seven *pheras* with a man I loved.

I thought of all this when we drove back home from dinner that night. *We have been together longer than they have, Brian,* I could have said, but looking at him sleeping next to me in the car as I drove down the bumpy road to our apartment, I knew it was futile. He didn't even make any money and at this point, quite honestly, I wasn't sure if I wanted to hang my hopes on a starving musician. I suddenly realized that marrying Brian had been a fantasy all along. In that moment, I knew I had been deceiving myself, but somehow, even then, I convinced myself not to give up on us. Things would be brighter if I went just a little further, I told myself. Looking back, it is difficult to say when we began drifting apart. I don't remember when I moved from being in love to being together for the convenience of escaping my pain.

I wonder if we would have drifted into marriage if this one evening hadn't happened. Papa had invited us to dinner. All day at work I worried about the conversation between Papa and Brian. They didn't seem to get along very well, especially after last time, when Papa had asked him, "So what do you plan on doing for a living?"

"I am a musician," Brian had insisted while Papa had glared at him.

On that fateful evening, I picked up Brian early from band rehearsal, making it a point to arrive half an hour early. I remember standing outside Papa's apartment, looking at my watch, fumbling in my purse to find the keys.

"Oh, let's just go in," Brian said and rang the bell.

No one appeared at the door. Brian punched the doorbell again, repeatedly this time.

"Stop, Brian. Maybe Papa's out. He'll be back soon. We are early anyway."

Brian made a face, walked back to the stairs, and sat down. I let my back rest against the wall and kept looking at my watch. When fifteen minutes had gone by, I began getting worried.

"Something's wrong," I told Brian.

"Yeah, right!" Brian said. "The dude must have forgotten he invited us."

I walked downstairs, set my things down, and climbed the fire escape. Brian followed me and watched me climb up. When I had reached the apartment window, he was there—Papa was

hanging there, from the ceiling fan; his eyes seemed to be dropping out of him.

BY THE TIME the cops got there, my mascara was running down
my cheeks. Brian stood with his arm around my shoulder looking like a lost boy, confused and scared. The paramedics arrived.
Red and blue lights flashed across the walls of the building.
People peered through their windows. The cop descending the
stairs looked suspicious, like the inspector who had once questioned me in Bombay.

"You're his daughter, you say?"

"Yes."

"And you don't have a spare set of keys?"

"I forgot them—at home."

"Hmm," he said, "don't worry. The paramedics are here."

It didn't take them long to declare Papa dead and shroud
him in a blanket. "I am sorry," they each told me as they took
him away.

Everything after that was a blur. The investigation revealed
that it was a suicide. An inspector came home and handed me the
suicide note that Papa had left—a small piece of paper that they
found on his writing table. It sounded more like a confession in a
diary than a suicide note.

*I can't bear it anymore. As if living in this foreign place without Tara's
Aai wasn't torture enough, the thought of not finding her is intolerable. I keep
looking for her.*

I was responsible for her. How could I? I just can't

That was it. Those were Papa's last words to me. I read it again. There wasn't a period after the last word. The *t* of the last word wobbled and tapered off, perhaps into another world, as if he could not wait any longer to leave this one. Who was he talking about? Which "her" was he searching for? Had he lost his mind? I should have taken him to a therapist a long time ago, when I thought he was depressed. I should have forced him to go. A sudden barrage of tears overwhelmed me.

One moment we have everything and the very next it all disappears. Everybody patted me on my back as they laid Papa's body for the last rites then cremated him. Papa's friends stood before me, now stripped of their ebullience, their faces dark and solemn like their clothes. Brian stood behind me taking phone calls as they placed Papa's body in the retort and closed the door, leaving him trapped between the bricks of the furnace. It was a modern crematorium, unlike the one we would have used in India, the one Papa would have preferred. Such memories are short and cracked; only a deep feeling of anguish accompanies them.

THEN ONE DAY, I was cleaning out the drawers in Papa's room and came across a stash of papers. The drawer rattled as I opened it. In the living room, I could hear Elisa packing away some things as she talked with Pete over the phone. There were bank statements, documents, and a roughly written list of phone calls made to Bombay over the last ten years. The bank statement showed checks made out to a detective agency in Bombay. I read them carefully, not knowing what to think, sifted through the rest of the papers—some faxes from the same agency. The subject line on them said, "Search for Mukta."

I read it again and again. It must have been a mistake. I sat on the bed looking outside the window, the fax in my hand, thinking about it. I could hear Elisa call, "Tara, where do you want me to put this?"

She kept asking me, calling out my name, then came looking for me.

"Oh, there you are. Couldn't you hear me?" she asked. "Where do you want me to put this?" I couldn't reply; I just sat there, looking out the window.

"Are you all right?" she asked, then walked up to me, sat beside me, and pulled the paper out of my hand.

"Mukta . . . she is the same girl, isn't she? The one in that photograph you carry around in your wallet."

I nodded, the tears in my eyes threatening to fall.

"It cannot be. They must have made a mistake. It couldn't be. She *couldn't* be alive, right?" I asked.

Elisa looked from me to the paper, her eyes wide. "I don't know, honey."

All this time, Papa had hidden something from me. And all along, I had agonized over the fact that *I* was the one who had kept things from him. That's who Papa had been searching for. He thought he had been responsible for Mukta's kidnapping. But why had he lied to me? Told me she was dead? I took the paper away from Elisa's hands, fumbled for the phone number on it, and dialed the number of the detective agency. The phone at the other end rang, echoing in my ear, but no one picked it up.

IT DIDN'T TAKE me long to decide. I talked to a real estate agent, put the apartment on the market and gave Elisa the power of attorney to sell it. I sold Papa's car, and transferred all the money that Papa had left to me to a new bank account in India. Even if I didn't have a job in India, it was a sizable sum, enough for me to live on for many years.

"You are crazy! To go looking for a girl who disappeared eleven years ago?" Elisa pleaded with me not to go. "Where are you going to stay?" she asked.

"Papa's kept the apartment in Bombay. All these years I had wondered why. But at least I can go back to it now. I'll stay there."

"Will you . . . will you ever come back?" Elisa asked softly, tearing up.

"I don't know." I shrugged. "Maybe if I find Mukta, then I can come back . . . I don't know," I repeated.

We hugged. I had made up my mind about leaving, going back to Bombay—the place where all this had started. I wanted to think I was going to Bombay because I wanted to find out why Papa had lied to me—why he had been searching for Mukta when he had told me she was dead—but that wasn't the reason I had decided to return. The truth was I had lived with what I had done for far too long.

"I need to disperse Papa's ashes in the holy river—Ganga. It's according to the Hindu rites," I told Brian.

"How long will you take to sort all this out?" Brian asked.

"A couple of months, and I will be back." I tried to sound convincing. I knew I was hoping never to return to the chaos of our relationship again.

As I collected my bags to leave, the urn with Papa's ashes

in my hand, I left my engagement ring in a box in one of the drawers beside my bed. I wasn't brave enough to tell Brian we were finished, that it had been over a long time ago. I couldn't bear to see in his eyes that I had abandoned our relationship the way I had abandoned Mukta years ago. So I emailed him from the airport, told him it wasn't him, that it had always been me.

CHAPTER 19

MUKTA
1994–1996

THE ROOM THEY kept me in had no windows. It was a small room—you could stretch your hands and touch the opposite walls. There was just enough room for a narrow bed. My only companion was a lonely lightbulb that stared down at me. I talked to it, cried to it. That was the only way to keep from going mad. Talking to something, anything, helped. Mostly I would sit down there and hope Tara and her Papa would somehow be able to find me. They were the only ones who would search for me, the only ones who could find a way out of all this. It didn't take long until I began waiting for the men anxiously, expectantly, so they'd come and take my loneliness away. It was strange—I felt guilty for welcoming a man, but it was such a relief to see a human face.

Some days I pressed my face to the wall trying to listen to the sounds outside. There was no way of knowing if it was morning or night. But if I listened carefully, I knew it was morning when I heard the sound of someone washing clothes, the banter of women, children giggling in the background—when the women here took respite from their nightly jobs. When I heard the drunken chatter of men, the tunes of Hindi film music beating loudly, I knew it was evening and it wouldn't be long before a man would be standing in the doorway once again.

ONE DAY, I was walking around that small room, my hands feeling the cracks in the walls, when a small piece of brick loosened and came away into my hand. I imagined writing with it on the wall. I thought I would paint parrots, pigeons, eagles—birds with wings that were taking flight—on the walls or maybe even write a poem. The one that I thought of the most was an awkward poem I had written for Tara. I don't know why the words kept spinning in my head; they floated around me and settled in my heart.

> No matter how bad the weather,
> How difficult the road,
> We will always be together,
> Climbing the hill,
> Wading through the rough waters,
> Always together.

Tara had laughed when I had read it to her. "That isn't a poem, silly," she had said. But they were words from my heart. I could have let the words sprawl across the walls, written them in bold so people could see I wasn't one to break. But I was so afraid that all I did was sit down in the corner and watch the paint peel off the walls and fall to the side. Day in and day out

I did this, the ceiling fan above me creaking, reminding me a world outside still existed.

On some days, I could hear the fervent pleas of another girl, feet running, a belt hitting flesh, the constant thumping of a head against a wall, the painful wails that bounced against the walls and remained trapped in them. My only contact with the outside world was with a girl who brought me my food twice a day and helped me clean the toilet in my room.

I soon learned her name was Aaheli, which meant "pure" in Hindi. The first time she told me her name, I stared at her and we giggled together at the irony of its meaning. I looked forward to the jingle of the keys, the rattle in the locks, as she appeared every day outside the doors bringing hot food.

"Don't worry, they only keep newcomers here to break them into this life. You know, you are one of the lucky ones. Since you didn't make any trouble and don't resist, Madam is allowing you this food. Some of the others don't even get food." She sighed. "What to do? We all have to work until we pay off our debts. But they won't keep you here for too long. You will soon get a room with windows. I heard something today." She gave me a wink.

That afternoon, when the doors opened, I had expected Aaheli's face, but Madam was standing there instead. I wondered what I had done wrong. Surely it was a complaint one of the men had made about me. I had heard from Aaheli that Madam rarely saw a girl unless she had an important lesson to teach her. So I sank into a corner, putting my hands against my face in case she decided to whip me. But Madam merely stood there and laughed. "What do you think I am going to do to you? You have made me quite some money in the last few weeks, and *you* haven't given me any trouble. I am moving you into another room. If you try anything, you come back to this room, you understand?"

I nodded.

"Besides, you are beautiful. If I take care of you, you will make more money for me than the other girls here." She patted my cheek. Then she turned and left, leaving the doors of the room open for the first time. It had been such a long time since I had seen sunlight. I remember how I sat there, watching the light filtering in through the door, drawing shapes on the floor. I remember how I crawled up to it, felt the floor, felt the warmth of it on my hand.

THE NEXT ROOM I was given had a barred window. Dust layered the windows, and pigeons sat on the sills, fluttering their wings; light danced on the ceiling. The sky was as blue as I had left it. The sun outlined the clouds for me that day. How beautiful it all appeared. Every morning I watched the *paan* and cigarette shops, the *daru* bars, the restaurants, even the chemists across the street close, and every evening, as the brothel opened for business, I would watch them open shop to serve customers. I would see drunk, naked men with beer-filled bellies fall on the roads, the street carts pushing past them, the hawkers calling out to people to buy their food.

Every afternoon, the children of the women living in these brothels ran amok on streets, playing marbles between overflowing garbage cans while their mothers gathered downstairs to wash clothes together at a public tap. Looking at them between the bars on my window, I often wondered if that was why my father had deserted me, because he knew what I would become.

SOON I JOINED in their banter and befriended many of the girls and women living here. I liked the afternoons when all of us got together and sewed our torn clothes or made new clothes for the children. It felt like those comforting times when Amma was there beside me, sewing clothes or cooking. These women seemed to know exactly what I was going through. When they asked me one afternoon why I got involved in this trade, I told them without any hesitation.

"I am a devdasi, a temple slave. This is what I was meant to do."

I didn't have to explain. They understood. Each one of us had a similar wound, a similar grief, a similar hope rising in our hearts. It was also easier accepting that I was a devdasi. Like Sakubai used to say, it was supposed to be our fate, so there was no point in fighting it. Fighting fate would only cause more suffering, I thought.

"I also was born into this profession," Aaheli said. "I am the eldest daughter in the family, belong to the Bachara community. Have you heard of it?"

I shook my head.

"For us—the women in our family—the truck drivers who pass on the highway are a regular means of livelihood. We have our houses along the highways so truckers can avail themselves of our services easily. I made one mistake—falling in love, thinking I could have a family. We eloped. He . . . he brought me here, sold me. I did not know then that when the brothel owners buy us, the money they give our kidnappers becomes our debt. It has been two years, and I still haven't paid my debt."

Another girl started sobbing. "I wish I hadn't accepted the mango juice from that stranger in my village. I was so hungry that day when the man offered to buy me something. I hadn't eaten in two days. I jumped at it and didn't think. He had drugged it, brought me to Bombay . . ."

Other girls spoke of the lives they had before they landed here, lives that had become mere stories now. Many of the younger girls like me would tease each other, animatedly weaving tales of nightly adventures with strangers; we would giggle when one of us said how good it felt. We forced ourselves to reinvent our tales, imbue them with hues of happiness, flourish them with colors of hope. Each of our stories was woven—with care—into our own cloak of delight to ward off the pain of those nights. We disregarded the wounds on our bodies: the gash on the forehead, the occasional swollen eye. It was better that way—reveling in stories of fantasy rather than facing reality. It helped us survive.

But there were the older, more experienced ones who admonished us for believing in such fantasies.

"I don't believe in love," Rani would chuckle. "We all just use one another. Call it love, hope . . . call it whatever you want; it isn't true."

"It is better to face the truth," Sylvie used to tell us, "than make up stupid stories. There will only be more disappointment later."

Rani was what we used to call a *moophat*—someone who kept mouthing off no matter how much trouble she got into.

She intervened when the younger girls got beaten, and took the beating herself. We all knew she had a good heart—she would be the first to clean the wounds on the younger girls and console them. But she never showed it in her words, seeming afraid something that rolled off her tongue would betray how sensitive she was. There were rumors her lover of three years had promised her marriage, but one day he had just disappeared.

Sylvie was a practical and grounded woman. She spoke when she saw an opportunity. She drank and smoked, standing with one hand on her hip, the other holding a cigarette, telling us, "I have been here longer than you girls have." It made us smile. She was smart though. Unlike the other girls, she would ask the men—her customers—for favors like foreign cigars, a radio, or jewelry she kept hidden in a secret place. Nobody knew of this secret place, and nobody so much as whispered about it. She wore fancy shoes with heels so high they were forced to announce her arrival. It reminded me of a cat with a bell. I used to like her *chalaki*—her cunningness. She knew how to get what she wanted.

Sometimes I told stories to the younger girls—stories I had read—and they listened to me in rapture. I told them love stories of Nala and Damayanti, of Lord Krishna and Radha—all stories I had read in the books Tara got for me from the library. I remember how the little girls with painted faces giggled. I hoped the stories cocooned them at night; after all, we were waiting for the love in those tales to become real for us.

I didn't resist or fight like many of the girls who were brought here. I knew that many generations of women in my family had been in this trade, and I didn't struggle against it. So I was spared the brutality many of the girls endured. Even then, I must admit that the thought of escaping crossed my mind. When the street was quiet, all the girls in the brothel were sleeping, and the security guards had dropped their attention and were snoring outside the doors, I would think this was the time I could escape. I'd think of Tara's strength and it infused me with so much energy. I struggled to think of a way out. I even thought I was brave enough to try to escape—a strange courage arose in me. I grabbed my things, bundled them up, and then lay on the bed wondering about this daring move I was about to make. I don't know why I didn't escape. Perhaps I needed answers to questions like: *Where will I go? What will I do for a living? What if they find me and beat me to death?* By the time my mind finished searching for answers, the din of the brothel had already begun and the opportunity to escape had passed. I felt like a mouse with the stupidity to think it could battle a cat.

Other days, I'd remind myself what Amma used to tell me—the color of our sky will be bright again, so I shouldn't lose hope. But watching the younger girls, especially those who were too young to understand any of this or know what they were getting into, filled me with deep sorrow. For a long time, I thought there was nothing I could do, that there was no escape. Then a simple encounter with a girl changed my mind.

It was a blazing summer afternoon, and I was reclining on my cot, trying to take my afternoon nap. Outside the voices were distant, muffled. The heat was at its height, and I had reached out for a cloth to wipe the sweat from my neck when a girl came running inside my room. This girl, no more than twelve, sat down beside me.

"Hide me, hide me," she said, her eyes darting from the doorway to me, hoping I would find a way out for her. I sat up and opened my arms to her. She flew into them, sobbing on my sleeve.

"Don't let them take me away," she whispered.

She didn't know the hug I was giving her was all I had to offer, a temporary solace from what was to come. It didn't take long for the men to arrive and snatch her away from my arms, leaving me with her tears on my sleeve. How tiny she looked as they took her away. I could hear her screaming all night. Intermittently some men laughed. I never saw her again.

"What do you think happened?" I asked Sylvie the next day when we were washing clothes.

"Who knows? She must have died. They must have thrown away the body. There is only so much a tiny girl like her can take."

I knew the casualness in her voice was a mere mask. And I told Sylvie I didn't want to think of it that way. I *would not* let myself imagine that the girl I'd held in my arms was dead. But Sylvie didn't respond and merely smiled at me as if I didn't know a thing. She was right. This little girl was the first I had seen. There were many after her, and as girls came and went, you could smell the sadness stripping the strength of each one, bit by bit.

I knew then that I couldn't live like this anymore. I had to think of a way to escape, but it wasn't going to be easy. I had to bide my time, wait for the right opportunity. And that day *would* come, I told myself. My only respite in those days was thinking of my time spent with Tara, hoping the life she had was many times better than this. I wanted to think she thought the same about me, but I didn't know if she had forgiven me. If only I could meet her once, I could explain to her again that I wasn't responsible for her mother's death. I knew she would understand. Or at least, I hoped she would. Maybe someday I would gather enough courage to escape from this place and be able to see her again. No matter what, no matter where we were, I wanted to think that Tara and I lived in each other's hearts.

CHAPTER 20

TARA
2005

THE SCENERY CHANGED quickly from the bustle of Mumbai city, from the slums and the high rises to the greenery of the countryside, as the train went through the Western Ghats. For a minute I thought I could already see the village of Ganipur in the pleasant light of day—the village where Papa grew up.

I thought long and hard for a couple of months before finally deciding to make a trip to Papa's village. The conversation with Anupam chacha had persuaded me to go to a place I had only heard of in Papa's stories. So I had asked Anupam chacha for my grandmother's address and set out that weekend. Raza said he knew somebody at the village who could guide me. So he helped Navin and me arrange for everything—the train tickets, somebody to pick me up at the train station, and an alternative place to stay at the village in case I wasn't able to meet my grandmother. I felt anticipation, a hope that the village was the way Papa had described it. Somehow, I was sure Salim had not brought Mukta back to this village. But what if there was a slight chance I could get some information about Mukta?

The station was more of a corrugated shed, a far cry from the railway station we had left behind in Mumbai. It didn't have a roof, just an elevated square mound of earth that served as a platform with a track running beside it. Passengers got down, walked the platform, and disappeared from my sight. I was the only one who stood there, not knowing which way to go. In the distance I could see a man waving at me. "Tara Memsahib," he called out, as he walked toward me.

"Sorry, I am late. Chandru, my name," he said by way of introduction, then helped me carry my suitcase from the platform onto a *tanga* waiting outside the station. Chandru continued to speak to me in broken English even after I started speaking to him in Marathi. I had forgotten how enthusiastic some people in India could get over speaking English; they continued talking in English even when what they said sometimes made no sense at all. It reminded me of something Papa used to say: *That's what the Britishers left behind for us—our fascination for the English language.* If Papa were here, he would have encouraged Chandru to speak English, to assert his authority over the language. I wished Papa were here, with me today.

I watched Ganipur—Papa's village—as it passed by me. Women carrying heavy pots of water walked on the dirt path we were on, alongside the *tanga*. The temple bells rang loudly, and women cooked outside houses with thatched roofs while their children played hopscotch in the afternoon sun. The sunlight shimmered off the water in the village pond where women washed clothes and whispered to each other as we went by. Cows grazed in the swaying green farm fields as I took in the air from this village. Half-naked children ran alongside my horse-driven carriage in excitement, and Chandru, my driver, made a futile attempt at shooing them away. The world of my imagination opened up before me, as if my childhood had returned and Papa was whispering the stories of his life in my ear all over again.

It was so far away from the hustle and bustle of a city like Bombay—just the way Papa used to describe it—calm and peaceful. I took a long breath. *One breath, and ah, the air was pure . . . so fresh*—Papa's words came to me. Chandru told me that the lower castes stayed far away from the village square. I had noticed their huts awhile back on either side of the narrow dirt road. Each of those huts must have been barely a room with a roof made of hay. It was where the sweepers and garbage collectors lived, he said.

As we neared the village square, the houses got bigger—concrete shacks with asbestos sheet roofs, their small court-yards housed their charpoys, cattle, bicycles—this was where the weavers, blacksmiths, carpenters, and barbers lived, I was informed. Chandru pointed out that the higher the caste, the better the house. Those were the houses in the distance, bunched in a corner—huge houses with red-tiled roofs, and some with gardens. We had to pass through the village square to get there.

As soon as we were in the village square and I saw that banyan tree standing in its middle, I knew this was the tree Aai had been talking about. I asked Chandru to stop by it for a while. This was where Aai had met Papa for the first time. I looked up and saw the sun peeping through the branches. I wondered how it would have been to spend my vacations in this village, meet my grandparents every summer vacation just like my friends did. Not very far away, I could see the bazaar. Heaps of vegetables were arranged in a medley of colors—fresh carrots, tomatoes, brinjals, potatoes, onions. Fruit vendors sat in the corner with heaps of red, orange, and yellow that teemed with flies. This was what I had missed in my childhood.

This was where Mukta was born and had lived her childhood. Why did she never tell me about her childhood in this village? We passed children sitting in an open space under the shade of a tree repeating the alphabets after a teacher, and I wondered if this was the school that Mukta referred to when she said that she wasn't allowed to go to school. "Don't mind my saying," Chandru interrupted my thoughts, "but you look so much like a girl from our village. Karuna, her name was . . . She ran away with the zamindar's son years ago."

"She was my mother."

He looked behind at me astonished, his whip in midair, the horse slowing down. "You are Ashok Sahib's daughter? So that's why you are staying at the zamindar's house? Malkin is your grandmother?"

"Yes."

"Malkin will be delighted to see you." In his excitement, he whipped the horses, making them go faster.

Maybe times had changed or maybe Aai was wrong about her village. Maybe they didn't take such cases of elopement or intercaste marriages as seriously as she thought.

"My Aai used to say that if she or I ventured into this village, we'd be killed just because she and Papa married," I told Chandru.

"Yes, it still happening here. Villagers killing women because they marry in the wrong caste. But your case, villagers may have forgotten by now. In any case, better not to mention to anybody. Not everybody loyal to Malkin, you see. And I also thinking you shouldn't stay for too long."

I sighed. Times hadn't changed as much as I would have liked them to but I was glad to be back, even if it meant it was for a short time.

Chandru stopped outside the gates of a sprawling mansion. The brick walls that ringed the house didn't seem to stop. I couldn't really see the house; only the roof was peering out at us. I got down from the carriage and stood outside, uncertain of what I was about to do, about what I was going to say to my grandmother, whom I had never met. Suddenly I wanted to meet my Papa's mother badly, understand why Papa had lied to me about so many things.

"You wait, I will call a servant from inside," he said as he knocked on the door. There was no reply.

"Malkin must have stepped out to the market with the servant," Chandru said, "or else the servant would have opened the door. She will be back soon."

I sat under the shade of a nearby banyan tree, waiting. In the distance, I watched a car come to a stop. A woman stepped out, her face barely visible behind the car door. Her servant stepped out from the other side and followed her, carrying bags of vegetables in both his hands. I watched as she asked the driver to run another errand, and he drove away. She put her key through the lock and unlocked the gates.

I could see her now, standing by the gates. Her face resembled Papa's, and her eyes were just like Papa's eyes—kind and warm.

"This . . ." Chandru motioned to me to come closer, "this is Tara Bitiya, Ashok Sahib's daughter."

She squinted in the sunlight and stared at me as I came closer. Her wiry, white hair was tied in a bun and the wrinkles on her forehead bunched together when her eyebrows rose.

"Hi . . . I'm . . . I'm Tara," I said, looking at her, uncertainty churning in my stomach. I shifted my suitcase from one hand to the other. For a second everything came to a standstill, all of us rooted to our spots not knowing what to say to each other.

Then she smiled kindly. "Yes, yes. I know. It's . . . I never thought I would be able to meet you," she said, opening her arms, her eyes welling up. I let the suitcase fall to the ground, and let her take me in her arms.

"Your father . . . he used to send me photographs of you when you were a child. I used to wait for his letter just to be able to see your photograph. Every year you would look so different, growing up away from me, in a different city." Her voice reduced to a sob. "Anyway, there is a lot we have to talk about, isn't there? Come in, come in. You can call me Ajji. How long have I waited to hear those words?" she asked, squeezing my shoulders.

Meeting my grandmother was confusing, like a dream that had suddenly become real. She led me into her home—a mansion. The courtyard was as big as the apartment complex in Bombay. The garden looked well tended. Roses—white, red, and yellow— flourished in every corner. A pipal tree stood in the middle of the yard. This is where Papa had spent his childhood. In all of his stories, I had never expected a house so huge. Suddenly, I felt betrayed. Papa had stolen a piece of my childhood.

"COME, LET'S GO to the living room," Ajji said.

The servant walked in with tea and placed it on the table. She patted his shoulder and he folded his hands in greeting to me. "This is Shyam. He has worked for me ever since his father died. His father was a loyal servant; he made Shyam promise he would take care of me in my old age. We don't have as many servants as we had at one time. Your grandfather was ailing for a very long time. The zamindari system in this village suffered in that time. I have two more sons, but they too escaped from this place—they couldn't take your grandfather for too long. Your Papa—he was the eldest, and he always stayed in touch. He wrote me a letter every month. Then a few months ago, the letters stopped coming. Something happened to him, didn't it?" she asked, her eyes filled with concern.

"Papa . . . he died."

She looked at the ground, fighting off tears, then nodded as she rubbed her knees. "It's a mother's worst dream, you know, not knowing if her son is alive or not? What happened?"

"He . . . he committed suicide . . . he . . . hung himself."

She looked away, her eyes filled up, but she quickly wiped them away. "What could I have expected? After all that happened? He was suffering deeply. I . . . always knew . . . something like this . . ." Her voice broke, and she ran inside.

I sat in silence, not knowing if I should run after her and console her. Shyam brought a tray of biscuits and set it on the table. I gave him a worried smile, and he hurried inside. I looked around. The ceilings were high in this aristocratic old house. The chandelier was like a colonial era lighting piece. There were many pictures on the walls of men and women in their traditional zamindar attire. There was a man who looked just like Papa. He had a regal mustache, and his eyes seemed to blaze with anger even in the photograph.

"That's your grandfather." Ajji pointed to the large photograph of the man who looked so much like Papa. I hadn't noticed her returning, but now she was standing beside me. "And all those other photographs—they are your forefathers. It isn't what it used to be," she sighed. "I am glad at least you could come back here. I've always wanted to meet you."

"I would have come a long time ago, except Papa told me that you were—"

"Dead. Yes, I told him it was better that way. Your grandfather was very . . . let's say not many got along with him. He was strict and careful about following all the rules. He would not have allowed you or your mother to set foot in this village. And if you did," she said, "it's not the same for women, you know. In this village when a woman elopes with a man, she and her children will be killed."

"Aai used to tell me that. She never wanted me to come here."

"I understand," Ajji nodded and sighed.

"Well, actually, I came to Mumbai to search for someone," I said.

"Who?"

"I don't know if you know, Ajji, but Papa brought a girl, Mukta, with him to Bombay a few years ago."

"Ah, Mukta. Yes, of course. She never spoke then, with all

that happened. I was the one who persuaded your father to take her along with him. You must have been about eight then? She was a local prostitute's daughter. Her mother was a beautiful woman, a caring woman, really. But when you are born where you are, as a prostitute's daughter, your fate is pretty much written the day you come into this world, isn't it? They are known as devdasis here—temple prostitutes. It's like an affliction in villages like this."

"Temple prostitutes?"

"Yes, these girls are traditionally married off to the Goddess and function as prostitutes to the zamindars. Your grandfather and his father—my father-in-law—helped perpetuate the myth, encouraged it, and why not? They were getting to enjoy women on the side. But I often wondered what happened to the girls, the eight- and nine-year-old girls who were dedicated to the temple and devoured by this tradition." She shook her head and sighed.

"Eight or nine-year-old girls? They become prostitutes? There is a tradition like that?"

"Yes, it still exists. Mukta was an inquisitive young child. When I saw her, I thought of you. Her mother went about saying that Ashok was Mukta's father. You must already know all this now. That's why you've come to search for her but . . ."

Suddenly the words, as she spoke, rose from her lips, broken and exhausted. "Of course, we could never truly find out if she was your half sister. There was no way of discovering that back then. Sometimes I couldn't help but wonder if she was my grandchild."

She stopped and watched my face intently.

"You didn't know," she whispered.

I walked to the window. Outside, the banyan tree stood majestically watching over all that had happened. When I looked up I could see the sun sparkling in the sky. It struck me then—was this place the one Mukta had talked about? The place where she had waited with her mother all through the night, waited for her father—*my* Papa—to walk through the gates of *this* mansion? I watched the sunlight streaming from behind the trees outside, clouds appearing intermittently—playing a game of hide and seek with me. I plopped on the sofa behind me. I felt paralyzed.

"IT WASN'T YOUR Papa's fault, you know . . ."Ajji sat beside me. "In his youth, your father fell for Mukta's mother—the temptation of beauty. It wasn't meant to be anything, he told me later, but like a thorn, it pricked his conscience. Then he met your Aai, and before I knew it, he said he was in love and was eloping with her. Your grandfather didn't know until the day after he eloped. He was mad with rage and told me I could never see him again. For years I begged and pleaded with my husband to let me see my son, and six years later he agreed. He came to see me a few times after that, always bringing with him the stories of the city, pictures of his family, of you, and I would wait—"

"Did Papa know Mukta was his daughter?" I interrupted, impatient to know more about Mukta.

She sighed. "He did not think she was his daughter. That was the problem. He had always known that Mukta's mother had been waiting for him, that she went around saying Mukta was his child. Your Papa refused to believe it. *Mukta can't be my daughter,* he used to say. Besides, he didn't feel for Mukta's mother the way he felt for your Aai. Your Papa was madly in love with your Aai. If he tried to help Mukta he would have had to tell your Aai. And he didn't want to hurt your Aai by telling her about his time with a temple prostitute. How could he do that to her?" She sighed. "As for Mukta, she suffered deeply. They did with her what they do with the other girls, got her married to the temple in a ritual and then they raped the child—those bastards, they hurt her. I was too late, the news got to me too late. By the time I reached there, the damage was done, and I had to call your father from Bombay. He was in a dilemma. He told me he wasn't sure she was his daughter. *'How will I ever know if a prostitute's child is mine? She could have another father. Mukta's mother could lie,'* he told me. I wouldn't listen to any of his arguments. I convinced him to take her with him anyway. There was no other way to save Mukta."

"No other way but to let her live like another street child in our home? She lived with us for five years, doing menial chores. If Papa felt, even for a minute, that she was his daughter, didn't she at least deserve an education? She could have studied, earned a degree, and had a better life."

Ajji looked up, sensing the anger in my words.

"You must understand, Tara, that your Papa didn't have a choice. It would have destroyed your family if the possibility of her being your sister ever got out. He was . . . confused. He wanted to protect Mukta and keep her home, but at the same time he couldn't give her an education and treat her like a daughter, because your Aai wouldn't hear of it."

Stray thoughts of my childhood came to me: Mukta following me, carrying my school bag, waiting outside the school, telling me she wanted to study, and sharing her hope of seeing her father one day. All of it could have been possible for her.

"Papa told you he wasn't sure if Mukta was his daughter. What if Mukta's mother wasn't lying? What if Mukta was . . . is really his daughter? Do *you* know for sure if she is my half sister?" I asked.

"Tara, when you *want* to see something, you see all the signs, whether true or not. And when you don't want to see . . ." She shrugged, tiredly.

"Then you don't know for sure?"

"No, I don't, but tell me one thing—does it matter if she is your sister?

"YES, of course it does."

"No, I mean will you stop looking for her if she isn't your sister? There must have been a very strong friendship between the two of you to keep you searching for her. Until now, you had no idea she could be your sister. Yet you came here all the way from America, leaving everything behind. Think about it." She laughed. "I have known real sisters . . . blood related . . . who could push each other over the cliff if given the chance." She laughed ruefully as if reaching for a memory in her own life. "So I ask again, would you stop looking for her if you knew she wasn't your sister?"

Her words made my mind race and travel to those moments Mukta and I had shared. The words that came out of me surprised me.

"No," I said, "I wouldn't . . . I . . . can't stop looking. But I think I need to know if she is my half sister."

She smiled. "I have something for you. Something your father left with me."

She hurried inside and returned with a letter, held my hand, and let the letter fall into it. "This was the last letter he wrote. You should have it." She smiled and retired inside.

I played with the letter in my hand, feeling its texture. Papa's writing. Papa's fingerprints were on it; it felt like Papa was back with me just for a little while. I opened the letter.

Dear Aai,
Pranaam,

Hope this letter finds you well. Both Tara and I are doing well in America. Tara wants to get married to a musician called Brian, and although I know she is planning to do it just to fill a void in her life, there is nothing I can do about it. She is all grown up now. And who am I anyway, to tell her how to live her life? Especially, if I have always lived my life the way I wanted.

There will always be one thing gnawing at my heart—not accepting Mukta as my own. That and the fact that I lied to Tara, told her Mukta was dead. But you know that, don't you? I always tell myself that I knew no other way of helping Tara forget all that had happened, especially after Tara's mother died. How long could we have stayed in India, searching for relief from our memories? I wish I could tell my dear Tara, tell her everything, but then I fear I will lose her; I will lose her credibility for me; the respect, the pride she has for me will evaporate. And what will she be left with? My burden?

I've always been inspired by Rakesh mama to do the right thing, to not hurt anybody, to make sure that everybody got a second chance in life. And I've tried so hard to live by it. When you persuaded me to take Mukta to Bombay, I didn't know what to do. I wanted to have a clear conscience, be certain that she wasn't my daughter, though at times I felt she was my daughter—the way she laughed, the green eyes she had inherited from me, the way she always thought about others before herself. But then again, my doubts would come up and I just knew that she couldn't be my daughter. I thought the best thing to do for her was to let her live in my apartment, with my family, and do some small chores. I told myself it was many times better than what her life was offering her. I thought that was the right thing to do. I never knew, hadn't ever imagined in my deepest dream that my Tara and she would grow up sharing things like sisters, that they would be inseparable from each other, the best of friends. When I saw them doing things together, sharing books or giggling together, I could tell it was time I accepted Mukta as my daughter. But every time I would wonder if a prostitute could ever really know who her child's real father is. Maybe if I had really asked myself, I would have known that I was ashamed to be a father to a prostitute's child. Perhaps I'll never really know if Mukta is my daughter but I could have been a father to her just the same.

All that time spent over all those childish debates in my head—what a waste! I wonder why I spent so much time debating whether she is my blood or not, when all I should have done is

*see her for the child she was . . . just that—a child! I should have
treated her like I treated my Tara. I wonder if I will die without
finding forgiveness.*

*Hope you continue to be as kind as you have always been
to me.*

Your loving son,
Ashok

I folded the letter, walked to the garden, and sat on the bench
outside. Flowers that had blossomed swayed in the breeze; the
azure sky looked down on me, the sun gleaming at this time of
the day. *Do we all hide things from people we love? Worry that if they find
out what we have done, who we really are, they'll just stop loving us?* I read
the letter again, went over Papa's words again and again, and
imagined him sitting beside me, reading it to me. I wept for his
troubled spirit, which had always been torn between accepting
a child as his own and choosing Aai's happiness. I looked up at
the sky and shouted at him in anger for not making the choice
of giving Mukta a better life. I confessed to him, to the emptiness around me, told him that if it hadn't been for my foolish
choice of getting Mukta kidnapped, our lives would have been
different, Mukta's life would have been different. And I hoped
that for both our sakes I would be able to find Mukta.

CHAPTER 21

MUKTA
1997

"Do you think you can help me? You have been so kind to me," I asked a customer. "Will you help me escape or tell someone that I need to get out of here?" I had thought it was the right opportunity to appeal to his kindness, but his eyes filled with fear.

"It's not any of my business—what happens here. I don't want to get into trouble."

He gathered his clothes and went away. I never saw him after that.

I had tried appealing to some good customers—kind ones—who I thought would never say a word to Madam, but perhaps it was a risk to trust them. If Madam knew what was on my mind, she would lock me up in that windowless room again. So for a while, I stopped asking for help and hoped that someday I would meet someone who could get me out.

I HAD COME to realize that most men who come here are either trying to escape something or are seeking something. Some men don't talk at all; they come here and go away as if they were performing a chore. Many talk about their lives, their wives, their children, memories they are leaving behind while visiting me. They show me photographs of their little children and beautiful wives and slur, *You are the only one who understands*. I've learned to smile and nod, but I always wonder why such seemingly happy men need to seek pleasure elsewhere. Perhaps we all have something to hide, something mysterious, deep and disguised behind our happy selves.

There was one man I loved very much—Sanjiv. Together we planned my escape.

I WAS NINETEEN when Sanjiv walked into my room and my life. I thought he was like one of those men who would sit by my side, show me photographs, and share stories of his life. In the very beginning, I thought he might be a good candidate for getting me out of this place. But that was before I fell in love with him. When he first came to my room, he stood by the door watching me, as if I were a mystery he was trying to solve. Tall and well built, somewhere in his early twenties, he stood there, smiling at me. I worried about the way I looked. The previous night a man had beaten me, and my face might have looked swollen. But it didn't seem to matter to him. He walked toward me and set a tape player by my side. He sat on the ground beside me and gently lifted a strand of hair from my forehead then tucked it behind my ear.

"Who did this to you?" he asked softly.

My eyes filled up. For a long time, no one had treated me so gently, with so much care.

"Never mind, if you don't want to tell me. Do you know what this is?" He tapped the tape player.

"Yes, a tape player." I had seen one in Tara's apartment. Her Papa liked to listen to it.

"Hmm . . ." He smiled and his entire face lit up. It made me smile too.

"I am an artist, a struggling one actually. I make music, and I thought we could listen to some music together. My name is Sanjiv."

Sanjiv, I thought, *like life, vast and expansive, mysterious.*

He clicked a button on the player and the music began to flow through the room—both of us absorbing it with so much hunger, so much thirst. For a minute, I traveled back in time, to when I was a six-year-old and music reverberated in our house in the village, and Amma danced like the true dancer she was, and I danced with her, my shy awkward steps no match to her perfect ones.

"Will you dance for me?" Sanjiv asked.

His black eyes sparkled with affection. It wasn't a command, not like when other men forced me to do what they wanted. The way he asked, it was as if I had a choice, as if such a thing could exist for someone like me. I could be brave and tell him no, and I knew he would be fine with it, perhaps even laugh it off. But in that moment, I was ready to do anything for him. I stood up, let my body sway to the music; my feet were miraculously finding rhythm, the delicate steps I had been so meticulously taught by Amma taking over for me. He stood up, took my hand in his, and swayed with me, our bodies molding into each other. My feet felt like they were off the ground, lingering in the air, and for the first time in a long time, I felt so light there was no force in the world that could bring me down.

"Hmm . . . you understand rhythm. Not many have the gift," he said and smiled.

We didn't make love that night; he said he didn't want to. He wanted to get to know me first, to get to know the artist hidden in me, because that was what was beautiful, he said. When he left that night, it felt like four hours had gone by too quickly. I wished and hoped he would stay a bit longer, but I didn't voice it. I was afraid if I showed too much interest it would frighten him, and he might never return.

I lived with that fear for several days, waiting for him to return. Most nights, when other men told me their stories, my mind drifted away from them, lost in that moment when Sanjiv and I had danced together, the rhythm running in unison through us the most natural thing on this earth. He arrived three days later, his tape player suspended on his right arm. I was delighted to see him and got up and ran toward him. He didn't smile; he laughed. I felt like a child running after a toy it had pined for. When I realized what I was doing, I made myself stop and watched how his laughter filled the empty room with happiness, pushing out the loneliness.

"You were waiting for me?" he asked mischievously.

"No, not at all."

We danced once again that evening, music filling our souls, uniting us in a way no one could understand or imagine. I was lucky to experience something so unique and blissful, to be with someone who shared that with me. He told me more about himself, how he had run away from home when he was eighteen because his parents had been too business-minded to understand his creative mind. They wanted him to be a businessman and take over his father's business.

"And do what? Sit in his office; do the same hopeless job day in and day out? I'd rather be dead. I create music in a small studio I have rented outside the Goregaon Film Studio. I don't make much, but some of my music tapes do sell, you know. It is not exactly well-paying, but I am comfortable . . . happy."

I smiled and offered to make him tea.

"What about you?"

"What about me?" I asked.

"What is your story?"

"Not very different from any of these girls. Now, do you want two teaspoons of sugar or one?"

I saw the disappointment in his eyes when I changed the topic.

"One teaspoon," he said and took the teacup from my hand. He smiled, and the disappointment of a moment ago was gone. My hand trembled as he took it in his, prompting me to sit close to him, my heart pounding so hard I could hear it.

"Well, whatever you tell me," he whispered in my ear, "you would still be the same to me. And if you don't want to tell me, that is fine too."

I thought for a while as he looked into my eyes. "My friend Sylvie—she calls me Sweety. But they call me by any name here—sweety, chameli, chanda—whatever the customer prefers. My . . . my real name is . . . Mukta," I whispered. The name sounded strange on my tongue, like I was talking about someone else, a little girl I had met long ago in memories I had left behind.

I told him about Amma, how much I missed her, about the house in the village, how I could never forgive Sakubai for what she had done. I told him about my father, the man whom I was confident I would meet and who, I hoped, would one day come looking for me. But most of all, I talked about Tara, the only friend I had ever had, who taught me how to read, let me have the small pleasure of walking her to school, of reading poems to her, of having ice cream.

"Amma named me Mukta, you know," I chuckled. "Since it means freedom, she might have thought I would have mine one day."

"You are my freedom from this world, my Mukta," he whispered, and gave me a peck on my forehead. As his hand touched mine, his body enveloped me. I knew there was nowhere in this world I'd rather be. I had spent many nights in the arms of a man, but this was my first night of making love with a man I loved. I didn't know until then that love could surprise me, melt my heart, and rekindle my faith in humanity.

AFTER THIS NIGHT, I didn't like it—in fact I hated it when another man touched me. Sanjiv's touch had ignited a new hope, a new enthusiasm for life, and no matter how much I told myself that I couldn't have love in my life, I had suddenly started imagining a new life, a life far away from this place. The hope for a family and children rang anew within me. But if I refused a man, I would be beaten, and then forced anyway. So I bore with it, until I could take it no longer.

I confided in Sylvie and Rani while we were washing our clothes near the water pump. Sylvie admonished me, "Don't fill your head with dreams. This is not just a job, it's our life now. The faster you get this into your head, the better off you will be. Don't you know what happened with Rani?!" Rani's tale of being spurned by a lover was widely used as a cautionary tale in our brothel. When *that* didn't prevent a girl from falling in love, all the women told the story of Suhana and her lover. Their bloated bodies were found floating in the sea near the Gateway of India, just because Suhana had escaped. She had married a customer and was living in her own home for almost three months until Madam's *goondas* caught up with them. No one knew if the story was really true but it resounded through the brothel, frightening any girl who dared to dream.

"When you're young, you fall in love; then when you get older, you realize it's just another stupid illusion." Rani told me, "I had someone too. Ajay, his name was, my first love. That was fifteen years ago, when I was sixteen. He was a thirty-year-old unmarried man, or at least that's what he told me. I couldn't believe my luck. He brought me flowers and chocolates, even took me to eat ice cream outside after asking Madam's permission. I was on top of the world. Oh, I thought I was different than all the girls. Special, you know. My fate was going to be different, I was certain. He promised me things—a nice home, a family. He wanted two children, he said. Then one day, he told me he was getting married to a good girl from a good family, one who could take care of the house. *What about me?* I asked. *What about you?* he said. *We had our fun. What did a whore like you expect?* He had me fooled for four years. After that, I haven't shed another tear for another man. " Rani told me, "Ask anyone here." She turned to some other girls who were wringing the water out of the clothes and slapping it on the clothesline. "Girls, tell Mukta here, didn't you all fall in love once and what use was it?" Then she turned to me, "Ask Leena there, about Vikram, or ask Chiki about Sohail. Do you want me to go on? These men they make use of our feelings, especially if you're young. Then they throw us away like dirty clothes."

Others nodded, as if they knew about me and Sanjiv. I might have looked confused. They laughed.

"Of course, we know! Anyone can tell! It's the glow of love on your face whenever he comes to visit you," Leena said.

I was horrified that they knew. Did Madam know? I asked them and they shrugged. If she did, I'd have to be cautious about us. I'd have to tell Sanjiv to stop visiting me. Tell him that he could find himself in trouble. I made up my mind to tell him the next time he visited me but every time he came up to my room, I'd tell myself I'd let him stay, just this one time. I blame love. It made me forget to be careful.

SANJIV SAID HE couldn't afford to come in every day; he didn't make enough to spend on me. He came in every Wednesday night, brought a red rose for me, and we had six wonderful hours together. He gifted me the *Gitanjali,* poems by Rabindranath Tagore. Every night we were together he would read one poem to me, and after he left, I would save the rose on the page he read as a reminder of that night together. We didn't have to declare our love; we felt it in the rush of blood in our bodies, in the bliss that soaked our spirit. For twenty weeks we did this—shared our ear for music, for poetry, and for silence. Then one day after we had listened to a beautiful piece of music, he said he wished he could show me the world outside, a world different from this. I told him not to worry.

"I have already seen it; Tara's shown it to me. But now, after four years here, it only seems like a dream."

"Still, I want to take you out there. Come with me, let's escape," he whispered, his eyes filled with longing for me.

It was a dangerous thought, and I didn't want him to think that way. It could jeopardize both our lives and the world we had built together in this spare room. But I must have longed for it too, because I didn't warn him, I didn't voice my concerns. It was not that he didn't know. I was sure he had heard of all those women who had been beaten badly or died from trying to escape. I told him of Suhana and he smiled, as if he didn't care, and when I looked in his eyes, I didn't care either. It didn't matter what risk we were taking as long as were safe in this illusion of bliss we had built for ourselves.

We hatched a plan to escape. I hadn't stepped out of this room in years other than once a month when I was allowed to go to the market with Madam and some other girls. But we were always accompanied by the security guards. I remembered what they had done to Jasmine, Maya, and many other girls when they had tried to escape.

Now here I was, trying to plan my own grand escape. When I looked at myself in the mirror I saw the same look Jasmine had when she was being taken outside to be killed. What she said that night echoed in my ears. *Sometimes one act of bravery is better than a life lived as a coward, as a slave.* It was then that I realized, it was *love*—love that makes you let go of all fear, allows you to float in life, throwing all caution to the wind. For the first time in my life, I did not fear death.

Sanjiv made a deal with Madam. "I want to take her out Friday evening, to the *mela*." *The fair*. It was brave of him, I thought, as I peered from the top of the stairs, watching Madam put a *paan* in her mouth, chew on it, and look at him closely.

"Sanjiv Babu," she said, "your father is a rich man, and that is why I allow you here. I know that even if you don't pay, he *will* pay to keep your name from appearing in the papers. Imagine what people would say if they knew a reputed businessman's son was rolling in this dirt. But this, asking to take Mukta out, is too much."

"Why? I am asking for one evening. I will bring her back next morning, and you know I always pay in advance. You can double her price if you like." Sanjiv sounded desperate.

Madam looked at him for a long time, and I thought this was it—Sanjiv had gotten himself in trouble. But surprisingly she nodded and said there would be two guards accompanying us. Madam came to my room after Sanjiv left, held my face tightly in her grubby hands, stared at me, and said, "Look, I trust you. Unlike the other girls, you don't fight. Besides, you have been with me for a few years. You know what your fate will be if you try anything."

As she spoke, I imagined our life together—Sanjiv and me. I could clearly see the beauty of the home we would have together, the children we would have. There was a voice inside my head saying I shouldn't trust him. He was just like the other men. *The lure of love is futile and disappears after a while*, Sylvie told me. But I wasn't listening.

The love I had sought so desperately was within reach now, I was sure. "Are you listening? Don't try anything," Madam's voice thundered.

I nodded. I wasn't listening at all.

We planned everything meticulously, chalked out the smallest detail—how to slip away from the bodyguards and make sure they did not follow us. The evening came like a sandstorm and all the details had become blurry to me. Ripples of fear ran through my mind.

Sanjiv put his arms around my shoulder and said, "If you look worried, they will know we are up to something."

I nodded solemnly, and we walked out of the brothel, the two bodyguards following us. At the fair, I tried to appear relaxed and enjoy the rides, watching the children on the merry-go-round as they shrieked in excitement. When I looked below us from the Ferris wheel, I could see the guards standing there among parents whose eyes lit up in delight as they watched their children on the ride. It was going the way we had planned. The trick was to get the men to see how much we were enjoying the rides, get them to relax and turn their attention away to something else. That way when we got the opportunity, we could slip out, right under their noses.

The plan was to go to Sanjiv's friend's house after we escaped and stay quiet for a while. Nobody would be looking for us there, and, within a few days, we would move to Delhi. Sanjiv had already let go of his rented apartment, and we had decided to stay at another friend's place in Delhi until we found our own apartment and settled in it. I had assured Sanjiv that once I was free, away from the eyes of the security, the brothel owners did not have enough resources for a nation-wide search.

Everything appeared surreal from the Ferris wheel: the stars that shone in the sky that night, the wheel that propelled us toward our potential escape, the sudden explosion of power inside us. When we got off, we ducked the guards, mingled with the crowd, and ran toward the entrance.

We hid behind a ride very close to the entrance. There was chaos there—the laughter of kids, the excited chatter of grown-ups, the smell of fried food and ice cream. A distance away, the guards were becoming frantic when they couldn't spot us, scan-ning the crowd with their eyes, pushing people as they made their way through. My heart was sinking, a certain dread filling it. Sanjiv nudged me and said, "Let's go." But I couldn't move; fear had taken hold of me. I couldn't move.

We sat there for a few seconds before I regained my confi-dence in us and in our love. I often wonder what would have happened if I had not felt that paralyzing fear. It wouldn't have given the guards an advantage over us. We might have disap-peared before they spotted us. But by the time we started run-ning away from this hiding place, one of them saw us. We were running out of luck; there wasn't a cab on that road so we had to run into an empty alley and hide there. There was no way we could come out in the open to hail a taxi. So with bated breath, we waited. I looked at Sanjiv one last time—his confident, fear-less face, sweat streaming down his forehead—in awe of what he was going through for me.

The next thing I knew, we were being dragged onto the street outside. I saw the man bash Sanjiv's head with a bat, and blood began streaming from his forehead down the sides.

"Please," I cried, "let him go!"

Sanjiv fell to the ground; I watched them beat the life out of him until his body could take no more. They dragged me away while I looked at his lifeless eyes one last time, the same eyes that had looked at me with such warmth for so many weeks, giving me hope of a better life. I knew as they piled me onto the backseat of the car—when I looked at the long road we were leaving behind, his body lying at the end of it, disappearing from sight into my memories—that the dreams I had of us together had always been an illusion.

"Look at this girl," Madam said, as soon as I set foot outside the car. "She thought she was brave enough to escape."

One of the men pulled my hand and lugged me up the stairs. I looked at his brown shoes covered with mud from the alley and the spots of blood that had spread on them like a painting of Sanjiv's dying moments. I looked at his eyes, determined to get me upstairs, unmindful of what he had done. Other girls—women I had known, befriended, and narrated stories to—stared at me in horror, clinging to the railing above.

I didn't see it coming. The sudden slam on my back, the thud of the metal rod against my bones, the repeated ramming against my body, the pain spreading through it like the roots of a tree must spread through soil—firmly, deeply. For a moment, I wondered if the pain was from seeing Sanjiv die, if the pain in my heart had extended through my body so that it physically hurt to be alive. But it was Madam, standing over me, letting out her anger on me. I collapsed on the floor, closed my eyes, let myself drift into the darkness.

MOST NIGHTS, I was in that same dark, windowless room as when they first brought me here; I was beaten every night—drugged and helpless—the way I was back then. Then one day I could hear screams, the shuffling of feet, and a thumping up the stairs. Sylvie opened the door of my room and stood there, while I squinted at the sudden light.

"Come on! It's a raid. The police are here," she said, gesturing to me to move.

I reached the doorway but was unable to move as fast as she could. My legs and my body still hurt from the bruises. The police caught up with Sylvie and me as we were trying to run down the stairs. They pulled us by our elbows, and we found ourselves in the police van, sitting next to the other prostitutes. Some of the younger ones were crying, their *kajal* dripping down their cheeks. The older ones knew it was just another raid, a routine one in which we would be jailed for a night and then released with a warning in the morning. It was apparent the police were bribed well by the brothel owners but still wanted to conduct a raid once in a while to make everybody aware that they were doing their jobs. But this raid was different; the police seemed determined to find something or someone.

"This is all because of your stupidity," Leena said to me in the van. Her eyes flashed with anger.

"Yes, it's all because of you. Didn't we warn you?! You had to go get involved with that wealthy man's son and try to escape with him. What did you think would happen?" asked Chiki.

I looked at Rani, who seemed to be staring in space, looking lost. Then, searching for answers, I looked at Sylvie. She sat there with a bored expression on her face and scratched her neck as she explained, "Sanjiv's father is giving this brothel a tough time; the police are here because he complained. He suspects this brothel had something to do with his son's disappearance. What they don't know is that they must have disposed of his body so far away that he will never be able to find out what happened to his son."

I looked at her astounded, thinking of that father who would never know what happened to his son.

"Don't worry," Sylvie said to me, patting my back, "there will be a few more raids, then they will quiet down. After all, the mafia owns the brothel. Who ever wins against the mob?" She gave a chuckle.

"But what about us?" one girl asked.

"Yes, what about the nights we waste sitting in jail? The money we could make will be added to our debt, and God knows how much longer we will have to keep working this way," another said, almost pouncing on me in her fury.

Sylvie shielded me. She grabbed the woman's hands as she advanced toward me and thrust her back into her seat. "Shame on you . . . on all of you! Haven't you ever fallen in love? Haven't you *ever* wanted to escape? So what if one of us had the guts to do something the rest of us couldn't?"

The women lowered their eyes now and became very silent.

I couldn't fathom why one act of mine had alienated them from me. I didn't know if they envied my audacity or if they simply worried about their own lives. We were released the next morning, and thankfully, there wasn't another raid. The brothel owners had suppressed it. But there hasn't been a day gone by that I haven't thought of Sanjiv or agonized over that evening we tried to escape, wondering if there was anything I could have done differently. I agonized just as the trees must grieve for their wilted flowers, like parched earth must feel separated from rain.

Years later, I would narrate this to another customer who was very fond of me. He listened very quietly to everything—how Sanjiv and I first met, how we fell in love, how I allowed it go on despite everybody warning me not to continue with it, how my stupidity got him killed by Madam's *goondas*. He listened and sighed.

"Didn't Sanjiv's father come here searching for him?" he asked,

"I don't know," I shrugged in response. "I heard it was in the newspaper for a while—that Sanjiv was missing but then when they couldn't find his body, it died down. But you must see what Sanjiv left behind for me."

I walked over to the wall and took a couple of the loose bricks out. I had saved the book Sanjiv gave me. It had been a while since I had taken it out; it was dusty and I blew on it gently, afraid I might hurt what was left of him. I showed it to this customer. He opened the book and scanned the pages.

"They are the poems Sanjiv read to me."

He nodded and flipped through the book. The dried petals

from the roses Sanjiv had once given me fell lightly to the floor and crumbled into red dust—the color of blood, the smell of blood; those thoughts of love came rushing back.

His lips trembled and he clenched them together. "I'm sorry," he said as he crouched down and tried to gather them.

"It's all right," I assured him. "I have to try and put them behind me just like my other memories."

CHAPTER 22

TARA
2005

I STOOD OUTSIDE Meena-ji's apartment on that cloudy morning, hesitant to ring the doorbell. Did Aai know if Mukta was my half sister? The answer frightened me. I knocked on the door. My heart raced when I heard the clinking of the chain lock, and a woman with gray hair opened the door partly, her face hidden behind the door.

"Yes?"

"Meena-ji?"

The woman opened the door farther now, leaned toward me, and looked at me carefully. Meena-ji's face had grown leaner, wrinkled with age, and her hair had lost its abundance. There was a flicker of recognition in her eyes. "Are you . . . ?"

"It's me, Tara."

"*Arre*, you look so much like her. How did I not recognize you? Come in, come in." She smiled and unlocked the chain from the door.

She pulled out a chair, waved at me to sit down, and sat on the chair opposite me.

"Such a surprise," she said. "I thought you had left India for good. How is your father?"

"He died a few months ago."

"Oh, *Bhagwan shanti de* . . . God rest his soul," she said looking upward.

We were quiet, not knowing what to say to each other. Then she got up abruptly, awkwardly, and said, "Let me make chai, get you some biscuits, *haan*."

"Don't worry about it."

"Look at you with your *firangi* accent and all. Have you forgotten we Indians never allow our guests to go hungry?"

I smiled reluctantly. She left me in the living room as she hurried inside. I wanted to ask while I still had the strength, before I changed my mind, but I waited instead. I looked around at the wall hangings that had been there for as long as I remembered. I could hear the clank of pots and pans in the kitchen, and before long she was out, wobbling into the living room, holding a tray. I stood up and took the tray from her hands.

"So what brings you back to India? Amreeka has so much to offer. Of course, whatever anybody says, this is always *apna desh*." *Our country.*

"Meena-ji . . ." I took a long breath. "Do you remember Mukta?"

"Mukta?" She took a moment to think. "*Haan* . . . yes, that village girl who used to trail behind you all the time."

"Yes, I wanted to know . . . to know if . . ." I stopped briefly to ponder what I was about to say and if it made any sense at all to bring it up.

"Yes?"

"I wondered . . . if Aai knew." There, I said it. I could hear the pounding of my heart, the quickening of my breath.

There was silence at her end. She seemed to understand what I was trying to ask. She looked away briefly outside the window, and my eyes followed hers. There was nothing to see but the bare sky.

"How do *you* know?" She sighed. "Did your father tell you?"

"No, my grandmother."

"We were never really sure. We only suspected. She looked so much like him, the green eyes, the fair skin . . . your Aai, she was an intelligent lady. I admired her patience. She had her suspicions when your father brought Mukta home. Her eyes were your father's—anybody could see that. But nobody said anything until that afternoon when your mother came knocking at my door. She sat right here on this floor, her head in my lap, sobbing all afternoon. She said if it were true, if your father had a child with another woman, what could she do? She couldn't dare ask your father if it was true. After all, she had nowhere to go. Running away from the village, defying her elders, she had invited a curse, she said. She had no proper education to rely on and then she had you to think of. How could she deprive you of your father's love? She had to live with it, she said, and as long as she lived, she did. It is all in our kismet—a woman's fate."

She sighed. I tried to feel the cool breeze on my face. We didn't say anything, just sat there for some time listening to the kids playing hopscotch in the courtyard, their excited screams throbbing through the air.

"She loved you, your Aai. There was nowhere else she would have rather been but with you," Meena-ji said. "And I don't know if I should bring this up, but for a while there was a question in my mind if she was Anupam's child—he had the same green eyes, too, you know. I told your mother, and for a minute she looked relieved. Maybe, she said, maybe Tara's Papa is being kind to Mukta out of the goodness of his heart, like he is good with all those orphans he brings home. Then she started sobbing again, said she was convinced that Mukta was your father's child."

I felt dazed. Her words seemed to assault me. To know that Aai had lived and breathed this fact that Mukta must have been my half sister, to know that she had died thinking that my Papa was a liar and cheat, was like getting the wind knocked out of me. I couldn't bear to listen anymore. "Thank you," I whispered, and placed my cup silently on the table and walked out.

Was that why Aai hated the sight of Mukta? Was that why she burdened Mukta with work? The thoughts that came to mind were disturbing. Before I knew it, I was on the street, walking, on and on, tears pooling in my eyes, blurring my vision. I was unaware of the crowd that engulfed me on this choked footpath. People walked by me, some rammed into my shoulder, some screamed behind me, "Can't you see?" And I wanted to scream back, tell them I couldn't see. For many years, I hadn't seen that my Papa was in such a deep dilemma. When we left for America, Papa had not just lost his wife; he thought he might have lost a daughter too. I had failed to see that; I hadn't recognized the terrible grief in his eyes. What a terrible

choice Papa must have had to make: leave for America so that
I could have a better education; a life away from the terrible
things we had experienced here *or* stay here and look for Mukta.
He had chosen me, my future. How had I not seen that? I had
also failed to see that Mukta just might have belonged in our
family. How many such children had we ignored or treated
badly simply because they weren't our blood or didn't belong to
the "right" caste?! How many such children continue to become
victims of our traditions . . . My thoughts went on and on and
I kept walking. Finally when my legs felt like lead, I sat down
on the steps of a shop. People bargained with the shopkeeper
behind me, sifting through a bag of grains, making sure it wasn't
contaminated with stones. Clouds began to gather in the sky,
dimming the light around me, and droplets of rain began to
fall. Two kids sat by my side slurping on their iced *golas,* giggling.
I didn't know where to go to escape from my memories, from
that girl in my past sitting beside me, pouring her heart out to
me on just such a rainy day. I fumbled in my purse, begged for
something to show up and give me an indication—a sign showing me a way out. I searched in my purse, threw out things—a
pen, a notepad, my makeup kit. Passersby stared at me as if I
were crazy. Then my mobile phone rang. It was Raza. Maybe *that*
was the sign I was looking for. "I found Salim," he said, when
I picked up the phone. I signaled to a rickshaw to stop to take
me to Raza's office.

On our way to Salim's apartment, we sat in a rickshaw that
bumped over potholes in the Mumbai streets. We stopped outside a building. I was about to enter it when Raza took me by
my elbow and led me away from it, toward a gulley.

"I prefer walking through this gulley. The street is so narrow that often rickshaws are a nuisance to the slum dwellers here," Raza said. I nodded and followed him.

"Tell me something, why didn't you tell the police? In fact why won't you tell them you know Salim is the kidnapper? It would make your job easier, wouldn't it? Rather than confront a man who had once tried to hurt you?"

I thought of the note, the one I had scribbled for Salim to take Mukta away, how it had rolled over and plopped into that gutter.

"I'd rather do things my way, I guess." I shrugged.

"He has something on you, doesn't he?" Raza stopped to look at me.

I met his eyes briefly and lowered my gaze.

"There is something you should know . . . I talked to Salim today. I think it isn't Salim who kidnapped Mukta, because that night in question . . . when Mukta was kidnapped, the police had arrested us. I remember now because I got the beating of my life. I remember it very well," he said.

"Are you saying the kidnapper is someone else?"

Raza shrugged. "You didn't see the kidnapper's face, did you? And from what you tell me, the kidnapper had the keys to your apartment. How could Salim have the keys?"

"He could have stolen them."

"Salim was with *me* that night," he repeated, gently.

"Are you saying it is futile going to Salim's place?!" I yelled. "Do you think I am a birdbrain who has nothing better to do in her life? What are we even doing here then? Why are we even going to meet him?"

"Because . . ." Raza began softly, deliberately. "Because, I think he may know more than he is willing to tell."

"Oh," I said, feeling embarrassed that I hadn't trusted him enough.

"Should we continue?" he asked. I nodded and walked behind him, quietly.

As I walked along these shanties, I could see people inside their homes, watching TV or chatting, the womenfolk cooking or cutting vegetables, kids playing. They nodded and smiled at me as if they were used to strangers walking by their door every day, peeking into the privacy of their homes.

People emerged from the slums and greeted Raza, "Namaste Raza Sahib."

Raza either waved or shook their hands and inquired about their well-being. People seemed happy to see him. It reminded me of when I used to hold Papa's hands and walk down the streets, the shopkeepers waving to him, greeting him, the same expression of gratitude in their eyes.

"You help them, don't you?" I asked as I followed him down the lane.

He looked behind. His eyes smiled for him.

"I *am* a social worker, and I *work* for these people. I can see you haven't been to this part of the city before." He held out his hand for me as I jumped across a gutter.

"No, I haven't. I've never seen so many people living in one room."

"Not even when you lived here?"

"No." I shrugged. "I guess Papa wanted me to see the good side of life."

"Hmm . . . I find it very fulfilling to help people who are less fortunate than me."

"Papa used to say that . . . it was such a long time ago."

He smiled at me affectionately. "You must miss him."

"Of course, I do."

WITHIN TEN MINUTES we had reached a dilapidated *chawl*. The bricks were showing through the wall, the cracks so deep I worried it might collapse on us. Outside, women were lined up with buckets and pots at a tap to collect water. I could smell the stink of the toilet we passed. Raza said it was the only toilet in this *chawl* that housed so many families. I climbed up the stairs after Raza. We finally stopped on the second floor, outside an open door.

"Here we are," Raza said. "Salim's place."

The door was open, like many other rooms in this *chawl*. Fear and anger waited to explode inside me as I waited outside his door. Around us, women chatted on the veranda and boys chased each other; washed clothes were on the railing, drying in the sun.

"Salaam, Aleykum Raza bhai." I could hear Salim's voice, his face hidden in the darkness of that room.

"Aleykum Salaam," Raza said and they hugged like brothers. Salim didn't acknowledge me, just invited Raza in. I walked behind Raza, trying to wave away memories of that evening. When my eyes had adjusted to the dimness of the room, I could see Salim's face clearly, different from the boyish face I remembered. Blackness had spread around his eyes now; a scar ran like a jagged line on his forehead and there were wrinkles on his face that deepened when he smiled.

"Tea or coffee?" he asked, looking at Raza and then me, inviting us to sit on the divan in the room.

"No, thank you," I said.

"Tara Memsahib, in my home you have to have something. We don't send guests away without having something to eat. It isn't a custom we follow."

"Chai will be fine for both of us. Thank you," Raza said.

Salim waved to someone in the kitchen and nodded.

"Tara Memsahib, all of us lost something in the 1993 blasts. Many of us Muslims were rounded up and beaten as though we were all to blame. So *forgive me* if I don't feel bad that you lost your mother."

I glared at him, the flashbacks forming a lump in my throat.

"Salim, we have come here for only one thing," Raza said.

"*Arre* Raza bhai, yes, yes," he said nonchalantly. He then turned around and shouted out a name, "Najma, Najma . . ."

A thin woman in a niqab appeared with a tray of biscuits and tea. I could only see her eyes through a narrow slit.

"My wife," Salim said while she carefully placed the tray of biscuits before us and poured the tea.

"We are looking for the girl who lived at Tara's place," Raza reminded him.

"*Arre*, but I don't remember very well," Salim said, calmly sipping his tea, looking in the distance, pretending to think. "I hear you are a great man these days, Raza bhai, helping people of all religions. But what makes you think I know anything about her? You think I kidnapped her, don't you?"

I felt like a scared cat, hiding behind Raza, waiting for him to say something.

"Salim bhai," Raza said softly this time, "she just wants to know if you know anything."

"Trust me." Salim paused and took a deep breath. "If I had done it, I would be the first to tell you, Raza bhai. I swear on Allah that I haven't kidnapped the girl. That night when she was kidnapped I was arrested by the police. Don't you remember?"

The look on his face, the way he convincingly told a lie, made my words erupt into the silence that followed. "You are lying. You were the one who took her. I saw you," I said, my voice trembling.

He looked at me and repeated very slowly, gritting his teeth, "I . . . haven't . . . done . . . anything." The look in his eyes was fierce. It brought back memories that left me gasping for breath. I was once again that little girl sobbing to get away from him. I got up and walked out the door, trying to catch the air around me, breathing in deep and fast.

Raza followed me and made me sit down. "Breathe, breathe," he said.

"*Arre*, I didn't mean to frighten you," Salim said, leaning against the door, his hands folded against his chest.

Raza turned around. "Shut up, Salim."

Salim turned around and walked inside. I turned to Raza. "He is lying, you know. It was him that night; he *was* the kidnapper." My voice sounded weary as I grasped at straws.

Raza nodded. "We should probably be on our way."

As we walked down the stairs, I wondered what I had expected from this meeting anyway. Did I really expect Salim to fall at my feet and apologize? I was a fool to have thought he would tell me where Mukta was, and yet there had been a hope that I would be one step closer to finding her. Just as we were about to descend the last step, we heard Salim calling out, *"Arre,* Tara Memsahib, don't be *naraaz.* I really didn't kidnap that girl." He gave out a laugh as we looked up.

He was standing against the railing, with a cigarette in his hand flicking the cigarette ash.

"I wanted to tell you that I saw that girl—and this was many years ago—at a brothel in Kamathipura."

CHAPTER 23

MUKTA
2000

THAT MORNING, A journalist came up to me, posing as a customer, trying to avoid the gaze of the *goondas* that guard this place. He said his name was Andrew Colt and he wanted to write my story in the newspapers, maybe even write a book about it. He told me he wanted to write about the kind of life we led here. I laughed and said the article would be read by thousands, maybe millions, over tea one morning. For a moment they will feel sad and cringe that a life like this exists. Then they will finish their cup of tea, greet their neighbors, and go off to work like any other morning as if nothing had ever happened. This has been happening for so many years, I told him, that small things like articles and books wouldn't make a difference to our lives.

He looked at me eagerly. He was young, strands of blond hair falling on his forehead. The yellow fluorescent lights gave his face a curious glow. He was a journalist from another country—curious about our lives. I'd met many like him. The last one said he was "passionate about spinning exotic stories for the entire world to see."

"I can help you . . . all these women here," Andrew told me now.

I sighed, knowing he was another one of those who *thought* they could help. But maybe he could help me find Tara. I brought out a bidi from my blouse, lit it, and inhaled the fumes, blowing smoke on his face mischievously.

"All right," I said, "but I need your help in finding two people. And whatever I tell you will not be for free."

He nodded. "Of course not! I will pay. And I will help you find . . . whoever you are looking for."

"How?" I asked, suddenly suspicious.

"How?" he repeated, his eyebrows raised.

"Yes. How will you help me find them?"

"I know people." He shrugged.

He might have been lying, but the longing in me rose again. This thing called hope, which I have been trying to lose for ages, has risen and fallen like waves in my heart for so many years. But what can one do. Hope is like a bird. It wants to keep soaring, no matter how much you want to tie it down.

I waved to him to follow me. "You speak good English," he said as I led him up the spiral stairs to my room.

"I am one of the few who can speak English here. It helps me in this trade. It is a gift from a girl I used to know long ago—Tara." He nodded but didn't say anything.

The stairs creaked under our weight. He looked around my bare room, his eyes running over the cracks on the brick wall behind me, finally settling on the barred window close to the ceiling. He took a deep breath and exhaled as if the place made him very tired.

"This room is six feet by six feet," I said with a show of my hands. "One of my customers measured it for me one night. He was drunk." I laughed. Above us, the whirring ceiling fan creaked. In the room next door, a girl moaned, a man's jagged breath in unison with hers.

"For a few years now I have been given a room with a window, so I am very happy. I can feel the warmth of sunshine in the morning. See for yourself," I said, sliding a stool to the corner, standing on it to peer outside. "It has been years since I have tried to escape, and Madam is now sure I am part of the family." I chuckled.

Outside, Bollywood music poured out from the *paan* bidi shops, instilling the promise of love and passion; prostitutes and *hijras* stood on the garbage-littered street below, trying to entice customers; drunks loitered in corners while the sky above us spread out onto another world—a distant, different world. The journalist was silent; his eyebrows knitted together. He watched me carefully.

"I am luckier than the other girls here. I found a friend who taught me many things, who gave me strength. Of course, I lost her like I lost everybody else who really mattered in my life, but in spirit she is still with me," I said, jumping down from the stool.

"What was her name?"

"Tara. I will tell you all about her, how I met her, how she gave me the courage to survive, but first you have to know what happened to me to understand how she helped me."

"Is she the girl who taught you how to speak English?"

I nodded. He sat on the cot in my room, and I squatted on the floor opposite him. He dipped his hand into his bag, bringing out a writing pad and a pen. I wished I could capture it like that—my life on pieces of paper, no more than a story.

"So what is your name?" he asked.

"They call me Sweety."

"You can call me Andrew."

I nodded and told him my story.

ANDREW CAME TO the brothel once every week, paid the brothel the money, but listened to my life story instead. By now, he knew everything about me—my childhood in the village, the ceremony, Amma dying, Sahib bringing me to Tara, and how Tara helped me recover from those days of despair. It was surprising to me that a man could sit before me and not touch me, that the story of a foolish, useless girl like me could be so important to him that he would pay the brothel to spend an evening listening to me. But of all those things, what was most surprising was when he arrived one evening with information about Tara and her Papa. *They had left for Amreeka, another country,* he said, *many years ago.*

"I'll find out more. I did an Internet search but there isn't much about them. It can be hard to find someone even on the Internet . . . I'll write to a few people in the US and see if they can find something for you."

I didn't understand what the Internet was and I didn't care to know anything about it. I was happy imagining Tara's life to be happier than mine—married to the man she loved, two beautiful children in her arms, and living in a country so far away that the pain of her mother's loss wouldn't venture close to her heart. I was very happy to hear that news, and indebted to Andrew for taking the time to look for her.

ONE EVENING, I was excited when he brought me a bouquet of red and yellow flowers. I smiled. "Sylvie once brought me flowers like these when I was in the hospital," I said, stroking the petals as they reminded me of another time.

"When did that happen? Was it the time they beat you up?" His eyes widened.

I smiled again. "No, no, when they beat us we learn to live with it; we recover on our own. I was in the hospital . . ." I paused as I poured water into a vessel and immersed the flowers in the water.

"I was in the hospital during one of my abortions," I said simply. The words rolled off my tongue like pebbles sliding off a hilltop, trying in vain to lighten its load. He remained motionless, scanning my face as if searching for a hint of sadness.

"Madam doesn't allow a lot of us to have children. She hates pregnant women. It's bad for business. Sometimes, I suppose, it can't be helped and you'll find children running around until they disappear into the brothel business."

"How long were you in the hospital?"

"A few days," I sighed. "Despite all the precautions we take, at times we just end up pregnant. So, most of us go through abortions. But you see, this particular time, I narrowly escaped with my life. Usually they call the midwife to perform it; we get a day's rest and then get back to work. If you repeatedly make a notch in a tree, it won't take long for the wound to penetrate deep inside and soon the tree will fall. My body was probably giving up; the midwife panicked, and they had to rush me to the hospital."

I won't lie—the idea of death had often crossed my mind. When they were stowing me away in a cab, loading me on a stretcher, rushing me through that pale hospital lobby, the nurses' faces hovering above me, I was afraid this was it—the end. I would never see Tara or her Papa again. Earlier, I had convinced myself finding them would never be possible, but it was at this point of no return that I realized finding them had always been my deepest desire, and I wanted to cling to life *just* for that.

A day later, when the darkness melted around me, Sylvie was standing there with red and yellow roses in her hands, staring at me as I lay in that hospital bed. Not many girls from the brothel wanted to be friends with me anymore, to avoid getting beaten badly if I tried to escape again. Sylvie was the only one brave enough to be there; she understood how painful it was to be all alone.

"It rained heavily outside when you were gone," she said, putting the flowers by my bed.

I watched the mist that had settled on the window after the rains, the dampness it brought into the room. And I watched Sylvie's face, how expertly she hid the pain she felt for me. When I held Sylvie's hands she burst into tears and knocked my hand away.

"You scared us," she said, sitting by my bed.

I tried to laugh. "I didn't think anyone would miss me."

She let out a laugh and wept some more. I wish I could have told her then that the comfort of her presence was what I would remember the most.

Upon my return, Madam stood at the bottom of the staircase while Sylvie helped me up the stairs, Madam's voice rising and railing about the hospital trip then fading in the darkness of the winding stairway. "You better not give me anymore trouble. I have spent enough on your hospital stay. You better earn it back for me."

Andrew listened quietly, scribbled in his journal. Just a few months ago, Andrew would have told me, *we should tell the police,* but by now he had seen too much, heard from too many of us. He told me that he had secretly complained to some social workers and the police. There were a few brothel raids for a while but as usual, it hadn't helped much. Madam just thought of him as another foreign customer and even if she knew that he was a journalist, I doubt it would bother her much. This brothel was her stronghold.

Andrew looked behind at the flowers as he left that day and I knew from his expression that he had had enough, that he wouldn't return for a long time. I wouldn't see him for years. After he left that evening, I thought of what Sylvie had told me after I was brought back from the hospital: Madam wouldn't have spent the money to pay the doctor's bills if it had not been for my ability to speak English. It attracted foreign customers, you see.

"Besides," Sylvie said, "your beauty is quite the talk outside. Otherwise, I don't think Madam would have spent even a rupee. Last year, the same thing happened to Leena, and Madam let her die . . . You're lucky, Mukta. Be grateful."

I was.

Over the next few months I tried to be careful. Sylvie helped me get the pill this time so I wouldn't get pregnant again. I had been on the pill many times before but either the pill would turn out to be fake or it just wouldn't work. So, abortion had been the only way out. For a woman, it's never easy losing a life that she could have brought into this world; a life that was crushed even before it had the opportunity to blossom. Sometimes I wondered about those little lives that I had lost. When I looked at children playing on the brothel grounds, I'd feel a deep void within me, as if an ache was spreading from my womb and reaching my heart. I missed those little lives that would have had voices, and little hands and feet and bright smiles if they had been allowed to be born. When I thought of this, it made me more determined not to lose another child if I ever got pregnant.

This time, the pills Sylvie was getting were from a trusted customer and we hoped that I wouldn't have to face another abortion. We giggled like children at the thrill of sneaking behind Madam's back to get those pills from that customer. Sylvie even managed to buy imported chocolates, and our dull afternoons exploded with the sweetness of it. Those were the small pleasures, along with the drugs they gave us, which kept me afloat for those few months. Those and Arun Sahib.

He was the main reason they didn't move Sylvie and me from brothel to brothel like many other girls. It was the custom in the brothels to keep moving the girls so if a kidnapped girl was sighted, she could never be found in that brothel again. He wanted to keep me in this brothel so he could regularly visit me, and I made sure he kept Sylvie here along with me. I met Arun Sahib three or four days after my trip to the hospital. He came into my life like a thunderbolt crashing down from the skies. His disheveled dark hair fell over his forehead, his bloodshot, brown eyes a molten mixture of anguish and anger, looking at me as if *I* could set *him* free. I gave him a faint smile, but he didn't return it.

"Hmm," he said as he came closer. His breath smelled of imported whiskey. Given what he has done for me, I want to lie and say he was a gentle lover that night but the truth is, he poured all his troubles into my body and didn't seem to care about my pain. He didn't say a word to me, didn't look at me, then grunted as he left.

He visited me every Thursday and never spoke much except to say, "It's true what they say. You *are* beautiful." Then he would hold my jaw tightly in his hand and continue: "Your eyes—they are the prettiest eyes I have ever seen." It seemed he had forgotten that was exactly what he had said to me the week before.

When I told Sylvie how he complimented me repeatedly and, strangely, said nothing else, she scoffed at me, asking, "Do you know who he is?"

I shrugged. I did not know. "He must be important and paying Madam twice as much as she could get for me in that hour."

"Twice?" Sylvie let her head fall behind as she laughed. "He wouldn't pay a thing and yet Madam wouldn't make a sound. Don't you know who he is? What world do you live in?"

I shook my head as my eyes widened curiously. Sylvie knew so much more about the world outside because she *insisted* on knowing more from her customers. Sometimes this got her in trouble, but most of the time she was the only woman who, despite staying in the closed quarters of a brothel, knew what was going on in the outside world.

"He is the *dada* here, the head of the gang who runs this whole place. He is involved in drug trafficking besides having this brothel business on the side. His *chamchas* come to collect *hafta* every weekend from every shop in this neighborhood, trying to extort money from shopkeepers for no rhyme or reason. He owns this place."

"*Haan?*" I asked in disbelief. Sylvie laughed loudly and for so long I thought she would never stop.

"You are such a fool. He is enamored by your beauty. The only thing that can tame a wild man is the charm of a woman. Haven't you learned anything in your time here?"

It was true. If I had the bold ways of Sylvie, I would have thrived instead of trying to survive. I envied Sylvie—women like her—who could comfort themselves with expensive things. I wanted to learn from them how to cover the gaping hole in my heart with silk saris and jewelry.

The next time Arun Sahib and I were together, I asked him if he could give me something special to remember him by. He laughed and the next Thursday brought me a shining gold necklace. He put the necklace around my neck and fastened the clasp. I stared at my reflection in the mirror and questioned whether I felt any different about myself.

"You are special to me," he told me, his reflection smiling at me. His words didn't seem to alter anything in me. I told myself it would take many such attempts to be like Sylvie, to try to find happiness in empty words and frills. In the days to come, Arun Sahib showered me with earrings, saris, shawls, bangles—but it never happened; it couldn't fix what was broken in me.

One morning Madam walked into my room, stood before me, and smiled. These days, she made a great effort to speak sweetly. She wasn't very good at it; it wasn't something she tried much in her life. I looked at her suspiciously. Her smile seemed against the law of nature.

"You still have debts to repay. All these *banarasi* saris and silk shawls, these earrings, this necklace will go toward repaying your debt. You understand, don't you?" She kept her smile as she tightened the necklace around her neck, gazed at her reflection in the mirror, then turned around and whispered to me, "Don't worry If Arun Sahib asks. Tell him you have left all this with me for safekeeping. Remember, it will free you of your debts."

I had been here for years, but I had never asked her when my debts would be repaid. Madam opened a book every month, and all the women in this brothel would sit before her hoping the day they would taste freedom was in sight. But that day never came, and we were too afraid to ask. So I let her keep the gifts, hoping someday I could convince Arun Sahib that Madam had taken most of his gifts to clear all my debts. He was the only one who could free me from this place. And if I was smart about it, maybe I could gain my freedom.

Soon Madam moved me to a better room—a room with more space.

"This room is for the more experienced of us. Don't think

you are one of them. This is all because Arun Sahib insists on treating you like a queen. God knows what *jadoo* you have done on him."

AS DAYS WENT by, Arun Sahib warmed up to me and started talking to me, telling me about his childhood, about his wife and kids who lived in an apartment in Mumbai. Some nights Arun Sahib narrated his tales of travel to me, talked about places like Dubai and America as if they were in our neighborhood; he conjured images in my mind that were prettier than the pictures I had seen in books.

"One day I will take you there," he said, his voice warm with genuine affection. Of course, I knew *that* would never be possible. Every man spoke like that when he wanted something.

"Do you think I will be free one day?" I dared to ask when he was in a good mood.

"Maybe one day I will just let you go . . ." he whistled, imitating a bird flying away. He laughed loudly, and I knew he was only humoring me. But even that helped give me hope.

There were days when he talked about the moments we could have together—traveling the world, walking down the streets of Bombay hand in hand, and I wondered why I did not see those moments the way he saw them. And I knew that in his own way, Arun Sahib had come to like me, perhaps even love me.

"Have you ever truly loved anyone?" he asked me once, scrutinizing my face, searching for the color of love.

I had a glimpse of Sanjiv then, sitting beside me and playing the tape, but that was years ago, and by now, I had learned to comfort myself in silence and never show how I felt. I looked into Arun Sahib's eyes and knew I could never experience the feeling of belonging I had found in Sanjiv. For me, Arun Sahib would always remain just one of my customers, an anchor keeping me afloat in the madness of this brothel.

THEN I FELL sick; the doctor who came to see me announced that I was pregnant. Sylvie shrank to the door in terror. Why hadn't the pill worked? Why was I pregnant? Madam stomped into my room, yanked me off the cot, and hit me repeatedly. "How do you think you will earn me money now, *haan*? You can't have this child. You hear me?"

I begged for mercy and pleaded with her, but she wouldn't listen. I didn't tell Madam that the last abortion had made my body very weak, and the doctor had told me if I tried to have another abortion, I might lose my life. Death should have been preferable to the life I was living. It would make me free, but here I was—hanging on to hope, wanting to bring another life into this cruel world.

"Let her have the child." The voice came from behind Madam; it boomed across the room. I actually thought I could see the clothes on the clothesline quiver, but it was only the breeze. Arun Sahib was standing in the doorway. It was a Thursday evening, and both of us had forgotten it was his time to visit me.

"What if I tell you it is my child?" He looked at Madam and blinked at her calmly.

"I-I . . ." Madam stuttered.

"I want her to have this child. You shouldn't have any problem with this."

"Yes, Dada, I am sorry." She walked out of the room, leaving me staring at him.

"Don't look at me," he said to me, putting up his hands, wiggling his head. "Don't expect me to provide for the kid. Do you know whose kid it is?"

I shook my head. I knew the child in my belly belonged to him. He knew it as well. What was the point in telling him anything? I was afraid he might get enraged, refuse to protect me. Who would believe a prostitute who sleeps with so many men? So I let it be, stifled the truth, and heaved a sigh of relief instead.

I EXAMINED MYSELF in the mirror every day of every month, caressing the growing bulge in my belly, noting the changes in my body—the flesh that had begun to line my body, my face that appeared fuller these days. I felt like a dainty plant becoming the trunk of a tree. Arun Sahib never caressed my belly or asked me how I was doing, but with time, he began inquiring about the child as if he knew this was his baby.

"If it's a boy, he can join me in my business," Arun Sahib kept telling me. I knew the fate of children born to mothers such as us. At the most the boy would join him as a pimp, bringing other girls into this trade, forgetting that his mother was once in this dirt. I never asked him what he would do if the baby was a girl. I feared to think about it. All I could do was wait and hope this life inside me found a better life—the dream *my* Amma once had for me.

CHAPTER 24

TARA
2005

RAZA STOOD BY the kitchen door in my apartment while I made tea. He had been in here many times in the last week, arriving at my doorstep to find out if I was doing all right. I had come to expect those few words of comfort he offered me every day.

"I came by to tell you I think I know of someone who can help. I spoke to Dinesh yesterday. He and his wife rescue women from brothels, ones who have been forced into prostitution."

"You think they will be able to find her?" I turned around expectantly, the tea simmering on the stove behind me.

"I . . . I don't know," he said, "but we have to try. Also, now that we know the kidnapper wasn't Salim, I can help you hire an investigator if you want to know who the kidnapper was."

"I've had enough of them," I said. I felt too tired to argue with Raza over Salim's whereabouts that night. I had always known, and still believed, Salim to be the kidnapper. In any case, I was the one responsible for Mukta's kidnapping. No matter what anybody said, one scream from me that night would have been enough to save her.

"What are you thinking?" Raza asked.

"Nothing. Yesterday I read an article about girls who were sold into this trade, and I tried to understand what Mukta's life must be like, what she would be going through. I read that they beat these girls if they refuse to do what they are told, even kill them. Do you think Mukta . . ."

I swallowed hard; I couldn't say the words. The tea on the stove boiled over behind me. I was still unable to bring myself to tell anybody that Mukta could be my half sister, my own blood.

"It is difficult, but all we can do is try hard to find her," he said softly, coming closer.

I nodded and felt the warmth of a tear run down my cheek.

THE DRIVE WAS long; the roads were filled with potholes, and clouds of dust loomed large over the streets from the construction nearby. Raza had hired a car to take us to meet Dinesh and Saira. The driver was a man in his early twenties who occasionally glanced into the rearview mirror and chatted with Raza as if he knew him.

"Memsahib," he said to me after a while, "if Raza Sahib not helping me, me lying in a gutter somewhere."

Raza laughed. "I just got him a job, nothing else."

"But me grateful or all those *harami* people making me sell drugs. I having no choice."

Raza leaned forward and patted his back. My heart softened just a little bit as I, too, began to respect all Raza did. The distance between Raza and me was decreasing with time. I took comfort in having him next to me, helping me, and he seemed to be well aware of it.

"They are a couple of hours away from the city, but the work they do here with the victims is remarkable," Raza told me as the driver deftly maneuvered the car around pedestrians. "They have another office in the city, but I want you to see this center they have built for the girls."

I lowered the car window and watched the downpour mercilessly drive the people of the streets into cold corners to huddle together. The raindrops felt cool against my face as the sky roared from dark clouds. It had taken a week for the news to sink in. For several days I had dismissed it, I couldn't imagine a life like that for Mukta. Now, as I watched people walk down the shiny, wet streets, holding umbrellas that swiveled in the breeze, I knew somewhere out there, on those streets, among all those people, I had to find Mukta, because I was the one who had ruined her life. The streets looked blurry now—whether from my tears or the downpour I didn't know.

"We're almost there," Raza said.

IT LOOKED LIKE a house with a huge courtyard. As we neared it I could see a couple of swing sets and girls playing hide-and-seek in the courtyard. The wide-open space of farmland around the center allowed the wind to howl around us. We left the car, opened the gates, and walked inside. The girls stopped playing and watched us with interest.

"Raza Bhai, how are you?" The man at the center folded his hands as he walked toward us. "Welcome, Tara Madam, I wouldn't have asked you to come so far, but this week we are at this center to look over some things and check if the girls need anything."

"That's all right. Thank you for giving me the time." I smiled and folded my hands in greeting.

"Dinesh," he said, introducing himself. "Let's go to my office."

Raza told me about the girls as Dinesh led us to his office.

"Did you know these angels not only rescue girls but also look after them for a few years, give them training in any vocation of their choice—teach them sewing, arts and crafts—so they can have a decent profession after they leave the center? And they provide legal help if they want to prosecute the people who kidnapped them."

Raza and I sat in their office that afternoon, on that muggy day, trying to recount my efforts to search for Mukta. Dinesh nodded and sighed as he listened. A short man with a bald pate and eyes that spoke volumes from experience, he explained to me that it wasn't going to be easy. His wife, Saira, sat beside him, draped in a blue sari with her hair tied in a bun. From the window behind them, I could see a group of girls doing yoga under the guidance of an instructor, the trees swaying in the breeze around them.

"I would suggest that you understand the way we work," Saira said to me as she nodded to a woman who placed tea on the table.

"Yes, yes." Dinesh nodded, picking up the glass of tea. "You must understand that usually kidnapped girls end up being sold to brothels. And then they are often moved from brothel to brothel. There are many brothels in Kamathipura, and we don't know which one she could be in," he said as he looked at me. "It has been eleven years since the kidnapping, so the girl in question may be too far lost in that world. It sounds cruel to say this, but we have to be truthful to ourselves from the very beginning."

I heard the wind rattle the windowpane and clutched my purse closer to me. "So I . . . I may never know what happened to her?"

"Yes, there is *that* possibility, which you need to be prepared for."

"The way we work" Saira interjected, "we have a number of employees, men who go undercover as customers and meet such girls, give them money, clothes, food so they trust us. These girls have been through so much. They are sold to brothels for as little as four thousand to five thousand rupees . . . uh . . . about one hundred dollars? They are kept in dark, windowless rooms and beaten regularly. They are scared."

Behind Dinesh and Saira, through the window, I could see the girls now—girls as young as twelve in a statuelike yogic posture, the smiles on their faces cleverly masking their anguish.

"Once we have gained their trust," Saira continued, "we try to explain to them that we can give them a better life. Then we, along with the police, carry out raids. Some of these girls are hidden in crates or behind secret doors—hidden so well it is difficult to find them. Sometimes they move the girls from place to place, between Mumbai and Kolkata, for example. Anyway, this time we will keep an eye out for Mukta. We will keep you informed about these raids."

"I would like to go with you on these raids," I said.

"I don't think that is a very good idea," Dinesh said. "It is difficult to—"

"But I have to go. I have to see this place," I interrupted.

My eyes must have looked desperate, even vulnerable, because Dinesh searched my face for a few seconds, then sighed. "You seem quite keen to search for a village girl. You were close?"

I nodded.

"I will let you know when we plan the raid," he said, relenting. "Raza, you can come too. Now, if you want to see the center and meet the girls, it will give you an idea of the work we do here."

After we thanked Dinesh and Saira, Raza and I walked through the center. I walked from room to room watching the girls as they studied in one room, sewed and knitted in another. Their expressions were calm and affable, and they smiled at me. I thought of Mukta—had she suffered like them? Did she have the same wounds? I hoped she was one of the lucky ones and had been rescued. As we left, the swing the girls played on creaked and the giggle of young girls began a rhythm of memories inside me. I wished that wherever she was under the sprawling wide sky, she had found something to smile about.

I WENT ALONG on the first raid. There were constables and police inspectors, social workers, and rescue teams—cars and jeeps parked a distance away.

"No, not a good idea," Dinesh told me when I insisted on walking through the lanes.

"Please, I have to," I persisted. "I have to see where she lives, and the place she has been for all these years, the room she has lived in—"

"It should be all right, don't you think?" Raza interrupted. "There are so many of us here."

Dinesh sighed, walked to the rescue workers, told them something, whispered to the inspectors in the jeep, and then walked back to us.

"We will walk down the lane so you can observe the place. The others will follow slowly. I will give them a call when we are ready." Dinesh told me, "We don't want to frighten the pimps or the brothel owners or they will hide the girls in crates. Now, Tara, are you sure you want to come inside the brothel? Many people find it difficult at first, to see such . . . hmm. I am just warning you."

"I am sure she will be fine," Raza said, looking at me. I nodded.

Raza, Dinesh, and I walked through the dimly lit, narrow alleys of Kamathipura. Some parts were swathed in yellow light from the streetlights and the stores lining the alleys. We crossed puddles of water left behind by a leaking faucet and passed garbage strewn on streets. The three-story buildings were old and dilapidated, looking ready to fall, and clothes swayed in the wind while scantily clad women peeked over them, watching us with interest. *Was Mukta one of them now? Those scantily clad women with the flowers in their hair and that face paint . . . waiting, hoping . . .*

My heart began crumbling with anguish, disgust. I had never seen a place like this before. Men loitered on streets with bloodshot eyes; women stood at corners in garish outfits and heavy makeup, some twirling their hair and beckoning passersby. *Hijras* dressed in saris smoked outside *paan* bidi shops, staring at us, letting out their torment in circles of smoke. Movie posters stuck on walls behind them depicted a life different than this. Bollywood music streamed through the area, cleverly masking the anguish that ran rampant here. Children defecated on the streets while some men were having a bath nearby. There was a man doubled over near an overflowing garbage can, muttering something to himself. The stench was becoming unbearable.

"Wait here," Dinesh whispered to us. "The rescue workers are right behind us, and the police will be coming shortly. I have given them a call."

We stood in a corner and watched. The place became chaotic as the police sirens came close, the shopkeepers hurriedly pulled down the shutters of their shops, and people began running away, throwing bottles on the streets so it would be difficult for the police to follow them. Raza and I were asked to sit in Dinesh's jeep and wait for the chaos to subside. Within moments, police barged into the old buildings and brought the women outside, herding them into police jeeps.

"We have to go in to see if they have hidden anyone. I don't think you should come in," Dinesh told us. "My team is trained to do this, to get the women and children out safely."

"I have to," I said, getting down from the van. Raza followed me.

The doorway was barely lit. Sweat lingered in the unventilated, dark pigeonholed rooms we passed, the corridors slippery and damp from broken water pipes. Yellow lightbulbs flickered in corners on the bare walls, the bunk beds in those rooms appearing to be reserved for prisoners. I couldn't take it anymore. I turned around and rushed outside. It was only when I was standing by the van, my arms tight against my chest, trying to breathe, that I noticed Raza next to me.

"Are you all right?" he asked. I nodded.

I could hear the calmness of his breath. He shifted as if suddenly becoming aware of his closeness to me, fished a cigarette from his pocket, pushed a match against the matchbox, and lit the cigarette.

"They'll be out soon." He smiled at me, blowing smoke away from me.

"Why are you always here for me?" I asked.

"What?"

"Nobody is helping me. Why are you?"

"Because, Tara . . . maybe I know what it is to be all alone . . . we all need someone when we feel alone," he said, flicking ashes to the ground.

I looked away not knowing what to say. Things had calmed down around us. This lane had suddenly become deserted and silent. Dogs rummaged in rubbish; cows sat peacefully on the street. The women in the police jeep had begun to speak quietly. I scanned their faces, watching, hoping for a familiar face hidden behind a coat of face paint, those green eyes I had once left behind. But all I saw were their careful expressions never crossing the border of a smile, the pain in their eyes lingering somewhere between a child and an adult—lost—as if they didn't know who they were anymore.

"We should go," Saira suggested, and Raza drove us back.

We waited at the center for Dinesh to arrive with the girls.

Saira, Raza, and I had gone ahead. I watched the volunteers help women and girls out of the jeep. Dinesh walked inside.

"We had forty-three prostitutes who were arrested today—twelve of them want to stay with us," he told Saira.

"What do you mean? Only twelve?" I asked.

"Some stay, some go back," Raza explained.

I ignored him and continued to look at Dinesh for an answer. "Go back? Why would anyone want to go back to that place?"

"Not all of them are forced into this," Dinesh told me. "We rescue only those who are forced into prostitution. But then, some of the girls are blackmailed into staying. They are afraid their parents in the village would be slaughtered if they came with us. Others—they don't know any other life; no matter how much we try to convince them there is a life other than that, they don't believe us. They have lost the ability to trust anybody."

"Oh," I said, still looking at him as if he hadn't answered my question.

He lowered his gaze. "No, none of them match Mukta's description."

"I don't believe you," I said and marched to the room where the women were asked to wait.

"Wait!" Raza shouted behind me. "You have to let Dinesh and Saira do what they are doing. They have been doing this for a very long time."

"Don't try to stop me!" I shouted back at him as I entered the room.

Dinesh and Saira followed me in.

"Do any of you know this girl?" I asked, flashing a photograph of Mukta and me at the Asiatic library. Those closer to me shook their heads and the others just watched me with alarm as I went bursting toward them. I had folded the photo in half to hide my face and focus on Mukta's face. But even as I thrust the photograph in their faces, not one of the women showed any sign of recognition. And at the end of it, everyone—including Raza, Dinesh, and Saira—was staring at me. I stood in that room full of women, silence and sorrow enveloping me.

"Don't give up hope," Dinesh said finally as he led me out. "We've only raided a couple of the brothels. There are more, and finding someone who was kidnapped years ago is going to take time. You must have patience."

CHAPTER 25

MUKTA
2001

THE BROTHEL WAS quiet today. It was the first day of the Diwali festival and the men must have been at home celebrating with their families. From my window, I watched the fireworks burst into the night sky, spreading their colors everywhere, traveling beyond the horizon into a world where Tara probably could see them too. Whenever I looked at the sky painted in so many colors, I always thought of Tara and wondered about what part of the world she might be in and if she still watched the sky like we once used to. I thought of that moment when my child would be born and put into my arms—I was sure I would have a daughter—and I would name her Asha. Only Tara would know as soon as she heard that name. It was a memory shared only by the two of us.

I thought of that day, back then. It was another day of Diwali—just like this one. Tara and I were teenagers. The air was filled with our laughter and giggles. I had drawn a beautiful *rangoli* outside their apartment, lit *diyas*, and painted those earthen lamps with designs. That morning, Tara and I were taking a plate of sweets to one of Tara's mother's friends who lived across the street. Everything around us was lit up, buildings painted and decorated; people waved at each other and said, "Happy Diwali!"

On our way, we saw a small crowd gathering at the side of the street. Out of curiosity we nudged our way to the front. It looked like a doll had fallen to the ground—fragile and small, wrapped in a white cloth. Mud on the side of the street formed a mound. There were paw marks on the side of it where a dog had dug the bundle out, pulling it with its teeth, unraveling it to reveal a face. There was a stench around this place, and I thought it must have been from the construction site not very far from here. The workers left the place dirty with leftovers from their lunch, and of course, there was the stench of their open toilets.

Tara wanted to pick up the doll so she walked ahead to touch it.

"Don't touch, don't touch!" a woman shouted. Tara and I took a couple of steps back. A man pulled us back firmly.

"What?" Tara protested. "It is only a doll."

"Shh," the woman cried, her eyes tearful and still focused on the doll. Another lady stood beside her and put her hands in the air, wailing like someone had died. We looked at her as if she had gone mad. More and more people had begun gathering around us, some sighing, some whispering, "Who would do such a thing?"

I watched their sad faces, thought about what they were saying, and stared at the doll for a brief moment. It took me a while to see what the others were seeing. It wasn't a doll at all. It was a child, an infant not more than a few days old. Before long the police came in their jeeps, shooed us away, and closed off the area of the construction site.

On our way back home we were silent, and I knew Tara was worrying about the baby as much as I was. That night I sat down in the kitchen, hoping the baby had found its way back to heaven. I wondered what it felt like to leave a world she had barely arrived in, to not know her mother the way I had known mine. Had she been glad to go away because she was a girl and her parents did not want her? In many ways, she was just like me. If she were alive, she would have known how difficult it would be for her father to love her, that the reason—the plain and simple truth—was that he *did not* love her.

Tara came to the kitchen that night, and I knew she couldn't sleep because of it.

"You can't sleep either?" I asked.

She shrugged and pointed to the sky. "Do you think we will find her there . . . the baby?"

"Of course. Look, there is a new star." I pointed.

"Do you think this happened to her because she was a girl?"

"Maybe."

"Do you think she had a name?"

I shrugged.

"I'd name her Asha, *Hope . . .*" Tara paused and looked at her feet. "If she were mine, and I'd never let her die. I would look after her." In the distance we could still hear the firecrackers bursting at this time of the night. We watched her—the baby in the sky looking down at us—until we fell asleep.

I THOUGHT OF that baby all through my pregnancy. And of Amma. It was incredible how much I thought of my Amma during my pregnancy. Her face, soft and delicate in my dreams, would smile at me and talk to me in her melodious voice. Her words were lilting, comforting. During this time I was crazy with joy, and my heart surged with love. Creating life had melted the iciness in my heart. Everybody could see it in the shine of my skin, in the rhythm of my movements.

But in the last few months, everything changed. My skin had become itchy and dry, flaking off like paper. The baby inside me didn't let me sleep. I lay in bed, staring at the ceiling fan that whirred above me. I would get up and let my fingers trace the outline of a water pipe that jutted out of the wall in my room. I stood on a stool to reach the window and watched the shadows lounging in the dark alleyway below my room. The more I became aware of the weight of this new life inside me, the more thoughts sprouted in my mind.

"You are concerned what will happen to the baby if it is a girl? But how are you so sure that it is going to be a girl?" Sylvie asked.

I shrugged and didn't reply. That was something I was sure of but couldn't explain. The burden of my thoughts was heavy, and I carried it with me wherever I went. I remember those last days of pregnancy. I had awful mornings of being nauseous and when I had to go down the stairs to the bathroom, the girls in the brothel gave me bitter looks.

"Make way, the queen is here," one of them would say, spitting on the floor as I passed.

"She thinks she is very lucky," another would remark.

"Why? She has Arun Sahib wrapped around her fingers. She can do anything she wants," still another would say as I passed.

Their words resounded in my ears. I must admit, at such times, I felt I was betraying them, refusing to partake of the pain we all had encountered together for so many years. In any case, the girls were right—I was lucky to be allowed no customers even if it was for a few months. No other girl could have afforded the luxury of privacy given to me.

I shudder to think what would have happened if Arun Sahib hadn't been in my life. Madam didn't like it that I was left to do nothing on most nights. So I was put to work sweeping and scrubbing the floors of all the rooms in the brothel, squatting beside the water pump downstairs, washing clothes, rinsing and wringing them while all the girls of the brothel piled their dirty clothes beside me. Then she stood over me, reminding me I had debts to clear. I didn't mind the hard work; it was way better than the life I had before I got pregnant, when the only thought in my head was *How many customers would I have today?*

"You should tell Arun Sahib that Madam mistreats you. It is not good to do so much work during your last few months of pregnancy," Sylvie warned.

It wouldn't have helped. I had heard Arun Sahib was an astute businessman, and Madam ran the brothel very well, earning him more money than the other brothels he owned. So at the most, Arun Sahib would have given her a warning, and that would have left Madam fuming. It wasn't a wise thing to do.

One night something stirred inside me. I could feel it while I slept. I could smell jasmine flowers, the smell of fresh earth after a pleasant rain wafting to me from outside the window. I could hear the baby's gurgles, see the innocence in its eyes. It was a dream because I woke up drenched in sweat. A dull ache had begun to surround my stomach; a throb had begun in my back. I stood up and inched toward Sylvie's room, the radiating waves of pain engulfing me as I doubled up outside. My pain synchronized with the throb of the music coming from her room. I looked inside. She shared this room with another girl, a curtain standing between their beds, a witness to what happened on either side. Sylvie found me lying on the floor and helped me up. She led me to a narrow, unventilated room that looked like a passageway. It was one of the many rooms I had my abortions in. This time I would be bringing another life into one of them. Sylvie asked me to lie down on a worn, tattered mattress, the red of it weathered over the years. I waited for the wave of pain to come again while Sylvie assured me that the midwife was on her way.

The midwife was new and inexperienced. Her name was Shaira, a young twenty-one-year-old who had another job at a beauty parlor. She told us that she had completed her midwifery degree recently but I had heard she was nervous when she had tried to abort Leena's baby and it had ended up being a mess. Leena had died. She was unlike Sheetal—the other, middle-aged midwife, who had years of experience. But Sheetal didn't come to this brothel anymore. Rumor was that Madam didn't pay her well for the last assignment and they had a falling-out. And then Madam hired Shaira, probably for free so that she could complete her degree by practicing on us. How could we rely on someone so young to bring new life into the world?

I feared for my baby and thought Madam was deliberately

trying to harm it by bringing in someone new. But Shaira turned out to be calm and collected, with a round *bindi* on her forehead and eyes so warm they could melt your heart. She tied her curly brown hair into a bun and washed her hands with the precision of a doctor. "You're in good hands," she said with a smile, and I no longer worried. *Maybe Leena had died because she was too weak to have another abortion or maybe she couldn't stand to lose another baby,* I thought.

I concentrated on the trickle of water on the walls of this room, on the paint peeling and falling to the side, and on the dampness inside. Sylvie got rags and water the color of dirt.

"I've boiled the water," she assured me.

My thoughts drifted to Tara. Would she be having a baby? I imagined an attentive husband standing by her, escorting her to the off-white walls of a hospital, the nurses and doctors hovering over her, assuring her it would be a healthy baby.

"You must push," the midwife told me as another wave of pain embraced me. I clutched the sides of the bed, took a big breath, smelled the dust in the air, and pushed.

This went on for several hours. Madam came by and asked Sylvie to get back to work. Soon it was only me and the midwife waiting in that lonely passageway to welcome my child. I must have screamed and wailed all night, waiting for the baby to emerge. She came kicking and screaming in the early hours of the morning, surrounded by the orange glow of dawn. She was so tiny when she was handed to me, her eyes barely open, her mouth constantly opening to let out cries from the shock of leaving my safe womb and arriving into this difficult world. Have you ever stared into the sunset so hard that you felt a deep connection with it? Felt the warm tingle of love, that overwhelming joy that crept inside you? That is what I felt when they placed my baby in my arms.

But that was also the moment when the shock at what I had done set in—I had brought an innocent life into a world that wouldn't treat her well. I had thought about this, but the dismay at my decision was apparent to me only when my child was born.

Holding my baby, wrapped up in that bundle of cloth, I had flashes of that Diwali evening when Tara and I had watched that fragile child wrapped in white cloth—the one who had died—being buried for being a girl. It was only now that I truly *understood* the mother who had let her own child die. I understood how she must have decided it was best for the little girl, despite her inner turmoil and the guilt of her dangerous decision. I thought of the name again—the name Tara would have wanted for my baby.

Tears fell from my eyes—from the fear of that memory or from the love that suddenly sprang in my heart for this little one in my arms, I didn't know—but I wept like I had never wept before. And I knew I could never be like that mother. I could never harm my child.

"What do you plan on naming her?" the midwife asked me, jolting me from my memories.

"Asha," I said. *My hope in this life.* My *only* hope.

CHAPTER 26

TARA
September 2006

I SHOULDN'T HAVE been here in the first place. It wasn't safe. It was a bad idea. Yet, despite all my fears, I managed to stand on this busy street, about to enter the Kamathipura area. Cars and buses honked behind me in the evening rush hour. Hawkers urged me to buy street food from their carts, and pedestrians rushed past me. I took a few steps away from that bustle and stood in a narrow lane between two buildings. If I continued down this road, I would find myself in the labyrinth of lanes they called Kamathipura. It was a dangerous, violent area filled with pimps and drug-addled men. Dinesh had warned me several times not to attempt to come here by myself. But it had been more than two years since my return to India, and after many brothel raids over the last year-and-a-half, I was tired of waiting for the next one to happen, tired of the hope that surged through me when the women were being rescued, and most of all, tired of the disillusion that assaulted me after not finding Mukta among them.

If Mukta lived here, she went into hiding during the raids. I hoped that if I came alone without the NGO or the police, and without the chaos they brought along, there would be a small chance Mukta would see me, recognize me, and not feel the need to hide anymore. It might have been a foolish, naïve plan, but it was a chance I wanted to take.

Above me, the orange rays of sunset scattered along the sky, and in the distance, I watched the *paan* bidi shops open for the evening. Young girls, some as young as ten, were slathering makeup on their faces, getting ready for their night's work. One of them—a girl about twelve with bright red lipstick and a red dress—seemed to notice me and began walking toward me. When she came closer I realized she wasn't looking at me at all but walking toward a pimp who stood a distance away. He was wearing a dirty white T-shirt with crumpled jeans. His unkempt hair fell over his shoulders. He glanced sideways but didn't look at me. I hid behind the building. Sweat rolled over my temples onto my neck. Had he noticed me here? I told myself to breathe. In the distance, I could still hear the hawkers peddling their goods. I could run out of here into the busy street and never look back. It was my way out.

I peered around the corner and watched the girl reach into her blouse and scoop out a few notes. She handed the money to the man. He stood there, his back leaning against a wall, and counted the money without lifting his head, while the girl returned to her place under an unlit streetlight. In the last year-and-a-half, during each brothel raid, I had navigated these lanes along with Dinesh and Saira's team, looking into the eyes of pimps and brothel keepers. I knew this place; I knew the escape routes. But what if I couldn't escape? Nobody knew I was here. I hadn't told Raza or Dinesh. They would have dissuaded me.

Standing there on that street, I knew this was something I had to do—if I could walk into danger to get Mukta kidnapped, I could definitely walk into this place to rescue her. Without giving it any more thought, I began walking toward it. The pimp continued counting his money and didn't look at me as I walked past. The Bollywood music got louder, and children giggled as they played tag with each other, circling women who sat on the veranda, making dinner on the stoves. Thick smoke rose from the stoves and mingled with the smell of country liquor and the stink of garbage. The women became silent as I passed by and continued to stare at me. The pimps had to be nearby, hiding in corners where I couldn't see them. All I wanted to do was walk around this place so Mukta could notice me, recognize me. I didn't need to talk to anyone here, just keep my head down and walk through the area. At least that was the plan. Then I saw a woman who stood by the building, nonchalant about my presence. One hand was on her hip and in the other she held a cigarette. She looked at me, and then looked away. There was something about her look, about the way she hid her urge to ask for help. I found myself approaching her.

"I am from an NGO," I heard myself saying.

"Here by yourself. No one else." She grinned at me and blew rings of smoke into my face.

"My name is Sylvie," she said. "That's my friend Sweety."

Sweety was talking to a man, giggling, and whispering something in his ear as she led him up the stairs. Her green eyes lingered on me for just a second before she continued whispering in his ear.

"What is it you wanting to know? I knowing you a journalist," Sylvie said. "You wanting to write article? Our story? Many coming here, but I not doing anything without any money."

"No, I'm not a journalist. I am here to help if you want it." She laughed.

"There are many who telling us they can help, but no one can help. It is stupid to think you can."

"I can really help you. But I am looking for a girl . . . a woman . . . she is—"

"I think you should go," she said looking over my shoulders. Her face had a sudden frightened look of a child.

"No . . . but I am looking for this—"

"What do you want?" a man's voice boomed. I looked back.

"Who are you?" he asked. Two tall, hunky men followed him.

"I am from an NGO . . ." I explained.

"I think you should go. We don't want people like you here." His bloodshot eyes looked me up and down. He scratched his cheek as he spoke. He smelled of country liquor.

"See, I don't want to cause any trouble. I am just passing through. I am from an NGO," I said, trying to convince him.

"That's what we don't like—others poking their noses in our business." His voice was louder now.

He signaled to two kids playing cricket in the middle of the street. Two dustbins posed as wickets. One kid walked toward us, dragging his bat behind him. The man snatched the bat from his hand and waved it around me.

"Look, I am . . . going." My heart was pounding so hard I could almost hear it.

"Now what is it that you want? Tell me again." The man advanced.

There was a sudden shiver in my legs as if I'd collapse. I felt lightheaded.

"I . . . I . . ." I slinked away from him. He took a sudden swing at me; I ducked and ran. But I had hardly covered a few feet when I felt myself falling. My feet had hit something heavy. My chin hit a rock and there was blood pouring out of it. My arms and shoulders hurt from the impact. A few feet ahead, I could see the bustle of the busy street I had left behind. Without another thought, I got up and started running. I didn't look back. I could hear laughter as I ran. I ran alongside cars and trucks, pushing pedestrians away from my path.

It seemed like I ran for a long time with a sudden super-human energy coursing through my body. Then I heard my name—several times. There was a car driving alongside me.

"Tara!" the man called from inside. I slowed down. The car slowed down alongside me.

"What's going on?" the driver asked, peering through the passenger window. I kept looking at the man inside.

"Are you all right?" he asked. It was Raza.

"I was . . . I . . ." I looked around me. I was quite a distance away from Kamathipura. How had I run so far, so fast? People were looking at me strangely; some even stopped to stare.

"Get in." Raza opened the passenger side of the car.

I was shaking when I got in. My hands struggled to close the car door. My clothes were soaked in sweat and felt cold against my skin. Raza didn't ask any questions, just kept driving until we came to my apartment. It was only when he stopped the car outside the gates of my apartment complex that tears started pouring down my cheeks.

"You shouldn't have gone there on your own," Raza said softly. His hands clasped mine.

I continued crying. Raza sat silently beside me.

"Let's go upstairs to your apartment . . . take care of those wounds for you."

I touched my chin. Blood had dripped down my chin and onto my clothes. My jaw hurt. In the car mirror I could see that my lip had swollen to twice its size.

"We can file a police report if you want."

"Why? I . . . just fell."

"Did they threaten you?"

"I don't care, I won't file any report. I've had enough of that." I stormed out of the car and started climbing the steps to Papa's apartment. Raza followed me.

I sat on the carpet in the living room of my childhood home, where Mukta and I had once played hopscotch, and cleaned my wounds with an antiseptic.

"Let me make some tea," Raza offered while I went to change my clothes. In my bedroom, I lay down on my bed and watched the ceiling fan whir above me. This was where I was lying when Mukta got kidnapped. Was the fear I felt today even close to what she must have felt? Did anyone deserve to have a life after they had destroyed someone else's?

I switched on my computer and sat at my desk. Pictures drifted on the monitor—pictures of Elisa with her baby sleeping in her arms, another of her baby in a Santa cap, smiling at her. I could almost hear the gurgle of the baby; feel the happiness on Elisa's face. I had sent my congratulations to her and Peter on the arrival of their firstborn just a few days ago. I liked to look at these pictures—my only respite from the side of the world I had been observing since the brothel raids began, my only way to believe that happy smiles and innocence did exist in some distant corner of the world. Today they were a relief to look at.

I should not have been this shook up after all that I had seen in the last two years. I had become actively involved not just with Raza's organization but also with Dinesh and Saira's organization. I volunteered to teach English to some of the rescued girls and women. At times, I had stayed behind at night and held the girls as they woke up terrified and cried in my arms. I thought of the girls I had met—some as young as ten—girls whose pasts would always be marred by something brutal, and yet they had learned to survive. I had learned something from them about life, about the way it lets you down and yet helps you move on. Their fortitude gave me courage, a hope that if they could survive what they did, Mukta could still be out there alive.

"WHAT WERE YOU thinking?" Raza asked, bringing me tea.

Our friendship had grown by leaps and bounds over the last year. In moments of despair, I knew I just had to look around me to find him by my side. It had been comforting—this friendship that we shared, our working together toward a common goal—going to food drives in the slums together, talking to the needy together, accompanying Dinesh on the brothel raids.

But how was I to explain the emotions that rose in me when we rescued those women? For me, it was almost as if the highest joy of being able to rescue a girl rested uncomfortably with the deep sorrow of having put a girl there.

"What were you thinking?" Raza repeated, and then sighed when I didn't reply.

"Let's go out to dinner. Have you eaten anything?" he asked.

I shook my head. He didn't give me a chance to protest. Within minutes we were walking down a lane, standing under the streetlight outside a food stall with open-air seating. I noticed it was actually a nice, neat place—a *dhaba*. Raza said the place was run by a north Indian family. Around us many table and chairs were arranged along the street. People were devouring their food, chatting loudly while the music played softly in the background.

"I know the search for Mukta looks dismal, but it will all work out, trust me," Raza said. "More than anything, I think, you have to let it go."

"Let it go?"

"Let go of the regret you feel for something you did such a long time ago. When you came to Salim to hand over that note, your mother had just died. Grief does that to people at times—you just can't think straight. Besides, there was nothing you could have done that night during the kidnapping. You were a child. So . . . let it go."

I hadn't realized, until then, that he knew—had known all along—my deepest, darkest secret, without my telling. I had failed to see him in my memories, standing right behind Salim, when I had sent the boy to deliver my note all those years ago.

All this while, I had been let down by my memory of him not being there that evening. Now his eyes were clear as he spoke, as if he thought what I had done was worth forgiving.

"It's all right," he said as I looked away. "We all do things we regret. Sometimes we just don't know any better." He looked up at the clear sky.

Raza and I had grown close, and it shouldn't have mattered to me that he was being honest, but my eyes burned with tears. "I don't want to talk about it," I said.

He shrugged and looked around, searching for a waiter. *Let go.* The thought smoldered inside me. "Maybe we should go," I said, my words like a rapidly rising tide.

"Why? You didn't like what I said? It's the truth, isn't it? Isn't that why you went all by yourself to Kamathipura today? You wanted to see what it felt like to be in a place like that; you wanted to feel the fear Mukta might have felt—the abandonment, the loneliness, the terror. Isn't that why you went by yourself? You knew it would be foolish to go looking for her by yourself. You would never find her that way." He glared at me. I gulped. He had read my mind.

"Look," Raza said, his eyes softening now, "you have to be patient. There is no point in putting yourself in danger. It's not going to help you find her. We are doing all we can."

"Well, it's not enough. You don't understand . . ." I let out a sob.

He clasped my shaking hands.

"I am here for you," he whispered.

His face was the same as when I had first met him more than two years ago. There was a furrow in the middle of his forehead that had deepened to form a permanent line and pockmarks on the sides of his face, a reminder of the scars left by his past. What had changed? Was it his brown eyes, which turned soft whenever he looked at me? Was it the look of concern when he saw me upset? Had *they* been trying to tell me a story all this while, one I hadn't been listening to? Why had he been so patient with me even though I knew he wanted to yell at me, admonish me for my stupidity?

"How you doing, Raza Bhai?' The waiter, a boy no more than eight, in a torn shirt, arrived at our table, carrying two glasses of water, and cleaned the table with a washcloth. I wiped my eyes quickly and made an effort to smile.

Raza put his arm around the boy's shoulder, "Tara, this is Chottu. Chottu, where is the shirt I brought for you the other day?"

"I wearing new shirt to school every day. Thanks you, Raza bhai, you sending me to school." His lips spread into a broad smile.

"Do you like going to school?" I asked Chottu.

"Yes, Madam. Very much," he said, wobbling his head. "I want to be a doctor when I grow up—help people, just like Raza bhai."

In his eyes, I saw the same zeal to study that I had once seen in Mukta's; the same glimmer of hope, of survival, flickered there. Sitting under the stars, being served food by an eight-year-old, I told Raza, "I won't ever give up, if that's what you are thinking. It seems like a lost cause. But I won't give up." Crickets chirped in the distance, as if trying to confirm what I was saying.

"I know you won't give up. I don't want you to." Raza smiled as he offered me a naan from the plate. "You know, when I see all these *goondas* on the street—these ruffians who beat people up—I go home and thank Allah that I met Dev Sahib. Otherwise I would have probably ended up just like them."

"Dev Sahib?"

"Yes, Dev Sahib. You know, I was born in a very poor family. Salim and I knew no other life growing up. The idea of a better life for us, the possibility even, was only through selling drugs and robbing people. It seemed like such a good idea then. We didn't know we were hurting people, or maybe we just didn't care."

I watched his eyes as he continued—looking away, lost in another time.

"I loved being seen with *goondas* like Salim; it gave me a sense of power to be part of the gang. With them, I wasn't as helpless as I felt inside. I joined them when I was eight, like many boys my age. I tried to learn the ways of the street, trying to decipher my life through it. I used to pick pockets very well, you know." He laughed at his memories of childhood.

"I sold drugs and got caught by the police a couple of times. I remember one time, how they made us take our clothes off, tied us naked upside down, and hit us with a rod. I still have the scars on my back. It should have taught me to stay away from the gang, but it made me more resilient, more determined to do better with the gang. I was fourteen when Salim tried to get hold of you in the middle of that street. I know I have apologized before, but whenever I look at you, I relive the guilt of what I did. I am sorry about that, I truly am. I was lost; I didn't know what I was doing."

There was pain in his eyes, regret on his face.

"You don't have to apologize," I said. "You've apologized enough."

"Allah was *meherbaan* that I met Dev Sahib. He rescued me when I was badly beaten in a police raid, and he and his wife nursed me back to health. I had never known a family before that. My mother was a drunk who slept on street corners and begged for a living, and I never really knew a father. Home was a cloth tent my mother had put on a street corner. We had to re-build it every time there was a strong wind, or when rain lashed too hard on the streets, or worse, when the municipality would drive by breaking all the huts because they were illegal. I must have been seven or eight when I ran away from her; I don't know what happened to my siblings. I did minor jobs—worked in restaurants as a waiter, helped shopkeepers carry their goods, garbage. I slept on a bench at night in the park, and when it rained I slept on the patio of a shop, the roof becoming my shelter for the night. Those were the good days when all I was worried about was one meal a day."

Raza stopped and sighed. The evening had turned into night. Chottu had cleared our plates and wiped the table; people around us had started dispersing and the food shack was dimming its light.

"Then you got involved with the gang Salim belonged to?" I asked.

"Yes. I was mostly involved in robberies, pickpocketing, minor thefts, and selling drugs. It is easy to use children to transport drugs. Nobody suspects them, and the police mostly let them go without doing a thorough check; all the while, the kids are carrying drugs in their undergarments. After some time you get used to it. I left behind that life once I met Dev Sahib. 'I will pay you a good salary if you work for me,' he said. I was fifteen years old, and despite my gratitude toward him for nursing me back to health, I couldn't let go of my old ways. He caught me carrying drugs twice, but he was a patient man and knew change didn't happen overnight. I found the work—carrying paper and other stationery from the shops to the office, carrying food his wife made for the slum dwellers—I found it all mundane and boring, far from the adrenaline rush I felt with the gang. But with his help, I persevered."

"What about the people you worked for? Didn't they come for you? I have heard it is not easy to leave a gang."

"You are right. But I had never climbed the ladder in the gang. When Dev Sahib discovered me, I was still at the lowest rung of the ladder in the underworld, and people above me couldn't care less if the bottom feeders left. I worked with Dev Sahib for a long time. Initially he made me run small errands for him. I would live with them—he and his wife, they treated me like a son. I became a part of his family. He had two sons and a daughter. I never knew until then what it felt like to have a meal with people laughing and sharing stories, talking about their day. It was like having a real family. Dev Sahib said I should go to night school and finish my education. I never had any education to begin with. He taught me all the basics so I could take exams that allowed me admission into the third grade. There were young kids all around me, and it was embarrassing at first. But I learned quickly and moved to a higher grade. He enrolled me in night school, and I graduated when I was twenty-four. I decided I wanted to follow in Dev Sahib's footsteps and become a social worker. I joined Dev Sahib and his wife in their task of keeping boys from being sold to gang leaders as beggars or girls being sold to brothels. The sight stirred something in me, and I realized there were things more important than me, that I could think beyond myself."

"And your wife worked with you."

"Yes, Naima was a social worker. Like me, she was rescued by one of the NGOs. She worked at the school, taught science and history to kids. I met her there. I have never seen anyone more passionate about helping the needy. She especially cared for the girls sold to the brothels here and worked with several of the NGOs here."

"So where are Dev Sahib and his wife now?"

"They were with Naima during the bomb blast."

"I am so sorry. How have you not told me all this before? We've known each other for almost two years!"

He smiled. "You didn't ask. And I didn't think you would be interested in knowing so much about me."

An awkward silence crept between us. I had been so absorbed in my own pain that I hadn't bothered to ask anything about him. Sure, I had often wondered what had persuaded a street *goonda* to grow out of the street life and run an NGO. But I had never asked why he had a change of heart. Perhaps, all this while, I hadn't cared enough about anything other than finding Mukta. I hadn't even told him about me, about what had happened for fear of opening up my wounds.

"So tell me about you," he said.

"What about me?"

He shrugged.

In that moment, I felt an urge to tell him everything—all that I had been holding inside, everything I had been guarding. I told him about Papa, about the happy childhood days I shared with Mukta, about the kidnapping and how I planned it, about the despondency I felt when I left India, and how when we landed in America Papa had become aloof because of his grief, about how hopeful I felt when I first met Brian.

"I met Brian in America . . . at a party my friend Elisa dragged me to." I laughed. "When I first met him, I had a feeling we shared something deeper, but it just didn't work out."

I told him about that evening when Papa hung himself. My eyes suddenly moistened with tears.

"Anyway," I continued, "after the funeral I found some documents in Papa's drawer. And I knew I had to come back to look for Mukta."

"I'm sorry you had to see your father that way," Raza said.

"There is something else I haven't yet told you." I paused. "In the village, I learned something from my grandmother, something about Papa—that he had a relationship with a village prostitute and Mukta could be . . ." I took a deep breath and continued. "That Mukta could be his child."

"Mukta is your half sister?" He raised his eyebrows.

"I don't know. I wish I knew for sure."

It was such a relief to have told someone. The shack behind us had closed long ago, and before we knew it, the sun was rising in the distance, spreading its light, washing away my worries, giving me renewed hope. We had spent the entire night talking about our lives, our troubles. More than two years had gone by, sitting on the sidelines of my life, watching it pass by me, and even though it looked like there was no ray of light ahead, I wasn't ready to give up, and oddly, for the first time in a long time, I felt like I wasn't alone.

CHAPTER 27

TARA
October 2006

NAVIN WOKE ME up early that morning, knocking on the door vehemently, speaking hurriedly, out of breath, as I opened the door. "Daddy is in the hospital; they say it is serious. Will you come see him? He's always wanted to tell you something."

"Of course." Gathering my things, I asked, "How is he doing now?"

"He is out of danger for now, but the doctors say"—his voice softened—"it's anytime now."

It had been almost two years since I first saw Anupam chacha so terribly weakened from cancer. Once in a blue moon, when I'd find the time, I'd visit his home, sit beside him, and read to him. We'd talk about our childhood memories, talk about Papa. Then once in a while, he'd stare in the distance and tell me he had many things to tell me. When I asked him about it, he'd clam up. I let it slide. I was sure the pain medicines were making his brain foggy. Navin had always echoed my reasoning, and I was surprised to learn that Navin felt differently about it now. I hoped Anupam chacha would be able to tell me whatever it was that was bothering him. I didn't want him to go like Papa did—carrying a heavy burden.

Before I left, I called Raza and asked him to pick me up at the hospital so we could drive back to Dinesh's center later. The hospital was situated between a market and a construction dump. The hospital smelled of antiseptics as the doctors and nurses rushed past us. The whitewashed walls reminded me of the time Papa and I had waited in hospitals just like this one, frantically searching for Aai.

"Room thirty-eight," Navin said, shuffling his feet and jabbing the elevator button.

I put my hand on his shoulder,

"No, no, I am not worried. My wife, Vibha, is with Daddy. He will be fine . . . I know, I know," he repeated.

"Oh, I forgot," he told me, standing outside as I got into the elevator, "I have to get some medicines; I will be back before you know it. Room thirty-eight, okay?"

I knew by the way he was looking away, hiding his face, that all he wanted was some privacy for his grief. I got out on the third floor and walked across the corridor, glancing from room to room, searching for room 38. A nurse hurried past me, and the tired visitors sitting outside other rooms glanced at me as I passed by them. Room 38 was at the end of the corridor. I stood outside the door watching Anupam chacha lying in that bed, tubes running in and out of his nose. Navin's wife, Vibha, was sitting on a chair beside his bed, knitting something. She looked up as soon as I entered the room and Anupam chacha gave me a small wave and pointed to a chair. Vibha dragged the chair toward the bed.

"He wants you to sit down," she said as if I hadn't understood.

I sat down next to the bed and took his hand in mine.

"Chacha, how come no one told me you were so sick?"

He gave a weak smile at my lightheartedness and tried saying something, but it came out as a croak. I helped him take a sip of water and looked behind me at Navin, who had entered the room, and his wife, who stood beside him. But they looked at me blankly, dismayed.

"We'll be outside, in case Daddy wants to tell you something in private," Navin said and nodded at Anupam chacha.

"Your grandmother must have told you by now." He sighed. I nodded.

"I don't think your Papa was ever sure Mukta was his kid . . . you know. I told him to let that kid go . . . just leave her at an orphanage or something. But your Papa was always the messiah. He yelled at me once . . . and said Mukta could be my kid. After all, almost every man in the village had slept with Mukta's mother. In the end, no one will ever know . . . I suppose, who the fathers . . . of such kids . . . are."

"Aai thought she was my half sister. She must have known. I don't know—" I said softly.

"It is my fault . . . whatever happened," Anupam chacha interrupted, his voice came haltingly. "I should have . . . never been tempted . . . to do . . . what I did."

"What, Anupam chacha?"

"After Navin's mother . . . died, I wanted to . . . fulfill her wishes . . . make Navin a brilliant musician. I . . . I would have done anything . . . to fulfill her last wishes. So much so . . . that I . . . I was blinded . . . with this dream."

It wasn't something I didn't know. "It's all right," I said, wiping the spittle from the side of his mouth.

"As much as I tried, Navin couldn't . . . reach the level . . . I wanted him to reach. I . . . I realized he . . . needed extra coaching . . . from the best teacher. It . . . would have made him . . . the kind of musician . . . I wanted him to be." He stopped and coughed. "The only problem was . . . my business wasn't doing well . . . and I couldn't afford . . . the fees . . . for the services of a good teacher. I . . . I borrowed heavily from . . . a man who claimed to charge . . . no interest. In my desperation . . . I wasn't thinking. In just a . . . a few months the man sent . . . *goondas* after me . . . asking me to return three times the amount . . . Then I understood . . . I had foolishly put . . . my son's life at risk . . . by borrowing from the mafia. So . . . so . . . one evening when I was walking back home . . . in the alley . . . a man called out to me . . . said he could help . . . I thought that was the answer . . . God was sending me. This man . . . this *goonda* . . . he spit the *paan* on the street as . . . as he approached me . . . said he knew how much I needed money. He said . . . all I had to do . . . was deliver a girl to them.

"At first, I said . . . there was no way I . . . I would commit a crime. There . . . was no way I would spoil . . . a little girl's life. He . . . followed me . . . asked me to imagine a life . . . where Navin is dead . . . all because I made the . . . the stupid decision . . . to borrow money. *Don't make another stupid decision . . .* he said."

Anupam chacha spoke slowly, softly. It came in waves, like

a man confessing to a priest. And I sat there silently, his words peeling off the wounds of his past.

"I was frightened when he came to me . . . day after day . . . reminding me of how I wasn't doing what . . . what was good for my son. He said the girl . . . was not a girl from a good family. *What . . . what difference would it make?* I thought . . . the girl didn't have a future anyway. He . . . he told me her name and I refused. But the next few days . . . it weighed heavily on me as . . . as if there was nothing else in life I could see . . . but my son . . . alive and happy. I told the man I . . . I would deliver the girl. Then one night . . . I heard you scream at Mukta . . . heard you unlock the door . . . say the devil will come for her . . . I knew your Papa would be fast asleep that night. He . . . he took sleeping pills in those days . . . after the grief of your mother's death had . . . had left him heartbroken. I . . . I saw my chance. I had a spare key . . . I easily entered your apartment. It is . . ."

By now, I could sense the warm flush on my face, see my hands tremble. I stood up and took two steps back. Everything was suddenly surreal; the sunlight poured from the window; this man sleeping in this bed couldn't be someone I knew. Anupam chacha raised his hand, tried to reach out to me, but I could only hear my whimper.

"It is the worst thing . . . I have done in my entire . . . life. Spoil a girl's life like that. What . . . what if she really was my kid? How . . . how cruel of me. God punished me for it. Navin told me . . . later . . . that he saw me that night. The hate . . . the hate I have seen in his eyes . . . for me ever since . . . he told me he didn't want . . . to sing anymore. And this cancer . . . it is my punishment. If I—"

I walked outside the room, his sentence unfinished, the words he uttered lingering in that hospital room I left behind. Navin watched me walk away and followed me.

"I told your Papa long ago, when he called once from America. I couldn't keep that secret, couldn't live with what Daddy had done. Your Papa broke all ties with us and never called again."

"Papa knew? *You* knew?"

"Yes," he said, lowering his gaze. "I am sorry."

I walked away.

I sat outside the hospital on a bench, watching the doctors go in and out, patients coming or going. In the distance I could see Raza walking toward the hospital. He stopped when he saw me sitting on that bench; his face tightened in pain as he looked at me. My tears made everything hazy. But I watched his pace increase. He sat next to me, and I took the photograph of Mukta and me out of my wallet, tracing my hands over the lines that had developed on it over all these years.

"This . . . forever . . . I . . . don't . . . know . . ." I said, my words trailing off.

Raza put a hand on my shoulder as my sobs came out in spurts. And I knew that, even though my words were incoherent, he still understood me. He pulled me closer, putting his arm around me. The tenderness in his eyes, in his touch, shocked me. I sobbed louder, huddled closer, my head resting on his chest, my tears soaking his shirt. I could hear his heartbeat, his slow, steady breath, smell his cologne, feel the touch of his strong arms around me. I let him hold me.

CHAPTER 28

MUKTA
2001–2006

"SHE IS SWEET," Sylvie said with a dismal, knowing expression on her face when she saw Asha. I was given a week to rest, feed my baby, and enjoy her company. After a week, Madam took her away and said, "You better get back to work. Who do you think is going to keep paying for your stay here?"

Every evening they took her away. I would think of her sweet gurgles all through the night, hear her cries as I went through the ordeal of my profession. I waited until morning for them to bring her back to me, to put her on my chest and feed her. But she survived—the little one. She must have had a stronger spirit than I had. With time she learned to remain hungry through the night, to stave off her hunger by sleeping. She adjusted her time to Madam's feeding schedule. I was amazed. In spite of being so little she adapted, understanding the world she was born into.

It must have been a week after she was born that Arun Sahib stood in the doorway, watching me closely.

"Don't you want to see her?" I asked.

"Who?"

"The baby."

Arun Sahib's eyes flashed with anger.

"Why would I want to see the baby? I come to see you, not some damn child."

I had to appease him, tell him I didn't have the ability to think before I talked. After spending the night, he stopped at the door and said, "Don't ask me such a stupid question again."

I should have learned my lesson from that episode, but I couldn't help feeling guilty for bringing my little girl into this wretched world. I watched children as young as four or five, born to women like me, running around freely, playing with other children in the dirty alleyway, not knowing the world they were born into, unable to understand there were pimps prowling around them, that the world surrounding them was full of nothing but men with just one thought on their minds. Then I would look at my baby sleeping on the cold ground, swaddled in hand-me-down clothes as tattered and soiled as my life, the light flickering on her luminescent skin, and wonder what she would have to endure in her life. So I didn't give up. I tried telling Arun Sahib that I didn't want her to grow up understanding anything of this trade. But he blinked at me as if he hadn't understood that I was speaking of his own daughter.

"He doesn't care," I told Sylvie once when we were washing clothes at the water pump downstairs.

"You are worried they will take her away from you. But don't you worry. You still have time. They are not going to do anything to her until she is eight or nine. You have time until then. We will think of something."

I wanted to think my child was like the flowers that bloom every summer no matter how hard winter has been on them. I wondered if I could stop time for her—hold it ransom until I was able to get her out of here. To delay time, I dressed my baby like a boy, sewed her tiny pants and shirts from some of my clothes in the hope that everyone around us would remain confused as long as possible. I wanted them to look at my child and forget she was born a girl. But time is like sand—the tighter I tried to hold on to it, the faster it slipped through my hands.

ASHA—*MY* ASHA—GREW UP to be an effervescent five-year-old girl, full of energy and surprisingly aware of her place in the world. She learned to adapt her moods to her surroundings. In the morning she would be like any other child, full of enthusiasm, asking too many questions. *Why do the birds fly? Why do dogs not fly along with them? Shouldn't God have given them wings so they could see the world too?*

"That isn't fair," she would tell me.

Her questions wouldn't stop. I didn't have the patience to explain everything to her like Amma had with me.

"That is how God made things," I told her.

To distract her, I would tell her stories of my Amma, of how we lived in a village in a house whose roof leaked.

"Can you believe I would watch the rain drops fall through the roof into a bucket and think the roof was crying?" She would giggle and look at me wide-eyed as I recounted my time with my Amma, fetching water, washing clothes, and cooking. I left out all the painful moments that were too difficult to recount, too arduous for her to understand. Then I told her about

Tara, about the first time I met her, how she came to my aid when I had no one to lean on, how she saved me from a terrible turmoil.

"What is turmoil, Amma?" Asha asked.

"I will tell you one day when you grow up."

"Did they do the same thing to you that makes so many women scream here?" She sat up, watching my face closely. I tried to hold back my tears. I had pretended that she was unaware of this life. The irony of it was, I realized, that our terrible lives were all out in the open. How could she have not known? And yet, I didn't want her to know.

"Amma . . ." She shook my hand, waiting for an answer.

I distracted her again—told her about my time with Tara— our time spent on the terrace where she taught me how to read, how she was one of the kindest girls I ever knew.

"But Amma, you don't read now."

"I-I don't get the chance. But if you meet her, you can ask her if she will teach you."

"Will she teach me?"

"You ask her. When you meet my Tara, never let go of her hand," I told her, though I knew there was no chance of ever seeing Tara again. But hope had great powers. It had helped me survive for so long. It would do that for her too. Someday the color of our sky would turn bright, I knew. I tickled her before she asked me another question. She cackled and giggled. But like always, I knew it wouldn't last long.

Every evening Asha became subdued as she got ready before the brothel began its business, wearing the only dress Arun Sahib had bought for her at my insistence. She took the small shoulder bag I filled with paper and crayons, one that Sylvie had stealthily gotten from her customers. Madam didn't question me about it, assuming Arun Sahib had brought it for her. Every day I would assure her, "Your Amma will be here when you return."

Every day she would look at me with suspicion, as if she knew it could be the last time we would ever see each other, and nod, the tears pooling in her eyes. I never knew where they took her. Once I asked her, "Is it a room? Where they keep you?"

She shrugged and scampered to get her crayons from her bag.

"Are they giving you food to eat?" I would ask often.

She would nod and refuse to tell me anything else. I knew from the way she came back every morning that she'd had nothing to eat or drink for twelve hours. Then there were times when Madam didn't have the time and gave her a sleeping pill to gulp down with some milk before shoving her under my cot. The men who visited me didn't seem to notice her. She was fast asleep anyway. I had become thankful for those nights when I knew she was in the same room with me, when I knew she would wake up every morning in the same room I was in.

Then one morning, the day Asha turned six, after I waited for her for more than three hours, they dumped her in my room. She was unconscious.

"She is sleeping," Madam said to me. Her bodyguards behind her looked at me but didn't say anything.

"What did you do?" I yelled after them as they closed the door behind them.

Sylvie and I had to throw water on her face. Sylvie went downstairs, boiled milk, and made her sip it. She came around in no time, the little one, but this was my wake-up call. I could wait no longer. Time was slipping from my hands.

"They drug the children through the night and keep them in a closed room down the street so they aren't much of a nuisance. They must have given her a stronger dose." Sylvie sighed as she squatted on the floor beside me. We looked at each other in horror, at the ease with which those words had spilled out of her mouth. Deep down, both of us had known. But not speaking of it had allowed us to avoid the truth for this long. But now, here it was out in the open.

"Sylvie . . . there has to be a way out . . . you . . . you have got to help me. I have to do something . . . for my child."

Sylvie looked at me for a while, took a deep breath, and said, "Let me think of something."

I nodded and sniffled.

She came to me the next morning while I sat in my room mending a rip in my blouse. I could see the fear in her eyes as she closed the door behind her.

"There is this man, a customer who came along two nights ago," she whispered as she bent down to sit by my side. "He was from an organization that saves women like us. That is, if we want to go, they will help us. Do you think it could be true?" She looked at the door afraid of being watched. We looked at each other with disbelief and considered the offer suspiciously.

"Who would want to save us?" I asked.

She shrugged. "I've heard that such organizations exist, but I thought it was false—a rumor Madam must be spreading to see what we do. If we escape, she could come after us and cut our throats."

I thought about it as I watched Asha sleep beside me, just hours away from being taken away for the day. And I knew—I knew this was a risk I was willing to take.

"What do we have to do?" I asked Sylvie.

"Nothing, just tell the man. He will organize a raid one night—"

"Arrest us? That will cause more trouble. I cannot—"

"No, no. Shh, listen to me. These raids are organized by his organization. They will take us away to his shelter. That's what he said."

"Okay, tell him then—"

"Are you sure? It could get us into trouble."

I nodded. I had no choice.

THE RAIN BEGAN to fall a few hours before the raid was scheduled. It was a light drizzle at first, then a disturbing downpour. The man who visited me that night was wearing dark brown trousers and a cream shirt and had arrived straight from his work. He said he was a waiter at a small restaurant outside the railway station and wanted to spend the entire amount he made in a month on me because I reminded him of his wife, whom he had left back in the village. I waited all night, listening to him, smelling the sourness of his breath, hearing his ragged moans in my ears, hoping that anytime now, my child would be free.

The raid never happened. When I finished work and my last customer left, I walked across to Sylvie's room. She was still with a man, and I was about to leave when I saw drops of red leaking on the floor. I entered the room. The girl in the next bed yelled at me, "*Arre*, don't you know you can't enter when we are with customers?"

I ignored her and walked closer to Sylvie's bed. My heart seized at what I saw; my hands and feet went numb, and I collapsed to the ground without a sound. The girl in the next bed came yelling after me, then went silent when she saw what had happened, her eyes widening in horror, her screams surrounding us. There she was—my dear Sylvie—in an embrace with a man, a knife wound through his back and her eyes so wide open, so far gone, that there was no sign of life inside them.

I don't quite remember how I managed to get back to my room. One of the girls must have pulled me up and helped me back, and they had probably given me something to sleep. When I came around, the police were knocking on all our doors. We lined up outside in the main area like we did on nights when men chose who they wanted to spend the night with. The policeman before us looked strict.

"I am Inspector Pravin Godbole," he said, waving his *lathi* around. "So what happened here today? Who is this girl who was killed? Do you know where she came from?"

He walked up and down, pausing briefly before each one of us, noting the expressions on our faces. Each one of us shook our heads and lowered our eyes as he looked at us.

Then Madam began to speak. "See, Sahib, I am telling you. This man was in love with Sylvie and wanted to run away with her. Sylvie must have tried to tell him she wouldn't escape, and he must not have been able to take the rejection. He killed her and then killed himself. Poor Sylvie . . . she . . ." Madam made an attempt to sob.

Everyone knew that was a lie. The man was from an NGO, posing as a customer; he was trying to rescue us—all of us knew the truth. The brothel keepers had got wind of Sylvie trying to escape and had killed the man and Sylvie. Even the police standing there knew this. It was so obvious. The police inspector looked sternly at Madam.

"Now, let's see what we can do for you, shall we?" Madam said with a smile. He returned her smile and accepted the bundle of notes she fetched for him.

"You have to do more than this if you want the case to go cold," he said, slipping the notes in his wallet.

"Of course, you can choose any girl you want from them," she told him, sweeping her open hand past our lineup.

I didn't see who he chose that night; my eyes were too overwhelmed with tears to see anything. But within days there was a thirteen-year-old girl who occupied Sylvie's bed and reprised the life that had once belonged to Sylvie, her screams dissolving in the terror of the night. Everything was forgotten, and everyone went about their work. It had become just another casualty of life.

Then the morning came that I hoped would never come. I waited for hours for them to bring Asha back to me, counting the number of times the ceiling fan made full circles. When I could wait no longer, I crept downstairs. Madam was sitting on the veranda with a glass of *desi daru*—country liquor—in her hands, a cigarette entangled in her fingers, the smoke rising from its end. I stood behind Madam, her back to me, as I collected my nerve.

"What have you done with her?" I asked.

She turned around and looked at me, her eyes red from the liquor and the smoke from the cigarette surrounding her.

"Wh-what . . . have you done with my child?" I repeated hesitantly. I tried to stop my face from revealing the deep fright clutching my heart.

She looked at me for a while, raising an eyebrow, then laughed and took a gulp from her glass. "She will be with you in a few days. Now go upstairs and get back to work," she said, motioning her guards to come at me. I ran up the stairs, back to my room. I could have waited and insisted on knowing what they were doing with her, but the guards would have beaten me for days. I told myself I couldn't afford to let my child see me that way—bruised and battered. Actually, it had nothing to do with my child seeing me that way. It tears my heart every day, more than anything else, that I wasn't brave enough to endure those beatings for my child. So now I wait every morning, standing on that stool, watching outside the window, waiting to see her face in the alleyway. And now they are sending me away to Sonagachi for a while, because I am creating too much trouble by asking about my child.

MADAM OWNED BROTHELS in Sonagachi too and she needed three older women to replace the ones who had run away. That's what she told us. Of course, we knew what "run away" meant— they had probably been killed trying to escape. In any case, there were too many of us in our late twenties and early thirties in this brothel in Kamathipura, and Madam said she wanted to bring some young blood into the place so she could earn more. So it was decided that we were supposed to leave at sunrise.

They loaded Chiki, Soma, and me in the back of a small truck. A strong, pungent odor assaulted our senses as we climbed in. There were rows of fish baskets stacked over one another and we squeezed in between them. Soma climbed in first and found a place at the far end. Chiki and I sat facing each other near the door. Only when they closed the door did we realize how enclosed this space was—darkness surrounded us, the only sunlight what could slip through a small vent. Chiki held her sari *pallu* over her nose. "Do you know how far it is?" she asked me.

I shrugged and peeked into the basket of salted fish next to me. I couldn't stand the smell. The fish were lying dead in there. *How they must have yearned to get back into water just before they took their last breath,* I thought. *Why do fish swim in water? Why can't they fly?* I heard my Asha ask. She loved asking such questions. The thought of her being far away from me brought tears to my eyes. I broke down and cried. My bitter sobs mingled with the roar of traffic outside.

Chiki wanted to leave her spot so that she could console me. But there wasn't any place to move. So she just leaned and patted my arm.

"It's about thirty hours," Soma said after some time, matter-of-factly. "You were asking how long it'd take."

"She just lost her daughter," Chiki explained to Soma.

"So?" Soma shrugged. "I lost my daughter too. Now she must be sitting in some brothel somewhere."

My sobs grew in intensity and Chiki admonished Soma.

"What did I say wrong?" Soma said defensively. "This is what happens in this brothel life. You accept it or you'll keep crying all your life."

We had forgotten that Soma had been brought to Sonagachi from Kamathipura a couple of years ago. Her seven-year-old daughter was also taken from her many years ago.

"Don't worry," Soma said. "You'll get used to being away from her. And I hope we stop soon. They aren't going to take us in this truck for too long. This is only until we get to the highway. After that, they'll ask us to get into another truck. They aren't taking all this fish to Kolkata. It's the same way they brought me in. Now, did you get something to eat?" Soma asked.

Chiki and I looked at each other, and shook our heads. Soma threw a bar of chocolate toward us. Chiki caught it.

"A customer gave me a couple of these yesterday." She shook another bar of chocolate. "You should always carry a snack on such long journeys. I learned last time that they don't care whether you're hungry or you're eating cow dung."

The journey took what seemed like more than a day. It went on and on. All we heard was the sound of vehicles whooshing outside, honking of traffic. Our truck hit potholes for the first few hours and sighed as the driver braked. Chiki and I managed by eating half a chocolate bar and sleeping for the next few hours.

When they opened the door, it was still sunny outside. And I had to squeeze my eyes shut as the sunlight fell on my face. It was late afternoon. Our driver, a scruffy-looking man who smelled of toddy, told us we had stopped at a gas pump on the highway. Outside, trucks drove past us on the highway, and cars tried to overtake them. On either side of the highway, bushes and trees swayed in the breeze.

"My job is over," the driver announced, and signaled to two other men. These men were young and fresh-faced but seemed to have done this long enough. They gave us strict instructions that we had to follow them. They made us walk to a restaurant on the side of the highway. The restaurant was small concrete shack with an outdoor kitchen. A couple of yards away, there was an even smaller covered space that functioned as the toilet.

At the restaurant, one man guarded the toilet door so we wouldn't escape while each of us went. They ordered food— some rotis and potato *sabji* for us. I kept looking at the highway, wondering if I could somehow escape and hitch a ride with someone. When I looked at Chiki and Soma, they were too busy eating their food and obviously not considering any such thing. I reminded myself that there was a better chance of finding Asha if I remained at Madam's brothel. Maybe, someday she would take pity on me and let me know where my child was. Besides, that was probably better than lying dead alongside the highway.

Later, the two men escorted us to another truck. This truck was empty. When I climbed in, I looked outside at the city we were leaving behind. Chiki and Soma seemed to have accepted the fact that they were being taken to a different city but Mumbai had so many memories for me—of Tara, of our time together, of those five happy years and more important, my Asha was lost somewhere there. I couldn't imagine life at another brothel in a completely different city.

"Here," one of the men said as they handed us each a sleeping pill. We were supposed to gulp it down with water. After we had done as they instructed, they closed the door and we started our journey again. I didn't realize that I had fallen asleep because when I came to, the truck was still on the highway. I could hear the vehicles outside. Chiki and Soma were still fast asleep. It took them a couple of hours to wake up.

"When will we get there?" Chiki asked. "I need to go to the toilet."

We shrugged, and waited.

When the doors opened, we were on a wide, busy street. We had reached Kolkata and slept through most of this journey. The two men pulled us out the truck and dragged us off this road into a narrow lane hardly four feet wide and made us walk in a line behind each other. In the distance, I could hear faint music, and the air smelled of alcohol— a familiar feel of the place we had left behind in Bombay. The streets were as squalid as the ones I had left behind. When we reached Sonagachi, women just like us were standing by the street, looking for customers. Some were sipping chai and chatting. The liquor shop was surrounded by men waiting to have their drink. As far as the eye could see, there were brothels in every direction, women peering at us from windows. It looked bigger than Kamathipura.

The two men stopped at a building. Some women looked at us from the balconies on the higher floor. This building had walls that were cracked and leaked water.

"Come in, come in. Hope they didn't give you too much trouble." a slender woman said to the men as she came running down the stairs. The men shook their heads, discussed something with this woman, took their money, and left. This woman, whom everyone called Aunty, took us up the stairs to a room. This room was rather large. It had a bright light and the walls had recently been whitewashed. We each had a bed in that room with a curtain in case we had customers. When I looked outside the small window, I could see similar buildings, men with similar intentions but different women. I had no idea until then that there were so many women just like me.

In early 2007, Andrew Colt, the journalist, came to visit me in Sonagachi, just about a year after my Asha was taken from me. He looked very different than when I had met him years ago in Mumbai—his sideburns had just about started to gray. Apparently Madam had told a few of the girls where we were—she'd threatened to send them away to Sonagachi too—and they had answered Andrew's questions when he came looking for me. I told him how they had taken my Asha away, hoping he could help me. As I talked about Asha, my eyes began to water without my knowledge.

"Didn't Arun Sahib do anything to find her?" he asked.

"Why would he bother? As far as he knew the child was never his; he wouldn't believe it if I told him. All we are to him is a way to make money."

"But he loved you, didn't he?"

"Love?" I laughed. "If there is one thing I have learned in this brothel, it is that love comes in so many different shades that it is difficult to find. It languishes somewhere between like and hate and can change color as a person wishes. Why else would I have these knife marks carved on my body—a gift along with all the other gifts he gave me?"

Andrew stared at my wounds.

"Will you help me find Asha and Tara? Tara, she is the only one who can keep Asha safe if I die."

"Yes, yes, of course." Andrew sniffled, then looked up at me, "What do you mean if *you die*?"

I sighed. "I think I have the same disease Amma had . . . Madam brings in doctors sometimes and they said I have to keep taking lots of pills. There is a lady from the NGO who gets them for some of us. But I . . . I don't know if they are of any help. ."

"I wish I was here. I would have brought you the medicines."

"Look for Asha and Tara . . . that's all I want now."

"I will do what I can." He nodded, then turned his eyes away and reached for a book in his bag. He gave it to me.

"This is my second book. It will be published in a few months. I wrote my first book a few years ago . . . It came out in in 2003 but I didn't get a chance to come back to India then. That one was all about the brothels in Mumbai. It didn't sell very well. But I wanted to write my second one—this one"—he pointed to the book—"especially for you and your friends. This one is mostly about the brothel you were in; it's about you, Sylvie, Rani, Leena, Chiki . . . I've included your stories here, especially yours—I've written about your Amma and Tara and Sakubai and . . . I wanted to give it to you."

It had been a long time since I held a book in my hand. It was heavy, perhaps weighted with our sorrow. The cover had the night sky spread across it, two girls standing next to each other, watching the stars shine in the sky—just like Tara and me.

"Read the title!" he said.

"The . . . Color of . . . Our . . . Sky." I looked up at him. He was reminding me of what Amma had always told me. He was giving me hope.

"Thank you," I said.

CHAPTER 29

TARA
March 2007

RAZA AND I sat back in the car, yet another night, and watched the chaos as it took over the brothel area, aware of how many lives were stowed away in the neighborhood's dark corners. I had been doing this for more than two years now, believing the NGO knew what was best and could ferret out information about the complicated brothel trade. After my life-threatening encounter at Kamathipura, I had realized I probably had no option but to rely on them. Now, beside me in the driver's seat, Raza lit up a cigarette and blew the smoke out the open window as I watched the confusion reflected in the side mirror.

"Navin came by the office yesterday and asked if he could be of any help. His son, Rohan, is almost five now, so he said he has more time on his hands," Raza said.

"Oh?" I said hesitantly. In the rearview mirror, I watched constables with their *lathis* driving away the drunks and the shutters of shops closing in a hurry. Female social workers were comforting prostitutes.

"He doesn't mean any harm. I think he just wants to make it up to you."

"Make it up to me?" I stared at Raza.

He shrugged at my anger.

"As if that is possible," I said.

"We all do things we regret," Raza reminded me.

I looked out the window. Not very far away, I could see Saira exiting the brothel with a few girls they had rescued, her team of social workers helping them climb into the van, talking to them in soft whispers. I thought about what Raza said. It had been a few months since Anupam chacha had confessed, but I still wasn't able to forgive him. I couldn't understand why Navin hid it from me. I had been avoiding him. For the first couple of months, Navin had apologized many, many times. He would come over with food that Vibha had cooked and beg to eat a meal together like old times. But I had asked him to mind his own business and shut the door on him. Even though he lived right next door and our paths crossed often, I'd just pass him by. I was actually glad to be rude. In my moments of fury, I wished Anupam chacha had been hale and hearty, so I could have handed him over to the police. That would have given me respite, watching him suffer in prison, being punished for the crime he had committed. But now that he was dead, all there was left to do was wonder about the desperation that might have prompted him to do something so evil. Was it similar to the desperation I had felt so many years ago when I had approached Salim to take Mukta away? Perhaps we *were* no different.

I saw Dinesh in the side mirror, walking to my side of the car.

"It will take some time," he said, knocking on the half-open window. "There is a girl in there who refuses to come out."

"How old?"

"Not more than five or six, I think."

"Why don't you lift her?"

"It is not that easy."

"Why?"

He didn't answer, but waved at me to follow him. I got out of the car to follow him inside the brothel. Standing outside, I was overcome by the same sickening feeling I had years ago when I had first entered a brothel. *This time, I am stronger,* I told myself. I had watched many girls rescued from this hell. I had consoled them in their agony. But I was wrong. Walking inside was like stepping into quicksand, getting sucked into a swirling vortex of despair. I walked through the long hallway, stood by a windowless dark room, and watched the bare walls and leaking roof as I had years ago, still smelling sweat mixed with incense.

"This way." Dinesh pointed.

It was dark, and the flashlight in Dinesh's hand was leading the way. There were many social workers gathered around a wall, and I had to push past them to see what was going on. Flashlights whirled around us, tiny circles of light moving across the wall like glowworms, settling on a small hole in the wall the size of an animal burrow. It was then that I noticed it—the movement of life inside. The two women from Dinesh's team—social workers—took turns lying supine on the ground, their face close to the opening, trying to coax a girl into taking their hand and coming out. This hiding place was too narrow, too small for any adult to enter. Even if one tried, one would barely be able to fit one's head in. They must have pushed this girl in there, squeezed her in through the tight opening. That was the only way.

"Let me try," I told them. The social workers moved out of my way. I told others to switch their flashlights off. It was scaring the little girl. I put my head to the floor, my face close to the hole in that wall, so she could hear me. I swung my flashlight in the distance, away from her face, but she shrank back farther into the hole, her eyes wide open and glistening with fear.

"Hi," I said to her. "I am not going to hurt you."

I could hear a whimper.

"I am not going to hurt you," I repeated, the words floating dismally in the darkness around us. I could hear the whispers, the subdued alarm in the voices of the social workers behind me.

"You must be hungry. Do you like chocolate?" I asked, fishing for a candy bar in my purse.

I held it out for her, the flashlight shining on it from my other hand. She looked at it suspiciously but didn't move.

"Tara," Raza said from behind me, "we can probably break a part of this wall to get to her."

"No, that will frighten her. Let me try."

"Is your name Tara?" the girl asked weakly, her eyes now wide open with curiosity.

"Yes," I said surprised. "Do you like my name? What's yours?"

"My name is Asha," she said excitedly.

"Hi, Asha. Can I be your friend?"

She was quiet for some time, thought about it, then looked

at me and asked, "If I hold your hand, will you take me to Amma?"

I clung to the opportunity, although I had no idea where her mother would be.

"Yes," I lied.

In a minute her hand was in mine, and she was out. She threw her arms around my neck and collapsed in my arms as if the comfort of them were something she had always been familiar with, and even as I brought her out to the car, she refused to let go of me. Her arms were tightly entwined around my neck. Raza drove us all the way to the center, the girl in my lap in the backseat, her head resting on my shoulder.

At the center, she refused to unclasp her arms from my neck. A nurse pulled us apart, and I watched from the end of the hallway as she took Asha to the medical station to examine her. She wailed at being separated from me, and the corridors throbbed with her screams. She bit the nurse's wrist, ran toward me along the hallway, her face stained with tears, and locked her hands around my hips.

I took her to the examination room and waited outside. Dinesh and Saira exited the examining room after a while.

"The doctor says she is suffering from the shock of being separated from her mother," Dinesh said, "of being locked up in the dark for such a long time. He has prescribed some vitamins. But she hasn't been harmed in any other way. I think it might be a good idea for her to stay with you for a few days."

I was shocked when Dinesh suggested that she stay with me.

"It is better this way," Saira added. "Once she is comfortable we can get her back here. She is in shock and seems very comfortable with you."

"But . . . but I don't know anything about taking care of a child. I—"

"It will be all right. You will manage well. You have been working with us for quite some time now," Dinesh said, patting me on the back. I looked around helplessly—at Dinesh's and Saira's encouraging looks, at the girl who looked at me pleadingly.

"It will be all right." Raza smiled, standing behind me. His gaze, firm and reassuring, gave me strength.

"All right," I said and got her into the car with Raza and me.

It was a silent drive back to my apartment, the girl sleeping in the backseat, Raza concentrating on the street as he drove, leaving me to my thoughts.

"I am not sure I can handle this," I told Raza as he parked the car outside my apartment complex and walked me up the stairs. The girl was sleeping in my arms, her chest falling and rising against mine.

"Yes, you can," Raza said as he dropped us off at my apartment. "You have been doing this for more than two years now."

I nodded my head as I let him in. I took her to my room and let her rest in my bed.

"You will be fine. If you need anything, call me." Raza smiled.

I was thankful for that smile. I watched him from the balcony as he walked down the stairs to the car. His tall form and broad shoulders grew smaller as he went farther away from me. When he was near the car, he stopped and looked up at me as if he had known all along that I had been watching him. He stood there waiting, as if he had always been waiting for me. I gave him a small wave of my hand. He waved back, slid into the car, and drove away. I watched the cars parked outside, the vacant spot he had parked in now as empty as the feeling in my heart. Raza had become such a constant in my life. We didn't just work together day after day for his nonprofit; we also went to the movies, held hands, and took long walks on the Marine Drive promenade. It was Raza who had taken me to Century Bazaar—the one place in Bombay I did not want to revisit. *You should go there,* Raza had said, persuading me to confront my memories. There were new shops that had sprung up, erected on the very land where many had lost their lives. We walked down the street lined with restaurants and shops, ate at an Udipi restaurant that had been damaged in the blast and resurrected. There were cracks on some of the older buildings and some missing trees—all evidence of the explosion. But other than that people had buried memories and moved on. Many who worked there and had lost loved ones preferred to remain silent. Raza and I had sat down on the pavement outside the bookshop where I had first promised Mukta I'd teach her how to read English. When I told Raza this, he held my hand and kissed it. It surprised me how comfortable I was with him doing that. It was strange, I thought, with Brian I had wanted to escape from my memories. I wanted to be a different person, far away from that girl who had planned a kidnapping. With Raza, I was able to be comfortable in facing my memories, I was able to relax. I wasn't running anymore. But when Raza kissed my hand, I had looked down and said, "I am glad we are such good friends." His smile had faded and he had let go. I *wanted* to think we were happy that way, with no pressure of being anything other than good friends. But on days like this, when I watched him leave, an ache crept into my heart, warning me he might leave me one day. I sighed and dismissed the thought, then went inside.

I watched Asha sleep that night. Bringing a child into this home was like inviting memories of Mukta back. In her sleep, she grabbed my hand, and I lay down beside her. As I watched the starry sky that night, I remembered another child. Asha—that was the name Mukta and I had given her—the baby wrapped in a white cloth and buried on that Diwali day. Did Mukta remember things the way I remembered them?

THE NEXT COUPLE of days were hard. Every time I tried talking to Asha, she sobbed. "I want to see my Amma. You promised you would take me to her."

"Well, do you know where she is?" I asked. Her eyes would fill up as she ran and cowered in a corner.

"What is her name?" I asked.

"Amma. I call her Amma," she shouted.

She hesitantly allowed me to bathe her and change her clothes. At lunch or dinner I would catch her putting food in her pockets or stowing it away in her underwear.

"You can always ask for more food if you want," I told her, but she looked at me and continued hoarding food in her pockets. I let her. At the center, I had learned it was the only way you could gain their trust.

On the third day, as I was consoling the girl, persuading her to come out with me, there was a knock on the door. I carelessly opened it to find Navin standing outside.

"How are you, Tara?" Navin asked.

I couldn't smile, couldn't return his warmth.

"All right, I suppose," I said, then turned around and left the door open behind me. He entered my apartment, his five-year-old by his side. Before I knew it, Rohan had rushed to Asha's side, asking her to play, and she held his hand, jumped down, and rushed out to play.

"Don't worry. They won't go far," Navin said.

I had a smile on my face before I realized it. "All this time spent cajoling and persuading her to come out with me, and Rohan does it in a second." I laughed.

"Children understand each other better than we adults can understand them."

"That's true," I said, thinking of the childhood Navin and I had shared, of the thoughts Mukta and I had read in each other.

"I came to see how you were doing." He looked at me. In his eyes, I could see concern.

"Are you all right?" he asked. "You don't look so good."

"I am just tired, I think, from Asha living with me for the last few days."

"I know. Raza told me how you rescued her. Know this, Tara: you are doing something very brave."

I didn't acknowledge his compliment, just looked at him blankly. An awkward silence settled between us.

"It's dark in here," Navin said, looking around.

"Asha asks me to keep the curtains closed. She is not yet used to the light. She's been held in a dark place for too long."

"Hmm," Navin sighed. "The things those girls have to endure in their lives! How evil of people to put them there."

The irony of the statement surprised Navin.

"What do you want, Navin?" I asked, narrowing my eyes.

"Forgiveness," he said, looking me straight in the eye. The word burned in my throat. *Forgiveness. Was it that easy to expect?*

"I want to say how sorry I am for everything Daddy did," he said, standing near the door, sunlight pouring behind him. "I am shocked . . . ashamed. Will you ever be able to forgive me?"

I recognized his expression—it was like looking at my reflection in a mirror, waiting to be forgiven. Tears burned the back of my throat.

"I know you mean it, Navin, but I . . . I don't know how . . . to forgive," I whispered, my voice coming out as a croak.

"I was a child, Tara; I didn't know what to do."

"I was a child too," I whispered and looked away, the tears burning in my eyes.

He shook his head, sighed, then turned around to go. In the distance, I could see Asha cackling on the swing set with Rohan.

"Maybe someday—just maybe—you will find it in yourself to forgive everybody—your Papa, my Daddy, me, and more than anyone—*yourself*," he said as he walked to the door, stepped out, and disappeared around the corner.

"Maybe," I whispered as I watched him leave.

FOUR MONTHS HAD gone by since I had brought Asha home. Raza and I were sitting on a park bench watching Asha do cartwheels, slide down the playground slide, and wave at us. She was coming out of her shell, although even now, she was occasionally afraid and pestered me about her mother. I was happy she mingled with other children so well.

"I think," Raza told me softly, as I waved to Asha, "you should send her to the center now. This was supposed to be temporary, just until she regained her confidence in the world. Dinesh calls me every day, telling me it will not be good for the girl if you keep her too long. If she gets attached to you, she will find it difficult to adapt to other people at the center."

He smiled as if he knew what I was thinking. It felt like Asha had always belonged with me. Sending her back to the center had been such a distant possibility for me. If I was honest with myself, in the last couple of days, I *had* worried, in fact feared, that the apartment would return to its stillness, the stillness that reminded me of the past and continued to haunt me. Besides, the last few nights when I watched Asha sleep in my bed after I had read a story, she would not let go of my hand and risk the chance of me leaving her behind. I understood that feeling.

"Are you there?" Raza's voice startled me.

"Yes, I am not so sure if that is the right thing for her—going to the center."

"This isn't about *you*, Tara. It's about *the girl*."

"I *know* and *the girl's* name is Asha," I said, my voice rising. The kids who were riding their scooters stopped to look at me.

Raza stood up and straightened his shirt, obviously upset by what I had said. "I think we should go," he said.

I knew he was right. She *was* probably better off with Dinesh and Saira, who knew how to take care of her, *and* with the children at the center who shared her pain. I called out to Asha and we strolled down the park, Asha walking between us, holding on to our hands, swinging between us. I told Raza then that he was right, that we needed to drop her at the center. He smiled at me.

ON OUR WAY to the center I thought about what I was about to do. I watched Asha slurp her ice cream cone in the backseat and wondered what it was that was driving me crazy.

At the center, Dinesh applauded me. "Leaving Asha here? Good decision. You know we saved the girl just in time. Couple more years and they might have sold her to another brothel; who knows what they would have done."

His wife, Saira, entered the office and said, "I heard. You are leaving Asha here? Yes, yes, it's better this way. I have been saying this for a couple of months now. We just wanted her to stay with you for a few weeks until she opened up since she was so fond of you. But if she stays any longer, she will become too attached to you."

I sighed. It was not just Asha who was getting attached to me. It was the other way round.

"See," Saira pointed out, "she is already making friends."

I watched Asha play with the girls outside and knew I had made the right choice. She was better off here with other girls her age. She would be able to settle in better, adapt more quickly. She would understand that her need to find her mother was shared by many girls her age.

I spent the evening with the girls, playing badminton with some of them in the courtyard. Dinesh ordered food from a restaurant and all of us sat on the grass outside and ate together. The smell of the food wafted in the yard as I watched Asha eat with the other girls, chatting loudly as children often do. I felt I was letting her down. I wondered what I would tell her. Raza squeezed my hand understandingly. After dinner, Raza and I stood outside, bidding everyone goodbye. Asha stood next to me waving a goodbye to everyone, too, expecting to come with me. The moment had come; I had to explain to her that I was leaving her behind. With dread, I bent down to face her.

"Asha, you must stay here. I am going away for a while but I will be back soon. They will take care of you here. See, you have already made so many friends. You can stay with them now."

Her eyes widened, tears filling them. Her face shrank and she kept repeating, "No, no, no." She clutched at my hand, and I felt a raw tug in my chest. *Was this the way a mother felt leaving her daughter behind on her first day at school?*

Dinesh picked her up. She resisted him, her arms flailing about her, her legs kicking Dinesh. "I cannot leave you. I am not supposed to let go of your hand," she wailed. The other girls watched the scene with horror on their faces, and Saira asked them to go inside.

"I think we must go. Standing here will only make it more difficult," Raza told me, his arm on my shoulder.

I turned around to go, smelling the sadness around us just like I had years ago in the storage room. I could hear the heavy sobs of a girl who whimpered through the night. The sky was sprinkled with stars on this night like it had been years ago when another little girl had lost her mother.

"Please." I turned back and faced Dinesh, who was still

standing there. "Let me take her with me just for one night. I will bring her back tomorrow morning."

Dinesh studied my expression for a while, then sighed while Asha whimpered between us. Finally he shook his head, defeated, and let Asha down.

"Just one night," he said.

I nodded. Asha wiped her tears, sniffled, and clasped my hand once again. In the taxi, I watched Asha sleep. I felt like she was the answer I had been seeking, and for a minute, everything fell into place. With her, I always had a feeling of familiarity, like we had known each other long before we met.

NEXT MORNING, I took Asha to the park. In just another hour's drive to the center, Asha would become one of those girls living at the shelter, waiting and hoping for their mothers to show up. People jogged in the park around us. Others walked their dogs. I watched Asha play on the playground, then looked up at the birds that chirped in the trees.

"You are sad," a voice said. Asha had stopped playing. She was standing by my side. I hadn't seen her walk to me.

She leaned by my side on the bench. "Amma used to be very sad too," she said, digging her feet into the soil. She looked at the sky, then looked at me: "Do you think I shouldn't have watched?"

"Watched what?"

"When they did things to her . . ." she gulped and twirled the side of her skirt. "Bad things. They thought I was asleep, that I had taken the sleeping pill they gave me, but I would throw it away, pretend I was sleeping when the . . . the men came. Do you think Amma was sad because of what I did?"

"No, it wasn't your fault," I said, pulling her close. She sniffled and wiped a tear that fell from her eye. This was the first time she had opened up to me.

"Then they took me away, kept me with the other children in a dark room. Now Amma will be sad because of me, because I am no longer there for her."

I took her in my arms and held her tight. She cried softly. She smelled of the sweet mangoes I had fed her for breakfast. The wind whooshed around us.

"See, Amma used to tell me when I hear the wind whistling in my ear, she is thinking of me. I can hear her now, can you?" she asked.

I looked at her face for a while; that was something Mukta had told me years ago.

"Amma said you would come looking for her, and you would teach me how to read and write, the way you had taught her, years ago."

"Yes," I said, laughing and crying at the same time; holding her tighter. "I'll teach you just the way I taught her."

AT THE CENTER, Dinesh was initially confused to see my beaming face.

"I am not leaving her here. She is my niece," I told him. I repeated all that Asha had told me. I had renewed hope, renewed strength that I was getting closer to finding Mukta.

"Yes, but still. Unless it gets proven she is your niece, I can't let her go with you. You don't even know if Mukta is your half sister in the first place. So unless there is an official adoption, which can only happen if we declare Asha an orphan . . ."

"Really, Dinesh? Look where we are standing. When I first came here, all people told me was how many kids go missing here, and there is no one looking for them. There is no report, no proper paper trail. Officials like to be bribed and are ready to produce false identity papers at a moment's notice. I have worked with you for almost three years. Do you think I won't be a good caregiver to the girl? And please, how many rules or laws do you think we follow to a tee. You and I both know that sometimes we have to bend the law to do some good."

Dinesh sighed and shook his head.

"Look," I said, and softened my stance, "let her stay with me. Isn't it better to have a home for a child than to have her stay at the center? How many children go without a home? Meanwhile I will file papers for the adoption. You trusted me with her for the last few months, didn't you?"

Dinesh looked out the window and then looked back at me.

"All right," he sighed. "But you will have to declare her an orphan, file the adoption papers, go through the system. I will see what strings I can pull."

"Thanks," I told Dinesh, wanting to jump for joy.

CHAPTER 30

TARA
October 2007

IT HAD BEEN three months since that conversation with Dinesh. I had filed Asha's adoption papers; the process was long and laborious, but I was hopeful. For the duration of the application process and until the adoption was approved, Asha had to stay at the center. But Dinesh allowed her to stay with me from time to time.

"This isn't something I normally do," he told me every time he let Asha stay with me. I knew he could get into trouble with the authorities over it, and perhaps I was also risking my application, but the lure of being close to Asha didn't allow me to think of the repercussions. Raza had also helped a great deal by contacting all the people he knew to expedite the process.

So when he called saying he wanted to talk to me about something important, I asked him to come over, expecting him to have some information on the adoption. While I waited for him on that dreary summer morning, I remembered the time when I couldn't wait to tell Raza the news. It had been just four months ago that I had stood before Raza in his office.

"Asha is my niece." The words had been so delightful as they slipped off my tongue. "She told me things only Mukta could know. I spoke to Dinesh, and he said he would help me adopt her."

He had watched my beaming face for a minute, momentary gladness passing over his face, and then had looked back at the door deep in thought. "You sound so happy. Good. Now if you find Mukta, you will be free to go to America."

"What? Why would I go back to America?"

Instead of answering my question, he had changed the topic. But his pain at the thought of letting me go hadn't escaped me.

Now, as Raza stood outside my apartment door, knocking on it, I suddenly wished he had asked me not to leave him.

"Hi," I said as I opened the door.

Raza burst in without acknowledging my greeting.

"There is a journalist, Andrew Colt, who got in touch with Dinesh today," he said, breathing hard. "He said he was interviewing prostitutes from a brothel for a book he has written. He . . ."

"Yes?"

"It's in his book," he waved it in front of me. "He's interviewed Mukta! She goes by the name Sweety. If he is right about this woman—if she is Mukta—then he says they've moved her to Sonagachi in Kolkata."

Was this just another hoax or was I really going to find Mukta this time? Anxiety filled me to the point I could not breathe. Raza put the book in my hands. It had a blue cover. *The Color of Our Sky*, it said.

"Sonagachi is another area just like Kamathipura but in Kolkata," Raza explained.

"Kolkata . . ." I repeated, as if dazed.

"Why don't you sit down?" Raza led me to the sofa.

"Dinesh and his team won't be able to come with us," Raza said, kneeling down beside the sofa. "They don't work outside Mumbai, but we can ask the help of another NGO there. I will come with you. We can leave Asha at the center for a while. What do you think?"

"No, we will leave her with Navin—she will be happy playing with Rohan," I said, "It's . . ."

"Yes?"

"*It's Mukta. It has to be. . . .* But what if it isn't Mukta? What if someone else, some other girl who knows Mukta's story told it to him . . . Or what if we're too late? What if . . ."

"Tara! You're thinking too much. In any case, it is a chance we will have to take."

BY THE TIME I had packed my bags, Raza realized he wouldn't be able to make the trip with me. He apologized, told me he was supposed to finish some work, but would definitely join me in a couple of days. I wanted to go earlier and meet Andrew Colt, this journalist who had interviewed Mukta. But I couldn't get plane tickets and chose to go by train instead. Andrew, was in Sonagachi, and I was to meet him first. If whatever he told me proved it was Mukta, Raza would be there by the time we prepared for another brothel raid in Kolkata. Raza said he knew somebody in Kolkata who would guide me. At the station, I boarded the train and stood by the door talking to Raza.

"I know you think it might not be Mukta, and you are worried that taking time out to go to Kolkata will probably set you back in your search in Bombay, but trust me, the raids will go on as planned. Dinesh will keep us updated. So don't worry, okay?" Raza said.

"Yeah. You're right. I think I am going on a wild goose chase all over again. After so many years of searching, I don't know what else to think."

"I know." Raza nodded.

"So what do you plan to do without me around?" I teased, trying to change the topic.

He looked away then swallowed hard, tapping his palm with his cell phone, and asked, "Tara, are we always going to pretend as if we are just good friends, that what we share isn't more valuable than that? I've waited to ask you this . . . for the right time . . . maybe when you've found Mukta, but I am not sure waiting any longer will help me."

I hadn't expected that. His eyes met mine as if speaking a language I had always been too afraid to utter.

"I-I don't know," I said, my shoulders stretching slowly into a shrug.

I studied his expression, afraid it would shatter like glass by something I was about to say. I took a deep breath and said it aloud in one breath as if spitting out something that had been stuck inside me for a long time: "Raza, I always lose people I love—one by one—I have lost them all."

It was the truth. He was as surprised as me but his eyes deepened into affection. "Tara," he said softly, "that's not a rule."

"*It is* a rule. Come to think of it, it is almost like a curse I carry." I tried to laugh but tears welled up in my eyes.

"So you are afraid you'll lose me?" He raised his eyebrows and smiled, pleased at the thought. "But if you don't give this a chance, how will you ever know?"

The train whistled and pulled away. I waved to him.

"Think about it," he mouthed to me and smiled as I left him behind.

HIS WORDS DIDN'T leave me as I slept in the train. When I woke up, I could hear the wind whipping through the windows. I almost expected Asha to be sleeping beside me, her breathing deep and peaceful. Then it came to me—I was on my way to Kolkata. I had left Asha behind with Navin. Navin had been thrilled that Rohan and Asha got along so well. Then I thought of Raza— what is it that Raza had asked me before I left? *Are we always going to pretend as if we are just good friends, that what we share isn't more valuable than that?* I sighed. He was right. I had been lying to myself for the last couple of years. If it had been another time—a time when there was no desperation, no guilt—it would have been easier to admit how much I liked him. But now, it didn't feel right to be able to find love. I watched the sky rush past me through the window. I was still thinking of Mukta when my phone rang.

"Hi," I said.

"Tara." Raza's excited voice surged through the phone. "I was able to speak to Andrew again. He said he could locate this woman, Sweety. When she told her story to Andrew, she said she was born in Ganipur and she was a temple prostitute's daughter. It can't be a coincidence, Tara. It has to be her. It has to be Mukta."

I felt numb. What was the name of that prostitute I had met a couple of years ago? The woman with green eyes who had looked at me while she had whispered in a customer's ears. I didn't remember her name now. For some reason, her expression had stayed in my memories, and I always regretted not being able to talk to her. Sylvie was the prostitute standing by the side of the street who had pointed her out to me.

"Tara, are you listening? My contact at the NGO is planning a raid on that brothel tomorrow night. We don't want to wait. If we are lucky they haven't moved her. She could still be there. Are you listening?" His voice rang with excitement.

"Yes," I managed to say. "I will meet him there."

All of it was surreal, improbable even. It had been more than three years of helplessly looking for someone I'd lost. Had I finally found her?

HOWRAH RAILWAY STATION was one of the busiest stations I had seen. As soon as I stepped outside, I could feel the intense heat, the stench of sweat mixed with the smell of fish. Romesh waved at me from a distance. He was Raza's friend I had worked with during one of the brothel raids in Mumbai. Back then, he had been looking for a prostitute—a young girl of twelve who had been trafficked from Kolkata. I suppose that's how NGOs worked, contacting each other for help in case the ones they needed to rescue had been moved to another city. This time it was Romesh's turn to return the favor.

"Welcome to Kolkata. Is this your first time?"

I nodded.

"Let me help you with your luggage. Raza told me how keen you are to find this girl. We met Andrew today, and he told us where Mukta is. We can help get her out. But we will have to act quickly."

He hurled my luggage in the van and asked me to sit in the backseat.

"Now that we've found her, Raza said he'd meet us there as soon as he can. He is flying to Kolkata."

The Kolkata streets were teeming with people—just like Bombay. I could smell the rotting garbage and hear the incessant honking of vehicles. It didn't take long to reach Sonagachi. It was no different than Kamathipura. I could see the women standing outside, trying to get the attention of men.

Raza joined us as we waited outside the brothel Andrew had pointed us to.

"I am going in," I told Romesh.

"Tara, I want you to understand that women like Mukta have known no other life for a very long time. It might take her some time, shock her that she is out. She may or may not recognize you. I want you to be aware of that."

"Don't try to stop me, Romesh. I am going in."

"Okay. We will wait for the police to give us the go-ahead. You can join the rest of my team." He sighed and walked toward his car, shaking his head.

Raza and I looked on from the car. The police had already entered the place and started getting the men into the jeep.

"Andrew was sure that Mukta would be here?" I asked Raza, looking at the ruin of a building.

Raza looked at me and nodded. "That's what Andrew said. He said she wasn't willing to leave because she has a daughter who was caught in the trade. You just have to tell her that Asha is with you. I am sure she'll want to get out then. Once you have her . . . would . . . you want to go back to America? I know you can have a better life there."

I looked at him, but he refused to meet my eyes.

"Raza," I said softly, "I don't want to go to America." My words were slow and deliberate. "I am staying right here with you." I took his hand in mine. He didn't look at me but tightened his grip on my hand.

ROMESH KNOCKED ON the car door.

"Let's go," he said, and we walked toward the brothel together.

"You will be able to do a DNA test now and find out if she is your sister," Raza said as we walked through the dark corridors inside.

"It doesn't matter anymore."

"But you'll never know if—"

"I don't want to know . . . not anymore," I said. "You know, when I read Papa's letter, the last time he ever wrote anything to me, I knew that didn't matter. Both Anupam chacha and he were caught in their debate about whose daughter she really was. And nobody saw her for the child she was. I don't want to make the same mistake again. Some bonds run deeper than blood."

"Then what will you tell her when you meet her?"

"That she *is* my sister. That she has *always* been my sister," I said, the steps creaking as I climbed them.

And I knew that the moment had come, the eye of a storm my whole life had whirled around. This was the moment I had waited for so eagerly—the moment when I could walk across to Mukta and take her home.

CHAPTER 31

MUKTA
October 2007

THERE WAS CHAOS in the air—the sudden scuffle of feet, those muffled voices outside. The man I was with seemed to know exactly what was happening without any explanation from me. He jumped to his feet, pulled his pants up, and buttoned them at his waist. In the dim flickering light, I saw the shame in his eyes, the shame of being in a place such as this. He gathered his clothes in a bundle in one hand, clutched them close to his naked chest, and ran out the door, his shoes dangling from his other hand.

"What are you doing sitting there? Let's hide," one of the girls said, peeking into my room.

I shook my head and smiled at her solemnly.

She knew what I was thinking and didn't insist. I watched her turn around and disappear down the stairs. I got up and tightened my blouse around my chest, pulled down my skirt, tied its draw-strings, and sat down, waiting for the police to show up. The raids had become a common thing. Every time the police broke into our brothel, their voices called out to us as if they had suddenly discovered that we exist. They find nothing. We are well trained to squirm into crevices, mold ourselves like clay into secret spaces. On occasions when we are caught, the police haul us into vans, take us to the station, keep us locked up for one night, and then we are back to work the next day after they are paid well by the brothel owner to keep their noses out of this business.

Every prostitute caught was freed only if the brothel owners paid her bail, a small amount compared to the money we made for them. But the money they spent on us was added to our debt. So there was wisdom in being safe, in hiding in those tiny places. I had done so several times, astutely avoiding the ones who raided this brothel.

This time I wanted to wait it out and ask the police if they knew anything about my daughter. A strange strength emerged in me. I was tired, and I simply didn't care if I was beat up, kept without food and water, or even killed. I had been quiet long enough, and I wanted to know where my Asha was. I owed her that much for bringing her into this nasty world.

I stood up and watched the street outside, watched how the routine commotion had come to a halt, how the bustling street had settled into silence. Some of the shopkeepers had closed their shutters; others had left them half-open and run away before they could be caught by the police. The men loitering about had vacated the place and fled, as if their reputations could be harmed further. The women who usually stood on the street beckoning such men had already been jostled into the police van. I saw them sitting in the van, their eyes scanning the building through the barred windows, seeking help.

"Are you all right?"

I turned around. It was a woman's voice, warm and calm, but I could see no one. I had expected a policeman to snatch me away from the window, drag me by my neck down the stairs, and throw me into the police van.

"Are you all right?" she asked again.

The lonely light that flickered in my room had been turned off and the darkness hid her. She switched on her flashlight but focused it on the ground. I watched her silhouette move in my direction. There was a man beside her. I hadn't seen him there.

"My name is Romesh. We are here to help you," he told me. I could barely see their faces.

"Yes . . . okay," I said softly.

"We will get you out of here," she said, and I walked with them toward an unknown destination. It occurred to me then that in my entire life, I had never questioned where people led me. Even now, I didn't ask. I walked down the stairs, following them. The flashlight that shone on the ground reminded me of the fireflies of my childhood, the ones that showed me the way out of the forest. In the glow of that light I saw the staircase, how it had rusted over the years, the peeling paint like skin falling off an old wound. The corridors were as dark as ever as we walked through them. Her hand led me to the door, and I had this sudden churning in my stomach, a feeling that I was leaving it all behind, the only life I had known for so many years.

As the door opened, a dozen flashlights were on us, the light dispersing the darkness around us.

"Switch them off!" I heard someone yell in the distance.

As the lights switched off one by one, I noticed the full moon in the clear sky, the clouds gliding away, parting for the moon to shine down on me, and I lowered my gaze. It was so overwhelming, the vastness of the open space around me, the sudden feel of fresh breeze on my face, that I couldn't breathe. I turned around and tried to flee, but the woman held on to my arm.

"You don't understand, I have to go back," I told her. "I . . . cannot—"

"Don't worry, we'll take care of you," she whispered. Her hands were on my shoulders; my tears fell on her hands, settling like dew drops on leaves.

She had a gentle smile. She reminded me of someone. "Let's go," she said.

I noticed the unibrow on her forehead, the round face, those keen eyes as she spoke to someone. How she looked like . . . like Memsahib . . . like Tara. How could she be in this place? I dismissed the thought, told myself I was in a daze and wasn't thinking clearly. When she turned to look at me, I realized I had been staring at her and looked away. When I looked back, her eyes were brimming with tears.

"Mukta?" she whispered.

Nobody had called me by that name in a long time. I watched her face, waited for her to say something else. She didn't tell me her name. She didn't have to. I just knew. I knew, but words didn't come. A whimper escaped me. She smiled through her tears as she drew me into her arms. It seemed like the old days again, when her touch, her breath of kindness washed away my pain.

"I have been looking for you for such a long time." Her embrace was warm and tight.

We didn't speak for some time, nestled in each other's arms. The street was silent; the eyes that surrounded us stared at us. I retracted from the safety of that embrace.

"I have to go back in there. I cannot come with you," I sniffled, my voice trembling as I spoke. "My daughter is in there. I have to find her."

"I know," she whispered, tucking a strand of my hair behind my ears. "Asha is with me."

I thought I hadn't heard her well. "Asha . . . I have to find her," I repeated.

"Mukta, we found her." She squeezed my shoulders and looked me in the eye. "She is with me," she reassured me again.

When I looked at her, I knew it was true. The world seemed to spin before my eyes. It was as if happiness was something I couldn't take. It was as if such a thing wasn't possible for me. I fell to the ground on my knees. She kneeled down beside me.

There were so many questions I wanted to ask, so many answers I seemed to need, and yet I gaped at her. Tears poured through my eyes and I looked down at my trembling hands. There must have been something good I had done to deserve this.

"Mukta, Mukta," Tara said, shaking me, "we have to go. Don't you want to see Asha again?"

"Yes, yes. And she is okay? I mean, is she eating well? Before they took her away, she had stopped eating—"

"Yes, yes, don't worry. We will take you to her." She smiled and held me in her arms.

THE FLIGHT TO Mumbai seemed very long. Tara was jabbering on about how Raza—the *goonda* who had once tried to hurt her in the streets—had helped so much with her search. She told me he had to stay back in Kolkata on account of work. I asked her if Asha asked about me.

"Always. Every opportunity she gets," Tara said.

I had waited so long to see my daughter that I was not even thrilled to see the clouds float beside us. It did not occur to me that I had always wanted to be on an airplane. Ever since Arun Sahib had talked about his travel, I had wanted to be so many feet up in the air. But all this—it didn't fascinate me now. The ride from the airport to the apartment wasn't very long, but my mind was ravaged with anguish. I longed to see my Asha. I worried about what had become of her.

THE APARTMENT WAS the way it was, so many years ago. The poetry of my childhood that ran free through the corridors; the songs that we had once sung made me feel like I was that ten-year-old girl again. But such a long time it had been. The echoes of our childish giggles had settled like dust over this home. The kitchen still had the smells of my past; the tree outside still stood strong, telling me how long it has waited for me. I looked at Tara, who stood by the door behind me, watching me with amusement.

"How long?" I asked.

"Hmm?"

"How long have you been looking for me?"

"Three years."

"So you aren't married then?" I asked.

She shook her head and smiled at me. "Came very close . . ."

Tiredness had sunk into her face like water seeps into soil, making it darker with its dampness. She seemed to have learned to conceal the distress in her eyes, but I could still see it; I had seen darker versions of it around me for such a long time. This was not what I had wanted for her, to waste her life looking for me, trying to understand the brothel world. After all, the life I've lived had always been my destiny.

"I thought you'd be married, have children, live a happier life than me," I said, looking away, twirling the ends of my sari.

"I *am* happy now." She smiled at me, held my hand, then walked to a cupboard and took out a stack of ironed clothes.

"Besides," she said, handing the clothes to me, "I think we will have plenty of time to talk about this. Don't you want to freshen up? Navin has taken Asha and Rohan to the park. They will be back soon. Asha likes Navin's son, Rohan, a lot—reminds me of Navin and my friendship. You'll see,." She laughed.

It didn't take long to hear my little one's giggles. I stepped out the main door and saw her—wearing new clothes, holding a little boy's hands, jabbering away in delight. She looked at me, stopped and stared at me, let go of the boy's hand, then ran the long corridor. "Amma!" she screamed and I heard her shrill cries as she called out to me. I bent forward and stretched my arms out for her. She smelled like the breeze—fresh and full of life, her moist breath on my neck a mere memory for the last many months.

"They are not going to take me away now, are they?" Her lips trembled.

"No, no . . ." I laughed through my tears and tightened my embrace around her.

AFTER ASHA FELL asleep, Tara and I talked like children once again, as if we had never parted. We sat on the floor, warm chai in our hands, the noise from the streets pouring through the window.

"Do you remember that poem I wrote?" I asked.

"The one I laughed at? Yes," she said, and sang it to me as the crickets chirped around us.

> No matter how bad the weather,
> How difficult the road,
> We will always be together,
> Climbing the hill,
> Wading through the rough waters,
> Always together.

"It sounds awkward when you sing it," I snickered.

"Hey, you wrote it!"

I laughed and she joined in.

"I thought of it so many times when they locked me in that dark room. I always knew it was you—you who would be there for me."

She leaned forward and caressed my wrist. "I searched for so long. How I longed all that while just to touch your hand again and now . . . it seems like a dream . . . as if you are . . . you are . . ."

"A ghost?" I asked.

We erupted into laughter again, the chaos of our lives momentarily forgotten. Then Tara's laughter turned into tears and her face acquired a sudden sadness. "I should have screamed that night, woken up Papa, the neighbors—done something to stop that man from kidnapping you. I should have . . ." Her voice faltered.

"Shhh," I said. "I saw how afraid you were. I saw your face while that man was taking me away. I didn't expect you to do anything. If you had, he might have hurt you or taken you too. Besides, you were a child . . ."

"Just like you! You didn't deserve this . . . this . . ."

She didn't say anything more, just sniffled. For a minute, silence took over our conversation.

"You speak differently," I said, just to break the silence, "a little like those foreign men who used to come visit me. I heard you lived abroad for sometime."

"Yes, I lived in America." She rubbed away her tears. "Papa took me after Aai died and after you were . . ."

"I heard. Andrew told me. Did you like it there?"

She thought for a while. "Yes and no."

She told me how heartbroken her Papa had been when they first moved there, of how even friendly people seemed strange to her.

"That's when I took to reading books and found that you were right."

"I was right?"

"Yes, books are better than the world we live in."

I smiled at the memory. It had been a long time since I'd held a book in my hands and shared it with her.

"Maybe I should get a book from the library, something you'd like to read," she offered.

"Maybe later. What about a husband? You didn't meet anyone?"

She laughed. "You sound like my friend Elisa, who is always eager to marry me off."

"Hmm, it was a dream I couldn't have for myself. So I wanted it for you. I wanted it badly for you."

Her eyes filled up as she gave me a wave of her hand, brushing away a thought. She continued to tell me about her life growing up in another country, about Elisa, who had become a dear friend, of how she met Brian, of how Sahib committed suicide. Her eyes moistened as she spoke of her Papa, and I remembered how dear he had been to her.

"So, how did you know to come looking for me?" I asked.

"Papa had been looking for you. I found some documents in his drawer."

"Why?"

She sighed and looked out the window. "I wish we—Papa and I—could have done things differently."

"Why? Whatever both of you did for me was more than anybody has ever done."

She looked at me closely, cautiously, then let out a deep sigh. "There are many things I want to tell you, but not now. We'll leave that for later. Maybe you should get some rest now."

She didn't insist on knowing anything about my life, perhaps sensing that my memories were too bitter to recollect, but I told her about Sanjiv, about Sylvie, who had been there for me, of Asha's birth, of all those better memories that managed to cover the bitter ones.

"Do you remember," she asked, "we used to tell each other

that we would always be together, even if I married and went away?"

"Yes, and by now you should have had at least two children," I said, and she giggled. Her laughter surrounded us, and I hoped this time it had come to stay.

I wanted to believe this world that I had returned to would never come to an end.

I HAD ONLY two weeks' experience of this new life when the phone rang. I was dusting the books in the library and flipping the pages of a book. Tara entered the library.

"Remember the hospital where we had your medical checkup? The doctor wants to talk to us about some reports," she said.

She didn't talk much on the way to the hospital. In the taxi, she kept clenching and unclenching her fists, smiling at me nervously. I wanted to tell her about my diagnosis—that I knew I had the disease that ravaged my mother—but I simply couldn't let her crumble at the news. I accompanied her to the hospital, keeping my diagnosis tightly tied up in my heart. At the hospital we sat down on the bench outside the doctor's office, and I told Tara that I could not believe my luck. What had I done to deserve this? To be able to live a new life? That's when the doctor came out, took Tara aside, and said something to her. Her face turned as grim as the sky gathering clouds during a storm. She sadly rested her back on the wall as if her body had become too heavy for her.

The doctor called me inside his office and asked me to sit down.

"Have you had recurring fever, loss of appetite?" the doctor asked from the chair next to mine.

"I have fever some days and don't like to eat, yes. They . . . they've told me about the disease," I told the doctor but looked at Tara.

"You know you have an HIV infection?" the doctor asked.

I nodded. "A doctor at the hospital told me a few years ago. A lady from the NGO would bring me the medicine."

"There are a lot of bogus medicines out there today. Do you remember the name of the medicines you were taking?" the doctor asked.

I shook my head. "They never told me. I just took the pills she gave me."

"I must be honest, there is no cure for HIV. But medicines can help you live a longer and healthier life. At this point, the HIV in your body hasn't advanced to a great degree but I am also obligated to tell you that if it spreads, AIDS is the final stage of infection and . . ." He left the sentence incomplete, and I felt my life hanging in balance in what was untold.

"What does it mean to have AIDS?" I said finally, looked at him and then at Tara, who was kneeling by my side.

"Don't worry," Tara whispered to me, "we will do everything we can to see that this disease has no chance to advance. Won't we, Doctor?"

The doctor nodded hesitantly, then gave me a prescription for medicines and a handout about how I was supposed to take care of myself. Both Tara and I left the hospital silently, as if the sheer stubbornness of our silence would bring us better days.

CHAPTER 32

MUKTA
January 2008

THREE MONTHS PASSED after the doctor gave us the news. Persistent headaches and coughs had troubled me, causing Tara to rush to my side at night. Each time I sent her back to her bed, reassuring her I was okay. I thought I was actually getting better. I didn't have the fevers anymore and the nausea had gone away but the dark clouds still loomed around us, as if AIDS could swoop down at any time and take me away. At such times, hope seemed like an illusion, like a delicate butterfly that flew away the moment you tried to touch it. Sometimes I woke up after midnight to find myself looking at Asha fast asleep beside me. I ran my fingers through her hair and traced my finger down her nose and her eyes, hoping I'd always have this memory. If everything went well, I would be able to live to see her grow up, go to school, get a respectable job, marry, and have children. I wanted to sit in her wedding *pandal* and shower her with good-luck rice. The one good thing was that we got Asha tested. I was relieved I hadn't passed my disease to her. When I thought about this, certain stillness surrounded me and my spirit soared, assuring me she would be all right, and I would always be right there with her.

"We should go to this doctor," Tara said, trying to show me another brochure she had brought along. "This doctor—he is very well known and is—"

"No more doctors, please," I told her. She looked at me surprised.

"In the last three months we have been to too many doctors. We have waited in doctor's offices only to hear the same thing the first doctor told us. Didn't the doctor just tell us yesterday my disease was stabilizing, that I could live a healthy life for many years? Maybe, I can see Asha grow up. That's enough for me. Why do you keep hoping for more? . . ."

She flung the brochure in the air and stomped out of the house like a little child. My words evaporated in midair. All day I waited for her to come back home, but she didn't return until late night. I noticed her only when I was making her bed—standing by the door of her bedroom. I continued pressing out the creases from the bedspread with my hand and waited for her to say something.

"You don't have to do that anymore. How many times have I told you? You don't have to do all the chores like you used to. You cook and clean, go shopping for vegetables. It's not good for your health." She folded her arms on her chest.

"No, no. I have to." I smiled at her. "No matter what you say, Tara, I didn't come from a good home, and I certainly didn't deserve a place like this. But your Papa brought me to this home. This is the least I can do." I stood straight and faced her, folding the blanket as I spoke.

She looked at me gravely and seemed to debate whether or not to say something. "There is something I have to tell you."

I watched her as she spoke.

"Papa. He came from the same village as you did. I went there recently—turns out . . ."

The look in her eyes scared me.

"Turns out that he was the zamindar's son."

My lips trembled. A memory of that evening came jostling to me: the evening when Amma and I had waited under that banyan tree . . . of the morning when I had run after my father as his car had sped away.

"Well, I might as well say it," she said, tightening her arms against her chest. "He . . . he had a relationship with your mother. There is a chance that . . . that . . ." She paused, swallowed, and continued: ". . . that you are my half sister." Her voice croaked feebly.

I closed my eyes and felt the heat of the words in my throat; my palms moistened, and I clutched the blanket closer to me. For a moment, everything around me seemed to have gone silent. I heard nothing, not even my thoughts, just the sound of my uneven breath running through my heart. Her eyes were still on me, looking at me nervously, as if I could crumble to pieces if she looked away.

"Are you . . . are you sure?" I asked her. The words came out carefully, as though afraid of themselves.

She shrugged slightly and held my gaze. Guilt and helplessness overtook her face. "Papa wasn't sure . . . but I don't know. We can find out—there are DNA tests—if you want to know for sure but—"

"But?"

"But does it matter? You *are* my sister. You've always been."

I looked into her eyes, then lowered my gaze, let the blanket drop to the floor, walked past her, and sat in the storage room. Thoughts ran amok in my head. The night was serene and the sky seemed to want to comfort me. But even they failed me on this night. My Amma's hopeful face floated around me. How many years had she waited for him? I remember that walk in the village where I had hoped my father would come and silence all those people who had berated us. Maybe Sahib was my father. Why else would he have taken a girl like me from the village to this city? Why else would he have been so kind to me? I imagined his face in all those memories where my father's face had been a thick, hazy fog. And I saw distinctly the man—Tara's Papa—as he had hesitated by the car that morning and looked behind briefly at me, seeming sorry to leave me behind. I was unsure if this was my mere imagination or a true memory. The questions that had been resting for such a long time came bursting out. Could he have given me a different life, a better life? If he had accepted me I would have been able to go to school, read, and write like all those children who attended school. Would I have found love? I certainly wouldn't have had this deadly disease. The thoughts teemed in my head. The pain, the anger, rolled down my cheeks. I drew my legs close and let my body fall to the floor. There was so much I had hoped for in this life, I thought as sleep drew its veil over me.

MY EYES OPENED to the warmth of the morning sun. I saw Tara stretched beside me, still deep in sleep. I watched the beams of sun push through the window, and I wondered about the way the night enveloped the day, holding it in its womb of darkness. Perhaps this anguish inside me wasn't helping me see clearly. I watched her as she opened her eyes, stretched beside me, and looked at me carefully, as if waiting for my decision.

"All my life, I have waited . . . waited to be told I was so-and-so's daughter so I could experience that shower of love a daughter basks in. But in reality your father, Sahib, did more for me than anybody ever has. He saved me from that village, gave me a childhood with you—one I would have never had otherwise. He spent his time looking for me after I was kidnapped."

I took a breath. She sat up and looked at me earnestly,

"I want to remember him *as* my father whether it is the truth or not. I want to remember the good moments, just the way they happened, not analyze it with some test."

She drew me into her arms, and I held her tight.

"Will you take me somewhere . . . somewhere I've always wanted to go?"

Her lips trembled. "Where? Ganipur—Papa's village?"

For a while I felt transported back to the village I was born in—Ganipur, to that house where the roof leaked, where I spun hope into stories about my father. I smiled at this.

"What? Why are you smiling?" Tara asked, scrutinizing my face.

"Nothing. You just made me think of my village."

"So where do you want to go if not there?"

"Amma used to say that when my father returned to us, she

wanted to go to Varanasi to have a dip in the Ganga River and wash away her sins. Maybe it will wash away *all* my sins."

"You haven't committed any sins, Mukta. Nothing that happened was your fault."

"Please," I whispered, "I want to go. My father has returned to me now, hasn't he?"

She swallowed hard and continued nodding.

RAZA MADE THE arrangements for us to leave and came to the railway station to hand us our tickets. I had only heard about him from Tara. She always spoke highly of him, even though he had threatened us when we were children. But I clearly saw the reason for her fondness.

"Wait here," Tara told me. She left the suitcases by my side and walked the platform toward him.

"Where is she going?" Asha asked, standing beside me with a concerned look on her face.

"She will be back," I assured her.

I watched Raza smile at Tara as he neared her and whispered something to her. Tara said something back to him and returned his smile. Their eyes spoke to each other as his fingertips touched hers. This closeness they shared was something I had always wanted for her. But a more surprising moment for me was when Asha's face lit up at the sight of Raza. She ran toward him and he picked her up in his arms and asked her if she liked the gift he brought her last time, like a father would ask his child.

"They've grown really close," Tara told me as she walked toward me.

I was still staring at both of them—a reflection of what I had always wanted for myself. He smiled at me and nodded his head but didn't say anything. His eyes were on Tara.

"Well, you be a good girl," Tara told Asha. "We will be back soon."

We boarded the train, my eyes still on Asha. She waved to me as the train sped by, and I wondered if it was a good idea to leave Asha behind. She was going to stay with Navin for a few days to play with Rohan, and Tara had assured me Raza would check in on her every now and then. Asha was worried I'd leave her again, but in the end, she had agreed to stay at Navin's place.

"Don't worry, she will be fine. Raza will be there for her," Tara told me from across the seat, reading my mind. I smiled at the way her eyes lit up at the mere mention of his name.

"You like him," I said mischievously.

She looked up in disbelief, a tinge of pink appearing on her nose and cheeks. She shrugged and waved it away.

"How come you didn't mention it before?" I pestered.

She sighed, but the expression on her face was pleasant.

"He asked me to marry him. I haven't given him a reply."

"Why not? What's stopping you? You'd better let him know how you feel; otherwise he might think you are going back to Amreeka," I teased.

She frowned. "Are you worried about that too?" she asked.

She raised her eyebrows, waiting for an answer.

"Will you go back to Amreeka leaving Asha and me behind?" I asked after a pause.

"No. I want to work with Dinesh and Saira. I want to be there for the girls at the center. But more than that, I want to be there for both you and Asha. I will look after you, I promise. Whatever the disease brings our way, I will be there with you every step of the way. You don't have to worry about that."

I was too overwhelmed to reply. She sat beside me and put her arms around me. We were silent for a while, watching the fog settle outside and lift with the warmth of the wind.

"And will you . . ." I asked, breaking the silence.

"Will you what?"

"Will you marry him?"

She sat up and laughed.

"Of course, eventually," she said softly as the train zoomed through the *ghats*.

VARANASI. THE RAILWAY platform was full of people— pilgrims and devotees—who had come to visit this holy place, to find salvation with one dip in the Ganges. The cycle rickshaw zigzagged through the labyrinth of crowded lanes, constantly honking at pedestrians. The street was noisy. Eager devotees tried to buy flowers and *puja* items from shops that lined the streets. Cows and goats rummaged in rubbish while the sounds of temple bells resounded in the background. After a while, the streets narrowed; we disembarked from the rickshaw and walked down the street, trying to avoid the overflowing gutters, cow dung, and sleeping dogs.

"Oh boy," Tara said, covering her nose with a handkerchief. "The road to finding God is tough!" She laughed in her hand-kerchief as she said this, but I didn't find it funny at all.

"It's the grief," I said.

"Hmm?"

"It's the pain people come with, the pain they wash off in this holy place. It rises like water evaporating into steam. It's grief; that's what it smells like to me; the heaviness of it lingers in the air."

She looked at me and put her arm around my shoulder. "You haven't changed, have you?"

"That's all I have ever had—the ability to see the beauty in small things, in people, in nature. It's the only thing that has helped me survive. Is that so bad?"

"No." She shook her head. "Not at all."

IT WAS ALMOST evening by the time we freshened up at the hotel and walked toward the *ghats*. There were people bathing in the water, shaving, washing clothes at the bank of this holy river as we took a boat ride to the *ghats*. We climbed the stairs, settled on the steps, and watched the domes of the temples nearby. *Diyas* set in marigolds glittered on the surface of the river.

"There is something I must confess . . . something I did . . . long ago," Tara said.

I waited for her to say something more.

"I thought there would be plenty of time to tell you this but . . ." She paused.

"If it's difficult, you don't have to say it," I said.

"No, I have to . . ." She swallowed hard and looked into the distance at the horizon. "This, all this . . . it's my fault. I-I wanted you out of the way. When Aai died, I wasn't thinking straight; I-I wasn't thinking at all. I went to Salim . . . asked him to take you away. Will you ever be able to forgive me?" She looked away, trying to hide her tears.

I sighed. By now, I was sure my destiny couldn't have been anyone's doing.

"Was he the one who kidnapped me then?" I asked.

"No, no . . . it was—"

"I don't want to know. I want to forget, Tara," I said. "What I am trying to say is, if it wasn't the person you thought it was, then how are you to blame? Why do *you* need forgiveness? It was just my past catching up with me. Madam was going to come after me anyway. She had spent too much on me to let me get away. Besides, I was born in a place like that; I had to return to it. All I remember is you holding my hand when I needed it, taking me into that world of stories I had never heard before, and pulling me into your childhood. If anything, you helped me out of it all, gave me a new lease on life, a childhood to remember. Most girls like me—born where they are—don't get that, and I am grateful to you for that. I am."

She looked at me suspiciously. "I don't know if I will ever forgive myself. I don't think I will ever live it down. Your life would have been so different."

"There are a number of times my life could have been different," I said, digging into my memories. "There are a number of people who could have made it different, but you were the only one who came for me. Generations of women before me were prostitutes, and if you hadn't interfered, stopped the cycle—saved my Asha's life—she would have become just like me. And all those girls, those women you help at the center, don't you see? You are doing a lot of good. So I don't want you to be hard on yourself—that is the last thing I want from you."

I touched her cheek and felt the moistness of her tears. She smiled wryly and wiped her tears on her sleeve.

"There was one person who did try to save you—Ajji—my . . . our grandmother. She convinced Papa to take you away from that village. I went to the village and she told me how she wished you had a better life," Tara said.

"Oh, it was her! She was the kind woman who rescued me after Amma's death."

"I think I'm going to ask her to come and stay with us for a while in Bombay. She will be very happy to see you."

I smiled, and wondered what I would have done if this kind lady hadn't thought of sending me to Bombay with Sahib. I would have never met Tara, never known Sahib, and never had a taste of childhood. I had so much to be thankful for.

We sat silently for some time.

"Now, would you want to scatter Papa's remains?" Tara asked.

"You should do it."

Together we walked on the edge of the riverbank. It might sound strange that the one person I really wanted all my life, the father I searched for all my life—my last memory of him was of his ashes. The ashes burst into the open space, scattered in the wind as Tara opened the urn. How long had I waited for the feel of my father's hand on my head? How long had I waited for his soft touch on my cheeks? Now, all I had of him were ashes settling around me in the water.

I felt light, floating above the smooth waters of this holy river, as I watched the snapshots of my life reflected back to me. I knew then that all those moments I left behind—the day I had first met Madam, the day Sakubai had not thought twice about selling me, the day Amma died before me, and the day I knew my father hadn't wanted me—would soon become blurry. This was the moment I would cherish: his daughters bidding him goodbye. I felt reassured in that moment that even if I didn't live as long as the doctors had predicted, Asha would be well looked after by Tara. It was only now that I understood the threads of life don't always weave the way we want them to; sometimes the pattern at the end of our lives is different than what we imagined it would be, and right now, I had nothing to do but be at peace with what was going to remain behind.

The sun was about to set and the sky was ablaze in colors of red. Amma was right. For women like me, our sky would be bright again. I knew. I could smell the hope.

"You have to wait for the night to fall," Tara said, pointing to the sky. "Once we have the night sky, you will be able to see Papa again. He will be one of the stars in the sky." She explained to me something I had once told her, something that I once so badly needed to believe.

"You don't believe me. It is true," she whispered, repeating my words. "You have to look hard enough. Our loved ones never leave us."

I giggled, laid my head on her shoulder, and watched the sky become ablaze with hope.

AUTHOR'S NOTE

The village of Ganipur is fictional and to the best of my knowledge doesn't exist on the border of Maharashtra and Karnataka, but there are similar villages in the area that practice the devdasi tradition and force young girls into the prostitution trade. The tradition of temple prostitution is especially prevalent in the poorer sections of society.

Although the characters in this story are entirely fictional, the idea for this novel germinated in my own experience of growing up with the daughter of a servant who worked for my family in Mumbai, India, where I was born and brought up. Her name was Shakuntala. When I first met her, she was a ten-year-old girl with striking brown eyes and shoulder-length hair. Most days, I would find her sitting in the corner of our living room unwilling to make eye contact with anybody. She was one of the inspirations behind the creation of the character Mukta.

If you are interested in reading more about the story behind the book and/or how you can help girls like Mukta, please visit me at www.amitatrasi.com.

Thank you for reading this book and sharing your time with Tara and Mukta. If you enjoyed this book, don't forget to review it so someone else can make this a part of their reading journey.

Amita Trasi

February 27, 2015

ACKNOWLEDGMENTS

I am deeply thankful to all the people who supported me while I wrote this book.

A very special thanks to my husband, Sameer—you have always encouraged and supported me. Thank you for reading multiple drafts of this book and for believing in it.

Many thanks to my wonderful editor, Rachel Kahan, whose keen editorial insight has been an invaluable asset to this book. To my hardworking agent, Priya Doraswamy, who worked tirelessly to make this dream come true—my deepest gratitude to you for your enthusiasm and unwavering support! Thanks to the the entire HarperCollins team who have worked dilligently on behalf of this book!

Thanks, also, to two more remarkable editors: Vrinda Condillac and Janet Hitchcock, for being so patient, and for your helpful advice. Your feedback was very, very encouraging.

A big shout-out:

To my first reader, Kala Ganapathy, who read this book many times over, every draft and every time I made the smallest change. I am truly thankful. You've always been a true friend.

To both my in-laws for their incredible kindness, especially to my mother-in-law, Sindhu Shankar, for reading this manuscript, and for your love and support.

To Bala Ramya Rohini—your help and support are peerless, as always.

To my parents, Deepak and Krishna, who brought me up to believe in possibilities, and my sister, Nandita, for being just who you are—my sister and good friend.

To my grandfather, the late Trasi Dattatreya Devrao, who told me stories when I was a kid and taught me the power of imagination, and to my uncle the late Sadanand Trasi, who always inspired courage.

To the rest of my family, who has had a promising influence over my life and who continue to love and support me: Gita and Arun Kumtha, Vivek and Sheela Trasi, Atma and Cynthia Trasi, Shanta and Ramesh Khambatkone, Subhir and Sanjana.

And last and most important, I am deeply grateful to all those women and girls whose lives and experiences have helped me create this book. My gratitude goes to organizations like Apne Aap Women Worldwide, Bachpan Bachao Andolan, Maiti Nepal, Prerana, and many other organizations worldwide who are constantly raising awareness and helping victims of sex trafficking. Thank you for making the world a better place for girls like Mukta.

GLOSSARY

Ashoka—a rain forest tree in the Indian subcontinent

Arre—an Indian expression of surprise or despair which can be loosely translated to "Oh my!"

Badam—Almond

Banarasi saris—saris made in Varanasi, a city that is also called Banaras

Bidi—a type of Indian cigarette

Bindi—a bright dot of red color applied in the center of the forehead

Burka—garment covering the entire body and having a veiled opening for the eyes, worn by Muslim women

Chacha—"uncle" in Hindi; i.e., father's younger brother. Also used informally to address father's best friend

Chai—spiced milk tea popular in India

Chaiwalla—a vendor who sells chai

Chamcha—a sidekick

Chapati—Indian bread

Chowkidar—watchman

Dal—a curry made with lentils and spices

Desi daru—country liquor

Devdasis—temple prostitutes

Dhoti—a traditional men's garment worn in India

Diyas—an oil lamp usually made with a cotton wick dipped in oil

Firangi—foreigner

Gajra—a flower garland made of jasmine flowers intended to decorate a hairstyle

Ghats—a series of steps leading down to a body of water

Goondas—ruffians

Gulmohar—Royal Poinciana, known for its flaming orange flowers

Haan—Yes (in Hindi)

Harami—Indian slang for bastard

Hijras—Eunuchs

Iced Golas—ice shavings slathered with syrup and sold by street vendors in Bombay

Jadoo—magic

Jaggery—a concentrated product of cane sugar

Jalebis—a deep-fried sweet that is soaked in sugar syrup; made in India

Josh—spirit

Kabaddi—a contact sport played in India

Kachoris—a spicy snack

Kalasha—a pot

Kurta—an upper garment worn by men and women in India

Lathi—Hindi term for a stick

Malkin/Memsahib—term used by servants for the mistress of the house

Moophat—brash, thoughtlessly expressive

Nada—drawstring

Namaskar—a salutation

Paan—a betel leaf with tobacco, chewed as a stimulant

Pakoras—a fried snack

Pallu—the loose end of a sari

Parameshwara—the Lord

Parathas—a flatbread

Pipal—a fig tree considered sacred in India

Pind-daan—a Hindu ritual performed after the death of a loved one

Pranaam—a form of salutation

Puja—a Hindu ritual performed as a prayer to deities

Pulao—a rice dish

Raga—a melody used in Indian classical music

Rajah—a king

Rangoli—a design made on the floor with colored powder

Rasgullas—sweetened ball shaped dumplings made of cottage cheese

Roti—an Indian bread

Sabji—a vegetable curry

Samosas—a fried pastry with savory filling

Taanpura—a string instrument used in Indian classical music

Tilak—a mark applied on the forehead

Tanga—a horse carriage

Udheyo—a form of salutation

Vaidya—a doctor practicing Ayurveda

Yellamma—a Hindu goddess

Zamindar—a landlord, typically an aristocrat who owns land

ABOUT THE AUTHOR

Amita Trasi was born and raised in Mumbai, India. She has an MBA in Human Resource Management and has worked with various international corporations for seven years. She currently lives in Houston, Texas, with her husband and two cats. This is her first novel. Visit her website at www.amitatrasi.com.